The Lost Prince

J.W. Webb

Acknowledgement and thanks to:
Catherine Romano, for editing
Julia Gibbs, @ProofreadJulia, for proofreading
Roger Garland, www.lakeside-gallery.com, for illustration
Debbi Stocco, MyBookDesigner.com, for book design
Ravven, ravven.kitsune@gmail.com, for cover art.

ISBN 13: 978-0-9863507-4-0 (Paperback)
ISBN 13: 978-0-9863507-5-7 (Digital)

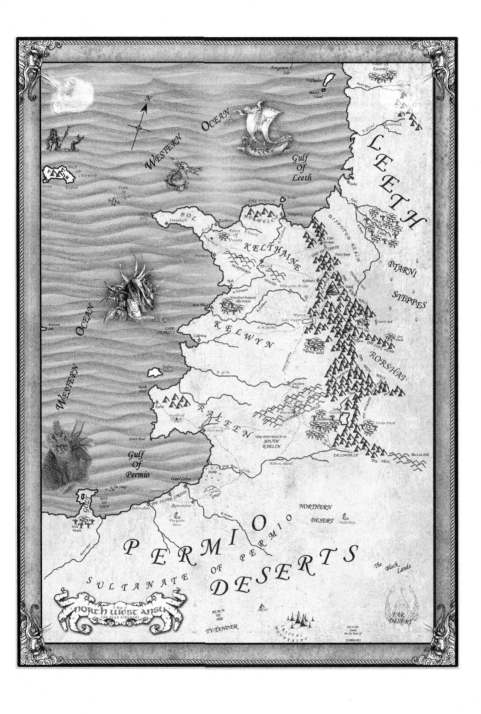

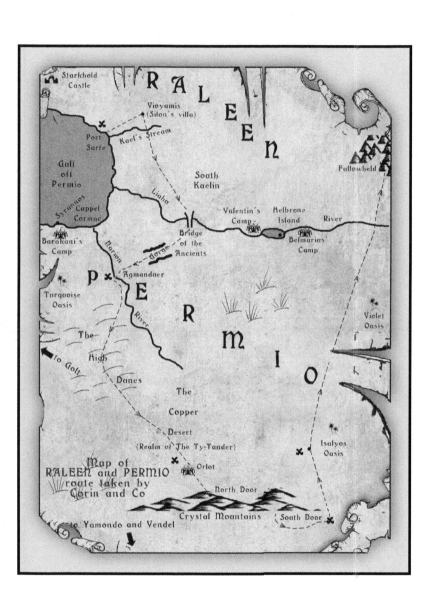

For my stepson Rhys
'A man to be proud of.'

Table of Contents

Part One

Raleen

Chapter 1

Rascals

Silon hated Permio. It wasn't just the noise and smell of the place, or the constant threat of danger. This desert country had a different feel to it than anywhere within the Four Kingdoms. It was always so hot here. Not to mention the stink and noise. Gone were the cool breezes that blessed his beloved vineyards in Raleen. The merchant was less than a hundred miles from his home, but he found it impossible to relax.

He was in Cappel Cormac—the stinking, festering home of every villain and cutpurse imaginable. And in this city Silon was a wanted man.

News had reached the coffee rooms of Permio's second largest city concerning the events in Crenna last month. Silon knew he had little time here and must return home quickly. Nor did he wish to linger, as every minute spent here was beyond dangerous.

The merchant waited restlessly for the contact he'd arranged to meet in this seedy place. A coffee house—dark, dirty and cluttered with unsavoury characters.

That man's choice, not his. Silon would have preferred somewhere quieter, perhaps nearer the wealthy quarter of the city. But he had bowed to the other man's knowledge. Besides this place was close to the quay, and ships sailed frequently across to Raleen. It wouldn't prove difficult slipping aboard one should the sultan's soldiers spot him. They would be very keen to apprehend him, those soldiers. The sultan in his wisdom had placed a price on Silon's head of two thousand crannels.

A tidy sum. All because he was suspected of smuggling contraband across the bay. It was just as well they didn't know his real business.

The room was harsh with voices and swirling smoke stung Silon's eyes, both tobacco and subtler substances. The smell of coffee beans and body sweat clung to his nostrils. Silon looked down with practiced disdain as a beggar held out a wooden bowl. The merchant signalled and the man was carried outside and pitched into the filthy street below. Cappel Cormac was a pitiless place. Any act of kindness would be noticed here.

Silon pulled the hood of his brown burnoose down over his forehead, shrouding his features. Quietly he studied the occupants at the tables around him.

Over to his right, a couple of swarthy merchants were speaking in furtive whispers, glancing up occasionally from their piping bowls of coffee. Behind them leaned a tanned handsome warrior, from Sedinadola by his look. He was flirting shamelessly with the dark-eyed beauty in the corner.

The tavern was busy with folk coming and going. Silon noticed the odd northerner sweating in the dusty heat and looking uncomfortably conspicuous. At the back of the smoky room sat a huge black warrior who appeared to be grinning at nothing in particular. He had a ferocious look and his teeth gleamed like perfect pearls. Silon locked eyes with the man briefly before dropping his gaze. It did not pay to stare too long in a place like this.

A soft sound. Silon glanced up carefully when the seat was taken beside him. He nodded slowly at the newcomer. His contact's face was deeply tanned beneath the scarlet shemagh. It was a hard face, lined with thin scars and dominated by a hooked nose. The eyes were coaly black and crow-sharp as they acknowledged the merchant of Raleen.

"I trust that you are fit, my old friend?" the newcomer asked in a dry voice hinting at the arid winds of the desert.

"Indeed I am, Barakani," replied Silon. "You look as vigorous as ever," he added. "I trust that your seven sons are all well."

"Yes," the desert chief grinned at Silon. "Their strength waxes alongside their impatience. Those boys have little time for our sub- tleties, my friend. They would prefer to act now, as indeed would I were the time right."

"That time draws close, Barakani," Silon leaned forward to whisper in the other's ear. "However, there is another issue I hope you can assist me with."

Barakani raised a shrewd brow. "If I can."

"Something has occurred which I did not anticipate." Silon leaned closer. "Something of great import. I heard voices in the mar- ketplace claiming a young nobleman from the north had recently passed through the city, seeking a guide into the deep desert. A strange request that, don't you think?"

"Very strange," replied Barakani with a secret smile. "You wish to know his identity—this youth?" The merchant nodded slowly and Barakani continued in hushed tones.

"He is your missing prince. I am certain of it. I had one of my men follow him through the city seeing he came to no harm. The boy was dressed shabbily and looked travelworn, but I would recognise Kelsalion's wayward son anywhere."

Silon smiled. "I sometimes forget how familiar you are with the northlands, my old friend. Is it true you served in the Tigers for a time?"

"I wanted to learn how you northerners fight should you ever invade our lands again," grinned Barakani.

"Well, I am in your debt," responded Silon with a sigh of relief. "The fool boy was mad coming here alone, I doubt whether he would have made it out of the docks without your help." "Maybe not," replied Barakani. "But the boy didn't seem that helpless. Strangely, everyone saw him and yet no one intervened—something unheard of in Cappel Cormac. And why would he come here? There are far safer places to flee to even in Permio. It's very odd."

"Odder than you think."

"Ah..." Barakani took a slow sip from his piping coffee. He glanced about the crowded room before continuing with a sour expression. "The sultan's soldiers are crawling all over this city; his supreme ugliness suspects everyone, not just northern merchants, my friend. I saw no advantage in the prince being taken to Sedinadola for questioning. So I bid one of my men escort him into the desert, as was his wish."

"Where was Tarin's destination?" asked Silon.

"He wouldn't reveal it. Said only that he desired seeing the Crystal Mountains in the far south. A transparent lie or else a most peculiar desire—I couldn't tell which."

"And risk the Ty-Tander's fiery breath!" Silon raised an eyebrow. "How bizarre. Stories concerning that beast have often been heard in the courtrooms at Kella City. Tarin will be well aware of the risk he's taking. And that prince is not known for his boldness."

"My own thoughts exactly," responded Barakani. "But just who has put him up to this, Silon? And why?"

"I don't know and it worries me, my friend," responded the merchant. Silon took a sip of his drink and sighed. "Another shadowy player in the game, I suspect. At least we can assume he's not an ally of Caswallon."

"But what would the boy's mystery helper hope to achieve by such a venture?"

Barakani winced as his coffee found a sensitive tooth. "Could it be what I think?"

"It might be." Silon smiled slightly and changed the subject, Barakani's hawk gaze was curious but he let it go. These two needed each other—diplomacy was about give and take, after all. And there were some subjects too dangerous even for whispers.

"I am awaiting friends from the north." Silon took another wary sip at his coffee. "Queen Ariane leads them, the same lot who escaped Crenna a while ago on Captain Barin's ship. They can't be far from Raleen now. That's if they managed to evade the Assassin's pursuit."

"Why would they make for Raleen? Isn't Ariane Queen of Wynais?"

"Call it a hunch." Silon sipped and smiled. "After the excitement at Crenna, roads from the sea to the Silver city will be watched tirelessly by Caswallon and Hakkenon, and it was agreed between us that Ariane would journey here after returning home. Thus my assumption being she skipped Wynais and headed due south."

Barakani grinned like an old wolf. "Rael Hakkenon won't be in a happy state of mind. He's not used to being thwarted so easily." The Assassin was well known and feared in Permio too. There were rumours that Rael had accepted contracts from the sultan himself during the latter's early reign.

Silon nodded. "True enough. My spies sent word from that island via pigeon to my villa the other week. A dangerous business for which I take some responsibility. Queen Ariane was involved and the mercenary Corin who I told you about. He in particular will be able to help us in this business as he knows Permio."

"The business being...?"

Silon smiled slowly. Barakani always like playing these games. The wily desert chief was well aware of Silon's gambit. "We have to find the lost prince before our enemies do. That will involve individuals with specific skills. Corin being one. I need your assurance of their safe passage through the dunes."

Barakani laughed quietly, "You ask much, merchant. The sultan's spies are even more commonplace than his soldiers. And there are northern mercenaries in Permio already. I passed them several days ago. A rough lot, I assume in the pay of Caswallon. Word must have got out to him of Tarin's intended destination. Though quite how I cannot guess."

"Gribble most likely."

"And who might he be?"

"A winged goblin—Caswallon's new spy. My people in Kella sent word about it."

"Interesting." Barakani let that one go. "The mercenary captain I saw looked familiar. Tall. Lean. Hard grey eyes."

"That will be Hagan Delmorier."

"The renegade Morwellan?"

"The same. You know him too?"

"I heard about his reputation during the war," replied Barakani. "A cold proud bastard they say."

"Aye, that'll be him." Silon frowned. Hagan hadn't wasted any time coming south, there were reports of his whereabouts in Kashorn village less than two months ago. Doubtless he was looking for Queen Ariane but fortunately had had no luck. It was just as well he didn't come across Corin an Fol. Silon needed Corin focussing on the task ahead. Hagan and Silon's former employee were not best of friends.

Silon studied the shrewd eyes of the man seated opposite him. Barakani was relaxed and at ease in the coffee room, despite a price on his head in this city that made Silon's two thousand crannels a paltry sum. Barakani wasn't called the Wolf of the Desert for nothing. He had earned his reputation, as had his sons—all seven.

"I know I ask a lot, old friend," Silon whispered. "But no one knows the desert as well as you and your boys. I see a real chance here. We can thwart the sultan's plans, placing you nearer to the throne of Permio—your rightful place."

"I will do what I can. When will your people arrive?"

"I don't know and that worries me. Time is short and I expected them in Port Sarfe over a week ago. I've heard nothing since they escaped from Crenna."

"Perhaps they were delayed."

Silon nodded and took a long controlled sip from his cooled coffee before continuing. "One final question."

"Go on."

"Did Tarin carry a sack upon his person? A small bag, perchance?"

Barakani shrugged, shaking his head. "Of that I know nothing. But it would seem unlikely—even those unwilling to gut the boy would have taken his belongings. This *is* Cappel Cormac."

"Yes, that's what I feared."

"Leave these matters with me, Silon." Barakani's crafty eyes were scanning the tavern. "We have said enough," he added in a whisper. "We are being observed, my friend."

"Who?" answered Silon without looking round.

"A large fellow, black skinned—most likely a warrior from the distant south. They occasionally visit to trade. This one looks a confidant bastard. He is sitting in the far corner behind you. He's clever—I only just caught his eye. A spy for certain."

"Yes, I noticed him earlier," responded Silon. "Think you he's in the sultan's pay?" he asked in a whisper.

"I do not know," responded the desert chief. "But this is Cappel Cormac. Few strangers here are who they appear to be. You and I included, my friend."

They spoke for a while in hushed whispers before finishing their coffee in a leisurely manner. Silon stood up, made a show of fastidiously dusting his faded brown burnoose and then quietly left the tavern. He waited out of sight for some moments, saw Barakani emerge, nodded briefly in his direction and then faded subtly into the crowd.

Silon was worried. He'd better be getting back to his villa fast. If by some miracle Prince Tarin still had the remnants of the Tekara on his person they were in with a chance—albeit a only fool's chance. But the idiot prince must be protected at all cost. And before they could protect him they needed to find him.

And why would he make for the Crystal Mountains if he didn't have the remnants of the Tekara? *No*, thought Silon, *Tarin must still have the shards.* It was the only logical explanation for his being here. But as to what mental state Tarin would be in after being holed up in Kranek Castle?

Silon would have to act fast. He needed Corin. Corin knew northern Permio better than he did. But where were they? The voyage south shouldn't have taken them this long. And just who had put Tarin up to this? Doubtless the same individual that freed the boy from the Assassin? And evidently some while before Queen Ariane's party arrived unwitting in Kranek harbour. It irked Silon that someone acted outside his circle of knowledge. A freelancer playing a subtle game. But just whose side was he on? And who was he?

The questions kept coming. Silon hurried down towards the dockyard, jostling his way through the bustling crowd. Angry faces glared at him as he shoved past, and skinny dogs snarled and yapped. Down at the quayside he spotted a Morwellan trader—one of the few that recently escaped the sack of Vangaris harbour. She was making ready to leave port. Silon suspected the vessel would stop off at Port Sarfe before heading north to winter at Calprissa now Vangaris had fallen to the barbarian fleet. Silon stepped up his pace turning into a narrow alley.

Too late he realised his mistake.

Footsteps approaching fast from behind. The sound of steel slicing air. Silon ducked low as a robed figure with a purple sash swung a tulwar at him from behind.

He slammed his right shoulder back into his assailant's chest, forcing the big man off balance. Then Silon twisted and rammed his knee up hard into his attacker's groin. The man buckled and Silon kicked him in the face, sending him sprawling. Silon turned to run.

Again too late.

Two other men had arrived in the alley. These blocked his way ahead. Silon recognised them at once. They were the sultan's finest warriors. The Crimson Elite, named for the long cloaks they wore in honour of their ruler. These approached at speed, barring his way. The first one swung his blade as he leapt at Silon. Again the whoosh of steel through air.

But Silon was ready. He grabbed the nearest soldier's outthrust arm with his right hand. Then pulling him forward, Silon rammed his left palm hard up into the man's nose, snapping the bone. The soldier sunk to the floor, the curved blade clattering beside him. Clutching his secret dagger Silon knelt, swiftly despatching the sultan's soldier with a slice along his throat.

The remaining soldier hung back, seeing his accomplice so easily bested. Then he grinned, seeing the first assailant regain his feet amid curses and, tulwar raised, approach Silon from behind. Silon was trapped in the dirty alley, his back against the wall. They closed on him slowly, each wishing to savour the moment. Their broad tulwars held ready and hatred burning in their eyes.

Silon braced himself for the deathblow. He shut his eyes.

Moments passed—nothing.

Silon heard a loud grunt of pain followed by a meaty thud and the sound of a body hitting the dusty ground. A brief clang of steel followed then another groan and thud. Then a heavy voice laughed and Silon opened his eyes.

Standing before him, outlandishly dressed and grinning broadly, was the huge black warrior from the tavern. Slung across his back was the most extravagant array of weapons Silon had ever seen. In his sinewy left fist the huge stranger clutched a gold-capped cudgel. That gold was currently stained with the blood of the two soldiers he'd just brained. The stranger grinned as he reached down, hoisting Silon to his feet. The merchant gasped, for the man's grip was like iron.

"I am in your debt," he coughed. "May I ask your name?"

"I am Ulani, King of Yamondo," answered the stranger. His voice rich, deep and musical. "I have been seeking a merchant from Port Sarfe by the name of Silon."

"Well, I'm happy to report you have found him," responded

Silon. Awhile later at the quayside, and after the merchant had booked his passage, the stranger told his tale. It was then that Silon realised their troubles had only just begun.

Chapter 2

Renegades

A beast's cry in the night. *Shrill* and eerie, unlike anything she'd heard before. What foul creature could own such a voice? There it came again, closer this time, a weird howl too high pitched for a wolf's cry. Something hunted—something close.

Shallan opened her eyes and blinked at the cold grey predawn light. She wanted to stay wrapped in her blanket, hidden and safe. But there was no safety for her anymore. She and her father were fugitives in an enemy land. Two weary strangers on the run. Shallan's face paled as howling broke out across the valley below where she and the duke lay nestled in the false security of their copse. More canine baying and barking, but these were not hounds or wolves. Shallan wanted to cover her ears and scream out loud. Instead she kept still, slowed her wild heartbeat, and tried to gauge their distance. There were many. And they were close.

Shallan rolled free of her blanket. The horses had gone—how was it they hadn't heard that? One of the bridles still hung twisted and broken from the branch she'd tethered her mare to late last night. Poor things, they must have been terrified. And now they had gone—bolted off into the gloom. Shallan blinked at the hoofprints a half score yards away. Tangled tracks on muddy ground. A light dusting of snow coated the earth, and thin rime in a puddle close by cast back the half-moon's white face as he spilled free of wary cloud. Shallan saw them then. Ungainly figures, distorted shapes shambling and jostling, barking and growling down in the whitened fields below. What they were, she couldn't begin to guess.

"Sorcery!" her father hissed in Shallan's ear. It was evident the duke had slept heavier than she, being exhausted from their ride the day before. He looked confused, on the verge of panic.

"This is Caswallon's work, daughter." Shallan's wild gaze locked with the duke. Lord Tomais did not look well this morning. The bitter cold. The long hard rides through rain and sleet. The loss and the failure to hold his city...his land. All were weighing him down.

And now these *things* were hunting them.

"There're getting closer!" Shallan clutched a thin wet branch of willow forming part of the withy thicket that had until recently hidden them so well. Terror gnawed at her breast, she felt sick and angry. Betrayed. They had come so far, done so well, she and her father. Almost they were at the border. Free Wynais, the silver city, home of her cousin Queen Ariane, was only two score miles south. But it was hopeless. These things (whatever they were) had caught their scent. They were closing fast.

"Father, we must flee!" Shallan tugged at his sleeve but the duke seemed fey. Trapped in the knowing certainty of awful death.

"No!" Shallan screamed. She slid the dagger from her father's belt as he stared hooked and broken at the horrors approaching the copse. Shallan bit her lower lip and readied the blade.

They'll not have us! First you, Father, then me...

Shallan raised the knife towards the duke's throat. He didn't even notice. He was far away. Lost. Shallan's hand froze as another howl erupted just a few yards below where they stood. Still clutching the thin blade she turned her head toward the baying din below. Her grey-blue eyes were determined, angry and half crazed with fear. Shallan could see them clearly now. Tall thin shapes—hooded, the features barely discernible. Then Shallan glimpsed the twisted dog face of one approaching creature and shuddered. Mostly they walked on hind legs, though some dropped and sniffed, clawing at the snow-crusted ground.

They were only yards away and the howling was everywhere. The wood was surrounded. Shallan knew there would be no escape. She gripped the knife harder, feeling its hilt greasy beneath her sweating grasp. The cold steel bit lightly into her father's neck. Tomais didn't flinch but a bead of blood showed bright on his collar. Shallan shivered when she saw it. The howls were rising in pitch. In seconds they would be torn apart. No time to hesitate. Must finish this...

Sorry, Father...

'NO!" a voice came booming through the trees. Shallan froze. A crash and thud. A bright light dazzling her vision. *What's this?* The creatures stopped momentarily in confusion as something heavy hit the turf to settle shiny at Shallan's feet.

A horn.

The knife fell from Shallan's fingers. The duke blinked, aside from that he looked like a dead man. The dog-things reared up slavering, hungry keen, no longer distracted. But Shallan no longer hesitated, she reached down, seized the horn with both pale hands. A thing of beauty, curving and tapering and two feet in length. A great tusk, mottled cream and grey, with wide hoops of rune-engraved silver. Had she time to look, Shallan would marvel at the ornate engravings on the silver bands. Though it was heavy in her arms, she had no trouble lifting it. Something was giving her strength and, raising the horn to her trembling lips, Shallan blew a long clear note.

The dog creatures froze at the edge of the copse—they seemed uncertain, puzzled by the horn's clear note. They started circling, barking and pawing at the earth below. They looked agitated, confused.

Shallan tore her gaze away from them. She blew again—harder. The note resonated through the valley. It gave her confidence. Beside her the duke stirred as one waking from a coma. Shallan's lips parted ever so slightly. She smiled. This time the creatures howled as though in pain. They snarled and barked in what appeared to be panic, tearing and snapping at each other.

Shallan raised the horn a third time. Again she blew even harder than before. Again the note silenced the valley. It silenced the howlers too. They lay motionless as though struck by invisible lightning, their snouts oozing slime, and dark steam venting from their lifeless hides.

Shallan felt the alien strength rush out of her as she gazed at the stinking corpses all around. She felt weak, exhausted and shocked. Her knees wobbled and she dropped the horn. But as the giddiness assaulted her, Shallan wrapped her right hand around a willow branch and held tight, taking deep breaths. The duke's eyes found the dead creatures. He blacked out again.

"What are those... things?" Shallan whispered to herself between breaths.

"Groil."

"What?" Had she more strength Shallan would have jumped in alarm. The voice was deep and came from right behind her. *Who?* But Shallan already guessed the answer to that. Slowly she let go of the branch. She turned, saw him standing there in silence with massive arms folded, scarce two yards ahead.

The Horned Man.

***

"You saved us." Shallan barely managed the words.

He shook his head—this stranger/friend from her dreams—his heavy face oaken dark, and the horns jutting out from behind his pointed ears. Much smaller horns than the one at Shallan's feet, but impressive nonetheless. He loomed close like a great gnarly tree, hugely muscled with barrel chest and corded thigh. He was naked save for the dark woollen trousers that clung to his thighs.

At last he spoke. His voice, though quiet, resonated through the trees.

"You saved yourself. I merely supplied the opportunity." The Horned Man watched her with those huge mysterious eyes. "You have the strength, Shallan. Few mortals can blow that horn." He smiled then. A sad, ageless expression.

A slight sound to her left. Shallan was relieved to see her father hunched and pale, staring as one stricken at the carcases below. Shallan felt a stab of pain as she watched him there. *Father, you are not well.* She let her gaze fall to the horn at her feet.

"This horn is yours?"

"No longer."

"Those...things?" Shallan looked up, saw that the Horned Man watched her still.

He spoke again, his voice sounding like wood smoke under winter rain.

"Servants of the other side." He turned away, showed her his back. Shallan marvelled at the width of his naked shoulders, taking in the huge corded muscles moving along his arms, enhanced by the fine tracery of blue tattooing darkening his oak-hard skin.

Shallan didn't know what to say. Beside her the duke shivered and clutched his cloak, if he saw the Horned Man he showed no sign of it. "Caswallon?" Shallan asked after stealing a glance at her father. He looked physically sick and about to pass out again. She reached out, supported his frail body.

"Perhaps now," the Horned Man responded, his dreamy gaze still on the valley below. Now and then a howl pierced the murk hinting there were more out there. All else was silent and still. "But once they served another people. A race long departed...like my own."

"We owe you our lives," Shallan said as her father blinked at the rain seeing nothing in the gap through the trees. "That horn..."

"It's a gift. There will be others."

"Why?" Shallan reached down and lifted the horn. Strange how it felt lighter this time. "A wonderful gift—wait!" The horned figure was departing—striding off at speed into the mist which had thickened to shroud the valley below.

"How can I repay you?" Shallan called after him.

Silence.

"Who are you? Why do you help us?" Shallan's voice was muffled by the rain. But he heard her. Looking down, Shallan thought she glimpsed him far below. He had turned his gaze upon her again.

"You're kin..." the Horned Man replied before turning back and vanishing in the gloom.

Shallan turned, hearing a soft thud. The duke had found his feet but was coughing up blood. He looked awful. "Those things are dead—thank the gods! But what killed them when they were almost upon us?"

"This did." Shallan held up the large horn and the duke's face blanched in horror.

"Throw it away!"

"What?"

"It's a thing of evil."

"It saved us! Did you not hear me blowing it, Father?"

"I heard a murmuring like night wind through winter trees."

Shallan rolled her eyes. She wondered if her father would ever return to the man he had been instead of this mess that slumped before her. She tried again. "Did you not see him father—the Horned Man? He saved us! His strength enabled me to blow this horn."

"I saw no one," muttered the duke, a crease of doubt lining his brow. "I saw nothing."

"But he was here, Father. I—"

A snort announced the horses' return. Shallan smiled as the relief flushed her cheeks. Both beasts appeared fine, though their eyes were wild and their manner still skittish. Shallan settled them and took the meagre provisions from her mare's saddlebag. The duke needed food. He stood swaying and gaping at the corpses already rotting below. Shallan lashed the horn to her saddle, determined to solve its mystery in time. Pursuing the discussion further today was fruitless. Time to move and get Father moving. Once they had eaten it was one last push. With luck they would skirt Kelthara without being spotted, cross the border and enter Kelwyn where her cousin ruled.

Ariane—that was another matter.

***

The fear had nearly broken him—back then. Almost he had lost his reason in that cold damp place. Naked and filthy and alone. Certainly he'd lost all sense of time. How long had he been incarcerated? Months? Weeks? Somehow Prince Tarin had clung to that tiny seed of hope. The stranger—Zallerak. He would come as promised and set him free.

But there were times when even that tiny hope was obliterated, down there in the numbing dark where the shadows mocked him. Being alone was bad enough. But when *he* came. Those were the times when the prince nearly broke.

Rael never touched him, but would appear in front of his face with angry torchlight and a lone huge guard. Those green eyes would feast on Tarin's terror. And Rael would whisper hints of what lay ahead for him. His face inches from the cage, the Assassin would smile and speak almost conspiringly as though he and his captive shared some huge joke. And Tarin would weep as his tormentor so eloquently described the many little *surprises* he had in store for the prince.

Then he would vanish without a sound, and the grim silent guard behind him, leaving Tarin alone with his terror. These were the worst times. But then the Assassin stopped coming.

Time wore on. The guard would arrive and shove cold gruel and stale water through the cage. They didn't feed him often—just enough to keep him alive. Tarin's young body was a mass of sores from his own filth. His joints ached from the damp and he was always so cold. The cage, though big enough for him to stand, allowed no room for lying down. What sleep the prisoner got was shallow and tortured by the promise of worse to come.

Then Zallerak came.

At first Tarin thought this another cruel trick of his captors. Somehow Rael had got wind of his ruse and had come down here to mock him. Tarin had cried out in terror as the tall figure of the bard loomed in front of him, pawing at him and muttering in annoyance.

Then the cage door clanged and swung open amid creaks. Deceptively strong arms hauled the stinking prince out to lie, weeping and shivering on the filthy stone floor of the dungeon.

"Wake up!" Tarin blinked through tears and then almost grinned like an idiot when it finally dawned on him that he was free.

"You...came..."

"Of course I bloody-well came—I said I would, didn't I?" The bard had lost none of his rasping wit. "There is need of haste here. Quick now don these garments, boy."

Zallerak produced a sack from somewhere and turned it upside down, spilling its various contents into a heap on the floor. Tarin gawped at trousers, a broad leather belt, boots, a green tunic and a heavy woollen cloak with a large copper brooch. Last of all a heavy hunting knife clattered on the cobbled stone beside the pile of clothing.

Tarin needed no further prompting. He rushed to clothe himself but struggled to stand in his weakened state. Zallerak assisted him until the prince was fully clad.

"You stink," Zallerak grumbled. "You'll have to wash in a stream once free of these mountains, I've only a little water and that's for drinking—sparingly, boy."

Tarin nodded happily. He was free and besides, no longer smelled his own stench.

"Hungry—or is that a stupid question?"

"Yes..."

"Here, I filched this from the kitchens." Zallerak, as if by magic, produced a large chop and shoved it into the prince's right fist. Tarin just stared at it in wonderment.

"Eat, idiot."

"Thank you." Tarin's weakened sense of smell caught a whiff of the pork and his stomach grumbled. Without further ado he tore into the meat, his aching teeth bleeding as he bit upon it.

"Slowly. Let your stomach adjust, boy," Zallerak urged him. "Small chunks—twenty chews a bite." The bard watched in the gloom while Tarin slowly consumed his chop. Zallerak grunted approval. Already the prince looked stronger. He had mettle despite his shortcomings. The bard had chosen well. The prince was strong in body, and his mind not as weak as most thought. He would do.

"You had best be on your way," Zallerak told him.

Tarin blinked through the murk. His eyes, though well accustomed to the dark, could see no way out of this dreadful place. He blinked again.

"What's the matter?"

"Where do I go? I don't know the way."

"Do I have to do everything for you, boyo? Want me to aim your prick when you take a piss?"

Tarin said nothing.

"At the far end of this oubliette is another passage, unused for many years. This eventually leads out to a secret postern at the northern edge of the mountains. It will take several hours so be sparing with that water. You will be hungry and cold but at least you will be free."

Tarin nodded and wished he had another chop to chew on.

"Once you're out in the open make haste for the coast—it's not that far. Drink and wash in mountain streams, there's still berries about so you needn't starve. The brooks will lead you to a river, shallow and swift. Wade it and follow the far bank down to a village on the coast. Got that?"

Tarin nodded.

"Good. Once there wait until dark and steal a boat. There'll be several scattered along the shore. You want a simple craft, small and buoyant with a single sail."

I don't know anything about boats," complained the prince.

"Time to learn then." Zallerak grinned at him. "Oh, I almost forgot, you will need this to guide your craft."

"What is that?" The bard had thrust a heavy circular object into Tarin's palm. The prince blinked down at it.

"A lodestone—so you don't get lost on the waves, boy."

"How do I use it?

"Learn."

That had been almost three weeks ago. Tarin had left Zallerak alone in the dungeon. He hadn't asked what the bard had planned. He didn't care, just wanted to win free of this terrible island.

And so he had stumbled the length of that dark tunnel at last emerging into the wide blue of a cold autumn day. That sudden bright glare had momentarily blinded him, causing Tarin to blink and stagger like a drunkard. After getting his vision back, Tarin had drunk long from a stream, its clear clean water reviving him. He'd stripped and washed until at last he felt almost a shadow of his former self.

He survived on meagre berries and such until he found the village. Once there Tarin raided a smokehouse, stowing strips of dried kipper in the pockets of his trousers. These he consumed while waiting for darkness beneath a hut until he could hear its occupants above snoring blissfully.

At that point, Tarin stole out and commenced scanning the beach. He soon spotted a craft suitable for his needs. Next came the tricky part. Tarin was still weak and he didn't have a clue what he was doing. Somehow he got the tub in the water and began thrashing about with an oar. It was challenge enough, even without the cold, wet and dark. He capsized twice and almost drowned, but at last cleared the heavy surge of breaker and paddled out into the deep.

Next challenge had been the short mast and sail. The mast he'd raised without much ado. But the sail was another matter. A triangular soaked pile of cloth with ropes attached. What went where?

As dawn greyed the skies, Tarin hauled the cloth up and got some basic notion of how the ropes worked. Then Tarin produced the lodestone and gaped at it for a moment. Another problem he had to solve. But eventually he fathomed that the needle inside the circle must point north, and so as long as he kept the left side of his boat facing in that direction he would eventually arrive at the shore of Kelthaine. He hoped. It was very tenuous, this sailing business.

During that crossing Tarin had surprised himself at how quickly he mastered every challenge. He soon discovered how to read the sail, adjust the ropes and alter course when the need occurred. He became deft at the tiller and studied his lodestone on the hour.

At last Tarin spied cliffs, distant and dark. Kelthaine, or else Fol—but land for sure.

By some miracle (or perhaps Zallerak's design) the prince grounded his craft just ten miles north of Fardoris harbour.

Now for the next challenge...

"Return to Fardoris and get the shards," Zallerak had told him back in the dungeon. "Make sure you gather them all. Once that's done make haste south to Kelwyn. Don't tarry there—keep journeying south."

"Where to?"

And Zallerak had told him and that had been another bad moment.

Chapter 3

Hints and Innuendos

I'm not going back there. *Corin an* Fol had had enough. It had been a crap day. And now Queen Ariane was informing them calmly of her plan to sail happily past her own country and fare further south. To Port Sarfe to be precise and then on to Vioyamis, his former employer's sumptuous estate.

Of all places. Vioyamis, home of Silon the bloody merchant and his meddlesome daughter. Corin had vowed never to go back there.

"What's your problem?" Ariane wore that lofty queenly look. Disapproving and vexed. Only two hours ago they had been so close.

"Nothing really." Corin knew he was defeated. No one else seemed to give a toss, and then Barin made matters worse by suggesting that staying clear from Kelwyn was sensible.

"It will foil His Nibs," the blond giant insisted later that day. "My guess is that Rael will split up and order they search the harbours between Port Wind and Calprissa." Barin closed one nostril with his thumb and blew vigorously through the other. He stood with Corin and Bleyne at the prow of *The Starlight Wanderer*. The meeting was over. They had their orders. The new glinty-eyed Ariane had vanished imperious inside her cabin. Corin had watched her shut the door behind her whilst he wondered which god he'd pissed off today. *And I thought you loved me.*

It was the evening of the second day since fleeing Crenna. Close by were Galed and Cale, now fast friends—although that didn't stop them quarrelling over their dice game. There was no sign of Zallerak. Barin was his usual cheerful self. They'd had fair weather since the Sea God's fog had lifted, and the air was warm for the time of year. It helped raise their spirits while they mourned the loss of Roman Parantios, the Queen's late champion whose self-sacrifice had enabled their escape.

"Will we be able to stay ahead of them?" Corin asked, determined to get to grips with one matter at least.

The Northman rubbed his blond beard and squinted at the sails. "I hope so. I suspect they'll search the coast as far as Raleen. That should give us a few days' grace hopefully—thanks to Zallerak."

Corin scanned the deck but saw no sight of the enigmatic bard/warlock/pain in the arse. Zallerak had kept a low profile lately. Corin asked Barin their best course of action.

"That Assassin's pride has been dented," responded his friend. "He'll not rest until we are in his hands. We'll need somewhere to hole up for a time and discuss our next move in safety. Silon's villa is perfect."

"If you say so." Corin stretched his back and yawned.

"What is it with you and Silon?"

"What has he said about me?" Corin glared at Barin suspiciously.

"Nothing. He just always looked in pain whenever I mentioned your name."

Corin barked a laugh. "Can't think why. You know I was shaft-"

A yell from above brought their conversation to an abrupt end.

"Arseholes in sight!"

"Where away, old chap?" demanded Barin, shielding his eyes.

"Far to the northeast!" responded Cogga, hidden by a flourish of sail. "Six of the fuckers!"

"Cheer up, Cogga, at least it's not the whole bloody fleet." Barin handed the wheel to Corin. "Hold steady on this course," the Northman told him.

Corin watched Barin stride across the deck, grab the rigging, and heave himself up the mast with an agility that defied his bulk. In minutes the ship's master had disappeared in the mass of taut sailcloth above. A few minutes later he returned, his expression resigned.

"There are six, Cogga's right. And they're led by *The Black frigging Serpent* herself." Corin shielded his eyes and followed Barin's directions.

"Do you see them?"

"No."

"Over there! Follow my hand!"

"You keep waving it about...oh, I see now." Corin could just make out six triangular shapes lifting above the waves.

"Sure it's them?"

"Who else?"

"Shit." Corin scratched his scar and pictured Rael Hakkenon's face with Biter imbedded in it.

I'm still here, Assassin.

"We'll change tack," responded Barin, "head out to sea for a while. I doubt they'll follow too close; the swells are bigger out there. Their small crappy ships could flounder." Barin grinned, impressed by his own wisdom. "We'll hold a western course while the light holds out. Then we'll turn south east and make for the coast of Raleen."

"Simple as that," Corin couldn't help saying.

Barin yelled at Fassof to change course. Swiftly, and for once without backchat, the mate passed the orders on. Within minutes the trader had swung to face the setting sun.

"Can you work the wheel for a while?" Barin asked Corin. "I need to go below, void my bowels and consult my charts."

"Oh sure."

Somewhere above his head, Fassof was swearing at Cogga and Cogga was swearing back. Bleyne was nowhere to be seen, and Cale and Galed had retired below after hearing about the ships. The decks were empty. Most of Barin's lads were either dozing or dicing, saving a couple up above with the mate and Cogga.

Corin was content alone with his thoughts. The salt breeze whipped his shaggy locks. He grinned, relishing its cold embrace and enjoying the responsibility Barin had awarded him. It felt good to be doing something useful. Lethargy pulled him inwards. Made him think about *her*.

An hour passed. Fassof told a couple of lads to keep watch and retired below with the rest, Cogga included. Corin watched the lodestone as he worked the wheel westward. He thought of his father long ago on those fishing trips. Had he felt like this? But he wasn't Corin's true father. Corin didn't know who his father was. He heard footsteps behind him and turning saw Ariane standing there.

It was almost dark and he could see little of her face. The young queen had the green priest's cloak draped over her shoulders with its hood pulled low, shrouding her features. For a time she stood beside him. Neither spoke. Corin shuffled awkwardly and feigned concentration. His leg brushed her thigh and quivered. He felt his face flush as something stirred below. *Too late for that, she's promised to another.*

"I need to speak to Silon," Ariane announced as though that explained everything. Corin grunted, feeling acutely aware of those dark eyes burning into him. He fiddled with the wheel and stared hard at the horizon.

"Look at me, damn you."

Corin turned. "Why? When all that brings me is pain."

Ariane sighed. She took a seat on a bench close by and tossed the hood. Corin noticed how the night wind ruffled her hair.

"This simply won't do."

"What?"

"All this moping and whining. I need you strong, Corin an Fol."

"I'd die for you—how can you say that? Like this is some business agreement."

"Well, it was to begin with."

"That was then."

Ariane's gaze softened. "Yes, and this is now."

Corin couldn't stand this any longer. "Bollocks is what it is. I love you and you love me. Bugger the Sea God!"

"That's not an over bright statement, considering where we are," she almost smiled.

"Well I'm not overly bright, as you know. But I do know what I want and it's you."

"We've had that discussion."

"Yes I know—we both have separate tasks. All part of some bigger fucking plan. All...total bollocks." Corin sighed like a venting kettle.

Ariane flashed him a grin. "You've such a way with words."

It was his time to grin. "And you're a fine one to talk, Queeny."

Ariane stood and rested a pale hand on his arm. "Hold me."

Corin tensed. "Is this wise?"

"Probably not, but at this moment I really don't care."

Corin reached for her but a noise behind stopped him.

"Don't mind me." Zallerak wore an amused, slightly smug, expression.

It had to be you.

Corin thrust Ariane away as though she were a serpent and glared hard at the bard. The queen said nothing but her eyes were lit coals. She swept Zallerak a frosty gaze, and ignoring Corin, left them to it.

"Ariane I –" Too late. She'd vanished below.

"Thank you." Corin awarded the bard a bleak stare and then cursed, noticing he'd strayed some way off course.

Corin savaged the wheel until he was back on course, ignoring

Zallerak. Corin could feel that uncanny gaze upon him. Enough. He rounded on the bard.

"What do you want?"

Zallerak raised an eyebrow. "Why should I want anything?" He was dressed in his finery again, the magnificent sky-blue cloak lifting slightly in the night breeze.

Corin was suddenly very angry.

"Just piss off." He bit the words out as though they were hot chunks of bile. He couldn't stop thinking about Ariane below in her cabin. What was the matter with him? Corin wanted to go below, bang on her door, apologise. He hadn't meant to shove her away like that. Again—too late. Corin checked his anger. It was a useless emotion when dealing with Zallerak.

"You must want something," he added in a quieter tone. "Why go to all this trouble helping us and that fool prince?"

"I want many things, actually," responded Zallerak, unperturbed by Corin's hostile manner. "Few of them concern you."

"I am relieved to hear it." Corin gripped the wheel with sudden violence as if he meant to break it.

"Relax, you're too hot-headed, boy." This time Zallerak's voice held none of its mocking tones. Instead sounded reflective—honest even.

"I'm sorry I interrupted your... tryst," he coughed.

"We were just talking."

"Yes. Well, *we* need to talk too. I know this business is hard for you, Longswordsman. It's always hard when the powers intervene with our little lives." Corin raised a quizzical brow but Zallerak continued as though he hadn't noticed. "It is bothersome having those Fates and old Oroonin lurking about, not to mention the other lot."

"And what would you know about all that?"

"Quite a bit. Your path is not what you believe it to be, longfellow. That young queen is not for you, my boy."

"So everyone tells me—including her."

"So...listen to them."

Corin was close to striking the bard, but something in Zallerak's cold, clear stare stayed his hand.

"I'm sick of your hints and schemes, wizard. Why are you helping us—really?"

For an answer Zallerak stared up at the starry sky above. He sighed as though this conversation was hard for him too.

"Everyone has to take sides," Zallerak said eventually. "We are all flawed children of the Weaver, the creator of the multiverse. The High Gods, my people, you young folk, all of us make mistakes. And some of us make big ones."

"So?"

"Every one of us is a tiny strand in the cosmic web, Corin an Fol. Most never know it. They are allowed to stay ignorant and content. But you, my friend, have been chosen for greater things. I know why Oroonin watches over you, boy. I also know that Morak fears you and has reason to do so."

Corin blinked. "Please enlighten me," he replied.

"We are all of us connected." Zallerak was waving his arms about in wild demonstrative gesticulations, but Corin's gaze remained fixed on the horizon. "Every action demands reaction," Zallerak said. "The Weaver's thread is very sensitive. He hears every thought."

"Alright, don't enlighten me. But answer this."

"Go on."

"That dog-thing... Morak." Corin spun the wheel again, the ship was drifting to port. "The Huntsman, the Fates. Why pick on me?" he demanded.

"I would have thought that obvious." Zallerak was staring up at the sky.

"Not to me."

"Where were you born?"

"You know where I was born. What nonsense is this?"

"And what happened the day you were born?" Corin looked blank and Zallerak summoned patience. "In Finnehalle and along the south Fol coast."

"There was a storm, they do say. A bad one."

"Ships were wrecked." Zallerak winked at him.

"I daresay."

"One ship in particular." Corin felt a shiver.

"What of it?"

"Your mother..? Your older brother... your aunt..."

"So what? They all died on a ship, I was washed up and reared as an orphan by the fisherfolk of Gol. And then they all died too. Happy fucking story."

"Your father isn't dead, Corin."

"I'm not listening."

"You never fucking do. But one fine day, my bonnie lad, you're going to have to wake up to who you really are. Any more questions?"

"Not for now." Corin's head was churning. Zallerak was right, he did shut things out. His childhood was a blur. No one had ever spoken much about that storm—why?

"The High Gods seldom reveal their intentions." Zallerak's tone had softened. He knew he had struck a nerve. "Oroonin is cunning. I suspect he has some glorious part for you to play in the ensuing war, but the Huntsman never shows his hand."

"Not unlike yourself," Corin couldn't help replying.

Zallerak turned toward him. Corin held those beguiling eyes in his steely gaze for a moment before turning away. Corin wondered what manner of being stood before him.

"Who are you, Zallerak?" Corin's gaze surveyed the glossy, black waters, shimmering beneath the stars. It was a beautiful night to be on deck. But that beauty was lost on Corin.

"You, Corin an Fol, are a persistent pain in the arse," Zallerak chuckled. "Wear anyone down, you will." He adjusted his cloak. "But then so was your ancestor when I met him."

Corin shut that out too.

"I am many things, Longswordsman. And yes, I too have a role to play in this situation we find ourselves thrust into. I can say no more at present, lest I send unwary words into the ether and alert our foes. They are always listening in."

Corin scratched an ear and yawned. "You sound like Silon—all glibbery and riddles."

Zallerak waved a dismissive arm. "If you survive the months ahead you will doubtless learn more. Suffice to say our paths run parallel for a time. Your enemy is my enemy—hence we are allies, if not friends. I would rather be friends. There is too much distrust in this world, and even I get lonely from time to time."

"You don't say." Corin guided the wheel. "But what's Caswallon's dog gang done to upset you?"

"You know there's more involved here, Corin, so don't act obtuse. My enemy is vastly more powerful than Caswallon, although he is not as he once was—thank the gods.

"Dog Face Morak. Of course, how could I forget?"

"I gave him a hiding back there on the island." Zallerak was waving his arms again. "I wouldn't have been able to do that if he'd had Golganak with him. His nasty spear. He'll rally though; Morak's not one to give up."

"I assumed you'd encountered that bastard before."

"Many times," Zallerak grinned suddenly. "We are veteran adversaries, the Dog-Lord and me. I could destroy him easily if he wasn't hiding in limbo. I cannot reach him there and to try to do so would prove my undoing. He is a creature of chaos and so limbo's void suits his purpose whilst protecting his ghost from any attack. Morak serves Old Night, the lord of chaos, and I serve -"

"You serve yourself," cut in Corin.

"And you do not?"

"That's beside the point—my goals seem transparent to all save myself." Corin didn't like where this conversation was going. "Don't get me wrong, wizard. I'm grateful for your aid. I don't trust you is all—no offence."

"Trust," laughed Zallerak. "What care I for that? Just accept that we are allies in this business."

Corin was about to press the matter when Fassof's shout cut

through his thought like a meat cleaver hewing chuck steak.

"You in control of that wheel or playing with your dick? We're way off course, Corin!"

"Sorry..."

Corin cursed, he'd drifted again—badly. The swell was hitting the beam. The thudding movement had brought the angry mate out on deck. Corin swung the wheel until the brig was back on course. Satisfied, he turned to confront Zallerak again but the bard was nowhere to be seen.

When Barin came on deck he found a moody companion at the wheel. Corin ignored his friend.

"Don't let Fassof get to you," Barin said. "He even shouts at me sometimes."

"I am not concerned with Fassof!" snapped Corin. Without further word he spun the wheel into Barin's huge paw and descended below deck like a storm cloud. Barin shook his head as he corrected their course again.

"I guess he needs ale," he said to himself."

Barin had changed his mind after consulting his charts. He now decided to keep to their western course for most the night. At sunrise he'd hearken south again. He hummed to himself cheerfully. It was peaceful here on deck and he was full of ale. Barin saw no sign of Corin, or anyone else until well after sunrise.

Chapter 4

Gribble

"Mr Caswallon's not happy." *This from the* goblin creature who'd just landed on his deck, and narrowly avoided being skewered by Scarn, the newly promoted first mate. "He ain't happy at all."

"What do you want?" Rael Hakkenon had only just regained composure after finally cutting through the fog that had swallowed Barin's ship, allowing the renegades slip his net.

"I was mid-flight," explained Goblin Gribble. "Just passing. Thought I'd drop by and share my wisdom. You should be grateful, Mr Assassin, you need all the friends you can get. The boss is vexed about all the nonsense on your island. Get off!" This last to Scarn who was attempting to spike the creature with his cutlass.

"Leave it," Rael waved Scarn back. Behind the mate the men had gathered wide-eyed to watch the winged ghastliness hop about on deck. "And, you lot, find something useful to do."

Scarn hesitated, his one good eye blinking at the hideous, squat, hunched horrible whatever it was, addressing his captain. "But that thing, lord, it's-?"

Rael shot Scarn a glint of jade and the mate slunk back and signalled the men to follow him amid mutters.

Rael wrenched his disgusted gaze from the Soilfin, and instead he held up the golden spyglass to his left eye and watched from the gleaming prow of *The Black Serpent* as the distant sails of *The Starlight Wanderer* sank below the western horizon. All damned day to find them and then lose them to dark.

Scrape, scrape. Gurgle and belch. Soilfins are not easy creatures to ignore.

"You still there?" Rael turned, awarded Gribble a withering gaze.

Gribble showed his fangs in what might be described as a conspiratorial grin." I am waiting to hear your excuses so I can report back to Mr Caswallon. After supper of course." The Soilfin licked its lips and made a vulgar sucking sound.

Rael set the glass down carefully. He fingered his rapier's hilt and narrowed his gaze. "You won't get far with my blade shoved up your arse, goblin." Gribble hopped along the deck and spat at him.

"No need for that, Mr Assassin. All friends here. No need to get your weapon out."

Rael summoned his last inch of patience. His hand dropped idly from the rapier. "Those bastards were aided by sorcery—tell Caswallon that. That's his department not mine. And tell him I'm going to catch them and boil the lot in a bloody great kettle, after I've removed various body parts with blunt instruments. I'll spare the little queen, though I'd be doing him a favour if I cooked her too."

"Will you save me some scraps?" Gribble shuffled closer and dribbled.

"Only if you make yourself useful."

"Doin' what? I'm pressed for time." The Soilfin looked pained.

"Track yonder vessel before the night swallows it, see what Barin's up to. Listen in and then fly back and inform me."

"I don't work for you, I work for Mr Caswallon," Gribble sulked. "I don't do private contracts."

"We won't tell him then, will we?"

"I'm not sure, sounds risky. They're a rough bunch."

"I'll let you chew on a big one, maybe even Barin Haystacks."

"Aw." That did it. Without further ado the Soilfin thrust out his grubby wings, flapped twice producing a sound like wet leather on wood, and levitated from the ship in one manic lurch.

"I won't be long," Gribble squeaked before circling twice and then bolting at speed toward the distant ship. The Assassin watched him go.

Gribble was back inside an hour demanding something to eat. Rael tossed him a ham sandwich fresh from the galley.

"That won't keep me going for long," the Soilfin complained, but gulped the meal just the same.

"What did you find out?"

"Not a lot."

"What precisely?"

"I lurked close, hid in a sail. The haystack was on the wheel nattering to the moody scarred one with the long blade."

"What were they discussing?"

"Beer mostly and women. Oh, and how shit their luck was. But mainly beer."

Rael slid his jewelled dagger into his left hand and rolled it across his fingers.

"What... else?"

"That's about it really, there was no one else around. Haystack said something about Port Sarfe, wherever that is."

Rael smiled ever so slightly. "What about Port Sarfe?"

"I didn't hear that bit."

"Listen to me, goblin. You're going to fly back there, lurk till morning, or else creep inside the cabin and wait until you can ascertain exactly they're planning."

"I don't do that sort of work," complained Gribble. "It's hazardous."

"It will prove a sight more hazardous if you stay here another second." Gribble complained again and this time added that he'd forward his grievances to Mr Caswallon. Despite that he complied, and within moments had voided his awful presence from the ship.

Rael sighed. He felt strangely weary, so ordered one of his men to uncork the brandy flask. There Rael sat for a time watching wave and sky as the wind cleansed the stink of the goblin, and falling darkness aided the strong drink lull his senses.

Morning came bright and clear. No *Starlight Wanderer* and no bloody goblin. Rael wasn't fazed. He'd already made up his mind. He was glad he'd split the fleet sending those other ships to cover Kelwyn's ports. Cruel Cavan was in charge of that lot so he needn't worry about Kelwyn. Rael decided he'd bid three sharks to sail further south hugging along the coast into northern Raleen, from where they'd join him later. Meanwhile the remaining two would follow *The Black Serpent* and cut straight for southern Raleen.

Rael smiled. "Scarn!" The one-eyed mate appeared. "I've changed my mind. Set course for Port Sarfe!"

"Aye, my Lord!" Scarn hollered the orders and *The Black Serpent* swung about. They'd head south west and cut Barin off. And if the goblin was wrong, so what? Rael would enjoy the trip anyway.

***

Gribble wasn't enjoying his trip. This little visit was far too risky in his opinion. The promise of a whole Barin to gestate seemed a long way off as he spent that chilly night hunched and muttering beneath a coil of rope on the aft deck of *The Starlight Wanderer*. Gribble didn't care for Mr Assassin. But there was something about old green eyes that got inside the goblin and made him shiver. It was usually the other way round with mortals.

Gribble's stomach gurgled. It would be light soon. Time to investigate then fly back for another sandwich.

***

Corin woke to a strange scratching sound close to the hatch above. He opened an eye, saw the boy Cale staring at him. "What is it?" Corin rolled free of his blanket and blinked at Cale.

"I can't sleep. I keep thinking about Crenna and Roman." Cale had been very quiet since their escape from Crenna. He appeared older than his fourteen years, although his red shock of mane was unkempt as ever.

"Are you going to kill that Assassin?"

"I have vowed to do so." Corin noticed that the boy's blue eyes were rimmed with red. Cale had loved Roman too. Corin smiled at the lad, feeling sudden warmth toward him. He remembered Roman's last words to the boy.

"You did well at Kranek," Corin told him. "You have a good heart, Cale, and a brave one at that."

"It's good that you're going to kill him," responded Cale. Most his spots had dried up. He looked healthier and fitter than he had when he'd joined them back at Kashorn. There were fresh tears in his eyes now. "Because if you don't then I will." They both turned to see the queen emerge bright and clean from her cabin.

"I would have tea." Ariane motioned Cale to look into that. She turned to Corin. "You two are awake early." Her tone was brisk and no softness spilled from her gaze.

"As are you, my Queen." Ariane ignored the formality. It didn't suit Corin and they both knew it. She glanced up, hearing a strange gurgling sound.

"What's that?"

Corin shrugged. "Seabird." Cale returned with a flask of hot tea. Ariane thanked him and made her way through to the master's cabin. Barin was sitting at table studying a chart. He nodded when the queen walked in. Behind her, Corin and Cale took seats. No one noticed the squat bulbous shadow squeezing through the hatch and creeping behind the door.

"We need to talk about the next stage," Ariane announced into her tea.

"Next stage?" Barin blinked up from his chart. "It's a bit early. Silon's house, you mean?"

"No. Of course Silon will be anxious to speak with us. Tamersane must have informed him of our quest by now. We will regroup at Vioyamis. After that respite we need prepare ourselves for another difficult journey."

"Where?" asked Corin, his eyes on the table.

"South, into the desert. Obvious, is it not?" Zallerak joined then at table. "We've a job to finish." An odd scraping sound announced movement outside the door, Zallerak glanced that way and his blue gaze narrowed.

"Can you elucidate, Sir Zallerak?" Ariane's clipped tone drew his attention back from the door. The queen glanced at Corin, who sat with arms folded and expression resigned. Beside him Cale looked excited.

"I will tell you what I can," Zallerak said. "After freeing Prince Tarin and showing him an escape tunnel from Kranek Castle, I bid him seek a nearby village and purloin a boat. Which I trust he managed successfully—I gave him a good compass so he'd find the mainland without much trouble."

Galed joined them, helping himself to a cup of the queen's tea and yawning. "Why's everyone up so early?" Galed asked.

"The boy's task was to relocate the shards of the crown," explained Zallerak, ignoring Galed as did everyone else. "Those little bits of crystal he had very sensibly buried at my bidding in a graveyard near Fardoris—just before his capture.

"After that, Tarin's plan was a stowaway passage to Permio. Purchase a horse in one of the desert towns with stolen coin, (or else steal a horse and not bother with the coin).

"Go seek out Croagon the ancient Smith-God who (rumour says), still resides below the Crystal Mountains." Zallerak scratched his long nose and drained his glass again. His mostly baffled and half asleep audience waited for him to continue.

"So with that in mind, I placed a ward of protection over his person when I sent him packing. Plan being, the fool prince could prepare the way for us to follow. He should have reached the desert by now."

"This is fucking ridiculous, if you don't mind me saying so," Corin muttered. "I'm not buying this crap and nor should anyone else. And I am not going anywhere near the fly-cursed deserts of Permio! Crenna was bad enough."

"Enough, Corin!" Ariane shot a withering glance his way and Corin slunk back into his seat.

"I'm just saying." Corin held Ariane's gaze for a second then shrugged.

"What care you about our lost prince?" Ariane asked Zallerak, her tone sharp. She was irritated by the way Corin was acting and chose to ignore him entirely.

"I must say I am most enamoured by your gratitude," responded Zallerak tartly. His large eyes had darkened to an angry violet and sparkled furiously under his heavy silver brows. "I save you all from the talons of that Assassin and his cronies and all you can do is criticise!" Zallerak drained his wineglass with sudden violence.

"Well do I remember why I shunned the world of men for so many years. You are all so churlish and self-centred!" Zallerak wiped his mouth on his silk sleeve fastidiously before releasing a large venomous belch. "That said, I am infinitely patient, so will resume under duress."

"Don't trouble yourself on my part," muttered Corin.

"I have been watching events unfolding in this corner of the world for some time," Zallerak glanced at the door again. "I knew Caswallon was up to something. So when he pulled his masterstroke in Kella City, I alone was ready.

"I sailed for Crenna a short while after the prince's abduction. I had other things to attend to first. Weaving a web of concealment I slipped into the Assassin's lair, taking note of young Tarin's dingy whereabouts. I let the prince suffer at Rael Hakkenon's hands for a while."

"That was good of you." Ariane winced, her tea had found that exposed nerve in her tooth again.

"The boy needed toughening up. A sharp lesson that should stand him in good stead. Then, when the time was right I freed Tarin and bade him be on his way with new instructions."

Scrape. Gurgle. Thud. As one they turned to face the door. It had creaked ajar just enough to reveal a clawed talon and scabby foot.

"What the...?" Barin gulped.

"It seems we are not alone." Zallerak stood up. "How long have you been spying, Soilfin?" The foot vanished and the door slammed shut. There followed a frantic scrape, knock and thud as Gribble vacated the hatch and capered awkwardly about on deck. Hoarse shouts announced the crew were onto him. As one the others followed Barin through the hatch, their faces (except Zallerak) a blend of confusion revulsion and horror. They emerged to see Bleyne pounce on the goblin and grip it with both arms. Gribble writhed and squealed in the archer's sinewy grip. Barin's crew gaped at the winged thing in horror before Fassof swore them back to work.

"What the fuck is that?" Barin managed his face a mask of disgust. Corin and Ariane just gaped, whilst Galed looked ill again. Cale stared at the goblin in macabre fascination. "It stinks," the boy said.

For its part, the creature was dribbling and spitting at them, its small red eyes defiant and malicious. It struggled and spat at Bleyne but the archer held it fast.

"Well, master Gribble, it's been a while." Zallerak loomed tall over archer and goblin. "How long have you been eavesdropping?" The creature hissed at him and struggled again. It seemed much more frightened of Zallerak than the rest of them.

"I was weary," the creature called Gribble said. Its voice put Corin's teeth on edge like a rusty saw scraping metal. And the thing's breath when it spoke was beyond vile. God's only knew what its diet must be like. "I've been flying all night—I'm shagged out. Needed rest, and somewhere to sleep."

"Shall I slit its throat?" asked Bleyne. The archer's tattooed left hand strained for his long knife, while his right arm locked on the goblin's scrawny neck. Gribble squealed like a cornered sow in a pit. Behind it Galed looked about ready to throw up whilst Cale's eyes were saucer-huge.

"Not yet," replied Zallerak, motioning Bleyne to ease back the blade. This the archer did reluctantly.

"Who sent you, my flying friend? Was it Caswallon or one of your original masters? Maybe the Dog-Lord himself?" Zallerak loomed close. "Answer me, goblin!"

But before Zallerak or anyone else could move, the creature Gribble twisted and jerked in sudden violence, wriggling free of Bleyne's grasp. The goblin bit the archer on his arm and clawed its way along the deck. Bleyne gave chase with knife in hand and the others were close behind him.

"Don't let it escape!" shouted Barin, diving after the Soilfin and narrowly missing as it scurried under a pile of nets, emerging seconds later out of reach with yet more spitting and clawing.

In less than a minute Gribble had scaled the aft deck, bit another sailor, whilst releasing a squeaky howl. The goblin turned and showed them its fangs and then after stretching its bat-like wings, leaped skywards up into the lightening sky.

But Gribble didn't get far. There came a sharp twang followed by a whish and a yelp of pain from the goblin. Bleyne had wasted no time recovering his bow.

Gribble's wings beat upwards in desperation. They steered steady for a moment, then faltered and folded inwards. With a weird shriek the goblin plummeted like a lead pebble into the ocean, colliding into the water with a sullen plop. In seconds Gribble had vanished from sight.

"Good shot!" applauded Fassof from somewhere high above. Galed, looking relieved, knelt to bind the archer's bloody arm with clean cloth. Satisfied there was no infection, he moved on to tend the other victim.

"Aye, but what was it I hit?" Bleyne enquired.

"It was a Soilfin," answered Zallerak. "An ancient creature, like the Groil spawned by the Urgolais. There were many of them once. Most were slain in the final battle, long ago."

"Did the Urgolais send it?" Corin had a cold feeling that Dogface was on the mend.

"Caswallon, I should imagine." Zallerak stood leaning on the rail, watching the swell that had swallowed the Soilfin. "Gribble was here because Caswallon's witch-sight has been compromised by my blocking strategy. We are in more peril than I thought."

"What should we do?" Cale couldn't help asking. He was slightly disappointed Bleyne had shot the goblin thing, horrible though it was.

"Make haste to Port Sarfe," responded Ariane. "Before Caswallon's on our tail again. I see no reason to change our plans now Bleyne's dealt with his spy. But we need to get there quickly. Enough idle chit chat, I for one am hungry. Is it too early for breakfast?"

That day passed without further ado. And the next the same. On the third day Barin ordered they change course again, this time faring south east toward South Head and Raleen. The seas behind stayed clear of craft. It seemed they had foiled the Assassin for the time being.

During the night they rounded South Head, Ariane saw the distant beacon flaring miles away on the headland. Raleen! They were almost there! As she watched through the glass she saw a huge shadow moving slowly along the dark line of cliff. A giant figure striding above the waves, His bulk occluding the beacon fire crowning South Head.

It might have been her imagination but Ariane felt heavy eyes staring into her cabin, but just then dark cloud squalled sudden rain at her porthole, and cliffs and figure were gone. Shivering, Ariane rolled into her blanket and closed her eyes. She prayed to Elanion the Goddess's Brother would wait awhile yet for her to pay her due.

Next morning they arrived in Port Sarfe.

Chapter 5

Port Sarfe

That same morning, nine tough-looking riders clad in fur and iron urged their steeds south through the arid terrain of northern Permio. They'd left Cappel Cormac three days ago and would soon be close to the bandit city Agmandeur.

Halfway through morning, they crested a rise and the leader summoned a halt. Ahead in the far distance the thin band of the Narion River was barely visible.

Hagan smiled. They had done well. But then Caswallon's 'gift' of charmed nourishment supplied by the contact had ensured the horses ride at breakneck speed, with need for neither rest nor water. The beasts had died when they'd reached Cappel. But that didn't matter to Hagan—they'd got them there in record time.

He turned to Borgil seated on a freshly stolen horse beside him. "A day, maybe two, we'll have crossed the bridge. Then it's on to Agmandeur and find the little shit. Double pay, lads! Remember what Caswallon's contact said!"

Caswallon's contact had found Hagan and crew in a tavern

just outside Port Wind where they had been charged to apprehend Queen Ariane's arrival into her country.

"Been a change of plan," the little creep had whispered in Hagan's ear. "Lord Caswallon's got fresh word of the terrorists' movements. Seems they are heading for southern Raleen."

"And we're to go find them, I suppose, that will cost your master back in Kella."

"You'll leave them be. Instead you will make for Permio where we have reason to believe Prince Tarin is to be found."

"Tarin? I thought the little shit was dead."

"Apparently not. And the renegade prince has something our master needs. A sack containing very important goods. Lord Caswallon says it's vital you recover said goods and stop the prince entering the desert."

"And why would Prince Tarin want to do that?" Hagan glared at the man. He didn't like spies and this one was oilier than most. "Why Permio of all places? And how did the little turd escape from Crenna?"

"Why and how doesn't concern you."

"Gold does."

"Feed your horses this nourishment,"—he'd tossed a small sack onto the table. "It will give them strength and halve your journey time. Feed them every morning and they won't need rest ere nightfall. Waste not a minute! Find Tarin and recover what he's stolen and you'll be paid double—more gold than you can imagine."

"I can imagine a lot," growled Hagan. A week later they'd arrived in Cappel Cormac. They'd ranged through the city for a few days until another 'contact' found them and informed them to make for Agmandeur.

∗∗∗

Port Sarfe was a sprawling tangle of honey-coloured stone, dug deep into steep sandy banks flanking Kael's Stream. Actually a wide river, Kael's Stream's sandy banks formed a lazy loop around the town, protecting it from south and east. The northern town was higher, built on the slopes of a low hill culminating in a wide dome-like crown and awarding sweeping views in every direction. Up there the barbican and walls dominated the skyline frowning on harbour and town. Port Sarfe was the busiest and largest of Raleen's cities. Atarios, the capital, was barely half its size.

Kael, Raleen's first ruler, had discovered the site and washed himself in the muddy waters where river met sea. Kael's Stream was named after him and the city's name (so legend says) was taken from his homeland Sarfania in long forgotten Gol.

Despite its chaotic construction, Port Sarfe was impressive on the eye: a maze of narrow winding streets, hedged by high sandstone walls, honey yellow in colour, and dominated by the oval turrets of the old castle and its barbican at the north eastern apex.

The port had thrived over the years. The last stop before Permio, and the sailor's last chance of grog and grope before Cappel Cormac. Port Sarfe was the last bastion of the Four Kingdoms. Despite that it had a nasty reputation being renowned for its seedy taverns and grubby brothels.

Corin loved it here.

It was a place he knew well, having spent considerable time gambling and sharing pleasantries with those nubile ladies who so often draped themselves around the quayside, soliciting and banter-ing with the sailors. Those whores were a tough lot—they had to be. Many a sailor had come to grief over chancing his luck in the dark alleys at night.

Raleenian women were famed for their skill with the knife. They could gut a man, slice his throat and lift his purse in a nonce, were he fool enough to close his eyes. Corin liked the girls here—they had a murderous honesty about them.

Silon's house being close by (only twenty miles or so), Port Sarfe had been a home of sorts for Corin during his years in the merchant's service. It felt good to be back here again.

Raleenians were a taciturn folk. Dark-skinned, soft talking and passionate. Their forefathers had followed the warlord Kael out of the desert wilderness some years after the arrival of King Kell and his sons. Kael's people like Kell's were survivors from the lost continent, Gol.

Independent and proud, they settled the arid region south of Kelwyn, naming it Raleen after Kael's beautiful daughter who tragically died on the eve of her wedding night. It was a roughly diamond-shaped country, bordered by mountains in the east and sea to the west, with broad rivers defining both its north and south boundaries. Raleenian rulers shunned the title of king and queen. They preferred to be known as warlords after their forefather, Kael. Despite that they had always been loyal to their overlords in the north, proving staunch allies and keeping a watch on treacherous Permio close by.

Once a Raleenian was your friend, he was a friend forever. That said, they were quick to anger and sometimes cruel. Port Sarfe was no exception, though the citizens of this southernmost city were considered decadent and lewd compared to other Raleenians. The well-heeled nobles of proud distant Atarios frowned on Port Sarfe, despite gaining wealth from its trade.

Not that the folk of Port Sarfe gave a fig about that. They delighted in luxuries and pleasures their northern kin shunned, considering such indulgence a sign of weakness and base character. Port Sarfe's citizens cared not what others thought, whether their own people or foreigners. They bathed themselves daily in the oils of intrigue, and revelled in vitriolic gossip. The markets here were more vibrant than any other town Corin knew. The men were dour and steadfast—canny with coin and quick with a knife. But Port Sarfe's women were sultry-eyed and olive-skinned. And even quicker with coin and knife. They wrapped themselves in scented cloth and drove their menfolk wild.

In Port Sarfe a man could acquire anything he wanted: gold, weapons or other, seedier things. The hot dusty streets rising from the harbour to the old barbican were a torturous maze of overcrowded mayhem. At night these streets became a lair of footpads and cutpurses.

It was only three days ride from the eastern gates of the city to the great Liaho River. That confluence marked the southern extent of the Four Kingdoms. Beyond the Liaho, the vast sandy dunes of the Permian desert marched southwards into areas unknown by decent folk.

That was hostile country.

It was a fine sunny morning. Corin stood by Barin relishing the warm air, as his friend piloted them skilfully into the harbour. It was rarely cold here even in winter—and it was still only late autumn.

Corin stretched and yawned; he'd stripped to his waist and was enjoying the sun's heat on his pink northern skin. His grey/blue gaze scanned the bustling harbour as they entered, then reached further out to the flatness of the coastal strip beyond. As he watched, a colourful flock of exotic birds winged north along the coast. Their harsh calls carried from the arid dunes framing the shore for mile upon mile. Beyond that lay a more fertile area of creeks, swamps, reeds and wildfowl.

This was the Liaho's sprawling delta. Around its glittering, snake-writhing tributaries sprawled a sallow treacherous marsh. A place of poisonous gases and steaming pools, impassable to all save a few native guides. Beyond the delta, the coast swept around in a broad arc fading from view before another river, the Narion, met the sea. Squatting on the far bank of the Narion's filthy mouth was the stinking fleshpot called Cappel Cormac.

"Fine view, isn't it?" Barin flashed a grin at Corin. The blond giant had also stripped to the waist. His massive chest was beaded with sweat under the morning's hot sunshine. He'd been humming a bawdy tune whilst guiding *The Starlight Wanderer* over to the harbour's occupied side.

Corin grinned in acknowledgement. He was itching to jump ashore. The warm sun had raised his spirits considerably since the night before.

"Port Sarfe!" He flashed a grin at Barin. "I had some times here."

"Me too in my earlier days." Barin released an enthusiastic fart into the harbour. "Those dark-eyed Raleenian lassies—feisty little beauties!"

"Treacherous," Corin added.

"That too."

Corin looked up at the distant barbican and honey-stained walls cordoning the glistening red-tiled roofs of the city. The lanes mostly wound up in that direction. These were narrow in places, some only wide enough for a single person to pass. They coiled around dingy inns, shops and bazaars, stables, tanneries and modest homes before reaching the barbican gates. Corin relaxed, for the first time since departing Crenna he felt almost content. Barin was right, why would Rael Hakkenon sail this far south?

Although the harbour was bustling with craft of every size and shape there was plenty of mooring space. They set to close to one of the largest taverns. Barin's choice of mooring was cause for concern for Ariane.

"I need to get supplies," Barin winked at her. "Stock up on ale and food and other gubbins. We could use some fresh lads too, though I care not to employ foreigners, so I think we'll struggle on that score. But I know a few useful traders here, and bargaining is always better with the fortitude of ale."

"And we'll need to glean some local information before we head out to Vioyamis," Corin explained lamely. He was thirsty this morning and determined to down a flagon or two. "*The Crooked Knife* is one of Sarfe's finest taverns."

Corin pointed to the nearest inn. A low-roofed, square building with small windows and doors resting ajar. "It will be ideal," Corin insisted. "We can break our fasts, and give Barin's boys time to re-stock the ship, fill their bellies with fresh food." Ariane's expression darkened further.

"With beer, you mean." Ariane was frustrated, deeming it fool-ish to linger in Port Sarfe with Silon's house being so close. But after such a long and troubled voyage she found small room for argument. These were her friends but bar Galed, none were her people. Despite that she spoke her mind.

"Well, make it quick! I don't think we should linger hereabouts. Port Sarfe is a dangerous place. There are bound to be spies abroad, both Caswallon's and the sultan's. And what if Rael Hakkenon got word of our whereabouts? We don't want to be trapped in this harbour, Captain Barin."

"Indeed not, my Queen," exclaimed Barin, grinning at her. She knew it was hopeless. His mind was on ale and nothing else. Corin's too—and the crew. The only allies she had were Galed and Cale. And Cale was weakening fast. "A quick stop then we seek out Silon." Barin winked reassuringly to her. Ariane nodded briskly before retiring to her cabin to make ready for their journey inland.

Barin turned to his men. "Come on, lads, you heard the queen! There're provisions to be bought and goods sold. We might as well make a profit while we're here."

Ariane heard that as she entered the hatch. She raised an eyebrow but refused to comment. "Just remember to keep your teeth together," continued Barin. "I don't want to hear anyone got drunk in my absence. And no fighting."

Cogga grumbled at that last comment and muttered something in his beard.

Corin noticed that his companions had all changed into lighter garments, supplied by Barin's copious wardrobe in the Master's Cabin. Over the years he'd acquired a fair range of clothing through trade and barter.

Barin offered Corin a silk tunic. The longswordsman sniffed at it, frowned and decided to stick with his leathers. Corin slung the steel shirt over his shoulders, strapped on Clouter's harness and slung the longsword and Biter in their scabbards. Within minutes he was sweating profusely.

I'll change at Silon's.

The merchant was a fastidious bather, and although Corin

considered excessive bathing to be unhealthy, indeed dangerous, once a month it helped to purge the soul. He had left some clothes at Vioyamis unless Nalissa had burnt them, which wasn't unlikely.

Corin glanced askance at Barin. His friend stood preening himself in the sunshine. The Northman had changed into black linen trousers and bright yellow silk shirt. He looked immaculate if a tad garish. He'd filled his arms with gold rings and spirals and wore a silver circlet on his brow.

"You look like a giant bumblebee—couldn't you find something less yellow?" Corin winced at all that colour.

"I like bright colours. And I'm to accompany you to Vioyamis," Barin replied. "I told you I wish to speak with Silon. I'll stay for a day or so then return here. Fassof will keep an eye on things."

"That's if Silon's at home. Last I heard he was in Permio."

"He should be back by now. Come on, I'm thirsty. Where's Bleyne?" Barin glanced around but couldn't see the archer. "Galed, old chap, are you coming too? How about you, master Cale? You could do with fattening up."

Cale grinned as he joined them on deck. Behind him Galed looked worried. He'd heard stories about this place and, like the queen, thought they'd be wiser making for Silon's house at once.

Bleyne was away purchasing arrows from a dealer on the quay. He returned heavily laden and joined them. Zallerak still hadn't surfaced from his cabin.

Barin's men set to work stowing sails and making fast. Fassof sent a few off to forage for supplies. One of them was Cogga.

"They'll be no drinking until the work's done!" the mate hollered after them. Cogga flashed a finger for reply.

Ariane re-emerged on deck. She'd changed into leather riding trousers, long suede boots and a short grey linen tunic, which left her tanned arms bare. Her hair had grown quite long since first Corin had met her. This Ariane had tied back in a neat bun. At her waist hung rapier and dagger. The queen looked stunning this morning.

"Are you sure *The Starlight Wanderer* will be safe moored in the harbour while we seek out Silon?" Ariane asked Barin, who had just jumped from the deck to join them. He had belted Wyrmfang around his broad waist and stood grinning in the sunshine. "She is a conspicuous sight."

"Fassof will keep an eye on things, my Queen," Barin insisted with a grin.

"Two eyes, I hope," responded Ariane. "We stop for an hour— no more." Ariane was determined their visit to *The Crooked Knife* would be brief. The sooner Corin and Barin, (not to mention Cale), were out of this town the better!

***

Taic was not having a good day. His head still spun from last night and his purse was woefully empty. That Raleenian bitch had relieved him of both wits and coin. He ought to have known better. Trouble was, he hung out with the wrong crew. One of whom was currently snoring on the filthy floor beside him.

Sveyn.

As usual it was all *his* fault. Where Sveyn led Taic followed, despite Taic being nephew to the island's greatest warrior, and Sveyn a lowly docker's son. It had been a good night though, what with the fighting, wenching, gambling and frolicking around. Taic hadn't had so much fun since he and Sveyn had left Valkador last summer, determined to make a name for themselves in the south. That hadn't really happened, instead the Northmen had become the favourite target of Port Sarfe's militia. All because of a little misunderstanding. Those Raleenian guards had no sense of humour.

Taic opened a bleary eye. Outside the sun's glare stabbed dazzling knives into his head.

"Ouch." Taic rolled to his feet, farted habitually and reached for the pitcher containing the stale remains of the ale he hadn't finished last night. He threw the contents of the pitcher over his head and belched. Revived, Taic turned toward Sveyn, awarding his friend a hearty kick.

"Piss off!" The voice was muffled but then Sveyn's mouth was half filled with dried vomit.

"Time to get up! Those militia lads will be back soon." Taic yawned across to the nearest table. On it was a plate containing cold rice and beans and a mug of ale—both items abandoned by a patron when the fighting broke out. Taic wiped the snot from his nose and stuffed the cold jellied contents of the plate into his mouth. He didn't bother with a spoon. He then reached for the adjacent ale mug and drained it in one. Behind him, Sveyn yawned, belched, wiped his mouth clean on his sleeve, and rolled grumbling to his feet.

"Was it a good night?" Sveyn looked awful this morning. "Did I miss something, it's all a bit blurred?"

"We're skint," Taic complained. "That dark-eyed bitch slit my purse open and legged it."

"Lucky she didn't slit your throat open." Sveyn lurched across the tavern sourcing food and ale. He found a half-eaten ham bone someone had tossed on the straw-covered floor by the front door. This Sveyn grabbed and commenced chewing.

"There is that," Taic nodded. "What happened to the other lads?"

"Still here." Two dark shapes stirred in a corner of the taproom. Taic and Sveyn had only met these two last night. Good lads though, and good scrappers. Wogun was as tall as Taic's uncle Barin, though wiry instead of broad. He was from the distant south, his skin black as ebony.

The other fellow, Normacaralox (Taic and Sveyn decided on calling him Norman) was dark-skinned too, but his was more of a dull ochre hue. Norman came from some obscure place east of Permio that Taic had never heard of. Both these two were older than Taic and Sveyn.

Norman wore a grizzled beard and sported a wide hooped golden earing in his left lobe. He carried a long curved blade. Wogun had seven earrings, all varied in colour and hue. He also kept an interesting array of knives strapped to his waist belt. Wogun smiled a lot. Norman didn't (which was just as well since he was missing any top front teeth). Both were seasoned sailors who had just arrived in Port Sarfe and, between contracts, had been enjoying the sights of the town when they had happened upon Taic and Sveyn. After that it had all gone horribly wrong.

The sudden rush of feet outside announced it was time they got moving. Taic recovered his axe from where he'd left it embedded in a post last night. Sveyn's five daggers were strewn across the bar, he vaguely remembered tossing them at people but had been too drunk to hit a barn door. Their new friends Norman and Wogun grabbed their own assorted weapons just as the door swung open and Port Sarfe's militia came crashing in.

"Morning, lads!" Taic grinned at the leader. "I think there's been a bit of a misunderstanding!"

Later, whilst his head stung from the vegetables hurled at him, Taic had time to reflect. The four of them graced the stocks at the southern end of the harbour, much to the locals' amusement. Taic even recognised the trollop that had filched his coin. She'd flashed him a gorgeous grin before sending an overripe tomato his way.

Bit rich that—in Taic's opinion. He closed his eyes. This was proving a troublesome morning.

But the afternoon was worse.

"Might have guessed I'd find you tossers here." A gruff voice close by. Taic's eyes blinked open. He recognised Cogga, Sveyn's hardarse uncle, scowling down on them.

That's not good.

"Uncle!" Sveyn grinned through the array of rotting squash stuck to his features. "I didn't know you were in town! Let me introduce me new mates, Norman and Wogun." These two grunted and bobbed their heads as best they could given their current confinement. Wogun waggled his massive hands and grinned. "You know young Taic, of course," Sveyn added.

"I know what a useless arse he is." Cogga glared at his nephew who for his part looked a bit crestfallen. "As are you, Sveyn. Well, holiday's over, boyos. Boss is short of crew, so I made a deal with my new friend here." The militia captain loomed into view and scowled down at Sveyn and Taic. "I parted with decent coin for you bloody pair," Cogga told them. "So it's back to ship we go and grafting."

"Work?" Sveyn looked a bit worried.

"Yes, work. It won't kill you." Cogga grinned at the militia captain who for his part didn't get the joke. "Get your shit together and get cracking," Cogga said, "we've stores to load before himself gets back."

"Himself?" Taic had a sudden sinking feeling in his belly.

"Your uncle Barin. Who else?"

That's not good.

***

The Crooked Knife was pleasantly cool after the heat outside. One of the more respectable establishments in Port Sarfe harbour. It actually had glass in most the windows.

Barin stooped to wipe his face on a tablecloth. He could never adjust to the heat down here. Up north winter was approaching fast. Valkador would already be coated in snow. He pictured Marigold with her long plaits and sharp tongue and then thought about his pretty big-eyed daughters. The youngest, Daisy, had given her a deal of trouble lately, (this from his last letter). She'd taken to hanging out with that wastrel nephew of theirs, Taic. When Barin next happened upon master Taic there would be words spoken.

Corin liked *The Crooked Knife*. He had frequented it often enough during his days with Silon. It was a large tavern with more than its share of drunks and wastrels, though these were generally better behaved than those idiots frequenting the dens at the southern end of town. 'The Knife' was empty this morning which well suited their purpose. Ariane hovered uneasy whilst Barin bid they claim stools near a window facing a side alley, a long table within easy reach.

Ariane remained standing but the men stretched their legs out. Barin yawned whilst Corin sought out the patron. He found him in the cellar.

Corin liked Rado. The innkeeper was a man of tolerant nature and sound wit. He greeted Corin cheerfully, recognising him in an instant.

"I thought that you had returned to Kelthaine, or was it Morwella?" Rado asked as Corin followed him back to the bar. He requested ale for his companions and chilled tea for the queen. She had sensibly declined the offer of wine at this early hour.

"One of us will need a clear head to speak with Silon," she had told them. At her left, Cale beamed his gap-toothed smile as he clutched his bubbling brew. He was one of the men now—part of an elite squad.

"Fol. You wouldn't know it," Corin was replying to the innkeeper's inquiry. "Rocky windswept country in the far north west."

"Never heard of it."

"No one has."

Corin recalled the last time he'd been in this tavern and tried to remember that girl's name. She had had a certain appetite and he'd learned a few new moves.

"I'm back here on business, Rado."

"So I see," replied Rado, "and in refined company too."

The innkeeper's shrewd brown eyes lingered a moment over Ariane's trim figure.

"Who's the lovely lady?" he asked without the narrowest hint of discretion.

"Some wealthy merchant's daughter from Kelwyn," Corin answered—glibly for once. "She requested we get out of the heat. So here we are."

"Silon knows her. I belief she is a distant relative of the old goat." He took a long pull at his tankard and sighed. "Still the finest brew in the south, Rado."

"We aim to please."

"Is himself at home these days?" Corin enquired casually. Silon was known and respected throughout southern Raleen—mainly because almost everyone owed him money, including Rado.

"Aye he is, though he only arrived back two days hence. Been lurking down in Cappel Cormac apparently." Rado was shaking his head. "Only the gods know why. In a right shambolic state he was. Unusual for him who's so fastidious about his person. I caught his eye down at the quay. Looked a touch stressed, so he did."

"Cappel Cormac?" Corin wondered what would possess the merchant to risk his neck in that sleazy den of treachery and deceit.

"So I hear. It's good to see you again, Corin." Rado placed a hand on his shoulder. "Let me know when you want to settle up, there's no rush."

Rado disappeared from sight to uncork another barrel for his guests. Whilst in the cellar, he mused over the dark-haired beauty at the table. One thing was certain; she was no merchant's daughter.

Rado grinned. He'd always liked Corin but the Longswordsman was a crap liar. He reckoned once again Corin had gotten into something deep. Rado spiked the barrel and clambered back up the ladder. Once back in the taproom he pretended not to listen.

"Silon's at home, though only just," announced Corin, returning to the table with a half grin. They still had the inn to themselves, most decent folk being hard at work, whilst the tavern loiterers were still snoring in their cots.

Ariane sipped her tea thoughtfully as men and boy guzzled their ale and ordered more. Cale's head was spinning a little and his eyes had taken on a glazed look. Even Galed was cheerfully bolstered with imported hops.

Ariane frowned at Galed. The squire had started to slur his words. Rado furnished them with a huge plate of seafood. This they consumed with vigour before sitting back in comfort. Outside the streets and harbour were a hive of activity.

"We had best be on our way in a minute," said Barin with a sigh after wiping his mouth. "It's only a score of miles to Silon's house. I told Fassof to expect us back tomorrow night with news of our next destination."

"What about Zallerak?" enquired Bleyne, who had recently joined them at table. He was dressed in his accustomed archer's gear and had purchased a new knife to go with his collection. Bleyne watched the open doorway as if he expected the bard to arrive any moment.

"A pox on him," responded Corin. "Let him find his own way to the merchant's residence."

Ariane glanced at Corin. She almost said something but instead looked away again, her sharp features flushed and those dark eyes troubled. Corin's lean, scarred face was tanned like leather. His dark hair was tangled and torn and he badly needed a shave, she decided. And those leathers must be soldered to his skin in this heat. She wrinkled her nose—questioned why she found him so attractive.

A noise turned their heads as the door creaked open. Zallerak stood at the entrance, his tall silhouette blocking the daylight. The bard had his sapphire cloak draped across his broad shoulders despite the heat, and his fine hair was tied back with a blue silk ribbon, which glistened in the morning sun.

"Is there a problem?" Barin asked the bard.

"Nothing really." Zallerak swept the Northman an ironic grin. "Just wondered if it's wise to idle away the hours in drink whilst your crew are under attack?"

Chapter 6

An Acquaintance Renewed

Barin leapt to his feet knocking the table, rocking it wildly and spilling ale and scraps to the rush-strewn floor. "Who?"

"The Assassin of Crenna of course." Zallerak rolled his eyes. "Who else were you expecting?" His long fingers tapped the door frame. "May I suggest a certain fluidity; his oiks approach this tavern as I speak. You had better drink up, my friends!"

Barin was already at the door, Wyrmfang gripped in his dinner plate hands. The Northman thrust past Zallerak followed by Corin, cursing under his breath with Clouter gripped sweaty in his palms.

Bleyne, watching their hasty departure, casually leant back and strung his bow, as if he had been expecting trouble all along. Galed and Cale were rendered sober in an instant. They both looked anxiously at the door. Cale's mouth was open. Ariane gave the boy a shove.

"Wake up! And you, Galed. Get a bloody grip!" Ariane cursed her choice of letting them come here. If only she'd listened to her instincts.

At her words Galed and the boy vacated the tavern, blinking stupidly at the glare as they stumbled out into the street. Behind them Rado scratched his head and sighed at the mess left by his hastily departed guests. It was alright—he'd send Silon the bill.

"Can't you do something, Zallerak?" Galed yelled up at the bard who stood hovering outside the inn's door.

"Have I not done enough? I've not been myself since leaving Crenna. Such exertions have their price. This time it is down to you—serves you right, loitering and lurking in grubby taverns with work still to be done. I suggest you pull yourselves together, people. I will see you in good time."

Without further comment Zallerak swept his blue cloak behind him and stormed aloof up the narrow side alley, quickly disappearing from sight.

"Where is he going?" Cale almost shrieked.

"I told you that bastard cannot be trusted," growled, Corin fingering Clouter and focussing on the departing warlock. "And here they come!" Corin swung the longsword in an arc and stepped resolute out into the alley.

Round two.

The sound of many feet could be heard approaching swiftly from the other side of the inn. Then a slim figure emerged in the entrance of the alley, his presence announcing that way was blocked. The Assassin smiled at them beneath the sun.

"Greeting, little Queeny, I believe we have unfinished matters to attend to."

"Run, Ariane!" Corin shoved her behind him.

"Bleyne!" Corin yelled in the archer's ear. "Take Galed and the boy. Make for the city walls; mention Silon's name and the guards there will help you. Fly!"

"But, Corin, what about..?" Ariane's face was close to tears. "I don't want to lose you too," she struggled to get the words out.

"You won't. I promise. Just go!"

Ariane hesitated for a moment longer, offered one last pleading glance at Corin, then she turned, chased Cale and Galed up the winding alley. Corin and Barin had no time to watch them leave. The Assassin's men were already upon them.

As she fled, Ariane stole a glance back down the street, saw Barin and Corin ringed by steel.

Elanion, please watch over those two fools—they are all I have left.

Ariane turned away, and weeping furious tears sped up the street towards the distant barbican from where she would alert the city watch.

Below the sound of ringing steel echoed around the harbour. Bleyne having crested a rise, turned and ushered them on. Ariane's strong short legs had already drawn level with Galed's.

Bleyne let them pass him. The archer was torn by indecision, his dark face taut and troubled. He'd an arrow resting on his bow and was wrestling with his choice: save the queen or assist Corin and Barin. At last he reached a practical decision. A clean shot would impossible from anywhere hereabouts, besides Ariane was the Goddess's chosen—his place was with her. Bleyne turned around, this time his friends would have to fend for themselves.

He shouldered the bow, and catching up with the queen, squire and boy, fled east and up through the dusty tangled streets of Port Sarfe.

***

Clouter met Rael Hakkenon's slim rapier in a blaze of sparks. Beside him Barin roared his battle cry and launched his bulk at the Assassin's men, gathered close behind their lord. There were at least a dozen of them. They were canny, this bunch, staying clear of Barin's axe. They kept their distance, goading and gesturing, trying to lure him back down to the quayside. One of them yelled at him.

"Hey, Haystack—we've already enjoyed gutting your crew and pillaging your tub! The rest of the boys are finishing off your ale." He grinned. "You're buggered, Northman." This one took a step towards

Barin who readied his axe. The pirate stopped, eyeing Wyrmfang warily.

"What's this—Big Bad Barin's lost his nerve? Balls shrunk, have they? Don't want to fight anymore? Shame, that." He turned and rejoined his laughing companions.

And of course Barin took the bait.

***

Taic dived low as the curved blade sliced air above his head. To his right, Sveyn butted a pirate and followed up with a stiff knee in the man's groin. Long legs Wogun was bludgeoning about with a huge club he'd produced from somewhere, and, cool as you like, Norman No Teeth was lobbing knives in all directions. It all made for a busy afternoon.

They fought alongside Cogga and Fassof the mate and the rest of the crew. The Crenise attackers had come from nowhere. One minute Taic and Norman had been sharing a pipe smoke whilst reflecting on their busy day, then the dirty knaves had leapt on board bold as you like. And now things had got out of hand.

Taic rolled to his left as a Crenise spear stabbed the timbers he'd just vacated. Taic launched his left foot skyward, taking his foe in the balls. The pirate stumbled on top of him, but not before producing a knife, and slicing hard for Taic's neck. That stab never came. Instead the pirate flopped as Wogun's club impacted his skull with a sickly squelch.

"Thank you!" grinned Taic and rolled free again. But it was no good. They were surrounded and more Crenise had just arrived from the harbour. Taic grinned at Cogga, who'd just dispatched a pirate with his jewelled knife.

"Glad we could be of assistance!" Taic heard shouts, someone roaring. That voice sounded familiar. Uncle Barin.

That's not good.

***

The Assassin's men were taken aback by Barin's sudden fury. They turned, commenced legging it back down to the harbour. Rael didn't notice them leaving, he was occupied elsewhere.

Barin tore down the alley, eyes blazing and Wyrmfang doing cartwheels. Emerging townsfolk fled into alcoves, women cried out, children hollered and pointed, and men stood gaping, all stunned by the fury of this axe-swinging giant.

The Crenise were in full sprint, they reached the harbour but not before Barin swatted four from behind with Wyrmfang—the gobby one first to go, his ugly head sailing past a shop window before plopping in the water.

Barin stopped as he reached the water's edge. The surviving pirates backed off again. No goading this time.

Glancing up with bloodshot eyes, Barin could see a score of pirates milling around his ship, Fassof and his crew hard pressed repulsing them.

The rage filled him again.

Kicking and cursing, hacking and sweeping, Wyrmfang whirling in bloody arcs; scattering foe, trader and wide-mouthed bystander like windblown leaves, Barin foamed at the mouth as he strode unchallenged to *The Starlight Wanderer*. Horrified merchants (who only recently had been chatting and dealing in a leisurely manner) panicked and fell over each other, eager to be anywhere as long as it wasn't in the Northman's path. The quayside emptied rapidly, folk took shelter in *The Crooked Knife* and behind the walls of any other sanctuary they could find. From these safe points they clustered gaping and mouthing expletives from the dust-streaked windows. Rado watched from the door of his tavern. The inn was full but no one was buying.

Five more pirates succumbed to Wyrmfang's steely kiss, their cloven skulls cracking like eggshells, and their tattooed limbs sent spinning through the air. Blood covered Barin's bright shirt and face, and his beard and hair were streaked with red. On he came. Three Crenise remained on the quay. These turned and fled.

Barin struck one from behind, splitting the man from left shoulder to right hip. The other two gained *The Starlight Wanderer,* tried clambering on board when Barin pounced on them. He'd stowed Wyrmfang and now held one pirate under either arm, both helpless as new-born lambs in that brawny grasp. All three crashed thudding onto the deck.

Barin hurled one fellow overboard to greet the eagerly waiting sharks—these having arrived moments earlier on cue. Many fins could be seen circling around the harbour in a growing frenzy. The pirate's agonised screams disappeared in a watery billow of crimson. In seconds he'd vanished beneath the frenzied brine.

Barin grabbed the other pirate by his throat with his left hand, whilst reaching down to grasp the man's belt with his right. He hoisted him high, and then rammed the struggling man's head into the main mast with a yell. The skull popped open like a rotten melon. Barin tossed the body overboard with contemptuous ease, letting the sharks feed again. He loosed Wyrmfang again and yelled at Fassof, whose wild-eyed glare had witnessed his captain's return.

"Took your bloody time, we've been hard pressed here!" Fassof yelled at him whilst lashing out at a Crenise.

"Stop whingeing and cast off! Let's get rid of these scum then we can sink that black tub over there!" Barin's axe swung toward where *The Black Serpent* was sitting serene on the water, just a hundred yards away with only a few men remaining on board the Assassin's flagship. The rest were bunched cursing at the other end of Barin's ship, showing their arses and jeering at his crew, another brief impasse having occurred after Barin's hectic arrival.

Barin glanced around. Mercifully there was no sign of any other enemy ships in the harbour. Barin had no illusions, the others wouldn't be far away.

Despite the odd bravo, most the Crenise were clustered like angry hornets on the aft deck. A half score desperate bunch shocked at how the tables had turned.

"Gut that filth and toss them overboard," Barin told his mate.

He wiped sweat from his brow and took hold the wheel. A large face grinned at him.

"Who the –"

"Hello, Uncle, let me introduce my new friend Wogun."

Barin turned slowly and locked gaze on his troublesome nephew Taic.

"You."

"I'll explain later," Cogga yelled in his ear.

"Can't wait," Bain glared at Taic. He recognised Sveyn, Cogga's cousin. Another idiot. But as for the other fellows standing beside them? One thing was sure, they weren't from Valkador.

Barin allowed Fassof, Cogga and the new recruits to finish the pirates. There was a brief clash of steel—the Crenise were trapped with little room to swing their cutlasses. They fought stoically but to no avail. Within minutes Fassof's vengeful posse had mopped the aft deck clean and commenced tossing the broken bodies of their foe overboard for shark bait.

Ruagon freed the bow line, and the brigantine eased away from the dock. Barin, feeling weary, the rage having worn through him, wrenched the wheel hard to port. Fassof yelled commands and his men stowed their weapons. These now took to the benches, commenced working the oars, their broad backs sweating beneath the merciless sun. Taic took oar next to Sveyn. They grinned at each other. It felt good to be on the ocean again. Behind them Wogun and Norman dipped oars and strained, blissfully unaware of Barin's quizzical glance.

"You said you wanted some new lads," Cogga growled in Barin's ear.

"I wanted useful lads. And from Valkador. Those two," he motioned toward Norman and Wogun, "appear a touch foreign to me."

"They're good lads. Bright too."

"Which is more than you can say for our nephews."

"They'll shape up."

"They will have to."

Slowly, majestically, the trader rounded on *The Black Serpent*. The Assassin's shark was quick to take the hint. Sleek and fast, (despite only half-crewed) she glided serenely out of Port Sarfe Harbour, *The Starlight Wanderer* closing fast behind.

And so the chase was on.

***

Rael ducked lithely beneath Corin's sweeping longsword. "You've some skill with that spike, peasant." The Assassin showed his patrician smile. "Not many longswords around these days. Impractical things and unwieldy. Easy to get behind, like—so!"

Rael's gleaming rapier swept around Corin's blade with a dazzling riposte. Corin leapt back, but Rael was on him again. The slim rapier darting hungry towards his belly with lightning speed.

Corin leapt backwards again, wondering how long he could keep this up. This bastard was quick. Lightning quick. Corin kicked out at his enemy in desperation, the rapier hovering scarce inches away, he knew his steel coat and leather would not rebuff a sword of that quality.

Corin spat in his enemy's face. "What's keeping you—losing your touch, Assassin?" Corin desperately parried another lightning thrust, bringing Clouter up barely in time. Corin was sweating hard, the big blade weighing heavy in his arms. He knew himself outmatched. Rael Hakkenon was the finest swordsman he had ever faced. His reputation was no exaggeration. It was depressing, he so wanted to skewer the bastard but couldn't get near him. Corin thought of Roman and his vow to avenge him. He spat again, and again blocked barely in time.

The Assassin smiled beautifully. He'd stepped back and held his sword vertical in mocking salute. "You look tired, peasant. Out of your depth. I think I'll let you get your breath back. No need to rush a good thing—heh?"

Corin was dimly aware of Barin's wild shouts resounding across the quay, accompanied by the panicked yelling of Port Sarfe's traders as the Northman hurried to assist his crew.

Corin closed on the Assassin again. He smote down hard at Rael's head, utilising the advantage of his height. Rael, still smiling, danced aside with effortless ease and then glided in close with another probing lunge.

That one nearly got Corin. He hurled himself backwards out of reach and grunted in pain as his back struck the wall of a building.

Rael wiggled the blade's point towards his foe. "Time's up, peasant. Nowhere to run." Rael was savouring this moment and taking his time.

Which was just what Corin wanted. He was hemmed in, cornered and outmatched, trapped with his sweating back hard against a wall. It wasn't proving a good day. And how many times had he been in this situation? Too many. So no change there.

Rael's grin widened. Corin looked worn out, resigned and defeated.

"And they said you were someone to worry about. I must say I'm rather disappointed in you, peasant." Rael flicked the rapier's needle point up at Corin's face. Corin slammed his head to the side and spat a third time.

"And such atrocious manners."

Cold sweat trickled down Corin's back and his old scar itched into his forehead like an accusation of failure.

But he wasn't done yet.

With sudden unleashed fury, Corin slammed Clouter down hard at Rael's neck. The Assassin danced aside and again levelled the rapier toward Corin's throat.

Rael looked peeved. He was bored with the game and ready to skewer this brute. But the Longfellow had a dreary talent for survival despite his clumsiness with that mile-long blade.

Rael creased his brow. Time to gut this lanky peasant and go see what his idiot men were messing about at. Why had they deserted him? By nightfall Rael would have skewered a few of them as well.

A was noise coming from the other end of town.

"What is that racket?" Rael asked Corin, who was now smiling back at him. "Oh, the city watch. So what?" Rael glanced peevish up the lane. Another blast. The long clear note of a horn sounding from the barbican above. Its clarion call sharp and defined above the din in the quay. And now from the direction of the castle came the sound of many voices shouting, followed by the pounding clatter of hoofbeat on cobble. The city guard had been roused from their slumber. Port Sarfe was suddenly alive with hoarse military shouts and blaring trumpets. Corin's grin widened.

Rael grinned back. Then his mouth curled down at the corner. Rael flicked the rapier at Corin's face but again he missed.

"You, peasant, are becoming tiresome." The horns were everywhere now. And the sound of rushing feet. It was time he got moving. Rael turned slightly to his right. Voices—the watch coming this way.

Corin seized the moment to take stock of his surroundings. Glancing left, he saw another grubby alley trailed off into gloom. He registered the alley in his mind and rounded on the Assassin again. He smiled.

"You're out of time, Assassin."

But the footsteps approaching fast turned out to be two of the Assassin's men. The biggest sported an embroidered eye patch and glared at Corin with contempt. Corin's grin fell from his face. This was looking bad.

"My lord, the city is alive with soldiers," Eye-patch said whilst glaring at Corin. "That bastard Barin's chasing your serpent out of the harbour. The crew got split up when the fighting broke out."

"Why is everyone so fucking incompetent these days, peasant?" Rael's rapier flicked toward Corin playfully. Corin didn't flinch. He was biding his time, seeing possible advantage in the current situation.

"Lord, we cannot remain here!" Eye patch looked worried.

"I am aware of that, Scarn, you one-eyed twit," responded the Assassin without taking his eyes off Corin. "As you can see I am currently preoccupied with this longshanks and his big sword. Wait there, I'll be with you in a minute."

Goodbye, Longfellow.

Rael's rapier darted at Corin's exposed throat. But Corin was ready, having anticipated the blow. He spun on his heels using the weight of his steel coated body to knock the rapier off course and unbalance his foe. Rael lurched forward. Before he could regain balance Corin seized Rael's arm, dragging the smaller man toward him. With a snarl Corin rammed Rael's face hard into the wall, Clouter gripped level in his other hand to ward off Scarn and the other pirate.

"Is it true what they say, Assassin?" Corin's eye was on the narrow alley that cut away to his left. "You prefer playing with boys and lack the equipment of a normal man?"

Rael Hakkenon clutched his bleeding nose and fought to quell his torrent of rage. His eyes blazed emerald fire. It was generally known that he had suffered dreadful torture at the hands of the previous lord of Crenna. That his manhood had been taken from him whilst he lay naked in the cold dungeons of Kranek Castle. But until this moment no one had dared remind him.

And now this Longswordsman, this rough-neck hick dared mock him.

Rael snapped his arms apart, breaking loose from Corin's grasp, his badly broken nose leaking blood as Scarn and the other man gaped in horror at their master's white-faced silent fury. They said nothing, a word spoken now could be a slow death later. Instead the pair waited in ashen-faced silence for their lord to close in for the kill. Rael's left hand gripped the rapier whilst his right reached down freeing his dagger from its sheath. He feinted with the sword then lunged the dagger toward Corin's left eye.

Corin dived sideways under that flashing steel as the dagger point scraped the wall. He pitched himself head first into the side cut, lashing out at the Assassin with a final, desperate sweep with Clouter. That big sword held Rael back for just long enough for Corin to propel his aching body along the side alley and up toward the city main. He ran like a hare harried by hounds, Rael's spewing insults following close behind as the Assassin and his men gave chase.

But Corin was used to legging it in Port Sarfe. His long legs soon gained him ground. He vaulted discarded piles of filth and clutter. Behind him Rael Hakkenon ranted like a madman, his customary cool demeanour usurped by a torrent of fury.

A common brigand had mocked the lord of Crenna. The rogue would pay for that. Rael would make a tapestry out of his cured, flayed hide. He'd wrench this Longfellow's head off with a blunt saw, scoop out the gooey contents and then piss in his hollow skull.

Corin an Fol. From this day on Rael would never forget that name. Grim-faced, Scarn and the other man hurried after their lord, gripping their cutlasses and wondering bleakly if they would get out of Port Sarfe with their heads still attached to their bodies.

Chapter 7

A Score Settled

Ariane sped up the hill. Beside her loped Bleyne, cool as ever, whilst behind them Cale puffed and a struggling Galed wheezed his way up the steep winding way.

After a sweaty, seemingly endless climb, they'd reached the eastern shelter of the city wall. They criss-crossed two lanes and followed its perimeter, hurrying towards the looming barbican. It wasn't far. They could see the round, flag-festooned, guard patrolled turret of the nearest tower shimmering above the sunlit rooftops.

The cityfolk stared at them askance as they ran. Most eyes were on Ariane, but a girl winked at Cale and the boy's red face reddened. He grinned back and she blew him a kiss. Then he thought about Corin and Barin and the smile ran away from his face. He ran on.

From somewhere close a horn sounded one long clear note over the city. Ariane guessed that Zallerak had alerted the guard. She didn't share Corin's view that the wizard had deserted them. Moments later she heard horses' hooves thudding out onto the dusty streets, together with the sound of many iron-shod feet marching forth in ordered fashion. The city guard had been raised.

About bloody time.

Panting and gasping at short breaths they trotted along the sun baked street until finally reaching the eastern flank of the barbican. Beneath its sandstone walls showed a gate house, turreted and square like the main holdfast above.

Within it were two soldiers, clad in polished steel and broad red tunics, helmets thrust under arms and their long ornate pikes resting redundant against the wall as they absorbed themselves in a game of dice. They appeared unconcerned that the castle had recently emptied itself of most the garrison. These two were evidently content with their role as rear guard.

They leapt up seeing Ariane approach, exchanged glances and one of them grinned. Ariane glared at him as she glided close with brisk strides. The queen was in no mood for challenges by such as these.

"Who are you, my lovely? What do you want?" The smiler still grinned at her though his sidekick blocked her advance with his pike.

"It's a bit hot to be rushing about." The pike wielder viewed her curiously.

"I am the Lady Salese of Calprissa," Ariane answered briskly as she regained her breath. She didn't have time for this. "These are my manservants, this worthy fellow my bodyguard." Ariane motioned toward Bleyne who viewed the men with little interest. "I am not used to such oafish behaviour when dealing with militia. Are you not concerned that your city is under attack?"

Smiler smiled. "Oh that. Probably just a drill, the watch get bored. I expect they'll drop by the taverns and sling a few drunks out. Nothing to worry about, sweetness. You, however—"

"Expect to be taken to your captain at once, so I can explain what I require from him." Ariane's tone left no room for discussion. The men exchanged uncertain glances but kept their pikes firmly in place. The nearest guard eyed Bleyne warily. Ariane had had enough.

"You will desist from this ridiculous posturing, and escort me to your captain at once!" She stamped her left foot. Again they exchanged glances.

"Begging your pardon, my lady," said Smiler, using a milder tone. "I'm sure you're very important. And are on important business." A broad yellow sash split his red tunic from left shoulder to right hip, marking his authority over his companion, "but I ain't heard of no Lady Salese of Calprissa. You come here claiming we have enemies rampaging through our city. Perhaps it's you that's brought them here, begging your pardon of course. But it does seem a bit of a coincidence, if you'll forgive my bold assumption, so to speak. Wouldn't you agree, Aric?"

Aric nodded his head slowly. "We can't be too careful, Roul."

"They are pirates, you bloody fools! Come raiding from the sea!" snapped Galed in indignation. He stood beside Ariane and was fretting about Corin and Barin fighting below. "They're lowlifes and brigands, intent on pillaging your homes and raping your women. Their leader is—"

"Enough, Galed, these two are blunt instruments." Ariane was drained of all patience. The queen stamped her foot harder this time in deep frustration and then looked up suddenly.

A newcomer had surfaced from the gloom of the gate house. Broad set, saggy jawed and lugubrious, his gold-trimmed purple tabard stating his importance.

"What nonsense is this, Roul?" The officer's leather-gloved hand rested on his curved sword and his dark eyes narrowed as he saw Bleyne's longbow slung across the archer's back.

"My captain, these—"

"I have already informed your guards of my identity, captain." Ariane interrupted with a sweep of her arm. "I've men fighting for their lives down there at the quay. They are fighting your enemies as well as our own. They'll be in dire need of assistance, whilst protecting your citizens from a plague of marauders out of Crenna."

The captain did not answer. Instead he stared hard at the angry dark-eyed, young woman who stood so confidently before him.

"Is this who you have been expecting?" He'd turned his head, addressed the question to someone hidden inside the gloom of the gatehouse.

"Yes," came the muffled reply. "Bring them in; I need to speak to the lady."

***

Barin's men sweated at their oars. Despite his misgivings the new lads were doing well, four extra pairs of arms working the oars was no small help.

But Taic and Sveyn? Barin had no idea those two were down here. Both were known for their idleness, unreliability and reputation for causing trouble. Barin had despaired of reining his nephew in years ago. Taic was a wild one. Sveyn was worse.

As for the other two. Barin had mixed feelings about allowing strangers on board, but after witnessing them fight and row he decided it only fair to give this Norman and Wogun a chance. If only for a little while.

Barin managed a smile. They were closing on 'the serpent'. He pictured the Assassin's pride and joy in splinters.

But not for long.

The sound of horns hooted through the city behind them. Barin turned, witnessed the city guard arriving on the quayside like angry ants, their red tunics and polished steel helmets blazing in the sun. Their officers shouted, and soldiers rushed to board skiffs and deal with the pirate invaders.

Barin watched them for a minute then swore profusely. Most of the small craft turned in their direction. These were heavily laden, resembling floating porcupines with the soldiers' pikes sticking out at all angles.

"Idiots!" Barin shook his hammer fist at the nearest craft. "That's the bloody enemy over there!" He pointed across to where *The Black Serpent* cut water some hundred feet ahead. Barin's wild gestures were lost on the city watch. On they came, at least a dozen boats heading their way, the rest racing to cut off the pirate ship. *The Black Serpent* had turned on her heels, making for the breakwater like a glossy sleek snake. Barin grinned evilly. They still had time. The Assassin's ship was directly ahead of them and they were gaining fast. He glanced down at the golden sea eagle's reflection as the gleaming ram sped beneath the water. He counted down the seconds.

But *The Black Serpent* was no ordinary ship; moreover these Crenise were Rael's best sailors. They'd heard about the events in Kashorn. They would not be foiled this time. Barin leaned forward yelling at his oarsmen.

"Come on, boys, let's cut her in half!" But then, with just fifty feet of water between them, and far swifter than Barin would have believed possible, *The Black Serpent* tacked half circle and faced the trader head on.

"Oars in!" roared Fassof but it was too late. The serpent ripped along the starboard side of *The Starlight Wanderer*, snapping oars like twigs, wrenching them from fists and dislocating arms and cracking ribs, in the grinding, scraping process.

Taic's oar splintered and split, sending him sprawling, whilst Sveyn broke two fingers as he tried in vain to hang onto his oar. Barin cursed as he watched the carnage. They had been out-played twice. The Assassin had stolen a march on them arriving here unannounced and now his crew had fooled them too. Barin wasn't happy.

The Crenise had retracted their own oars at the last moment, allowing their sleek hull to slide alongside the brigantine snapping oars like twigs. Once clear of *The Starlight Wanderer's* wake, the lean vessel tacked again.

Now the serpent faced open water, her single black sail taut and full, while the trader floundered behind in confusion. Like a swarm of steely beetles the skiffs rounded on Barin's ship. They'd given up on the pirate craft, *The Black Serpent* having almost cleared the breakwater.

Barin swore and kicked the gunwale, snapping a clinkered panel. Fassof barked orders like a demented hound, he'd lost a tooth in the collision and was spitting blood and curses at everyone in range. The trader lurched seaward. Those still in one piece assisted their injured, others were replacing broken oars where they could, or else hastily fixing the old ones. The shouts of the city guard announced their closing proximity. Barin was still swearing and kicking things.

"Those soldiers are closing." Fassof's red face glowed like a beacon. His eyes bored into Barin's. "Any ideas?"

Barin glared at him and then nodded. "Hoist some canvas. Let's put an end to this farce."

"Unfurl the lower main!" Fassof yelled. "I don't want to lose track of that ship!"

Within minutes the big sail had trapped some wind and the brig pulled clear of the pursuing pike men. But it was too late. *The Black Serpent* had cleared the harbour. She was speeding ahead, keeping tight to the sandy shore. The narrow pirate craft was built for raiding these shallow waters. *The Starlight Wanderer* dared not steer that close to the beach, her deep-sea keel ensured she stayed in the middle of the harbour. Thus she trailed behind again.

Barin sighed. He was calmer now, reflective even. He shook his head in resignation; at least they were out of reach of the soldiers' pikes and halberds. None of the guard had crossbows, an oversight on their part but one Barin was grateful for. He gazed back at them where they sat yelling and waving their weapons furiously as their skiffs slipped to stern.

Bugger off!

Barin glanced skyward, wiping sweat from his dripping brow. He'd slung the silver headband in his cabin and doused his head in a bucket of sea water. He looked almost human again, though still blood-splattered, shaggy and mean.

Above, his men unfurled the rest of the sails; wind filled these too. Once again the silver sea eagle fluttered high over water. Fassof handed him a horn of mead, the mate's face was a mask of dried blood.

"So? What's the damage?"

"Just buggered oars and a few cracked ribs. Nothing as won't mend." Fassof spat a gobbet of bloody phlegm on the deck. "Most the lads seem alright."

"My nephew still in the land of living?"

"If you mean that skinny yellow-haired twat down there, then, yes."

"Good. Get the bugger working and his friends too."

"Will do. But what about that?" Fassof pointed to *The Black Serpent* just visible beyond the harbour's arm. "Do we chase her into nightfall?" Fassof's frizzy blood-crusted red hair gleamed like polished copper in the afternoon sun.

"No," replied Barin, scratching his ear. "Just mark where she goes, Fassof. Then steal inshore, make for that small smugglers' cove we used to frequent in the bad old days. You remember the spot?"

"Aye."

"Make for that and lie low for three days. Send some healthy lads ashore, have them coppice young trees to replace those damaged oars. And, Fassof."

"What?"

"Keep a lookout on the headland, there's a good fellow. That Assassin will be lurking somewhere close by. That's if Corin hasn't gutted the little shit."

"What of yourself, captain?" asked the mate, pulling at a second loose tooth. He'd have to borrow the carpenter's pliers for that one.

"I've business onshore," came Barin's reply.

***

Corin slammed Clouter in its scabbard and sped through the filthy alley, his enemies close on his heels. The track was scarce wide enough for two men to stand abreast, weaving backwards and forwards between shabby, faded whitewashed leaning houses.

Rubble and clutter barred his way, rats wriggled and scurried under his feet, their enemies the cats peeking at him warily from their nearby hideouts. Clothes hung on twine across his path, drying in the heat. Corin tore them down in desperation and hurled them behind him into his pursuers' faces.

Corin unsheathed Biter as he ran, weaving left and right crossing from alley to alley. He cursed once when a cat got under his feet, nearly tripping him. It spat at him then hissed and bolted. A glance back revealed the Assassin gaining on him.

Fuck!

Rael kept pace with his quarry, but Scarn and the other man had fallen behind, their faces red with exhaustion as they panted in the heavy heat.

Rael wasn't panting. He was ice cool and closing on his prey. The lane twisted sharp, Corin tripped on a loose cobble, regained his feet but slammed into a wall. Rael was on him then, diving low for Corin's legs.

Corin twisted out the way and lashed out with Biter. Rael rolled free of the steel and danced back on his feet. He had no room to swing his rapier, instead Rael stabbed his dagger viciously up at Corin's face, Corin ducked and the dagger point wedged itself in the wall's mortar.

Biter sliced towards Rael's neck. The Assassin tugged his dagger free just in time and trapped Corin's sax with its guard. He pushed hard, forcing Corin back into the other wall. The two faced each other. Rael swore at Corin and Corin swore back. Then Scarn and the other one came crashing in and the chase resumed again.

The alley opened on another. Corin turned left, saw another cut and turned into it. This one led down towards the harbour again. Corin could hear shouting and horns blowing below. He ran on without turning. No point, he could hear Rael's feet padding the cobbles close behind.

Corin entered a wider street leading to a busy marketplace. The Assassin followed heartbeats behind. Corin hurdled a table laden with fruit. The seller cursed him and leapt back, arms flailing wide. Corin seized a water melon. He turned, launched it at the Assassin.

Rael ducked, but the fruit vendor was not so quick. The melon exploded into his head, much to the humour of his fellow peddlers.

Corin ducked and weaved, pulling awnings down in the Assassin's path. Rael hissed as he kicked them clear. Behind, Scarn and the other pirate had entered the marketplace. They were already being accosted by angry peddlers.

Corin heard the rap of armoured feet. *Now what?* Soldiers were running down the main street towards them. He turned, lashed out at Rael Hakkenon's knee with a vicious kick and then upended a table of cheese in his path.

The Assassin dodged round the table, ignoring the pain in his knee. A back glance revealed Scarn and the other idiot being pursued across the market by the city guard. The watch looked conspicuous and clumsy in their ridiculous red coats. Rael despaired at their dress sense. He yelled at Corin's back.

"You cannot escape me, peasant! Slow down so I can start murdering you!"

"Bugger yourself!" came the reply.

Corin collided into a cheese stall. The vendors leapt up in outrage, but he twisted and sped past them.

Rael wasn't so lucky.

Two large cheese peddlers barred his way; the biggest, a bearded sweating brute of a man, clutched a heavy cudgel in his greasy palm. Rael's left hand jabbed hard into his stomach. Grunting, the big lad slumped to the floor.

The other man's fist flew at him, but Rael danced aside, arcing his elbow into the surprised man's face. There was a sharp crack as the nose split open and the second cheese peddler collapsed on top of his prone comrade.

Rael grinned. A small thing but any pain inflicted gave him cheer. He turned, gazed about. Where had that longfucker got to? There was shouting everywhere, traders were yelling at the watch and pointing to where Rael stood.

"Scarn! Where the fuck are you!" The city guard was running

toward him. Rael yanked his rapier free. Time to go. He turned, then blinked as an arc of steel slashed hard at his face. He leapt back but not quite far enough. Rael yelled as Biter tore open his face.

Rael's head flew back. He spat like a lynx as his handsome features exploded in a river of bloody pain. Corin smiled, he readied Biter for a second blow. He had narrowly missed slicing the Assassin's throat but instead had slashed Rael's face wide open, leaving a deep welt from right eyebrow through both lips to chin. Rael's ruined face oozed blood and splattered down on his expensive garb. Rael gurgled more in outrage than pain. Blood obscured his vision. That didn't matter, he knew where Corin was standing.

He blocked Biter's second thrust and lunged back with the slim sword.

Corin was caught off guard by the speed of Rael's attack. He shifted left in the nick of time as Rael's rapier scored a slice along his arm. Corin grinned in relief. It was just a flesh wound.

"You missed me!" Corin's grin widened. Rael Hakkenon resembled a contorted parody of what he had been. "Spoiled your looks, heh Assassin! That was for Roman Parrantios! Remember the kiss of Corin an Fol next time you admire your pretty features!"

Rael's lips splattered blood as he tried to reply. He wiped his eyes clear and saw soldiers everywhere. He faced a quandary: stay to skewer his enemy and get skewered by the watch, or else leg it back to his ship and plan a rematch. Tough call.

Corin heard the stomp of heavy feet behind him. The city guard and traders had been avidly watching their fight, exchanging views on who would win. Deeming the show over, the watch advanced on Corin and Rael with levelled pikes.

Corin grinned at Rael and Rael glared back. Another day then. Corin rammed Biter into Rael's midriff but the Assassin jumped clear. The watch crashed forward, all steel and kerfuffle. Corin found a gap between pikes and raced for the far end of the market. In seconds he'd vanish down another side cut. A dozen guards broke off from the main squad and ran after the fleeing longswordsman.

Rael stoked his anger and watched the guard file out to block his escape. The remaining watch circled him, their long weapons probing. They were taking no chances with this dangerous bastard. There was six of them and they were careful. It didn't make any difference. They all died.

The first fell with the Assassin's knife in his throat, as did the second clutching his belly in disbelief and crumpling to the floor. Rael's rapier danced its cobra death, slicing through pikestaffs and killing two more. Number five got close, but Rael's dagger slid down the pike taking the guard's fingers and then lancing into his throat. The last one turned and legged it. Rael legged it after him and skewered him from behind. Rael glared at the strewn tables and gibbering, accusing traders. There was no sign of Corin an Fol.

More heavy feet approaching.

Another troop of scarlet-clad pikemen had entered the marketplace after hearing the tumult. They saw their dead comrades and, outraged, hastened to cut off his retreat. Rael turned on his heels, floored a couple of stunned traders, kicked out at a dog that snarled at his legs and was gone. Within minutes he'd flitted back into the labyrinth of streets behind, distancing himself rapidly from the chaos in the marketplace.

Rael sought solace in a dingy doorway once he'd lost his pursuers. He could hear them crashing and yelling two streets away. Their voices grew quieter. Satisfied he was safe for the moment, Rael carefully wiped the blood seeping from his face with a black silk handkerchief. Then he squatted, calmly took out the needle and thread he always kept stowed up his sleeve as defence should his fine cloth fray.

Rael stitched the scar, working down from brow to chin. The pain was nothing: it focused his mind. As he worked the needle, Rael thought about the peasant that had scarred him for life and broken his nose. Longswordsman Corin an Fol. The brigand Caswallon had told him to kill.

And kill him he would. In due course. It was just a question of when and more importantly how. Corin an Fol. Rael would cherish that name. He'd think about it every day, on the hour until he had his enemy naked and bound before him. Then, very slowly and with intricate care, Rael Hakkenon Master Assassin would take his revenge.

Chapter 8

An Old Friend

Barin stood at the prow of his vessel whilst Fassof steadied the wheel. *The Starlight Wanderer* rounded the southern, rock-strewn tip of the small bay that thrust seaward protecting the city's harbour. To the south, Kael's Stream rushed to greet the ocean in a chiming whirl of spume and spray. It was late afternoon and still very hot. Far out to sea, the sail of *The Black Serpent* was only just visible in the hazy sunlight.

Barin's mood had calmed to pragmatic reflection. The day could have gone better but things could also be a lot worse. He hoped Corin and the queen were alright and that the Assassin lay gutted in an alley. Barin had taken stock after their elopement from the harbour. Fortunately Raleenians were lethargic sailors. There would be no pursuit from the city at least. Port Sarfe's harbour commissioners relied on trade and kept few war boats. Barin had spied two galleys when they'd entered this morning but both had been undergoing repairs.

He turned to his crew. Ruagon the cook had splinted the broken bones, rubbed salve on deep cuts and bolstered the crew's spirits with fresh food and copious ale. This last having been fortuitously purloined by Cogga, Taic and Sveyn from the harbour master's stores just before the raid on their ship.

Barin counted heads. He had lost two men during the fight, but had gained four—though two he deemed useless and the other two foreign, thus untrustworthy despite Cogga's endorsement. Barin traded with foreigners, had friends from other lands, but until now had never employed anyone overseas.

He determined to keep a sharp eye on Wogun and Norman. Both big rough-looking lads. And very foreign. He'd keep a sharper eye on Taic and the other idiot. Or rather Fassof would while Barin was away.

Barin watched as the trader rounded the point in a bright flourish of sail. To port, half a mile away, was the mouth of Kael's gushing stream. Once free of its eddying currents his men would heave to and await their captain's orders.

Barin had tossed his blood-spattered silk shirt into the harbour, deeming it no longer fit to wear. Instead he'd donned a tight leather tunic over close fitting goat-hide trews. Once again he strapped the huge axe across his back. He then stooped to tie a cord of braided leather around his forehead. It would keep his hair from impeding him on this next venture. Satisfied, Barin strode to the prow. Fassof stood waiting with Cogga and Taic, of all people.

"You got nothing to do?" Barin glared at his nephew.

Taic beamed. "Just wondered if you needed a companion, Uncle."

"Nope." Barin turned to Fassof. "This should do it,"

Fassof nodded his approval. "Will they return, do you think?" The mate cast his eye towards the tiny black sail on the horizon.

"Almost certainly," responded Barin with a nod. "I left Hakkenon to Corin. We got parted. Whatever followed, I doubt the little shithead made it back to the serpent. Those maggots won't go far without their leader, and his other ships must be lurking close by."

"Let's hope Corin slew the bastard," growled Cogga, fingering his jewelled dagger. "Corin's efficient with that longsword of his."

"So is the lord of Crenna—with his rapier," responded Barin with a bleak stare inland. "Too efficient."

To their north, Barin could see the turrets of Port Sarfe's barbican peering-hazy in the distance, over the rocky ridge beyond the river. The rest of the city was hidden from view by dunes and surging surf, and the sounds of the harbour drowned out by the rush of urgent water beneath them. Barin hoped Corin was safely reunited with the others. He would know soon enough.

"This will do fine, Fassof," Barin told the mate after dispelling his gloomy thoughts. They were leeward of the river's southern shoreline, as close to its sandy banks as they dared venture without grounding on hidden shoals.

"Await me at the arranged point," Barin said. "And keep a wary eye out for our pirate friends. I will return as soon as I've spoken with the merchant and have some answers regarding our next voyage."

"I thought we were heading north again later, wintering at home."

"That's the plan, Fassof—but you know what Silon's like."

Without further ado Barin turned to face the shore. He straddled the rail, linked his brawny arms together, holding them high over his head. Seconds later he'd plunged headfirst into the salty embrace of the bay of Permio. Within moments his bold strokes were cutting water towards the nearest stretch of beach.

The mate and his companions watched their captain swim otter-lithe towards the sandy shore. "What's this latest business with the merchant about?" Cogga asked him.

"Buggered if I know," muttered Fassof. "He don't tell me much." He turned, awarded Taic a hard stare. "You still here?" Taic took the hint and returned to his chores.

"He's not a bad lad," Cogga whispered as Taic left them. "Just a bit misunderstood. Sveyn too. I was a bit wild at that age."

"You still are a bit wild."

"Hmm. And I thought I'd mellowed."

Just before last light Fassof steered *The Starlight Wanderer* through narrow jaws of sandstone into the hidden cove they'd used in earlier years. It was scarce more than a jumbled collection of sandy rocks forming a wide circle, fenced shoreward by a stubby coppice of stunted cedars, and seaward by low sandy bluffs. Well hidden from prying eyes.

The crew tossed anchor. Early next morning they would be about their tasks, the hale repairing and shaping new oars and the injured resting up, while they awaited the return of their captain. Fassof took first watch. He crested the nearest knoll, and shielding his eyes, gazed far out across starlit water. Nothing stirred on the watery horizon.

Barin was a strong swimmer. He'd wasted little time reaching the sandy beach and hadn't spotted any sharks. He coughed and spluttered his way up the bank, shaking off the excess drops of salt water as he went.

From here Barin could avoid Port Sarfe easily enough. He'd lope up stream for some miles, ford the rock-strewn river at a place he knew, and then make his way northwards to Vioyamis—Silon's villa.

Barin glanced up as gulls swooped and mewed above his head, their sharp eyes watching him with avaricious curiosity and their harsh cries berating his efforts. Barin ignored them. By dusk he had crossed Kael's stream and was heading north in great bounding strides. To his left the square, distant walls of Port Sarfe bulked skyward. Barin was too far away to see the guards patrolling the battlements. Not that he cared about that.

***

Ariane tensed as the guards led her and her companions into the murky gatehouse. She felt panic welling up inside, remembering the trap at Kranek Castle, and fearing another.

But there was no alternative. The queen steeled herself. It was so
gloomy in the gatehouse, hard to see anything clearly after the bright
sunlight of the street outside. They entered a back room where a fire
crackled on an open hearth despite the heat.

Huddled by it on a bench was a man, his features hidden by the
deep folds of a heavy hood. He was slight in build and slouched idle
in his chair. Ariane frowned. There was something familiar about
this hooded stranger. Behind her, Bleyne silently slipped his knife
into his palm.

"That knife won't be necessary here," said a voice she recog-
nized instantly.

Goddess be praised!

Ariane laughed in relief. The stranger stood with hood cast back.
His face was hard and sun-darkened and his eyes shrewd glints of jet.
The hair close-cropped and silver. In his left ear sparkled a diamond.

"I've been expecting you, your Highness," Silon smiled coolly.
The guards shifted awkwardly and Bleyne watched on without expression. Cale wondered if this was the merchant they were meaning
to visit, Galed's relieved smile affirmed it.

The captain of guard looked puzzled; he exchanged a questioning glance at the merchant.

"It's alright, Dornal, I'll conduct matters from here." Silon nodded towards the door. The captain hesitated for a moment then took
the hint. Dornal motioned to his men to follow, and po-faced closed
the door behind him.

"Corin is in danger," blurted Cale before anyone else could
speak. "And Captain Barin. *The Starlight Wanderer* has been attacked!" Silon's gaze drifted over the boy.

"And you are?"

"This is master Cale—a loyal and trusted aide," announced
Ariane. Silon raised an eyebrow but said nothing.

"You are familiar with Galed," continued Ariane, "this is Bleyne
of the forest, a skilled archer and good friend." Silon nodded towards
Bleyne who for his part barely shrugged. Again Silon looked slightly

puzzled. Then the door opened and a guard brought in piping hot cups of tea. Ariane waved him away. "There is no time for this nonsense."

"Relax, my Queen. Enjoy your tea." Silon motioned they take rest on couches in the corner and imbibe at leisure. "Everything is in hand. The city guard has put paid to the surviving Crenise—though I think Barin did for most of them. *The Black Serpent* was last seen fleeing the harbour with the Northmen hard on its tale."

Ariane glared at him. "Please, take a seat, Ariane. This is excellent tea and will sustain you."

"What about Corin?" Ariane reluctantly seated herself whilst motioning the other three to do the same. Bleyne remained standing.

"There was confusion at first to who exactly the enemy was," Silon explained in a quiet voice. "Some of the militia here aren't that bright. But when I arrived I soon straightened things out." Silon paused sipped his tea again. He studied their anxious faces and smiled.

"As for Corin an Fol. When is he not in trouble? I've known that one for years, why do you think I'm so grey? He has a talent for surviving so I daresay he's alright. I sent someone to recover Corin from whatever mess he's gotten into, so don't worry, young master Cale." Silon motioned for the boy to drink his tea.

Cale was unconvinced. And he wasn't impressed with the tea. Beer would have been preferable. "He was fighting the Assassin, the one that killed poor Roman."

Silon nodded slowly. "I assumed Roman was dead since you haven't mentioned him. A sad loss. But Corin is still alive—that I promise you." Cale subsided.

"What of these soldiers, are you sure they are trustworthy?" Ariane hinted towards the door. "Port Sarfe militia aren't beyond taking bribes. Hakkenon knew we were here so most likely Caswallon does too." She sipped her hot tea and traded a worried look with Galed, who was clearly thinking along the same lines. Meanwhile, Bleyne's cool gaze surveyed the street outside.

"Their trust is assured, Ariane, please relax," replied Silon losing patience. "As you know, I possess a certain privileged position hereabouts. The captain and his men answer to me and nobody else. Caswallon's insidious reach has not yet filtered into Port Sarfe's streets. People are rough in this town, that I grant you. But they're loyal. Anyone asking pert questions and I'd know about it. We are safe for a while."

"Are we?"

"For now. Certainly we've little time. Caswallon's web deepens. His dark mentor feeds his ambition and furnishes him with Groil creatures, and other even more unsavoury troops. My brave contacts inform me that Kella is an evil place these days." He forced a smile. "Rest here a while, you've had a busy time. And don't fret. We shall await that rogue Corin in this very spot. He shouldn't be too long. Once reunited, I will escort you all to my villa. The distance is short, as two of you know. There are enough horses stabled nearby awaiting our needs.

"Get what rest you can, there is much to discuss tomorrow. I will be holding council in Vioyamis. Among the guests will be General Belmarius and Duke Tomais of Vangaris. The latter arrived in very poor state late last night, accompanied by his sad-eyed daughter, Lady Shallan."

Ariane felt a cloud cross her when she heard that last name.

Lady Shallan of Morwella.

As young girls they had been rivals in love. Shallan was so beautiful men were stupid around her and yet she never paid heed to any of them. Proud, dreamy and aloof. Ariane had never liked Shallan.

Another thought darkened her mood further.

Corin.

And Shallan. Ariane knew his reputation with women. He was such an idiot on that front. She stared sourly into her tea cup. If Corin was still alive (and Goddess please let that be so). If he so much as glanced at that willowy waste of space tomorrow, she'd kill him herself. Ariane might be promised to the Sea God but she wasn't ready to lose Corin to another. Especially *her*.

***

Corin sped up the hill pursued by half a dozen puffing guards waving an array of nasty weapons, and cursing in their southern accents. Despite his predicament and aching bones, Corin grinned. This was just like old times. He wondered if Lania still kept a room on the Street of Dark Vales. She'd been a rare one, that Lania. He must be somewhere near her place. Those had been the days! If only he had more time. Then Corin thought of Ariane, the lad Cale and his other comrades. Corin's face grew sober again. Those foolish carefree days were gone forever. He had responsibilities now.

Corin knew most of these streets. He led the soldiers on a merry dance up towards the barbican. He hadn't a clue how he would escape from the city, but would worry about that later. What mattered was to keep moving—don't let them get too close. He'd have a hard job explaining his actions with a pike shoved up his arse.

And this lot were angry.

Crossing into another street, Corin lost his pursuers for the moment. He crouched, gulped in deep breaths then cursed when excited shouts announced he had been spotted again. This time it was a colourful troop of horsemen cantering noisily down the cobbles towards him, the riders' long lances held ready.

Bollocks! They've unleashed the bloody cavalry.

Cursing this new development, Corin ducked back into the street he had just emerged from. Blocking his way was a soldier sporting a wicked-looking halberd. The man grinned at him and swung. Corin caught the halberd's shaft with his left hand, he pulled the guard towards him and rammed his head hard into the soldier's nose. The guard crumpled and Corin booted his groin.

That's you done, big lad.

But then three others appeared and jabbed their pikes toward him.

Can't go forward, can't go back. This was getting tricky. Corin slammed Biter in its scabbard and reached down warily to retrieve the groaning guard's halberd. A bloody great thing but they had their uses. Corin jabbed back at the guards jabbing at him. They backed off and looked at each other. No one wanted to tackle this lunatic single handed, and there was scant space for a rush upon.

Corin grinned at them; he thrust the weapon forward and spike down into a crack in the cobbles. They watched, confused. Corin took a little run up then launched his lean frame upon it, and then hoisting himself skyward let go one hand, this he waved about like a flag before grasping the iron gutter above him. He dropped the halberd and swung the other arm up until his free hand caught the gutter. Corin grunted and swung about like a horny gibbon, legs dancing, arms straining, and face reddening. Despite all that he pulled himself higher.

But unfortunately the gutter was rotten.

Fuck...

Corin crashed to the ground with the broken gutter accompanied by feathers, mud, sand, dust, sparrow shit, and brackish water, most of which connected with the closest pikeman's face.

Corin followed that up by kicking said guard while he thrashed about, then seizing his chance, Corin leapt skyward again, this time without the aid of a halberd, instead he rammed a foot into a window ledge and scampered frantically up the side of the building. Adrenaline is a wonderful thing. So is incentive. It's amazing what a man can do with a bunch of hairy arse militia bearing down on him with spiky things.

Corin's legs started slipping, he swung his arm out just managing to grip the eaves of the roof with three fingers. Tiles cracked beneath those fingers as Corin hurled himself up onto the sloping pitch. It was a hard thing to do what with Clouter, Biter and a steel shirt weighing him down. The soldiers milled and cursed below, poking their pikes and halberds up at the madly dangling feet above their heads. Falling really wasn't an option at this point.

Corin heaved his long frame out of their reach, ripping more tiles off for better grip on the trusses beneath. These he hurled down on the cursing soldiers until they backed off again.

"Bunch of tossers!" Corin yelled down at them.

Tenuously and cautiously, Corin crawled up the fragile gable like an ungainly spider. At last he gained the ridge and swung a long aching shank over to straddle the rooftop.

Phew...

Corin stood up carefully, holding his arms out on either side for balance. The guards were still shouting but he could no longer see them.

Corin reached the far end of the roof ridge, and quickly half slid, half clambered down the other side. Grabbing the eaves he leapt, arms flailing, onto a slightly lower adjacent roof, landing with a painful thud and cracking more tiles. He shakily regained his feet after a struggle. At least this roof looked stronger. Corin dared run along its edge. This time he hurdled the ridge and leaped onto the next roof.

Progress at last!

"He's getting away!" a voice shouted somewhere behind him.

"After him!" boomed another. The sound of heavy feet and hooves passed beneath him. Corin rested for a moment, regained his breath behind a severely cracked chimneystack. There weren't that many chimneys in Port Sarfe (it being hot), but Corin was grateful for this one.

For several minutes he waited until the footsteps faded and the voices trailed off. Then Corin laughed—he had lost them again! He rose too quickly. Lost his footing and took a wild grab at the stack, cursing as the sandstone bricks came free in his hands.

Whoops...

Down Corin tumbled, arms flailing, crashing to the floor. He cursed and covered his head with his hands. Bricks rained down upon him, bruising his already sore body and nearly knocking him senseless. Dazed and somewhat giddy Corin stumbled up, shook the dust from his soot-stained body and spat a tooth across the street. That had hurt. But at least he'd lost them. Then he heard that familiar sound. Hoofbeats approaching. It seemed the cavalry had found him again. This was becoming tedious. Corin studied his options. There weren't many left.

He turned, watched as a single rider approached in a leisurely manner. Corin had no idea where the others had gone.

Corin freed Biter and wiggled it about but he was exhausted. His right arm hurt from where he had landed on it and he was a mass of cuts and bruises, but nothing appeared broken. Corin waited sour-faced for the horseman to arrive. He couldn't see very well, the sun was in his eyes.

When the rider emerged out of the sun's glare he glanced down at the filthy scowling swordsman with an amused expression on his face. Corin's gaze narrowed. This horseman didn't look like one of the city guard; indeed he didn't resemble a Raleenian at all. This rider was dressed in an elaborate green tunic, laced with gold braid that covered his frame from broad shoulder right down to the soft suede riding boots with their decorative silver spurs. He looked like a proper ponce in Corin's opinion.

The stranger's long hair was as gold as barley and it sparkled in the afternoon sun. The face was young, good-natured and handsome. The rider had a smug look as though pleased with himself.

Up yours too.

Corin spat blood and waggled Biter at the rider who still watched him in amused silence. He assumed this was some rich nobleman's by-blow who had decided to join in the chase, purely for larks.

"Are you going to sit there like a pompous twat or challenge me or...what?" Close by came the shouting again. Mainly swearing announcing the watch had collided with the horsemen and both were blaming each other.

The handsome rider cupped an ear and smiled. "They seem a bit unorganised," he said, ignoring Corin's challenge. His big horse snorted and clumped the cobbles. The gaudy rider leaned forward in the saddle and grinned raffishly.

"Actually, I've come to help you, Corin an Fol," he said, then turned in his saddle to watch the street behind him. "We had best hurry else they sort themselves out and get a plan together. They are quite decent fellows normally, but seem to be holding a grudge towards you. I cannot think why." The rider held out a gloved hand for Corin to mount. His smile was welcoming. "Don't you remember me? I'm disappointed."

Suddenly Corin laughed, recognising the rider. It had taken a long hard stare, the horseman looked different from when he had last seen him, weeks ago among the ruins of Waysmeet village.

"Tamersane, yes, I remember," grinned Corin. He leapt onto the chestnut stallion's broad back behind the rider. The horse gave a derisive snort and turned to stare reproachfully at this added burden he now carried. Suddenly Corin found himself laughing.

"Thunderhoof, you old bugger! It's good to see you, my fat friend. Have you missed me?" Thunderhoof rolled his eyes and snorted again. At a word from Tamersane he started to trot along the narrow street. There was no sign of the soldiers anywhere and the shouting had subsided. They must have given up at last.

Thunderhoof led them up to the barbican gates. The cheerful Tamersane chatted as if they were on an afternoon's jaunt through the country, and not risking certain incarceration if spotted. His face darkened once, when Corin informed him of Roman's death.

"He was a fine man," said the rider, "like an older brother to me." Corin added nothing. He thought of Rael Hakkenon—wondered if the Assassin still lived. Corin hoped so; he was not finished with him yet.

***

Ariane leapt up in joy when she saw her cousin arrive with the Longswordsman intact. She hugged and kissed Corin, and Cale laughed at his dishevelled state. The queen turned to Tamersane.

"I have missed you, beloved," she said. Corin was not sure whom she meant. He cast a dark look in Tamersane's direction but the blond horseman failed to notice.

Silon waited inside. Corin greeted him coolly; the merchant seemed as amused as everyone else at Corin's shambolic state but chose not to comment.

Instead, he ushered them all through the gate to where the other horses were tethered. They mounted swiftly, Cale took a seat behind Tamersane, whilst Corin reclaimed Thunder. Silon saluted the captain and his men, thanking them for the assistance. They said nothing, just stared reproachfully at Corin.

Dornal recalled the tall ruffian from earlier days. It seemed he was still a troublemaker. He shook his head and wondered why it was that handsome ladies were always drawn towards these worthless scoundrels. It vexed him but in a week he got over it. He scratched his arse, and then returned to get the latest report from his men. Rael Hakkenon of Crenna had escaped them for now. But if he returned with his marauding filth, the soldiers of Port Sarfe would be waiting. Their vigilance second to none.

They cantered down the dusty road. Behind the sun set crimson and the red roofs of the distant city gleamed as though on fire. Wispy strips of cloud raced across the darkening sky as evening descended. The miles passed with relative ease. Soon they had entered a fertile valley of olive trees and vines, swaying gently in a light breeze as nightfall descended. They wove their way through the valley. Grapes still clung to the vines hanging above the road despite the lateness of the year. Corin gazed up at them as they rode beneath. Silon had always been fortunate with his crop as he had with most other things.

Some moments later they crested a hill. Cale gasped when he saw the merchant's glistening villa. There it stood in stately splendour, serene and tranquil under the watchful gaze of the waxing moon. Cale decided this Silon merchant to be very important. The thought pleased him. Cale liked important people. One day he would be important too.

As ever Corin was impressed by Silon's villa. He'd always been slightly envious of the white marble manse, surrounded by its cut lawns and ornate statues. Vioyamis, it was called; named after some obscure wood nymph Silon claimed had frequented this valley in distant olden times. It was a ridiculous story that Corin had always refuted. Now he wondered.

Ahead, sharing the road with Silon's mare, trotted Ariane's horse. She was so relieved. Only two things nagged her: how had Barin fared? And just what would she say to Shallan when she saw her in the morning? Still, they had done well yet again, Ariane told herself, and at last had arrived at their next destination. Tomorrow they would finally glean some answers.

When they arrived at the villa, Zallerak was waiting with crystal glass in hand. They all chose to ignore him. Far behind a single horn sounded the all clear. Having seen the pirates off, the bold citizens of Port Sarfe resumed their visits to the copious hostelries, filling them swiftly and talking of the eventful day that had passed.

In *The Crooked Knife*, its patron Rado was surprised to receive some silver coin from a stranger who mysteriously announced that the 'queen' was in his debt and would call again to thank him. *Queen?* he thought, *whatever next?* then quickly forgot as voices demanded beacons of ale. *The Crooked Knife* was very busy that night, and for several long nights after.

***

The lone figure waited on the clifftop watching as the sun set like oozing blood beneath the ocean. His ravaged face still stung and his mood was blacker than ever. High above dark clouds scurried westward over water. The evening wind whipped the frayed sleeves of his studded tunic, but Rael said nothing as he brooded beneath that sullen sky.

Hours passed. The Assassin watched in silence until his black ship slid ghostlike into the bay below. It was not over. It had scarcely begun. He would start with his captain who had left him stranded in the city, a simple flogging would do for now as the man had his uses. Rael laughed, thinking of Scarn and the other fellow's head adorning the castle walls some miles to the south of him.

They should have kept up with their leader, fat bastards, instead they had let themselves be caught by the vengeful watch, and had met their fate, the fools.

It had been a mistake entering Port Sarfe alone but then he hadn't trusted that goblin, and had bade his other vessels patrol the Raleenian and Kelwyn coasts. It didn't matter. They would be joining him soon enough.

Rael raised the storm lantern high above his head. In slow sweeping motions he swayed it back and forth, at last seeing *The Black Serpent's* lanterns answer in turn.

He would sail north, gather his fleet and then the hunt would resume once more. This time there would be no escape for *The Starlight Wanderer* and her barbarian crew. Then after that victory he would go ashore and seek out the renegade who called himself Corin an Fol.

Chapter 9

Vioyamis

That night Corin bathed in scented water as servants scrubbed his back and tried valiantly to get a comb through that tangled maze of hair. Afterwards he thanked them and bid them begone, rising steaming from the piping bath and glimpsing his reflection in the polished silver mirror. The blue/grey eyes staring back at him had a haunted look. His face was leaner than before, the scar whitened beneath the deep tan. He looked older.

Corin sighed, he reached down to the crystal basin, retrieved a sharp knife and tugged at his beard, sawing at the mass of curly dark hair until more of his face was revealed. Satisfied, he dressed swiftly in new garments given him by Silon's retainer, and then joined his companions in the main hall.

Cale laughed when he saw Corin, and Ariane raised an eyebrow at his smart apparel.

"I knew there was a face hidden behind all that hair," she told him.

Corin shrugged and managed an awkward half smile. He accepted a cold glass of wine from the merchant and without more ado took seat by the vine-draped balustrade overlooking the magnificent gardens.

Vioyamis. Silon's villa. Stately and grand and spacious and serene.

All wasted on Corin. As always Vioyamis left him with a feeling of emptiness, as though Silon's wealth mocked him and found him wanting. Everything was order here, so precise it irritated him. Corin looked around at the sumptuous furnishings, the crystal statuettes and ruby-studded vases that paraded the airy hallways, cooled by breeze-driven ceiling fans. No dust mote dare settle here. There were bright ornate tapestries on the walls and paintings of intricate designs. Priceless rugs from far off lands carpeted the floors. Vioyamis never failed to impress. For that reason alone Corin disliked it. Silon was one of the most successful people he knew whereas he, Corin...

Two swords, a horse, a gold brooch, a bow, and a pair of stolen boots that still leaked.

Capacious and airy, the villa was built on the flat crown of a gentle knoll, commanding wide sweeping views across vineyards and gardens below. Its white marble walls could be seen for miles around, standing elegant and majestic above the freshly cut acres of green turf. Swan-regal, the villa's wings spread out on either side housing Silon's many visitors and his score of silent servants.

Polished glass and marble reflected the sunlight. Vioyamis blazed like a grounded star across the fertile fields reaching up to greet it, still lush despite the lateness of the year. Obsidian statues watched with blank unseeing eyes from shady courtyards as servants and retainers passed silently to and fro.

Above were crystal lanterns, swaying and flickering, their silver light chasing shadows from the walls. More crystal lights glimmered at the corners of tall trellises framing the rose-clad walls. Behind the terraces were sleepy hallways opening to reveal wide verandas draped with more intricate tapestries of silver and gold, each telling a tale of days gone by.

Outside Corin could hear the soft chiming of crystal waterfalls cascading down to wash through sweeping ferns lining the gardens below. Silon's manse was a harmonic blend of filtered water, polished walls and distilled careful lighting. Corin wished he were back in Port Sarfe.

Corin thought of Silon's sultry daughter. He wondered what had become of Nalissa. She had been the reason why Corin had left the merchant's service. A misunderstanding that had ended with a bitter quarrel between the merchant and his daughter—and Corin stuck starkers in the middle. Corin had departed the next day, cantering off in a cloud of anger bound for Finnehalle far away. Nalissa had pleaded with him to stay, then at his stiff refusal lost her temper, announcing she would ride to Atarios in the north and stay with her cousins—who at least liked her even if no one else did. Her father had not spoken of her since, and there was no sign of Nalissa here tonight.

Probably just as well

Corin wiled away that evening playing an intricate form of draughts with Tamersane and losing badly, much to his annoyance. Tamersane appeared to have more than his share of good luck, Corin decided. He was handsome as ever, tall with long fair hair kept neat and smiling mouth and laughing eyes. His teeth were far too white and even, in Corin's opinion.

And Tamersane's dress sense was ambivalent. He favoured bright colours, this evening being no exception, with turquoise silk shirt and olive leather trousers, and soft grey suede boots that folded over at the top. Though Corin had scrubbed up valiantly he felt like a tramp next to this boy. Apparently Ariane's cousin was a big hit with the ladies at court.

Tamersane had an easy tongue. He was charming company and took little seriously. Corin considered him a bit of a ponce. But then Tamersane was young, still in his early twenties whilst Corin was a very old thirty summers, particularly this night. Tomorrow, the Kelwynian informed him (after thrashing Corin at draughts a third time), there was to be a council held by Silon and the queen and some other important guests that would arrive in the morning.

"I cannot wait," Corin had replied.

It was late when Corin retired, bidding the annoyingly cheerful Tamersane a grudging goodnight and making for his room, still kept ready for him at the western wing of the house. Queen Ariane and Galed were already asleep, both exhausted after the hectic business in Port Sarfe, although Cale was still wandering around with a gormless expression. The boy had hardly spoken all evening, so stunned and star-gazy was he by the grandeur of Silon's house.

Corin grinned, noticing Cale's newly close-cropped sparkling ginger hair and clean scrubbed face. Cale looked pink and plucked. The queen had evidently had someone work on the boy. Corin messed Cale's hair and bid the boy goodnight before retiring to his room. He gazed around, remembering the last time he was here with Nalissa giggling and Silon crashing in on them. That evening hadn't ended well. Corin closed his eyes and tried to forget what an idiot he was. Silon's dreamy villa seemed so very quiet compared to Port Sarfe's bustle and the constant grind of Barin's ship. Corin fidgeted and rolled about but eventually dozed for a time.

***

He awoke sometime before dawn to the sound of dogs barking and hushed voices exchanging hurried words. Corin smiled in relief, recognising the booming voice of Barin trying unsuccessfully to be quiet in the hallway. Elanion be praised! His friend was still alive. But what of his ship? Corin looked forward to comparing notes with Barin about it later in the morning.

Corin was about to roll over and go back to sleep when subtle movement outside caught his eye. He slipped out from under the soft silk sheets and peeled back the velvet curtain. Something or someone was watching him from the darkness of the garden. A shadow within a shadow, hard to define and swaying slightly. Corin could feel the things invisible eyes boring into him in that horribly familiar way.

Corin froze. He felt a sudden chill and noticed a score of new shadowy shapes emerging from Silon's hedges. The figure watching him flickered and vanished before Corin could be sure he'd seen it.

He blinked, saw the other shadows turn and vanish into the gloom, making for Vioyamis's main entrance away to the right. Before they'd disappeared Corin caught a glimpse of dog snout and serrated blade. *Groil. We are under attack!*

Corin heaved his naked body from the bed and yanked his leather trousers up his legs, buckling his belt tight. He didn't bother with smallclothes, but instead unlatched the window, swung up into the orifice and half fell out, before reaching back to grab Clouter from its resting place by the door. He prepared to jump but froze when a new sound filled the morning.

Hooooo halloo!

The blast of a horn sounded close by. Corin vaulted to the ground and sped along the path. *Hoooo!* The horn sounded again, louder this time and accompanied by the ghastly baying and howling of what must surely be the Groil. Something or someone had beat him to it! Corin sped along a path, cursing the bushes blocking his vision and stabbing his face. The howling rose to wailing shrieks, he heard hounds bark and distant voices.

Hoooo halloo! The horn blasted a third time and the howling subsided to a weird whimpering followed by sudden silence. Corin crashed through the hedge, rolled, and tore Clouter free from its scabbard. He froze at the scene confronting him.

Three people were standing on Silon's front terrace. One was the merchant himself, another was Barin. The third was a tallish woman clutching a long twisted horn. She wore a long white gossamer thin gown and her hair was strewn dark across her face. Her feet were bare and her ankles showed slender and pale. Corin caught more than a glimpse of enticing curves beneath that gown.

For a second he stood gawping, wondering if this was Silon's wood nymph come to life. Corin wished she'd turn around so he'd get a look at her face. She didn't oblige. But rather stood as one stiff or frozen in time.

Close to her bare feet lay a half dozen bodies, Corin didn't have to look to know these were the Groil decomposing already. The stink was proof enough. Baffled but fascinated (mainly at those curves and that dress) Corin strode forward, Silon glanced his way and Barin raised a dinner plate hand in greeting. The woman hadn't seen him yet. She appeared deeply troubled, her gaze locked on the stinking dog-corpses below.

"Where are the rest?" Corin slammed a fist into Barin's open palm. "Glad you're in one piece," he smiled whilst glancing at the strange lady in the gossamer dress.

"Good to see you too, Longswordsman," Barin grinned, seeing where Corin's gaze was focussed. "As you see we've had a spot of trouble. Things could have got out of hand if this brave lassie hadn't joined us." The woman shook her head hearing that. At last she turned, brushed the hair from her face, and awarded Corin a quizzical glance.

"My lady," Silon frowned at Corin. "This is the mercenary we spoke about."

The woman said nothing but her eyes watched Corin for a time before turning away again and feigning disinterest. Corin felt a sudden shiver, like a ghost riding on his back. Haunted stare, her eyes, grey/blue almost matching his own. Her face ivory pale, symmetrical and oval. The lips full and slightly parted, and that wild chestnut hair cascading down her back. A haggard, tired face. But a beautiful one.

I know you...

"Corin an Fol," continued Silon sharply. "May I present the Lady Shallan of Morwella?"

Shallan. Where had he heard that name before?

"Where did he say she came from?" Corin whispered in Barin's ear as they returned to the villa. Silon had sent guards and hounds to scour the gardens and fields beyond. They'd returned with no news of the remaining Groil. Six of the dog creatures were dead but the others had vanished like morning mist. Sorcery. It had to be sorcery. But then Corin was used to that, and besides, he now had other things on his mind. The woman who glided gracefully beside Silon, her arm locked in his.

"Morwella, she arrived with her old man the duke the other night apparently." Barin saw the way Corin's gaze was on that white shift and pale curves. "Quite a beauty, heh."

"She seems a bit stuck up."

"Methinks that lady has much on her mind."

"And what's with that bloody horn? She must have a fine pair of lungs?"

"That and other things. No doubt we'll learn later," Barin smiled at Corin. "I must say you look a splendid sight this morning, Longswordsman. I suggest you go get scrubbed and dressed before you scare the servants away."

Later that morning Corin found Silon standing alone at the main entrance of his house. The merchant nodded seeing Corin, and motioned him approach.

"You've done well." Silon allowed his lips to form a slight smile. "Queen Ariane holds you in highest regard. I'm quite impressed, Corin an Fol."

Corin wished he'd known just what Ariane had said to Silon. He ignored the merchant's probing gaze and instead admired the view across the gardens.

"We were lucky. Except Roman of course."

"He will be sorely missed."

"He is already." An awkward silence followed. Eventually Silon broke it.

"What troubles you?"

"Oh nothing really," Corin choked an ironic laugh. "Just Groil stalking us in our sleep, the Assassin knowing we were at Port Sarfe, despite our thinking we had eluded him. The joyous prospect of venturing to Permio to scoop up some idiotic prince. And then there's the queen..."

"The queen?" Silon's gaze narrowed knowingly. "Regrettable.

But Ariane did what she had to do."

"She told you then."

"Aye, she did." Silon's expression made Corin wonder what else Ariane had told the merchant.

Corin smiled bitterly. Again he was caught in the middle. "I saw that creep Morak this morning. Leastways something that looked like him, and felt like him."

"More likely one of his brethren," responded Silon, who also knew all concerning the fight at Kranek. "I like to hope the Dog-Lord's still licking his wounds. But one cannot be sure, and we now know there are others. Rorshai scouts claim to have seen ghoul-like dog creatures high up in the mountains. The Rorshai are not the kind of people to imagine such things. Olen Valek lies close to the northern boundaries of their country."

Corin had heard about the Rorshai. They were a fierce secretive people living in clans east of the mountains. They were rumoured to be the finest horseman in the world. They were also rumoured to be cruel-hearted killers.

"The old ruins?" Corin had heard of Olen Valek too. Most people had. "I heard they are closer to Wynais. Has anyone actually been there?"

"Zallerak has."

"Well, there's a surprise," Corin chuckled wryly. "So you are acquainted with the... bard?"

"You don't like him."

"I don't trust him."

Silon laughed. "You don't trust anyone, Corin an Fol."

"It's why I'm still alive."

"I need you to stay that way." Silon rubbed his diamond earring and stared hard at Corin. "We'll speak more of this during the council."

"One last thing."

"Which is?"

"What's the duke of Morwella doing here with his smiling

daughter? And what's with that bloody horn? How could such a thing kill those Groil? Is she a witch?"

"I daresay you'll find that out later too. Oh, and be respectful in their presence, Corin. They've been through a lot. And I know how you like Morwellans. The council commences in an hour, I will see you then."

***

The light spilling in from outside failed to lift his spirits. But then Yail Tolranna had little to be happy about of late. Every day the doubt and fear tore into him. Was he right in doing this? What if he was caught? But then he had to do something and what real choice was there? He loved the queen more than anyone. But Ariane had abandoned her people by leaving on that fruitless quest. The queen was headstrong and courageous. But she was rash and foolhardy and Caswallon was on to her.

And as for her advisors. Where were they?

Dazaleon was old, as blinded by his devotion to the Goddess as was his queen. Roman was dead, the contact had informed him of this after receiving word from his master. There was no one else. Certainly not that soft fool Galed. As for Tamersane, Yail's younger brother had crashed in on Tolranna on his way south to that meddlesome merchant in Port Sarfe. They'd quarrelled heatedly and Tamersane had departed inside the hour.

Besides, Yail was doing this for his queen as well as his country. To protect both from the coming storm. The inevitable invasion from the north. Caswallon's army was mustering, so the contact said. The spy from Port Wind. There will be a massacre unless the city is handed over.

"Open your gates to Kelthaine, Captain Tolranna," the contact had said. "Your people, and more importantly your queen will be spared. You have Lord Caswallon's word on this."

So what choice did he have? Caswallon's army had recently been reinforced with fell creatures and soon would fall upon Kelwyn like hammer striking tin. The contact had taken pains to explain to Yail just what had happened to those valiant royalists up in Kella City. Torture and slow cruel death.

There had to be another way.

Ariane would never understand. Yail Tolranna, passionate loyalist and fervent patriot, would be branded traitor forever. By queen and countrymen alike. Unjustly—when he was the only one who could save them from themselves. The parchment crinkled under his palms, he hurled it to the corner. Tolranna couldn't bear to look at its contents any longer.

A letter from Caswallon. Coded and discreet. The spy had delivered it in person this morning. The words read thus:

Tolranna

My patience runs short while my army grows stronger.

I am a reasonable man but grow weary of your queen's perverse animosity.

Only your prompt actions can save Kelwyn. I will not be mocked.

I trust you will comply with my latest instructions.

I await your swiftest response.

You will inform my man who will then contact me via bird.

Caswallon

Chapter 10

The Merchant's Council

The bells sounded in Silon's courtyard, announcing it time. A scrubbed and freshly garbed Corin accompanied Barin to the main hall. Two smartly dressed servants attended the doors with polite smiles and nods. They ushered the two men in and bade them take their seats. Corin could see there were only three spaces left around the table. He wondered who would claim the last one. The table was large, oval and highly polished. It dominated the ornate hall. Upon it were crystal vases of wine and water, together with silver bowls of exotic fruit.

"Last again," muttered Barin under his breath and Corin repressed a smile. Neither had hurried to get here. He took his seat whilst stealing a glance at the other occupants of the room.

Queen Ariane was looking radiant in a pale green dress that shimmered slightly when trapped by sunlight. She was sitting opposite Corin, a delicate necklace of emeralds gracing her slender neck. Her dark hair looked glossy and her pale face intense. She talked quietly to Tamersane who slouched to her right, lazily nodding at her words.

Corin had never seen Ariane looking so queenly. He smiled her way and she nodded briefly before returning her attentions to her cousin.

To Ariane's left were seated Galed, dressed in neat dun velvet, and young Cale in smart blue trews and matching jacket. Corin was surprised by the boy's presence. He hadn't expected Cale to be at the council—urchin as he was. That said, the boy had scrubbed up well. The southern sunshine had dried his spotty chin—he looked quite presentable.

Galed's brown eyes met Corin and the squire nodded slightly. Beside Galed perched Bleyne, his tattooed face inscrutable as ever as he listened in to the queen's words.

Corin tensed when he saw the swarthy character seated to the left of Bleyne. A stranger—and from the wrong side of the Liaho by his look. Corin stared rudely across the table. But if the stranger noticed he gave no sign.

He wore a full beard, the face beneath artful, crisscrossed with thin scars; his long black hair held up by a scarlet cloth wound tightly around his head. The southerner was clad in a loose white gown with brightly striped baggy trousers of various fading colours, beneath were pointed silk shoes, which turned up at the front.

A man of the desert. At his side, supported by a jewel-encrusted belt, hung a curved scimitar with ornate silver hilt. Corin's frown deepened; he had fought against men just like this stranger in the wild lands south of the Liaho. He questioned Silon's wisdom in letting a Permian inside his walls.

Corin listened when the merchant introduced the man as Yashan, leader of the Sundhami, one of the many tribes that roamed the vast southern deserts. The Permian nodded curtly, he caught Corin's hostile eye and smiled slightly. He had a dangerous smile. Corin smiled back, equally dangerously, then casually turned his attention to the other guests.

At Corin's right was seated a burly individual in his middle years. He owned a large red face, dominated by a broad flat broken nose and bristling mustachios, these drooping down either side of his ruddy chin in the favoured style of Kelthaine. Corin needed no introduction to this man. Here was one known and respected throughout the Four Kingdoms.

Belmarius, lord General of the Bears, the once revered second regiment of Kelthaine—now ostracised and driven south by the usurper, Caswallon. The big general grunted in Corin's direction as though vaguely recalling him from somewhere.

Adjacent to Barin and Corin was seated Silon, looking splendid in gold-trimmed navy silk—his diamond earring, like Ariane's dress, trapping the sunlight.

To Silon's left was seated a noble looking man in his late middle years. His face elegant though thinly drawn. He appeared haggard, and his moist blue eyes held a haunted expression. He wore a long tunic of scarlet trimmed with gold, but that rich garb looked as faded as its owner. Silon announced this to be Duke Tomais of Vangaris.

Corin hardly noticed him. Instead he was looking at the woman beside the duke.

The Lady Shallan.

No longer wild-eyed and rigid. Rather she appeared regal and stern, her expression haughty, as if she didn't want to be here. Corin's gaze soaked up every inch of her. The long autumn tresses, those blue/grey witchy eyes. That oval face and pert nose, full lips and elusive smile. She caught his gaze and nodded slightly. Corin grinned at her and she turned away, irritation showing in her eyes..

Beside him, Barin muttered something obscene under his breath. Ariane's foot struck savagely out at the Northman, but her eyes were focused on Corin, currently staring stupidly at her cousin from Morwella.

Ariane had expected this. Shallan invariably brought out the worst in men. Even experienced courtiers got flustered by her pale beauty. And Corin wasn't remotely subtle. Ariane wished she had something hard to hit him with. Instead she kicked Barin again, who was chuckling in Corin's ear.

Ariane had seen her cousin last night but they hadn't spoken, though the Morwellan had smiled at her. As always Ariane felt second best. She studied her childhood rival with a critical slantwise glance. She looked a dream, did Shallan. That cascade of glossy chestnut, those perceptive dreamy eyes, the bluish grey of northern seas. Her features serene perfection with a dusting of freckles and high cheekbones, not to mention those full red lips.

Her cousin's body was all curves, the skin ivory pale beneath the silky blue dress that so lovingly caressed it. Between her breasts gleamed a chunk of amber carved in the shape of a bear and supported by a heavy chain of gold. Chain and pendant sparkled in unison as Shallan smiled politely at something Silon said. She seemed unaware of the eyes watching her, but Ariane knew her better than that.

Shallan was a consummate actress who knew well how to play to the crowd. As a girl she had been moody, evasive and capricious, whereas Ariane had been straightforward and blunt. It was part of the reason why Ariane had always disliked her back then.

When her cousin spoke it was always in measured tones. Shallan was clever, a thinker, her voice soft but compelling. Some three or four year older than Ariane, but as young girls they had known each other well. The Morwellan beauty was taller than the princess by a head.

Ariane forced a frosty smile at the Morwellan before darting daggers at Corin. She hated the fact that she loved him so much. It was intolerable. But what right had she to complain? Corin was a free agent. She had thrown away any chance they had by pledging herself to Sensuata. Since then she had acted cold towards him. Not that there had been any choice. But that didn't help her now. Shallan and Corin, the thought of that made her want to scream. Ariane quelled her wrath. She determined henceforth to ignore Corin, Barin and her cousin. They were here to discuss business after all.

***

Shallan had never understood why her cousin so disliked her. She had always tried to be friends with Ariane, but they just hadn't got on and her royal cousin's sharp glances announced nothing had changed. Not that that mattered to her at this moment.

Shallan was exhausted in body and mind. Worn down by their arduous journey, the Groil attacks, and her constant worrying over her father's health and state of mind. She masked those worries well and smiled politely as she was introduced to those present at the table.

She and her father had arrived at Vioyamis two nights ago. Both shattered, their horses limping and their food supplies clear out. The duke had almost fallen from his saddle, his relief and weariness combining to drain the last of his reserve. Silon, considerate as ever, had seen to Tomais's needs at once, allowing the duke to retire early that night. He and Shallan had stayed up discussing the situation back in Morwella. The duke had rallied a bit since then, rest and comfort helping him to mend.

At least the last part of their flight had proved uneventful. They'd reached Kelwyn, stopped briefly at the Silver City without announcing their presence. They had stayed in a quiet inn, bought new mounts and, after brief respite, rode south for Raleen.

Shallan had been so relieved when they arrived here. That had changed this morning when the dog-things attacked. Had they followed them from the north? Surely not?

Shallan had woken early. Some alien instinct compelling her to dress quickly and venture outside with the horn clutched in her pale palms. She hadn't been surprised when she saw the Groil emerging snarling from the mist. Almost she had expected them. As before, Shallan had blown three times and they had fallen clawing at her feet. The Horned Man's gift had saved them a second time. That horn was her only comfort in a maelstrom of troubled confusion.

Shallan smiled politely as the droll Tamersane whispered blatant compliments across the table. Shallan knew Tamersane of old and he hadn't changed. She liked him despite his easy manner. Tamersane acted shallow and glib but it was all a façade. He was sharper than most and ever a sunny companion—not like the queen, his second cousin, (they shared a grand-uncle apparently).

Shallan listened mostly to her father and Silon. She ignored Barin and Corin, who were evidently coarse fighting men. She had come across that type before and held little regard for them. And the man Corin reminded her of Hagan Delmorier, the infamous outlaw and brigand. Though this Corin had kinder eyes. She'd noticed him gawping at her and wondered if he was soft in the head. Then Shallan noticed how Ariane's gaze often fell on him. Suddenly she was interested.

***

Before the council commenced they ate a splendid lunch comprising of three courses amid light discussion and general banter. Lord Belmarius, after hearing Silon's introduction, gruffly asked Corin why he had left Lord Halfdan's Wolves. He hardly listened to Corin's reply.

After the meal, Corin scanned the table, his fingers fidgeting whilst he waited for his glass to be filled. As ever Silon's servants were skimping on the wine. That merchant hadn't got rich by giving things away.

Barin looked at his empty glass with a bleak expression. "What are we waiting for?" he complained to Corin.

Corin shrugged. "After dinner speech?"

Just then, Silon stood up. He cleared his throat, was about to speak when there erupted a loud kafuffle from somewhere outside. Dogs barked and whined, and voices shouted in alarm. Corin wondered if the Groil had come back. He was getting decidedly weary of the Groil. Silon seemed excited.

"Please excuse me a moment," the merchant waved a hand apologetically. "I believe our final guest has arrived. He had some prior business to attend to and warned he might be late. Hence we ate without him." Silon wiped his tanned face with a silk kerchief and vacated the room. He returned minutes later with his mystery guest.

Zallerak.

Corin scowled at the bard, whilst Shallan, her father and the dour Permian all looked puzzled by the appearance of this very tall, wild-eyed newcomer.

Zallerak took his place at table to the left of General Belmarius. He smiled at the general who for his part looked baffled and annoyed.

"He's a bard," Corin whispered in Belmarius's ear as if that explained everything.

Zallerak looked resplendent. Even Corin was impressed by the long flowing shirt of marvellous hue that shimmered from colour to colour as he shifted. The bard's long silvery gold hair was combed back and held in place by a pale circlet of dazzling crystal. He gave Corin an ironic smile before nodding to the queen and (after Silon's introduction) the duke and his daughter too.

"At last we can start." Silon spread his hands wide. "My Queen, Lord and Lady, Sir Zallerak the Bard, Lord General and you others, my friends. I bid you all welcome to this council. Many of you have arrived here through great perils, seeking answers. A bold strategy against the wave of evil descending on the Four Kingdoms.

"This world Ansu is in dire need. The Urgolais necromancers have returned, we were visited by one this very morning and his Groil creatures. We need to act while we still can. Time is short."

Silon paused to beckon a servant to bring more wine before resuming in heavy tones.

"Kelthaine has fallen into darkness," he said. "Caught in the web of Caswallon and those he serves. Only Car Carranis and Point Keep remain free of the usurper's claws. And they cannot hold out forever. General Perani, Caswallon's new sheriff, has crushed all opposition in Kella. Next he'll turn on Kelthara where a few brave stalwarts still hold out. Those poor souls have no chance."

"But what happens next? Caswallon has a large army growing by the day. Not only an army of men, but rather a force of Groil and worse things. They will come south soon. That is inevitable."

"My Bears wait at the river, vigilant as ever!" snapped Belmarius.

"We cannot fight both Permio and Caswallon. What of Halfdan? Where are the Wolves? Not all were butchered during the coup."

"Alas, I fear it is time for our news."

It was Duke Tomais who had spoken. His quiet voice weighed down with woe.

"A messenger arrived in Vangaris three days before we departed from the city. He was mortally wounded; he'd been waylaid by mercenaries who fight alongside the barbarians of Leeth.

"Before he died he told us that Point Keep had fallen to Leeth, and these invaders now threatened Car Carranis. He said Halfdan was dead. And that Lord Perani had sent him our way with the promise of aid. We now know that to be a false promise from a false general.

"I thought the messenger delusional and suspected these just to be brigands led by that villain Hagan. Foolishly I didn't believe the connection with Leeth. I do now. With brigands in mind I sent riders south and east to scout and scourge, led by my three sons. They returned two days later with bad news.

"On approaching the Gap of Leeth they'd espied a host gathered at the edge of the forest and saw a dark trail of smoke rising up from behind the northern foothills of The High Wall.

"I fear the messenger spoke truly about Point Keep at least. I believe Halfdan's mountain fortress has indeed been taken." The duke shook his head in resignation, took another sip before continuing.

"But we had scant time to worry about that. Daan Redhand's ships arrived two days later and set fire to our fleet, just as his father's brigands whooped and crashed their way into our streets. King Haal has attacked on two fronts, his fiercest warriors taking my city whilst his main force marched on the Gap of Leeth.

"Vangaris's bastion walls were breached by fire and stone, we had little time to spare on the thoughts of others. The barbarians were slaying anyone who moved. Had we not fled then we would have perished too. That night terror reigned in Morwella and bright flames rose skyward as inferno consumed Vangaris!"

Tomais's face was almost tearful as he recalled the horror of his and his daughter's flight from the harbour; were it not for her intuition he would have perished in those flames. Despite that they had barely escaped with their lives.

"Only Car Carranis remains free. I sent my people there—those still living. My sons and the surviving soldiers were to help bolster the garrison there, led by Starkhold of Raleen—your countryman, master merchant."

Silon nodded. He was well acquainted with Starkhold. The former warlord's lands weren't far north of Port Sarfe. Starkhold was respected and feared. He was also unpredictable and stubborn with a reputation for rash decisions. He'd fallen out with the leading houses in Atarios. They'd sent an assassin. Starkhold killed him and responded by sending his own knife wielders into Atarios's streets. The result was a bloody feud that lasted ten years, ending in Starkhold's exile from Raleen. He'd sought refuge up in Kella. Then, after serving for five years, Starkhold was given charge of Car Carranis. Mainly because nobody liked him and those living in Kella viewed Car Carranis as the edge of the world.

Starkhold was unbreakable, they said, but Silon knew that wasn't so. Starkhold's chink was his pride. He would never bend, which meant that he could break. And if he broke at Car Carranis all was lost.

. Corin found it hard to believe that Halfdan was dead. That old fox was a survivor. But if Halfdan was dead then Corin would avenge him. The High King's brother had been kind to Corin back when few others were. But it wasn't just that. Corin felt a loyalty and bond to the Wolf leader, despite leaving the regiment. He shook his head in denial. Lord Halfdan was alive. He had to be.

Across the table Ariane was watching him. She placed a pale hand over her glass when a servant tried to fill it. "If Car Carranis falls Caswallon will have King Haal of Leeth at his walls within days," Ariane said. "I doubt his sorcery and army of fiends could hold back that horde."

"He'll buy them off," Corin said. "That's all they want, those savages. Gold and plunder and promises of more. That bastard Caswallon probably invited them into Kelthaine. I doubt he likes this Starkhold, so let Leeth deal with him, and for a reward offer them Wynais and Kelwyn to spite Queen Ariane." The queen awarded him a sharp look but Corin continued unabated. "That way Caswallon wins his war without using his own forces. And if Leeth turns on him, Caswallon still has his army and his spooky friends. It would explain why Perani was tardy sending aid."

"I fear that you are right, Corin an Fol." Ariane's eyes were still on him as were those of the others. Even Shallan was watching him with interest, Corin couldn't help noting.

"Kelwyn and Raleen united lack the military might to rebuff Caswallon's Kelthaine, let alone Leeth aiding it. Our countries would fold under such heavy odds."

"Then we cannot let Car Carranis fall!" Belmarius slammed his huge fist into his palm. "It's simple enough! I will send word for my force to march north at once under the cover of darkness! My Bears will steal upon Caswallon's goblin army, destroy it and then turn northeast to assist Starkhold. We might be outnumbered but with the element of surprise—"

"That is precisely what Caswallon expects you do to," said Corin, surprising himself as he criticised the fierce general's passionate proposal. "His spies are everywhere, one even found us on board ship."

"I can be in Kelthaine before the king of Leeth has his breeches done up!" answered Belmarius, glowering at Corin. "So don't fucking lecture me, boy!"

"It won't work," answered Corin, undeterred. He noticed Lady Shallan was studying him with interest. He smiled briefly at her and then guiltily glanced in Ariane's direction, but the queen appeared lost in her thoughts.

"Well what do you suggest, young fellow?" Duke Tomais asked Corin while Belmarius snorted in derision.

"Skirt the mountains, general." Again Corin held their attention. "March your army beneath the Fallowheld, then cut north-wards through the Heel. Within three weeks hard march you could be at the Gap of Leeth, coming from a direction the enemy won't be expecting."

"That would entail passing near Darkvale and skirting the plains of Ptarni," Silon said. "Not your best idea, Corin. And there is the Rorshai. They are unpredictable."

"It seems fucking obvious to me!" Corin glared at Silon, angered by his dismissive tones. "Fuck the Rorshai and fuck Ptarni. Caswallon is our enemy not them." Shallan couldn't hold back a laugh hearing Corin's language. She received a grim look from her father. Tomais had small love for foul-mouthed mercenary types.

"I spoke of Darkvale also. That wood is no Forest of Dreams, Corin an Fol." Silon pinned Corin with a hard stare. "A real horror dwells thereabouts. An ancient evil matched only by the ruins of Olen Valek.

"Nightmares come alive in Darkvale, they say the Witch Queen still resides there. Even Morak is no match for Undeyna. That forest is a tangle of madness where a man's worst fears will manifest and then follow him under those witchy groves rending the flesh from his bones. Passing near Darkvale is not an option."

Corin shrugged deflated, "It was just a suggestion."

"Not a good one. Besides, I have contacts in Rorshai. Some of their riders have seen lone warriors from time to time watching them from the eastern steppe lands. Ptarni scouts doubtless planning raids. There is trouble brewing out there as well. We cannot afford to get caught up in that."

"What about Permio?" Barin enquired. "The moment this general withdraws his boyos from the Liaho, that shithead sultan will creep across the river and pounce on southern Raleen."

"Barin's right, Silon, we've seen it all before." Corin noticed that the desert warrior Yashan was watching him thoughtfully beneath those dark hooded eyes. Beside him Cale's blue eyes were agog. The boy was eagerly absorbing all this information.

"The sultan has more immediate worries than the acquisition of Raleen." Yashan spoke for the first time. He exchanged a knowing glance with Silon.

"Permio is somewhat unstable at the moment," announced Silon in reply to their puzzled faces. "An unrest that I and some others, including Yashan here, have been able to encourage over several years spent scheming in the stifling heat of Cappel Cormac and Syrannos. A difficult and dangerous task. But a necessary one. We need Permio as an ally."

"Some chance," Corin almost laughed in disbelief. He'd spent years fighting south of the Liaho. The only Permian you could trust was one with your knife embedded in his neck. Not that he was prejudiced in any way.

"The sultan is strong, but he can be defeated. There are those secretly seeking to bring him down. Foremost is Barakani, so-called Wolf of the Desert. A man Yashan knows well and deems worth the knowing. Do I not speak sooth, Yashan?"

"Indeed so," answered the Permian, his eyes shrewd and calculating. "There is a great distrust of the sultan in my land," Yashan told them, "and his favoured guard the crimson cloaks of Sedinadola are hated by we free folk of the desert. Barakani has only to ask and the tribes will set aside their many feuds and come to his assistance."

"Well, so what," rumbled Belmarius. "Even if I take young Corin's advice, which I at least deem fairly sound, Darkvale or no Darkvale." he nodded in a surprised Corin's direction, "Just how long can Car Carranis hold out against the numberless might of Leeth? Starkhold is tough but not known for his predictability."

"Starkhold will hold as long as he has to!" said a strange voice. Corin had forgotten about Zallerak.

He'd been uncommonly quiet until now. They all turned to see that the bard had vacated his seat and stood staring airily towards the distant lake at the southern end of Silon's vineyard. The small figures of workmen could be seen toiling away beneath the warm late autumn sun.

"What a splendid spot you have here, merchant. I should like to explore your grounds at some point if you grant me leave."

Belmarius frowned, irritated by Zallerak's casual manner. He looked at Corin.

"Is he taking the piss? This is a council meeting not a fucking garden party."

"He does this," replied Corin. "It's why we love him." Belmarius shook his head and Barin sighed as he poured himself another glass of wine.

"So?" Corin turned to Zallerak, who was still gazing dreamily at the garden. "What's your view, wizard? You've offered little to this gathering thus far."

"Corin's right," Belmarius again. "We plain talking, fighting folk have little time for small talk and nuances!"

"Which is exactly why you are so predictable," retorted the bard without turning from the window. Belmarius's face reddened in rage but Zallerak ignored him. When he continued his voice was sharp and commanding, allowing no interruption. Cale gulped and even Bleyne sat up and listened to the words.

"This is a council of fools!" snapped Zallerak. "You skirt the surface and solve nothing!" He drained his wineglass and demanded another before slowly regaining his composure. He sighed, and then continued in a softer voice as if patiently berating a small group of likeable, yet rather simple children.

"The Tekara must be reforged," Zallerak declared. "This is the crux. When the crown is whole again. Then, and only then, general, can you even dream of throwing down Caswallon. Then and not before! While the crystal shards are scattered there can be no hope in resisting this tide of evil. We need the Tekara back and whole."

"Is that why you sent its broken bits deep into the desert, with only a witless prince to protect it, in a vague hope that he might overcome assassins, Groils, goblins, and bugger knows what else; his task to persuade an ancient being (that's probably dust by now) to aid in gluing it back together?" Corin wasn't fazed by Zallerak's grand tone. He'd heard and seen it all before.

Zallerak looked in pain. "My hopes are not vague, Corin an Fol, and I at least have an idea of the challenges that lie ahead. I freed Tarin and sent him into the desert, yes. Both Caswallon and his master were so intent on watching your queen's every move, they gave scant thought to the wayward prince, believing him safe in the Assassin's clutch, as indeed he was until I intervened, at no small cost to myself.

"Even Morak deems the Tekara a side issue now. He seeks the black spear Golganak, and may the gods help us if he finds it! Still, I suspect he was angry that Caswallon did not seize the remnants of the crown and destroy them when he had the chance. As for the young prince being unprotected," Zallerak eyes burned into Corin's but the Longswordsman held his gaze.

"I told you that I placed a charm on Tarin so none might do him harm. I deem that should hold until he is deep beneath the Crystal Mountains. Tarin is our bait and a useful decoy for my own mission—catching Morak and his people unawares and destroying them utterly. With that task accomplished we will be able to assist Prince Tarin in his search for the Smith."

"We?" asked Barin, thoughtfully scratching his beard. "Who exactly are we?"

"Not you, big fellow. Your way lies north," Zallerak told him. "Well, after a brief diversion." Barin frowned at that. "Corin an Fol shall accompany me together with Bleyne here, and young Tamersane (with his queen's kind permission of course)." Tamersane looked up in surprise on hearing his name while Bleyne shrugged, but Corin was having none of this.

"I told you, Zallerak." Corin rose to his feet, flushed-faced and angry. He leaned forward, his hot palms gripping the chair back. "I wish for no part in your schemes. Nor you, Silon, for that matter, or anyone else with fancy ideas. I fought the Permians for years— they cannot be trusted." Yashan smiled slightly beside him. "The Huntsman take you and your plots, I'll not be part of it!"

"Don't be dense, Corin. You are already part of this as I have told you before," said Silon, rewarding Corin with a measured glance.

"Yashan shall be our guide into the deep desert," continued Zallerak, completely ignoring Corin's outburst. "He knows it well and can steer us away from the sultan's prying eyes. Hopefully Barakani will be keeping most of that one's soldiers occupied further west, so we can slip through unnoticed."

Corin punched the chair, sending it spinning. Both Ariane and Shallan were watching him intently but he was past caring.

"I want no part in this folly! Let me accompany Belmarius to war—or else sail north with Barin. I have already played a greater part in this crown business than I promised. Tamersane," he motioned to the younger man who was nodding his head in approval, "Don't be party to this madness!"

Tamersane was about to respond but Bleyne cut in first. Corin looked up in alarm.

The voice wasn't Bleyne's. The archer's lips moved but it was a woman that spoke. Corin gasped; he recognised the melodious lilt of Vervandi. For an instant he saw her sitting before him, her green/gold eyes coolly measuring his own.

"Try as you might you cannot flee from your weird, Corin an Fol," said the husky voice then in an instant she was gone.

Corin found himself staring stupidly at Bleyne's puzzled face. Nobody else seemed to have noticed anything untoward.

Behind him, Tamersane mentioned some creature called the Ty-Tander and whether they would encounter it but Corin wasn't listening. He felt suddenly very foolish and confused. His eyes met Lady Shallan's; he didn't smile this time.

"It must be reforged in the Lost Cavern," Zallerak was saying. "Beneath the giant crystal itself. Only Croagon the blind Smith has the knowledge to do this. That old god must be awoken from his slumber deep beneath the mountains so that he can aid us." Zallerak spread his long arms wide with excitement.

"The fires of his smithy must burn white hot again! The crystal of the Tekara is unlike any other precious stone, except perhaps Callanak the sword of legend, and few know what happened to that worthy blade. Both were made from the purest crystal," Zallerak enthused, "artefacts mined deep beneath those mountains many millennia ago. That crystal's more malleable than steel, you see, harder than granite and lighter than silk. A unique substance containing elements of earth power—the same as granted to the Aralais by the ancient gods, for the crown was conceived by their thought.

"And with the Tekara whole again," Zallerak was even more excitable now and had commenced pacing the room, "We can seek out the remaining talismans, especially Callanak. I suspect that sword resides still on Laras Lassladan, an island far to the north of even Barin's Valkador. Then," Zallerak insisted waving his arms, "When we are thus armed and strong again, we can destroy our enemies at our leisure."

"What the fuck is he talking about?" Belmarius had risen to his feet also and was biting his moustache and snorting.

"Bugger the Urgolais, whatever they are! It's Caswallon and Leeth we need bring to heel! Haven't you been listening, bard? It's all very well seeking this Smith god (if he even exists, which I doubt). But what of Kelthaine? Much good will it serve us all to regain a crown and lose a fucking kingdom!"

"It's already lost." Silon's face was resigned.

"Which is why you, my good general, will take Corin an Fol's advice," announced Zallerak with a curt wave of his right hand. "Surprisingly sound advice for so slow a brain." He winked over at Corin who had taken to his seat again, fingering his wineglass amid smoulders.

"You'll march northeast, general," continued Zallerak. "Lead your army up out of Raleen. Stay close to the Rorshai Heights, thus avoiding both Darkvale and any probing Ptarni scouts! The Rorshai will be watching but they'll not intervene. They are a strange lot, granted, but they could yet prove worthy allies." Belmarius puffed out his cheeks. He was lost for words. Who was this idiot? "So, Zallerak, you're a general now as well as a wizard and bard? Your talents are limitless." Corin smiled. He had calmed down after another wine and ignored the heated exchange, instead he looked across at Shallan and she smiled briefly back at him before lowering her gaze.

"I *was* a general once," responded Zallerak. But Corin ignored him. Instead he caught Ariane's baleful glare and felt ashamed. Perhaps he should venture off into the desert for a while, things were getting complicated round here.

Outside a gentle breeze wafted through the cobbled courtyards, lifting leaves on slender boughs and burnishing them in golden sunlight. Late afternoon had arrived and they had resolved nothing. Silon decided everyone needed a break. He suggested they convene again an hour from now.

As the others wandered out into the gardens, Corin sat staring into space. A light touch on his shoulder turned his head. "You're quite taken with Lady Shallan, aren't you?" Ariane stood over him.

"Er...no."

"She is a strong woman. You could do worse."

"You're reading things that aren't there."

"Am I? We will see. I will miss you, you rogue."

"I'm not going anywhere."

"Yes you are. Your longsword will be needed in the desert. You're the best man I know, Corin, that's why Zallerak chose you."

"I belong at your side," Corin replied lamely. "Not his. With Roman gone you need me as a...protector, if nothing else."

"I can handle myself and I need to return to Wynais—keep a close eye on Caswallon's moves. I miss my city and my people, Corin. I will be just fine. Yours will prove the toughest task."

"I will always love you."

"I know that, you fool. I also know that our paths lead to different roads. Don't fight your destiny, Corin. We both know what it is."

"Do we?"

Ariane looked up as Cale joined them. As ever the boy steered close to his queen. "These gardens are awesome," Cale told them. Corin looked at the boy and sighed. "I promised Roman I would see you safe."

"You have done that and more," Ariane told him. "Enough for now, the others are returning."

As Silon's guests reclaimed their seats, Cale grabbed Ariane's sleeve. His voice was insistent. "If Corin is off to the desert then I'm going with him."

"Don't be ridiculous. You, my boy, are coming back to Wynais with Galed and myself. There you will receive schooling in etiquette and courtly manners—all that's involved in becoming a noble squire."

"Why? There's a war coming and I could be useful. I don't need an education!"

"Yes, you do. Besides, you're far too young for battle."

"But I was fighting in Crenna," Cale pleaded. "I want to be a warrior like Corin. I want to own a longsword and fight bad people." The boy's eyes caught Corin's wry sideways glance.

"You, shithead, couldn't lift a longsword."

"I could if I worked out."

"Enough, Cale!" Ariane's hand rose with abrupt authority, closing the matter. Cale pulled a face as he took a seat beside her. "The council has resumed."

"It's stony for many miles." Yashan informed them about Permio's terrain whilst blowing smoke through his nose. He'd asked Silon's permission to light his pipe, and with the host's blessing sent whirls of wispy smoke up into the ceiling. The tobacco was blended with something sweet, it made Corin's eyes water and his mind wander dreamy. Not ideal at councils.

"The lands between Liaho and Narion are awash with bandits," Yashan explained. "I know most of them. They'll not trouble us." Belmarius snorted and Corin raised an eyebrow.

"The real desert lies beyond the River Narion crossed by most at

Agmandeur. We will make for that walled city. I have a friend there who will supply us with capacious water gourds, camels and food for the deep desert terrain. Agmandeur is a free city—the sultan's boys tend to stay away."

"What's a camel?" Cale asked Corin.

"A horrible horse-type thing with lumps on its back," replied the longswordsman.

"South of Agmandeur the dunes rear up, higher and higher for many leagues," Yashan told them. "Beyond these towers of sand lies the Copper Desert, realm of the Ty-Tander. We do not go that way! Instead we'll follow the Narion southeast towards its source, making for a remote rock called Orlot. That hill's flat summit awards a clear panorama of the terrain leading to the Crystal Mountains. Those legendary peaks lie some leagues south of Orlot. That is where I will leave you. The land beyond Orlot is forbidden to the tribes. Legends speak of fiends dwelling beneath those mountains."

"Oh that's good," said Corin. "Anything else we need to worry about?"

There followed more discussion and considerably more wine before their various courses of action were finally decided upon. As evening beckoned they reached concord. Not before time, in Corin's opinion.

General Belmarius would leave in the morning and venture east with his most prestigious regiment (he'd insisted on sending a small force of four hundred elite horse rangers to accompany Ariane, despite her assurance that she didn't need them.)

"My Queen, I insist," Belmarius said. "I would see you safe to Wynais. Stay here until they arrive. Captain Valentin will lead them, he's one of my best."

Ariane thanked him. Captain Valentin's rangers were camped just three days' ride away on the northern banks of the Liaho. Silon would send a pigeon there right away.

Duke Tomais and his daughter Shallan would return north aboard *The Starlight Wanderer*. Barin would find a safe cove for them to disembark and slip through the hills to Car Carranis—taking Silon's news from the council to Starkhold so that the Raleenian warlord knew he wasn't fighting alone.

Once he'd parted with his passengers, Barin would return north to his island home. There he would hold council with his clan chiefs and raise a levy against Leeth. They would raid Grimhold—Haal's castle town. Once he found out, the king of Leeth would be so enraged he'd abandon his siege of Car Carranis and march north—so Barin told them.

But first Barin would sail south and deposit Silon in Syrannos, where the merchant would seek further word with Barakani, ensuring the desert chief's planned coup stayed intact. The Raleenians, Silon told them, would keep watch on events south of the Liaho.

That left the desert quest. Yashan would guide Zallerak, Bleyne, Tamersane and Corin an Fol deep into Permio, on the hunt for the Smith Croagon and disgraced Prince Tarin of Kelthaine. These five would depart in the morning with Belmarius. They would bid farewell to the general at the Liaho crossing.

Despite his earlier outburst, Corin was resigned to the task ahead. He was glad that Tamersane would be with them. The thought of being stuck in the desert with no ale, and Bleyne and Zallerak, and this Yashan for comrades was enough to leave him witless.

Decisions made, the council concluded. Silon's guests retired to enjoy the evening. One by one they filtered off to gardens, rooms and terrace. Corin, alone again, found himself wandering the deserted corridors of Silon's villa. He needed time to think. Although the council had gone on forever he'd had little time to absorb the result.

Another foolhardy quest. Why had he signed up to it despite his protestations? Vervandi appearing hadn't helped, seeing her face occlude Bleyne's had sapped his confidence and burst his bubble. Again he was being played for a fool. Corin passed the kitchen and drained a half-filled wineglass he found abandoned there.

I need air.

Chapter 11

The Gardens at Dusk

Outside, light was fading fast. Evening had fallen starry and serene. Corin took to strolling out into the quiet peace of Silon's expansive gardens.

A lone bird sang for a time then all was still. The sweet scents of jasmine and honeysuckle rose up to greet Corin, reviving his senses. But not lifting his mood. He strode across the lawn towards the long ferns fanning the steep bank, before descending and vanishing into the shadowy maze of vineyard below. Tall columns of cypress stood silent as sentinels as he walked beneath.

Past those silent trees, the clear water of the lake darkened to spilt ink. Corin saw the tall figure of Zallerak standing there framed by swaying reeds. The bard was fingering his harp and gazing dreamily out across the water, idly watching the restful ripples chase each other along its darkening surface.

As he played, wisps of mist rose up from the lake's surface. It was a haunting sight and an eerie sound. Corin tried not to listen to the clear melodic peel of music drifting up towards him. The harp song was beautiful yet sad. It spoke of days gone past. A splendour long forgotten. And a world that he would never know.

Corin turned away.

He still distrusted Zallerak, but now believed the bard needed their help as much as they needed his. Zallerak was an enigma. Only Silon seemed at ease in his presence, but then Silon was almost as bad as the bard. Barin was right, they were both clever players in some complicated game.

Corin pondered on Zallerak's late arrival at the council. What was the real connection between him and the dog creature, Morak? One day he would know.

They were like two sides of the same coin, and although Zallerak was highly favourable compared to the hideous dog-thing, Corin suspected the bard to be equally manipulative and just as ruthless as his enemy. Time would tell—he just hoped he'd keep the skin on his back over the coming months.

Corin shook his head irritably. What was wrong with him this evening? He blamed Zallerak's melancholy music. Corin liked a healthy jig—not this woeful dreary plucking. He sighed; took to strolling again. Down the ferny path toward the silent orchard grove below. He needed a clear head—space and time to think. That wasn't happening at the moment.

Corin stopped, hearing soft footsteps behind. A twig snapped and whoever it was paused. Corin wished they'd go away. He suspected Silon or else young Cale sought his attentions. Deciding it useless to ignore them, he turned about.

A hooded figure watched him from the dusky gloom. Corin froze, wishing he had brought Biter with him. Then when the hood slipped off her head Corin recognised Lady Shallan of Morwella.

***

Shallan had listened to the words spoken at the council with growing concern. She felt out of her depth. Nobody had mentioned the Groil attack this morning, she'd caught up with the bard Zallerak, asked him whether he thought Caswallon was onto them. He'd evaded the question instead, stating that these Groil had come from Olen Valek in the mountains, a place she'd never heard of.

"They are servants of my enemy the Dog-Lord," Zallerak had said. "It's true that Morak sent many to aid Caswallon but I believe our visitors last night serve their original master. I drove the rest away after your horn killed those six. A useful tool, my lady." Shallan hadn't replied.

She had hoped that by arriving here they would glean some answers. Instead she felt more confused. Enemies everywhere and Caswallon's claws tightening by the day. Shallan thought of her beloved city crumbling beneath the hungry fires of Leeth. The library destroyed. Her favourite place—so much ancient lore and knowledge lost to the ignorance of hate. The sweet memories of her long dead mother sewing contentedly in her room. All buried forever beneath a pile of ash.

She felt fury too. Vengeful loathing. How dare they burn her city! Murder her people! Sometimes Shallan wished she were a man. Were it so, then she would pursue the king of Leeth and his foul sons to the far corners of this green world and tear their bloody hearts out! She had hoped to receive aid or at least assistance today. Instead she'd been faced by confusion, and a group of people clutching at straws.

Shallan was disappointed. She'd reported her opinions to her father and Tomais had replied that she was naïve, and that their only hopes lay in travelling as far from Kella City as was possible. Caswallon had already won, the duke told her. It was a view she wouldn't subscribe to.

But then Shallan had never seen eye to eye with her father. Not since her mother's sad demise. Though she loved him, his daughter never really trusted the duke. There were things he'd never told her.

Bad things and difficult things. Something had happened between her parents rendering the once beautiful stately duchess haggard and frail, and resulting in her untimely death.

It had left the mourning duke stern and rigid—impossible to reach. That had been years ago but the strain still showed on his face. So when they had safely arrived at Vioyamis, Shallan had been more than ready for new company.

Instead she'd woken to Groil howls.

And she hadn't expected to encounter her cousin Ariane. That had been a complete surprise as the young queen was rumoured on some wild sea venture beyond Kelthaine. For her part Shallan had masked her emotions and feigned friendship, but the queen had proved frosty as ever.

The two had never got on since the unfortunate business with Ladislaw, the handsome, glib courtier eventually outlawed for embezzlement.

A rake and villain he proved. But the teenage Ariane and twenty-year-old Shallan had both mooned after him. Though Ariane more than Shallan. When Ladislaw's attentions favoured Shallan the young princess took it ill. Not that Shallan got any satisfaction in that quarter. She was stiff and remote and Ladislaw soon gave up on her. But the damage was done.

And now she was here with this strange company. Some she knew but most she didn't. Tamersane reminded her just a little of Ladislaw with his easy smile and sunny laugh. But Tamersane was a good man unlike the other.

Galed she remembered as one of King Nogel's scribes from earlier days visiting her cousin in Wynais. A fussy irritable little man. General Belmarius she knew also from her childhood. But who were the others?

Bleyne confused her; she'd been alarmed hearing his home was the haunted forest close to the borders of her country. Elanion's forest—nobody went there.

The ginger boy Cale was evidently quite bright, although he

looked like some wastrel Ariane had collected on the way; as a young princess she'd had a penchant for stray cats and puppies. Ariane seemed to view this lad in the same manner.

Yashan's tribal features were frightening to behold, as was Barin of Valkador with his huge bulk, wild hair and grizzled beard. But Shallan had warmed to the Northman as the day wore on. Barin appeared a decent sort despite his girth and dishevelled looks, and had a kindly glint to his eye.

Shallan didn't know where to start with Zallerak; she would have to probe Silon about that one. These guests of the merchant were so unlike the people she had known in Vangaris. Those polite smiling whisperers with never a hair out of place.

But it was the dark-haired warrior type with the scar on his forehead that fascinated Shallan. This one was unusual. Quite out-spoken for a commoner. The Longswordsman. (Apparently he had a very long blade, which had caused Shallan to raise an eyebrow when Tamersane had told her).

"I so look forward to seeing it," she'd replied without thinking what she'd said. This Corin had the manners of a tavern brawler. And his face—though raffishly appealing—had a dour set to it. He reminded Shallan of a bad-tempered hound who had recently had his bone confiscated. He didn't seem one for smiling a lot. But clearly he was no ordinary mercenary, and Tamersane had told her how Corin knew Hagan and how they were bitter foes. But it had been when Shallan noticed how often Ariane glanced upon this Corin that she became curious.

Ariane loves this man. Why?

Corin an Fol: the name meant nothing to her except to announce he hailed from that bleak promontory west of Kashorn, where only poor fisherfolk dwelt. But as Shallan studied this Corin she came to see the strength in him. And when he spoke with such passion at the table Shallan began to comprehend why her cousin appeared to have fallen for this man.

Corin was attracted to her, of that there was no doubt. It was something Shallan was accustomed to. Shallan flirted subtly when in the mood. She'd not been in the mood of late. Not for many months, in fact. Besides, he wasn't her type. But then again, nor were most men. She'd trapped his gaze a few times, seen the colour of those stormy eyes. Blue/grey, much like her own. Northern eyes. Moody. Strong. Intelligent and perceptive, though haunted with self-doubt and irony. Shallan saw the anger surface so frequently in that gaze, but also she glimpsed a compassion and clemency buried beneath. This was a strange man. A contradiction.

Shallan had listened in interest when Corin first spoke out in anger. She noted how he alone (save perhaps Silon,) seemed undaunted by the weird, wild-eyed Zallerak.

Corin an Fol, Shallan decided from that point on, was worthy of her full attention.

And he would be gone tomorrow so she would make the most of him tonight. Try and find out what went on inside that rough head. Shallan felt a wicked little shudder of excitement. It wasn't like her to act in this way. Usually she was remote. Austere, even. And it wasn't that she wanted to spite Ariane again. This was something else. A kind of fascination for a type she had never encountered before.

Her arduous voyage had hardened Shallan. The Horned Man had hinted at her fate. Shallan knew she was different and that circumstances had changed for her. Not only externally with the war, but deep inside her hidden self. The horn and her power over the Groil creatures had given her new confidence. Her intuition had grown as her vanity faded.

The world outside was turning in on Shallan. The future so uncertain, death alone could be relied on. Shallan assumed her life would most likely prove short. The nets of the enemy were tightening. She might no longer be helpless and there were brave people here. But their chances of defeating Caswallon were woefully slim. Strangely that no longer worried Shallan.

And for once she needed male company (not her father's) and

perhaps, she allowed, Shallan needed love too. Love: a complicated word for so few letters. It was something she'd never really understood. Bizarrely, Shallan knew intuitively that with this Corin she could gain rare solace. A moment of light and joy in a world ever darkening and closing in. She recalled a phrase she'd read long ago written by an unknown hand; 'Time scatters seeds to the wind, life is but a moment flowering'.

With those words in mind, Shallan took it upon herself to follow Corin an Fol when he left the house. After all, what had she to lose?

***

Corin stood frozen with a peculiar expression on his face. He couldn't think of what to say or do. He managed a lopsided smile and,

"Hello."

Shallan smiled back and Corin felt a tingling sensation up his spine.

"I saw you leave the villa. I don't know why, but I followed you here. Hope you don't mind." Her smile fled as a shadow haunted her gaze. Corin felt a twig snap below his feet. She was so beautiful standing there, her long chestnut hair spilling free of the hood, and alluring figure hinting at him behind that cloak.

"Ugh? No—it's fine. I was feeling a bit forlorn."

She raised an eyebrow.

"I was just going through stuff in my head," Corin explained. "It's all a bit of a worry, this gallivanting about..." His stance was stiff and awkward, Shallan noted how uncomfortable he looked.

Shallan nodded. She turned her head, tilted it back slightly, listening to Zallerak's harpsong still wafting in and out from the lake shore. "It's a beautiful sound is it not? I wonder at the words though."

"It gives me the willies."

"It is strange—yes. Eerie." Suddenly the music stopped and a watchful silence settled over the orchard. It was quite dark now. Somewhere close an owl hooted twice.

"So where are you off to alone in the dark?" Shallan asked him, whilst wondering why he was still looking so uncomfortable.

"I like being alone particularly after noisy council meetings."

"And you've no doubt attended many." Shallan's smile was ironic.

Corin fiddled with his foot, broke another twig and, almost reluctantly turned his full gaze upon her. He noticed how her hair lifted with the breeze, while those dreamy eyes...

"I never got on with Morwellans."

Shallan chuckled. "You certainly have a way with words."

Corin looked worried. "I was going to add that you are my first exception—my lady."

"I'm honoured. Truly."

"Why *did* you follow me here? I'm not easy company—not like Tamersane."

"Who says I desire easy company? Rather I admire strength, Corin an Fol, and I see that strength in your eyes. I would share your company and thoughts. That is all. And I don't bite."

"I should hope not," Corin chuckled. "Care to stroll a while?" He offered her an arm and she obliged with a quirky grin. "What's the story with that magic horn?" Corin asked after a moment's silence

"It was a gift from an old friend."

"A useful one," Corin smiled but Shallan didn't respond.

Together they strolled beneath the apples and on through an orange grove. Silon's gardens seemed endless. They wandered for a time in silence, both wrapped in their thoughts, then on reaching an open field Shallan suggested they turn back, make for the lake shore.

Corin still didn't know what to say, despite that Shallan appeared relaxed and content on his arm. In thoughtful silence they approached the lake's surface.

They stopped by the lapping water. Shallan knelt, felt its clean touch, letting the water run through the gaps between her fingers. Corin watched her. He noted how the amber pendant glistened on its chain. He fidgeted and glanced around then picked up a pebble and sent it gliding over the water. It skimmed five times before plunking beneath the surface. Corin was relieved to see that Zallerak had gone. Hesitantly he broke the silence.

"I don't want to leave tomorrow," Corin said then.

"I would that you didn't have to." She reached up with her left hand and traced the length of his scar.

"How did you acquire that?"

"When I served in the Wolves there was an officer who didn't care for me."

"I trust you paid him back."

"With dividends."

Shallan's fingers caressed his hair and her face hardened.

"You ride into peril, Corin an Fol," she said. "Despite that, I wish I was riding with you. Doing something, anything to stop that evil bastard Caswallon."

You ride into peril...

Corin was shocked hearing those words again after so long. His mind fled back to the hag by the river. He shrugged indifference.

"An occupational hazard, my lady." Corin's gaze was fixed on the lake. "Were it down to me," he told her, "I would sail north with Captain Barin and your father—help defend Car Carranis."

"You still can—after the desert business. Car Carranis will hold for months."

Corin didn't respond. Shallan changed tack.

"Queen Ariane is very beautiful is she not?"

"Indeed she is and courageous too." Corin was feeling awkward again. He wondered where this was going. He'd never had this trouble with tavern wenches.

"She's fond of you."

"We've been through some sticky times." Corin coughed then looked intently at the shadow of a swan preening itself by the far bank.

"I can see why." Shallan was smiling now. "You don't share her bed?"

"It's not like that," Corin coughed. A bit forward, that question, in his opinion. "Besides I'm a commoner, such a thing would be frowned upon."

"And that would stop you? I think not." Shallan smiled. "I also think that you, Corin an Fol, are the most uncommon man I've encountered."

"Certainly I'm confused. Shall we walk on, my lady?"

"Call me Shallan. And yes, lead on."

More walking in silence. Corin thought of the queen and what she had said only a few hours earlier and the awkwardness grew. If Shallan sensed his discomfort (and surely she did) then she didn't let on.

They skirted the lake before turning back towards the distant villa. High above, a remote star hung like a diamond, its argent sparkle mirrored in the lake. Corin knew it as Ardemei—the star of hope.

During their sojourn Corin made feeble attempts at conversation. Shallan hardly responded and seemed lost in thought. Corin moped despondently. This beauty was impossible to read. One moment she was smiling and teasing, the next dreamy and remote. Corin cursed his lack of courtly skills. Tamersane would know what to say this woman. Roman would have done too. Why was he so fucking useless?

They reached the place where Zallerak had been playing his harp. From here the track led back up toward the cypress lawns.

It was there by the water that she kissed him.

"I don't want to sleep alone tonight." Shallan's voice was husky and a trace of tear stained her right cheek. Corin stood silent as one carved from stone.

"I'm sick of being lonely, Corin an Fol. My country is in ruins and my city sacked. My mother's dead and my father's dying—his soul that is. Understand that I'm not usually like this. But I feel so alone tonight."

"My parents are dead too," Corin relaxed at last. This woman was his friend. They had something—he wasn't sure what. "Though now I'm not convinced they were my parents. I don't know who I am, or rather I'm trying not to discover." Corin smiled then. "We are two lost children—you and I."

"But we have found each other, at least for this evening. A brief moment of solace amidst the chaos."

"Brief indeed. We part on the morrow."

"Then let us make the most of tonight."

Corin grinned hearing that— and pulled her close. Gone was his doubt, his awkwardness, his confusion, all replaced by a hunger. A yearning to love and protect this beautiful woman standing beside him. Corin stooped, kissed Shallan long and hard, one hand stroking her hair, the other questing below.

Shallan stiffened. "It's been a while –"

"For me too." Corin fumbled with her cloak pin, and freeing it allowed the woollen garment to float to the ground.

Beneath that she wore a russet tunic of fine linen and a calf-length skirt of softest leather, her long legs bare beneath. Corin worked at the laces of the tunic with his left hand while his right went venturing below. Shallan relaxed: she wanted this. Needed this. She laughed and he kissed her again. They fell on the grass, missing the cloak by a yard. Neither noticed.

Shallan moaned as Corin's probing fingers slid up between her thighs. She deftly unlaced the drawstring of his trousers and smiled as his sex sprang forth.

"Now I see why they call you a longswordsman."

Corin thought about replying but speech was beyond him. But then it *had* been awhile come to think of it.

A little while later they lay entwined, their naked bodies pale beneath the stars. Neither spoke. Both were lost in deep thought. After a moment Corin fidgeted, grunted and rolled free.

"I'm not happy about leaving you tomorrow."

"As long as you don't forget me," Shallan smiled up at him.

Corin studied her small firm breasts, her athletic body and the moist patch of dark hair between her thighs. He felt his manhood rise again.

"I am in danger of forgetting everything else at the moment. But we had best return, my Lady Shallan. It's getting late and your father -"

"Will be worried—yes I know." It was her turn to feel awkward.

"Corin, I'm not usually so...forthright."

"Me neither," Corin lied. "Place and time—lack of time. Chemistry. Needs must."

She chuckled. "I will see you again—won't I?"

"Yes!" Corin blurted the word out. "Shallan, I know this sounds shallow and contrived coming from a man like me. But...I think I love you, even though we've only just met. It's like I've been hit by something profound. A thunderbolt or else a missile. My legs have gone wobbly and I feel queasy inside. I swear I'll stay loyal to you... whatever."

"From any other man that would be shallow, ridiculous and woefully inadequate. From you..." Shallan chuckled again. "From you it is pure poetry, Longswordsman."

They dressed quickly and then started the walk back. It was quite late now and Silon's lanterns flickered dreamy in the distance. The two walked arm in arm, silent as ghosts. Shallan's face was pale, her eyes pensive again. Her mercurial mind clouded by sudden doubt. Corin also looked troubled and kept glancing at the bushes. He saw the concern in Shallan's face.

"What is it—what's wrong?" Corin asked her.

"Just a familiar feeling. I think someone is watching us. Come on, time to go in."

Shallan gripped his calloused hand as he led her across the cypress lawns toward the lantern-lit veranda.

As they approached the entrance to the left wing Corin felt the invisible weight of immortal eyes following him across the garden.

He turned slowly.

Vervandi stood there framed by two tall cypress trees, her green dress rising and falling softly in the breeze. Her feet were bare, Corin noticed. Her hair long, wild and free. Almost a shadow, she watched them in silence. She wasn't smiling.

"Who is that strange woman?" Shallan squeezed his hand in sudden alarm. "Is this place haunted?"

"I don't know," Corin lied, wishing his words were true. He turned away, urged Shallan inside. Vervandi said nothing, just watched them go.

"How intriguing," Shallan whispered as Corin, moody again, led her inside the house. The scent of jasmine was almost overpowering by the door—that and Shallan's hair. Almost the copper of Vervandi's but just a touch darker. Beneath the lantern's glow they could be mistaken for sisters. A strange thought, that, and a troubling one.

Corin opened the door that led through to the hall.

"I must go," Shallan whispered. She kissed him—softly this time. "Else Silon will set his hounds upon you for fear of my ravishment!"

"Damage already done. Perhaps I could slip into your chamber in an hour or so. I can be discreet when need calls."

"You will have to be," she smiled. "And you'll have to find my room. And I might be asleep by the time you do."

"I'll take my chances." Corin kissed her mouth and they parted without another word. An hour later, and after considerable fumbling and creeping around, Corin an Fol sneaked into Lady Shallan's chamber next door to her father's. Happily she wasn't asleep.

***

Queen Ariane had witnessed her cousin's quiet departure from the house that evening. She'd seen Corin wander out just before—it wasn't hard to guess Shallan's destination. Her cousin was fascinated by the Longswordsman. She was subtle but Ariane had read the signs.

Shallan had won again. Ariane managed a wry smile. That girl was in for a rocky ride. As for herself, Ariane felt no bitterness. Just regret that things hadn't worked better between Corin and her. And that the fates had been kinder. At least Corin could find love again. As for her...

Ariane knew Corin loved her in one sense. But theirs was a different love, particularly after her pledge to Sensuata. Ariane realised that now. But it wasn't just that. Almost they were like brother and sister, despite being queen and rogue.

"You'll miss him," said a familiar voice beside her. Galed had joined her at the window. Together they'd watched the evening descend on Vioyamis.

"I've still got you, Galed," she smiled at her servant and friend.

"You will always have me, my lady," he replied. "But I have watched you over the last weeks. I know how much you care about that oaf."

"You like him too, Galed. Despite your words."

"He has an ungainly charm, I'll grant you. Though I fail to see what you ladies see in him—great unwashed lump that he is."

"Corin is strong," she answered, "and we'll need strong men in the days to come."

Again Ariane thought of Roman. She prayed silently to Elanion that Corin would be safe in the weeks ahead; after all he was so reckless and headstrong.

"He is the toughest man I've ever met." Ariane's glance had followed the lakeshore to where Zallerak could be seen playing his harp.

You're a lucky girl, Shallan of Morwella.

"He is tough—especially between the ears," responded Galed but added quietly,

"I will miss him too."

Ariane turned, smiled at Galed. Over in the corner Cale was fast asleep, not having made it to his room. The boy had had an exciting day. He lay there a motionless lump—just a crop of ginger tangle showing above the blanket she'd thrown over him. Ariane smiled. She'd big things planned for that one.

***

Vervandi waited in silence as she felt the shadow of her sisters emerging from the gloom behind her. "You risk much with this one." That was Urdei's giggly voice. Vervandi turned to see the young blonde-braided girl grinning impishly up at her. "He is interesting though. But is he worthy?"

"Corin is worthy," answered Vervandi. "Though he tests me."

"He is a fool!" cackled Skolde. Her withered features showed stark beneath the trees. "He thinks with his groin like all men do. They are all fools!" Her voice trailed off before returning seconds later.

"Has the evil one left?" Urdei enquired of her sisters.

"Yes, Zallerak drove him away this morning. Just as that dopey girl's horn destroyed his dog-soldiers. Morak's strength is not yet great enough to confront Zallerak for long," responded Vervandi.

"But others are coming, sister. Morak's kin are stirring." Urdei puffed her cheeks out to look important. "And Old Night's heinous spawn multiply in their caves beneath the earth." She giggled. "Don't rely on that dry stick Zallerak. He also is not what he once was. His power also wanes."

"Zallerak!" rasped Skolde. "A foolish name. Still, wise is he to keep his true identity hidden from these twitchy mortals. Were they to know...?"

"Corin doesn't trust him." Urdei's eyes were mischievous lamps of cobalt. "But then he's smarter than the others, more instinctual. For a mortal anyway—they're all so stupid."

When her sisters didn't reply the blonde girl folded her bare arms in front of her chest and blew out in vexed exaggeration. "I'm bored, Vervandi," Urdei complained to her sister. She stamped her feet on the turf and huffed. "Let us leave this world of stupid men and pathetic moon-gazey women. We three are needed elsewhere."

"You go," replied Vervandi. "I'll join you both soon."

"Have a care, sister," Skolde rasped. "Don't place too much hope in the heart of this man. They are all weak inside!" Scolde's abrasive voice faded into the night as she and her sister departed. Vervandi watched them go in silence.

She would stay awhile yet to see the first outcome at least. She had staked much in this affair. A cold smile curved her full lips. Let the mortal maiden have her moment, Corin an Fol would have need of her soon.

Trust nothing, Longswordsman—least of all your heart.

A shadow crossed her vision. Vervandi looked above; saw the ethereal face of Elanion, her mother, reflected in the stars. The Goddess's words echoed across the hillside.

The chosen one must not fail us, daughter. The time draws nigh!

"He won't," she answered. "He has Zallerak with him—and Bleyne. This is but the beginning, Mother."

Then that is well—much depends on this mortal. He is the fulcrum. The nine worlds spin ever faster and the scales of balance rock as the last storm hastens nigh. Your uncle wakens beneath the mountain. And I don't trust your father either. Oroonin will thwart us if He can in His eagerness for war. He is lurking somewhere near, I can feel His presence. You must tread carefully, daughter!"

The husky voice of Elanion trailed off like distant thunder. Dark clouds scurried occluding the stars. The Goddess had gone. Still Vervandi watched the villa in silence. Let her father shake His spear as He led that ghastly host across the void, forever seeking lost souls to serve Him in the quest for eternal war, while beneath the earth Cul-Saan the First Born stirred in violent answer.

Neither Oroonin nor Old Night would claim the soul of Corin an Fol. That belonged to Vervandi and her sisters. They were the Fates. The deciders.

Urdei: girl child full of hope—the past that should have been. Vervandi: the passion and inspiration of here and now. And Skolde: futility—the future where all things fade to dust in time. Vervandi's green-gold gaze searched the heavens for her father but saw Him not. *I know you're out there, Crow-gatherer. You'll not win this one, Father.*

***

The Huntsman laughed, hearing His daughter's words.

You know nothing, child. This is the reckoning. All mortals must side with me against my brother. Living and dead—both shall gather when I call. You children are connivers but no match for me. Only I can see both ways.

From His lofty lodgings in the clouds Oroonin had watched amused as His scheming daughters weaved their intricate webs. Clever little spiders, those three—blood of his blood. More like their mother, though. Beside Him Oroonin's hounds bayed excitedly, their eyes feverish sensing battle's commencement. The time was almost here.

The Huntsman brandished His spear high so that the sun glanced triumphant off its tip. He laughed loud at His daughters' games—so transparent. They meant little to Him, those petulant offspring. They had their uses sometimes. But only when their mother stayed out of it.

He was the Lord of Ravens. For millennia the Huntsman had watched and waited for this final confrontation. He was on nobody's side and no one was on His side. True, He hated His brother who owed Him an eye. But Oroonin had little love for the others either. Telcanna the Sky-God in particular vexed Him. As for His father. Gone. Wherever the Weaver weaved it wasn't around here. This universe was neglected. Someone had to tidy up the current mess.

Yours truly.

So whilst His kin grew soft and indolent amidst the surety of their starry halls, He, Oroonin, had plotted and prepared. Let His siblings be content in their eternal bliss, the fools.

Only Elanion challenged his purpose, but then His wife had always been difficult. It was part of the reason why they no longer shared planets. He missed her sometimes though. Theirs had been a long relationship: sister/brother, husband and wife. Giantess and hermit. Warlock and witch. The games they had played! But Elanion was too tied to this world whereas He was free to hunt again.

So let it begin!

Chapter 12

The Warlord

Joachim Starkhold watched the early morning mist creep up the valley. Within minutes its wispy tendrils reached the lower walls of the city, obscuring sight and sound. Starkhold hated fog but at least the day ahead promised to be a dry one. Over the last few days the granite bastions of Car Carranis had been assaulted by icy winds wielding great lumps of hail. Here in the northeast corner of Kelthaine, winter had arrived.

Starkhold's gaze was relentless. His face hard and uncompromising as the city walls—finely chiselled, noble and hawk-lean. His hair was close-cropped and skin-dark, weathered from years of Raleenian sun. Those hard brown eyes revealed little.

He stood motionless, a figure carved in stone watching the mustering fog below the walls. Starkhold thought he could discern dark shapes moving within the swirling mass, but couldn't be sure.

There were muffled voices. These were accompanied by the grinding of wheels as the barbarians led their wicker chariots out of the dark forest lining the ridge in the east. That ridge sloped down steep from the northern foothills behind Car Carranis, until both forest and hill stopped abruptly at the edge of a wide level plain.

The Gap of Leeth was only partly visible today. Smooth and featureless it ranged south for twenty miles, culminating at the foothills of the misty heights known as *The High Wall*. Hidden amidst those distant peaks lay Car Carranis's sister fortress. Point Keep. Starkhold had received no word from that quarter in months.

At dawn's departure the mist had cleared north of the Gap just enough to reveal row upon row of tall pines spearing the fog roof like the pikes of countless silent sentinels. They were only visible for minutes before the fret returned.

Though he could see little, Starkhold heard muffled sounds rising and fading through forest and Gap. Among them: the grind of wheel on stone, dark voices shouting, the thud and crunch of steel-shod boots, the drumming of hoofs and the baying of hounds.

An army on the move.

For three days shaggy warriors had led their stunted ponies into the Gap of Leeth, filling the grassy plain with their encampments. More were coming. The creak and scrape of the roughhewn wains set Starkhold's teeth on edge. The chariots of Leeth announcing the Northmen had come.

Two years ago no barbarian leader would dare enter the Gap of Leeth, no matter how large his force. But things had changed—and not for the better.

The whole area was now alive with noise and activity. Last night the enemy's campfires had pierced the murk like a thousand winking eyes. Occasionally warriors would approach the walls, stare defiantly up at the fortress, while behind their kin sang brutal songs in their guttural tongues.

But this morning the fog was denser, hiding them and distorting the sounds. Yesterday when the fog lifted Starkhold had tried gauging their numbers. It was impossible as there was no end to them. He guessed a host comprising more than one hundred thousand barbarians filled the Gap. And still more were marching out from beneath the trees.

The lord keeper of Car Carranis rubbed his stubble-grey chin. He was tired, bone weary. He'd slept fitfully, if at all, over the last week. Joachim Starkhold wondered how long his city could hold against such vast numbers. He had scarcely a thousand men, though his strength had been recently bolstered by the arrival of the three sons of Duke Tomais. The boys had fled the ruin of Morwella, bringing with them two hundred spear-horsemen. But their arrival had brought problems too. With the cavalry had come nearly three times that number of women and children, all fleeing from the recent destruction of Vangaris and the ongoing invasion of Morwella.

More mouths to feed, thought Starkhold. Worse than that, water would become scarce during the certainty of the long siege ahead. They could dam the streams in the foothills but the enemy would be watching up there too.

Car Carranis was a fortress city not a sprawling town like Kelthara. They hadn't the infrastructure within these walls to cater for all these folk who didn't belong here. They would sap the supplies, there would be bickering and fights. Starkhold kept a tight rein on his own people—but this lot? Joachim Starkhold couldn't begin to guess how many more stragglers would arrive from the wild lands behind the mountains. The current situation was untenable. And things would only get worse.

One large party of Morwellan refugees had brought news of Lord Halfdan's end. Starkhold had assumed it already; he'd glimpsed the telltale wisp of smoke columning out of the mountains across the Gap, and guessed its meaning. There would be no help from Point Keep. That had been almost two weeks gone and still the barbarians came.

The last messenger from Kella City had promised aid, but Starkhold trusted not the smiling words of Caswallon the Usurper. He knew that Car Carranis stood alone.

Joachim Starkhold turned sharply as steel-shod shoes scraped the smooth stone flags behind him. He waited for Ralian his Captain of Guard to approach, grunted to acknowledge the tall man's salute before returning his gaze to the misty assault below. "They keep coming," Starkhold said. "One can only surmise King Haal has united all the warring tribes of Leeth so they can parade themselves like so much offal below our gate."

"Let them come, lord." Ralian's dark eyes were defiant. "Their numbers mean nothing!" The hawk-faced captain's golden earring gleamed against his dark beard. Ralian hated this waiting game; he was spoiling for the fight.

"Their numbers mean everything." Starkhold returned his gaze to the fog.

Unswayed, the captain leant forward and spat over the parapet. "Car Carranis has never fallen," Ralian said. "It is the mightiest stronghold in the Four Kingdoms, my lord."

Ralian rubbed his gloved hands together to banish the morning chill. "We've enough supplies to endure the hardest of winters—even with these cursed refugees. Let Haal's filth throw themselves against our walls and break! Car Carranis will hold!"

"I hope you are right, captain. I for one am not convinced." The former warlord's hard face bore the signs of many conflicts; Starkhold had always relied on his own strength and judgment. He liked Ralian—the boy was a fighter—but lacked his optimistic view of their chances. Against such vast numbers no city (however strong) could hold out indefinitely.

Peering below, Starkhold noticed that the mist was thinning to smoky wisps, its long shadowy fingers retreating from his walls. Above a pale sun was emerging, shedding light on the legion of pines flanking the north east. Starkhold's head hurt. He felt weary—drained. The waiting game ever turns the mind inward.

I hope they attack soon...

"Now that Point Keep has fallen we stand alone," Starkhold said. "Caswallon's Kelthaine is rotting from within; the other lands will follow now that the Crown of Kings is no more. The carnage has only just begun," Starkhold sighed and turned to face his second.

"We are on an island fortress, Ralian, surrounded by a sea of foes. We have weeks, perhaps months, before our supplies run out and disease and famine and fear take hold in the city.

"And they seem in no hurry. King Haal might be a savage but he's a cunning one. Haal knows this tense waiting game will sow seeds of fear inside our walls. Sap our resolve. There will be no glorious victory here, captain."

"Then we shall die fighting, my lord!" Ralian's eagle-sharp eyes stared almost longingly at the shaggy figures emerging from the mist below. The young captain's hand gripped the long sword at his side. "The men are ready for anything."

"They will need to be." Joachim Starkhold pointed across the Gap. "Look, the mist is nearly gone!"

The two fighting men watched captivated as the last smoky strands of fog curled back and faded from the morning. Far above the battlements the wintry sun cast restless shadows across grey stone.

Beyond and below the mighty gates of Car Carranis stood an army so vast it was as though they were on a castle of sand, soon to be washed to oblivion by the swiftly returning tide.

Warlord and captain watched and all along the walls soldiers watched with them. Hard-faced men: Raleenians, Morwellans and loyal Kels—all resolute. Resigned in readiness for the long fight. Word soon spread that the fog had cleared. Soon the soldiers were joined by their loved ones and children. Then came the stragglers from Vangaris. Within an hour almost every citizen stood gazing down with dread from the present safety of the city walls. It seemed that everyone wanted to witness what had come.

As the city watched on, a leader rode forth from the ungainly mass of warriors below. This rider was huge in muscle and girth and clad in black iron and bulky fur. He wore a king's crown, a gold band of spiralling spikes set high upon a helm of black steel, the hair showing beneath was tangled and long, and the beard dishevelled and greying.

King Haal of Leeth had come to announce his presence to the city. At the king's waist hung axe and sword. He sat astride a pale horse; both his iron-gloved fists gripping the ashen shaft of a long pole.

Starkhold's keen gaze narrowed. He had encountered King Haal many years ago, even before the murderous prince stole his uncle's throne. That had been during Joachim's wayward youth and before he owned title and deeds to the Starkhold estate. As a freebooter he had entered Grimhold Castle (Haal's stronghold) with twenty fighters and a train of stolen gold. Back then the Raleenian freebooters had traded with Leeth and Valkador braving the long coastal voyage north. Starkhold and his men had served as escort to a wealthy merchant from Atarios who had long sly dealings with Leeth, and who often travelled in the Northlands.

Starkhold's memory of Grimhold was bleak. A dark granite fortress covered in ice set in the heart of a bitter cold forest. He'd seen Prince Haal ride out on a hunt—a big man, cruel and hard. Even back then. He hadn't changed overmuch, save perhaps he looked crueller and harder, his hair greyer and his face paler and lined.

Haal's tattooed cheeks were stained blue beneath the gold crown, and his bare sinewy arms glittered with stolen gold. The king's war beast stamped and blew as its master mocked the defendants watching him from above.

King Haal raised the pole he held high over his head with both arms parallel. From it trailed a dark banner. A gonfalon flapping and dancing in the chilly breeze that had recently risen to dispel the last of the mist.

Starkhold's heart sank as he recognised the snarling wolf emblem of Point Keep. Halfdan's banner. The king held it aloft for several minutes, as behind his chieftains jeered and roared shaking their spears in unison, and striking their multi-coloured round shields with great axes and clubs.

Their king was laughing now so they laughed too. Then Haal

slammed the pole down on his knee, snapping it in two. The horde roared their approval as their king cast down the broken banner, trampling it into the dust with his horse's iron-shod hooves. Starkhold's mouth tightened. So much for Lord Halfdan and the Wolf regiment. Point Keep had fallen to the barbarians and the High King's brother was surely dead. No great surprise.

Then Haal turned, raised a gloved hand, the leading finger pointing up at the occupants of the fortress above. His hand fell in a swift chopping motion and again his army roared with approval. Over a hundred thousand voices yelling and shouting filling the Gap of Leeth like a sudden storm.

Starkhold said nothing. He watched as three horsemen cantered forward to flank their king. These were huge men (even bigger than Haal), their bodies covered in armour and their faces hidden beneath iron helmets. But these three needed no introduction. Their reputation announced them as no herald could.

Here upon proud steeds were seated the three hated sons of King Haal:

Vale, known as the Snake Prince due to his reputation for catching venomous snakes by hand and whip-snapping their necks; Corvalian Cutthroat, and worst of all, Daan Redhand himself. They too raised armoured fists; they too brought them down in swift chopping motions. The message was clear; Point Keep was destroyed and Car Carranis would follow.

Starkhold remained in post throughout that morning, taking neither breakfast nor respite. The enemy milled about below like disturbed termites, the nearest just beyond the range of his bowmen. The furthermost flanking the distant trees.

Car Carranis's archers lined the outer wall four hundred strong, each armed with fifty shafts.

Not nearly enough, Starkhold allowed. Yesterday the garrison sergeant had ordered great vats to be filled with boiling tar and oil, ready to be poured through the murder holes above the barbican when the first attack commenced. He had three mangonels oiled and ready, once loaded the machines would hurl rocks down onto the teeming foe below. His artillery men stood primed and waiting, ready to rain death down on any overzealous attackers.

But no attack came that day. Instead the steady grind of saws and the even thud of hammers echoed like thunder across the Gap of Leeth. Until dusk and beyond, deep into nightime, they thudded and grinded, and the cityfolk covered their ears. Great drums rolled adding to the cacophony, heralding the countdown to doom.

Starkhold resumed his post at first light after only three hours rest. He scowled, witnessing the wooden siege towers slowly taking form across the Gap.

Much nearer and creaking in front of the castle gates was a huge scaffold, its erection completed in the early hours. From the high gantries hung the naked bodies of thirty men, their sightless faces gazing up in warning at the city walls. Dried blood smeared their legs, making it apparent to all watching that their genitals had been removed.

Captain Ralian snarled like a trapped beast. He rapped his sword pommel on the battlements in fury, despite their tortured bodies the young captain clearly recognised the blind faces of the scouts he had sent out only last week.

Starkhold said nothing. He had expected this. The Raleenian warlord watched their enemy's progress with accustomed calm as that day faded into another. On and on the great drums rolled and still no attack came. Crows hovered above, some settled on the gantry to feed.

Beyond the gates the mutilated corpses of the scouts were starting to stink, this despite the winter chill. Time passed. Starkhold's mind drifted. He thought of his home, far away in sun-bathed Raleen. It was a shame he would never see it again. Starkhold shrugged, it didn't really matter, but it would have been nice to return just once before the end. Then the next day dawned to reveal row upon row of wooden chariots lined up in front of the walls.

And so at last the assault on Car Carranis began.

Part Two

Permio

Chapter 13

Beyond The Liaho

Twenty leagues from Starkhold's former estate a cluster of riders sat their horses beneath a sizzling sun. The hour was early but already hot.

Corin an Fol sat astride his stallion Thunderhoof on the broad marble base of the merchant's grand terrace. He was restlessly waiting as Silon's various guests gathered to say their necessary farewells. It seemed to be taking forever. Not that Corin was in any hurry to leave. But if you've got a shit job to do it's best to get on with it.

Corin's fists gripped the saddle pommel, he flexed his thigh muscles and tensed his buttocks. It had been some while since he'd last ridden.

Corin was once again dressed in his travel-worn leather with steel shirt, although he had removed his heavy cloak, rolling and tying it to Thunderhoof's flank in a neat bundle. He knew it would come in handy as it got cold in the desert at night.

Clouter was slung across his back and Biter hung at his side with the hunting knife. He'd purchased two new throwing knives from the merchant who kept a ready supply of such things. The yew bow he'd lent Tamersane was thrust into Thunder's saddle holster, together with a quiver of twenty arrows. An impressive sight, Corin looked alert and sharp, but beneath that mask of confidence, confusion still clouded his head.

He caught Shallan's eye briefly and she rewarded him with a bright smile. They had not spoken since last night, (or rather early this morning, when he'd slipped out of her rooms with a fond farewell). Shallan now accompanied her father again, together with an escort of a dozen soldiers that had ridden across from Port Sarfe at first light. These soldiers would accompany Queen Ariane and her party through the city before turning east on the road to Atarios and beyond. Once they reached Atarios they would be bolstered by a further two hundred horsemen. This last arrangement was down to Silon's prompt response to the queen's needs, and for her part Ariane was more than grateful.

Barin would say farewell to the queen in Port Sarfe, together with Tomais, his daughter and Silon. At the town quay they would await his ship's return to the harbour. Silon had sent a rider out the previous night to inform Barin's crew that they were once again welcome in Port Sarfe. Barin surmised Fassof would already have *The Starlight Wanderer* under sail.

Throughout last night soldiers had lined the headlands along the coast as far south as the Liaho's delta keeping watch for pirates, but none were seen. Rael Hakkenon, it seemed, was licking his wounds elsewhere.

Corin patted Thunderhoof's flank as he said an awkward farewell to the queen and Galed, who had been given new horses from the master of the house. Ariane looked stunning this morning—a young warrior queen dressed in flared navy trousers and suede tunic, over which she favoured a short hauberk of glittering steel rings, the rapier gleaming at her side. Behind Ariane, Cale fought to hold back

tears. Corin winked at the boy and Cale managed a valiant smile.
"Look after yourself, you rogue," smiled Ariane, her gloved left
hand resting slightly on Corin's shoulder before their jostling steeds
forced them apart.

"My thoughts will be with you," Ariane told him. Corin noticed a
slight dampness lining the rim of her eyes. A part of him felt heartily
ashamed about last night, although a greater part cried out in joy. He
was torn—caught like a moon-gazy hare between these two bewitch-
ing women.

He *did* love Ariane, but lying with Shallan had eased his soul in
a way he'd never known before. Her touch, her smile, her lips and
subtle scent. Everything had felt so right. Corin could think of little
else this morning.

"You too, my Queen," he managed eventually. "We'll meet again
in due course—of that I'm sure. You're the best, Ariane. May Elanion
watch over you in the days ahead."

Ariane glanced across at Shallan who was avoiding her gaze this
morning. "You've a deal to live for now I deem," Ariane spoke softly,
and if Corin heard her he didn't answer. He seemed edgy, awkward—
lost in thought. Ariane smiled wryly. It was the old pattern repeating
itself again. The game Shallan and Ariane had always played and the
outcome inevitably the same. So be it...

I am a queen.

"Farewell, Corin an Fol." Ariane smiled at him briefly then
turned her attention to more important matters.

Barin strode up and thumped the brooding Corin on the chest.

"Take care, Longswordsman," he grinned as his hand ruffled
Thunder's mane.

"Don't have too many adventures without me, and keep an eye
on that crafty wizard!" Barin's glance shifted to the other side of the
terrace where Zallerak stood consulting with the desert warrior,
Yashan.

The bard/magician had donned his sapphire cloak. Corin also
noted that Zallerak carried a long spear, the broad point sparkling

like polished glass in the morning sun. There was no sign of his harp; perhaps it was hidden behind the ample folds of his cloak. Zallerak's silvery gold hair was swept back and contained by a simple steel circlet. He looked like a peacock, preening himself whilst the desert warrior looked on.

Corin shrugged. He punched Barin affectionately in return.

"Aye and you," he replied. "Have a care with that unwieldy hatchet, and don't pick any fights on your way home, you've noble passengers to mind. I will expect to see you in one piece when I come and visit your daughters!" He clasped his friend's dinner plate hand and shook it hard. "Mayhap I'll run off with one of them!"

"They wouldn't like you," countered Barin. "They prefer real men, fair-haired handsome bearded giants like me." In a softer voice he added. "Besides, it appears to me that you have already chosen where your heart lies, my friend. I don't know how you do it, Longswordsman, but you have two lovely ladies fretting over you this morning."

"You are observant as usual." Corin glanced over to where Shallan sat neatly upon her mare surrounded by the city guard. She was speaking with the queen as her duty bade her. Neither woman looked comfortable.

"I have eyes," answered Barin. "Farewell, Longfellow."

The outgoing party rode through the quiet vineyard together, most kept to their thoughts, though Cale who had recovered his humour questioned Silon on the wily ways of merchants. Silon raised an eyebrow once or twice. The queen would have to watch this one. Cale the guttersnipe was no simple urchin.

Birds sang on the swaying boughs of trees and late bees hummed busily amongst the morning blooms. Behind them Vioyamis's white walls glistened before disappearing behind a hill.

Tamersane, trotting next to Corin, glanced back to get a last look at the house. His young face was cheerfully thoughtful. The Kelwynian noble was garbed in a long polished mail shirt over soft leather trousers and vest. He wore a dun-coloured cloak of fine wool despite the heat. At his side hung a broadsword and long hunting knife. A steel helm rested jaunty on the pommel of Tamersane's saddle, and a new bow with accompanying arrows sprouted from the saddlebags. He looked like a young prince off to some country joust.

Corin cast a weary look in Tamersane's direction. He was a peacock, but at least would prove good company, which was more than could be said for his other companions to the desert. Behind them, Bleyne sat on his beast in accustomed silence, his tattooed face as usual revealing no emotion, the long bow and arrows slung across his back and a leather cloak flapping behind him in the warm breeze.

They passed through Silon's fields reaching the road to Port Sarfe and beyond. Here they reined in. Just a few miles west the sandy walls of Port Sarfe's Barbican shimmered in the sun. They'd reached the crossroads where the road from Silon's villa met the broad way that would serve Zallerak's party on their journey south to distant Permio. The riders sat on their steads in silence. Time to part and go their own ways.

Corin's head was heavy with thoughts of the journey ahead; he met Shallan's gaze again, caught the glistening of a tear. She mouthed a silent brave farewell. For the briefest instant Corin's eyes locked onto hers. He felt the electricity of that contact: sad and joyful. Then she turned away.

Corin watched after her for a moment longer then he too turned away. Ariane witnessed that exchange. Corin nodded in her direction. The queen raised a hand in farewell, Corin saluted her, and then without further fuss bade Thunder follow the other five horsemen already heading south along the dusty road towards the desert lands, and Elanion knew what else.

Corin turned in the saddle, gazed back just the once; saw that both Shallan and Ariane watched him still, as did Silon and Cale. Corin waved and saw their hands lift in answer. He mouthed a curse about his fate and bid Thunderhoof turn, canter and catch up with the others.

"Hey, old lad," he told the horse, "It looks like we're stuck with each other again." Thunderhoof flicked an ear. "I know," said his owner. "It's going to be fun."

Throughout that day and the next the five horsemen rode south, fording Kael's stream and passing like grey shadows through the empty land known as South Kaelin, the troubled border country between Raleen and Permio. A bleak arid region, desolate and open. The scene of many an ambush during the Second Permian War.

It was very warm. Corin had tied a dark strip of cloth around his head to keep his long hair in place.

Beside him Tamersane had stowed his cloak and now sported his expensive leather sheaved ring mail above a linen shirt. A broad studded black leather belt supported the Kelwynian nobleman's long sword and curved hunting knife.

Yashan was dressed as he had been at the council, save that he now wore long boots instead of pointy shoes. Bleyne the archer was wrapped in his habitual leathers, the long bow slung across his back and slender knife at his side.

The heavyset Belmarius rode encased in steel like a mobile fortress, an iron mace hung from the belt at his side and a broad square helmet occluded his features.

Only Zallerak stood out, draped as he was in his magnificent blue cloak, the long spear resting easy in his right hand. The bard's mercurial eyes studied the stony country as they cantered south. Already he worked on a plan.

The terrain became even more arid when they approached the Permian frontier. Here and there were scattered clumps of trees, but mostly this was a land of sandy hills and hot dusty valleys, where lolling goats watched them pass with lazy curiosity.

On the morning of the third day since their departure from Vioyamis, the six riders arrived at the old stone bridge that spanned the Liaho River. Corin marvelled at the sight as he always did. He couldn't comprehend the skill of the ancients who had built it. Over fifty foot high, the bridge reached up and out across the wide muddy river, in a single unsupported span of sparkling stone. It favoured neither rail nor post, and at twenty feet wide allowed the swift passage of armies.

For many years men had fought bitterly (himself included) back and forth across this bridge, their blood spilling on its shining stone. Yet still it stood there untainted by either time or conflict. A defiant symbol of an age long past.

Yashan rode ahead scouting the way. He returned after a few minutes announcing the far bank deserted and their crossing into Permio unchecked. It was here that General Belmarius bade them gruff farewell. From here Belmarius would make his way eastwards alone along the northern bank of the river, to where his army was waiting at their encampment on Helbrone Island. On the way there he would divert to Valentin's camp, order his second to lead his rangers north with the promised aid for Queen Ariane.

The five remaining riders dismounted and led their horses across the gleaming bridge; despite its girth the bridge was worn by ages and safer to cross on foot.

Behind, the brown ridges of South Kaelin faded distant into shimmering haze. Corin, glancing back, watched the tiny beetle figure of Belmarius disappear behind a rocky outcrop that marked a bend in the river.

Corin thought of the risks they were taking coming here. He pictured Shallan's lovely face and Barin's bluff smile, and then thought of the queen's courage as she faced the Assassin in his hall, and of little Cale, her most ardent servant who so wanted to become a fighting man.

"Stay alive, all of you, until I'm back," he muttered to the wind.

Corin studied the country greeting them as he led Thunderhoof across the old bridge alongside his companions. Their horses' hooves clattered noisily on the smooth surface of the bridge. Tamersane's eyes widened when he glanced down at the broad expanse of river so far below.

"Reckon there's crocodiles amongst that sludge," he said to Corin.

"That and worse," replied the Longswordsman.

"What's worse than a crocodile?"

"Sea pikes—they swim up from the delta. Shred a man's flesh in seconds. That and foot-long salt leaches that slide inside your private parts and commence sucking."

"Then best we don't fall off this bridge," grinned Tamersane.

"What are the women like in Permio?"

"Dark and hairy with foul tempers."

"Sounds like we're on a fun trip."

The bridge's apex awarded sweeping views of the lands around. Westward, the Liaho was split in two by a dark island cloaked in forest. Beyond that a hazy region of marshland showed tall reeds and stunted trees, occluding either bank before vanishing in shimmering murk. This was the beginning of the great swamp that straddled the river's delta for miles on either side before finally reaching the sea. A dreary realm of strange fowl and poisonous gases, where weird creatures were rumoured to lurk in dank pools and glowing fungus festered on rotting wood. It was a place best avoided at all costs, though Tamersane seemed fascinated by it.

They remounted at the south bank and again checked the terrain. They were in Permio. Enemy country. They must needs sharpen up. Corin cast his scout-trained eyes along the dusty ridges ahead but saw no sign of movement. Beside him Yashan appeared relaxed. Corin wondered whether they were wise to place complete trust in this Permian, despite the tribesman's affable nature. Corin liked Yashan well enough, but found it hard to confide in him. Permians had ever been cunning foes.

They rode till dusk darkened the way. Stopping for the night, they set up a sparse camp at the bank of a stony stream. Bleyne snared a leggy hare and this they spit roasted over a discreet fire.

Water was not a problem in this region, though that would change once they entered the real desert south of Agmandeur. Corin gazed at his companions' faces as they prepared their blankets for sleep. Nobody had spoken much; even Tamersane seemed oddly thoughtful, as if dwelling on the enormity of their task. The handsome Kelwynian idly watched their tiny fire whilst Bleyne fed it dry faggots from a dead tree nearby, before wandering off to take the first watch.

Zallerak had kept his own counsel since leaving the merchant's villa. He looked lost in thought sitting dreamily buried in his cloak, huddled cosy under the thorny arm of a shrubby tree. Corin yawned, checked Thunderhoof had enough water and then rolled over to sleep.

The dream came almost immediately.

***

Blood dripped down walls and filled the gutters of the streets. Close by someone screamed; a desperate sound cut short by the guttural growl of some nameless beast. Thin alien shadows stalked deserted streets. Blood was everywhere. Corin lay in a pool of blood; he did not know whose blood. Maybe it was his?

A figure stood above him. A cowled figure—the dog snout thrust out with nostrils flaring and damp. Yellow eyes glared out from the hood and a stench of gallows filled the air.

Corin couldn't move. His body was a block of ice. Looking up he noticed the dog creature was stroking, almost caressing something in its blackened claws. An object so dark it was difficult to define.

Then he saw it. A shadowy spear: a black needle of pain, its serrated leaf two foot in length and six inches wide, tapering off to a fine needle point. The shaft was long: paradoxically it shimmered, and yet seemed to suck darkness into its essence from all around.

Corin felt terror consuming him as he gazed at that spear. He knew somehow that the weapon was sentient. That it watched him, gauged and mocked him.

Golganak…once more loose on the world.

Corin felt the cold eat into his bones and the fear scrape inside his head. He closed his eyes, then opened them again as searing pain lanced into his belly. Morak had stabbed him with the spear! Corin voiced a silent scream as black fire erupted in his veins. The Urgolais lord stooped and drooled on all fours over his prey. Morak raised his spear again, and again it fell and once more he screamed.

Then the pain vanished: he was spinning through air infused by light.

I am no more...

But Corin was alive—could feel the thumping of his chest as he fell free through space. Minutes passed, seconds, hours?—Impossible to know. Corin opened his eyes to blinding brightness and heard Vervandi whisper behind him.

"Seek the sword of Light. Only with Callanak's aid can you defeat the master of the spear."

"Why me!" he cried out but she was gone. Gone too were Morak and the dreadful spear. Gone were street and dripping blood. And gone the impossible brightness of that nothing place.

Instead Corin stood at the prowl of *The Starlight Wanderer*; with him were others that he knew and loved, and strangers too. The sea below was dark and fathomless, above the sky hung heavy with metallic clouds. These scurried past, iron grey and full of doleful voices.

Rime coated the decks of Barin's ship. It clung to the stays, and long icicles bearded down from the furled frozen sails. Great mountains of ice loomed ahead and on either side of their narrow passage, grinding and booming. Beyond these an island rose sheer and serene.

Corin yearned to reach it. He could see it was summer there. The mountain/island's steep summit was crowned in golden rays and a rainbow spanned the peak. He looked closer, somehow his eyes pierced the rock of that summit and Corin saw within.

A cave cut deep inside that mountain. This Corin entered without knowing how. Glowing sconces led to a hall of light. Corin walked toward that cavern. He entered within.

On the far wall of the cavern hung a sword of blazing crystal, its ethereal beauty filling that place with throbbing light. A multi-coloured coruscating light; silently the glaive beckoned him forward. *Callanak—Sword of Light.* Corin approached the weapon, reached out to touch it. And then the sword spoke to him.

"*Take me.*"

As it spoke Callanak's colour changed from rose pink to scarlet. "*I know thee for my master! Take me; together we can cleanse the stench of Old Night. Take me, Corin an Fol, chosen of the gods!*"

"*No!*" he heard himself shouting. "*I'll have no part in this; I'll not be a pawn to your wishes!*"

Behind him a dark voice laughed like distant thunder.

"*Pawn you already are,*" said the voice, "*but you are my pawn and I watch over you.*" Corin turned, saw the single eye of the Huntsman blazing down on him from the sky above. All about Oroonin thunder roared, and the stars spun crazily in the heavens. "*Take Callanak, mortal warrior, it is your destiny! As my chosen champion you stand to gain much.*"

"*I will not!*" Corin cried before darkness descended on him again and he knew no more....

***

Corin awoke with a start. He stood, shivered and shook himself, glancing about the camp wild-eyed as if expecting a score of dog-faced foes, but all seemed as it should be.

He could smell the sweet smoke from Yashan's pipe and guessed the tribesman must be on watch somewhere nearby. A desert habit, that pipe. Most Permians found recreation by inhaling the fermentation of certain toxic plants. Corin had tried this once but it made him woozy.

Corin looked at his sleeping companions. The hour was late. He cursed vehemently, re-wrapped himself in his cloak, and stubbornly rolled over, within minutes sinking back into sleep.

Thankfully this time he didn't dream.

It seemed to Corin he'd barely closed his eyes when Tamersane shook him, announcing it his turn to take watch.

Corin trudged over to the edge of a steep bank, from where he could descry any movement in the rocky land around. Nothing stirred. The night was silent and starry. Corin stretched out with his back to a shrub. He watched the clear moon, trying to relax. But the harrowing dream still hung over him. Corin thought of Shallan and their brief time together. That seemed like a dream too, although one he would happily revisit. But thinking about Shallan made him think about Ariane, and things got complicated in his head again.

I love two woman. Neither are here. Instead I've an idiot noble-man, a taciturn archer, a warlock and a weed-smoking tribesman as bedmates. Corin switched his thought to far off Finnehalle. He thought of Karin his mother, (although she wasn't really his mother and he didn't know who his mother was). Corin remembered the old tune she'd sang on those clear bright mornings as she watched her husband take to sea.

Finnehalle by the sea, a fairer place could never be,

Where white caps dance and sea birds call,

Where lanterns guide them home to shore.

Where forest tumbles over cliff, as ocean greets the sky,

Where fisher's craft dance blue on blue as nearby porpoise sigh,

Where stars alone will witness my love's return from sea.

Finnehalle my home, work and rest.

Come back to me. Come back to me!

Corin pictured the lanterns swaying down by the water's edge; he felt Shallan's slender hand in his own, as together they entered *The Last Ship* and Burmon greeted them with a broad smile and two full tankards. Shallan seemed the sort of girl that could drain a full tankard.

What's that?

Corin jolted out of his reverie. Something stirred out there. A black speck in the distance growing bigger, filling the night sky. Somewhere a great distance away there came the sound of hoofbeats and horns.

The Wild Hunt!

Corin gaped at that speck in the sky, his idle imaginings forgotten in an instant. He shivered as the shadow crossed the moon. That shadow became a host approaching at speed. Hounds bayed and horns bellowed, filling the sky with clamour.

Then he spied the Huntsman pale and ghostly on his dreadful steed. In their master's wake loped huge pale hounds, their eerie bays echoing horribly through the night sky. Behind the rider hurried the host. Dead souls everyone—the Huntsman's children.

Down and down they descended through the starry dark, spiralling and swooping ever nearer, until Corin could discern the faces of the doomed and hear their desperate cries. And it seemed to Corin then that they were calling out to him.

"Come to us, warrior!" They beckoned and he gasped to see Roman's face among them beseeching him with the rest.

"Roman!" Corin cried, waking his friends with his hoarse shout, but Roman's face had vanished in the multitude that shuffled forlorn behind the giant hounds of Oroonin. The Huntsman raised a great horn to his head and blew; *hoo hoo!* And the host passed high overhead. Slowly, as they dwindled, peace returned to the sleeping land. The sky paled in the east. At last morning had come.

Chapter 14

Nomads

"What in the nine worlds is happening?" gasped a white-faced Tamersane as he cowered from the ghostly apparitions departing through the blackness above. Bleyne fingered his bow nervously while Yashan held his head in his hands. The tribesmen were a superstitious lot and Yashan was greatly alarmed.

"The Wild Hunt rides out!" Zallerak stood gaping up at the sky, his eyes hard and jaw set resolute. "The time is upon us, Caswallon's war has begun!"

The stunned companions watched the astral host trail north like a dust comet and then vanish from view. Nobody spoke for several minutes. At last, Corin dragged his stricken gaze from the sky and glanced wild-eyed around at their camp. The horses needed attention so he ventured over as no one else seemed in a hurry.

The poor beasts (excluding Thunder who just looked miserable) had been clearly terrified by the apparitions, but fortunately they had been well tied, and after a few placating words, followed by oats and some water, they settled down again. Corin looked at Thunderhoof and the horse snorted snot.

"I know—it was a rough night for me too," Corin grumbled.

"We had best get moving," muttered Yashan after they had moodily nibbled a brief snack of dried bread and dates, courtesy of Silon's fast diminishing kitchen fare. The five companions weren't carrying many supplies as they were expecting to spend the next night with Yashan's friend inside the walls of Agmandeur. Not that Corin held high hopes in that direction, but time would tell.

"How far is the city, Yashan?" enquired Tamersane, trying to keep his hand steady while scraping his sharp hunting knife across his chin, and wincing when he nicked the flesh. It wasn't the ideal time to shave but Tamersane was most particular about his appearance. He wasn't convinced the women here were as ugly as Corin had hinted. You never know when you need to make an impression. Gods forbid him ending up with a face like Corin's—all grizzly-frowns, muscle, scar and sprouting hairs.

"We should make the gates by nightfall, if we leave now," answered their guide. Yashan still appeared shaken. His tough desert face was filled with doubt after seeing the sky rider (that was what the Permians called the Huntsman). "If we can make it," he uttered under his breath.

"We'll get there," said Corin. "It's not the first time I've encountered yonder spook. Whatever game that Huntsman is playing, I think he needs us alive to participate in it."

"Oh, well that's good I suppose," grinned Tamersane. "Encouraging. We can take heart from that, friend Corin." Tamersane might be smiling but no one else looked happy. Zallerak was away staring at the morning. Bleyne, as usual staring blankly into space, and Yashan staring hard and quizzical at Corin.

"What's up with you?" Corin caught his eye. Yashan did not reply at first. He continued staring at Corin strangely for a moment longer, his dark eyes respectful and troubled beneath the scarlet burnoose.

"Marakan?" he asked eventually.

"What?" Corin was unnerved by the tribesman's quizzical stare.

"It means chosen by the gods," responded Yashan before

mounting his steed in a single, swift flowing movement. "You, Corin an Fol, are Marakan. You might save us yet."

"Don't you start," Corin growled, before vaulting onto Thunderhoof's back and striking the horse's flank with a hard slap. Thunderhoof snorted in reproach then stoically trotted off to rejoin the road.

They made good progress during that morning, the road they travelled being well constructed, once a busy trade route, and still often used, despite the many conflicts fought amongst these sandy hills. Their spirits rose, it was not too hot and they had the road to themselves. Miles faded behind them as the dusty day wore on. Most were content to ride and think. Tamersane, however, was curious.

"What manner of city is Agmandeur?" the Kelwynian enquired of Yashan as the tribesman led them southeast at a steady trot. "Is it like the vast decadent fleshpots of Syrannos and Cappel Cormac?"

"No indeed." Yashan's sharp gaze swept the brown hills ahead. Their guide still seemed edgy as if he expected trouble at any moment. Nonetheless he answered the fair-haired rider readily enough. "Agmandeur is a frontier city," Yashan told him. "It stands on the northern edge of the desert and has a fine view across the dunes. It is a bartering centre for the many tribes roaming the vast expanses beyond. Though most are bitter enemies, they cannot carry their feuds beneath the city walls. Violence of any kind is forbidden in Agmandeur."

"The women...?"

"Devout. Noble. Fiery."

"Brothels?"

"There aren't any."

"Oh..." Tamersane crinkled his nose in disappointment and no longer pursued the subject. Yashan managed a wry grin and Corin laughed at the Kelwynian's mournful expression.

"You'd only catch something nasty," Corin said.

"What of the sultan's soldiers?" enquired Bleyne, surprising everyone with his sudden interest. The archer seemed oddly cheerfully and at ease in this dusty hot environment, so unlike his forest home.

"They will not trouble us inside the city," answered Yashan with a curt shrug. "Once we are beyond its walls in the deep desert? A different matter."

"The sultan doesn't approve of Agmandeur," Zallerak cut in. He was riding a few yards ahead and had been listening in. He looked relaxed in his saddle, the cloak flapping behind him like a blue cloud.

"Its citizens pay no taxes to Sedinadola and the warring tribes are forever raiding his sumptuous caravans! It's an outlaw city really."

"A man has to earn a living." Yashan's hawk like features revealed little. Corin noticed that Zallerak now had his small golden harp hanging from a silver belt at his waist. So he had brought it. For some reason that comforted Corin. The bard continued enthusiastically remonstrating about their certain perils ahead, as though he were looking forward to encountering them.

"Agmandeur is under the sway of Barakani and his seven sons," Zallerak announced. "The old bandit also calls himself the lord of the desert. Somewhat presumptuously, in my opinion."

"Sure he'd love to hear your opinion."

"What's that, Corin an Fol?"

"Nothing."

Corin's war-trained eyes scouted the country as they wound their way around arid hills and ducked through stunted woods. Towards afternoon the hills rose up, becoming much steeper before splitting in two swallowing the road ahead.

Beneath these jagged crags lay a sharp ravine. Into this cleft the road led them in a series of dusty twists, like a sleeping snake coiled under the sun. Rocks and bushes shouldered the pass, affording a wealth of concealed protection to any would-be raider.

It was dangerous terrain. Corin could see why wealthy merchants never crossed this region without a score of paid protectors. This was bandit country and an ambush could happen at any time.

Corin kept a wary eye on the rugged outcrops leaning toward them from either side. Yashan said the tribes would let them be, but what other enemies lurked in these lands? Corin thought of Morak and his recurring dream. He shuddered. Zallerak's party were seeking the prince and the Tekara, but what was seeking them? He pictured a host of dog-lords hefting black spears and snarling unmentionables. Best not to dwell on such things.

Yashan led them on at a steady canter through the twisting rocky sandstone until they cleared the pass, much to everyone's relief. Once again the landscape levelled out, the slopes falling away to north and south.

Corin slowed to a trot, shielding his eyes with his hand as he studied the country ahead. For miles it appeared dreary and uninspiring, scrubby bushes, stone and sandy soil, though some way off he caught the sparkle of moving water.

"That is the river Narion," announced Yashan, reining in and pointing southwest, as the others joined him whilst allowing their hot mounts a brief respite and munch at stubby grass. "You can just make out the stone walls of the city beyond the river."

Corin let his gaze follow the guide's direction until he espied the sandy walls of a town.

Agmandeur—at last their destination was in view.

They were about to spur their horses forward when the sharp-eyed Bleyne stopped them. The archer had seen movement on the road ahead.

"What is it?" Corin asked, fingering Biter's hilt. He had learned to trust Bleyne's eyes.

"Looks like one of those merchant caravans," replied the archer with a shrug. "It must be several miles long."

"Are there any soldiers with them?" Corin had no desire to encounter the sultan's elite guard in their own domain.

"There are warriors there, yes, but they look like hired men," responded the archer. "Yashan tells us that the hounds of Sedinadola wear crimson cloaks. These fellows appear randomly dressed and scruffy—bit like you, Corin."

"Thanks."

Bleyne continued to survey the approaching column. All Corin could descry was a large cloud of dust and a few ambling carts. Once again he marvelled at the archer's piercing vision.

"Had we best seek cover?" Corin enquired of Yashan, but it was Zallerak who answered him. The bard also had astounding vision: he seemed satisfied that this was indeed a large merchant train heading for the Four Kingdoms, or perhaps the remote lands beyond Ptarni far to the east.

"They will have stopped in Agmandeur," said Zallerak. "We can glean knowledge of the road ahead."

"Are you expecting trouble, Sir Zallerak?" Yashan still had a profound distrust of the bard. Like Corin, Yashan believed Zallerak knew more than he gave out. He half suspected trouble would descend on them like a plague of angry wasps once they entered the deep desert. Still, the wizard's words were wise for once. They might as well see what lay ahead, he told them.

The five riders waited at the small rise just beyond the ravine. The horses fidgeted as did Tamersane, while the winding train of caravans wove their dusty trail towards them. Corin studied the brightly coloured wagons trundling, grinding and bumping behind the sweating horses. Other ungainly beasts carried silken robed merchants and fighting men who eyed the distant horsemen on the ridge with professional calm.

"What are those ugly creatures?" Tamersane enquired of Corin. The young Kelwynian was amazed by the sight confronting him.

"Camels," answered Corin. "Desert beasts. The Permians often rode them during the wars across the borderlands. They are very tough and have little need for water, carrying it as they do in those fleshy mounds on their backs."

"They look repulsive." Tamersane wasn't impressed.

"They are useful, though somewhat bad tempered."

"Do you think there are any women hidden in those canvas wagons?" Tamersane's expression brightened, eager to encounter whatever lay beneath the billowing brightly coloured cloth.

"One or two, I suspect," answered Corin with a grin," though they're most likes worse tempered than the camels."

"But more comely..."

"Marginally." Corin was glad Tamersane was here. The handsome Kelwynian was an easy companion and Corin found himself liking him more than the others.

The five watched with palms resting lightly on weapons as the colourful cavalcade approached. Three riders rode ahead on the unwieldy camel creatures, which snorted and spat at their horses as they drew near.

"Hideous brutes," muttered Tamersane. He couldn't disguise his disappointment as there didn't appear to be any women about. Still there was always Agmandeur, he mused, and he might get the odd grope if he awarded them his irresistible charm. Of course he might get his organ sliced off too. But sometimes you have to optimize advantage. Tamersane smiled in welcome as the three riders halted their camels just yards ahead.

The scarlet-robed man on the leading camel was a portly girthed merchant clad in silken cloth, and sweating profusely and miserably beneath the afternoon sun.

About the merchant's opulent hide hung the stale smell of sweat fused with day old perfume. This one looked oily and artful and Corin remembered why he so disliked merchants.

The other two riders were dour-faced fighters—northerners by their look. Mercenaries and hardened killers armed with swords and crossbows. They sat on their camels uncomfortably as if they would be more at ease on the back of a horse. Corin couldn't blame them either. The merchant's men eyed the five strangers with patient distrust.

Their greasy boss was all smiles though. He showed no surprise at encountering strangers on the road and greeted them with an elaborate bow.

"Greetings, friends, you are far from home!" The man had a high-pitched nasal voice and Corin disliked him instantly. Zallerak though, responded with an open smile.

"Indeed we are, master merchant," proclaimed the bard. "I am Lord Bormion of Kelthara and these are my worthy followers." Corin's stomach growled at that. "I had heard that the markets of Agmandeur were second to none, and thus decided to venture here myself. My own country is rather damp and chilly at this time of year, and I so hate the damp."

"Indeed the markets there are wonderful." The merchant's shrewd eyes watched them like a hawk. "However, we have with us a fine selection of riches bound for distant Shen and the eastern lands—a journey of many months.

"You are welcome to peruse at your leisure, Lord Bormion. We shall be setting up camp soon, as I prefer not to travel under the cover of darkness." The merchant waved his fat arms to usher the first wagons past as they rattled and banged their way up the dusty hill.

"Let me introduce myself," he beamed with a smile that reminded Corin of a lizard that had just consumed something twice its own size.

"Sulimo of distant Golt at your humble service!"

"I am honoured," responded Zallerak. Corin wondered how much longer these pleasantries were going to last. The afternoon was drawing on and there were still many miles to go before they reached that city. "However," continued the bard. "I have set my mind on entering the walls of yonder desert city before dusk. You will forgive my untimely haste, master Sulimo. A hot bath calls, I feel."

"Of course, Lord Bormion, I understand completely." Sulimo looked relieved on hearing this. He waited impatiently for the last wagon to pass in a cloud of dust before he resumed his words.

At Corin's side, Tamersane was still desperately trying to discover what lay hidden inside the brightly painted train, but it was impossible to see.

"Are the roads west busy, master Sulimo?" Zallerak enquired, watching as the wagons sauntered off before vanishing behind the tumble of hills that hid the ravine.

Corin looked behind him and tensed suddenly. There were at least a dozen fighters, most carrying crossbows, watching them from the nearest hillcrest. Corin was alarmed, he had not seen these men before and assumed they were Sulimo's scouts.

"Indeed yes," Sulimo was saying. "The western desert is crawling with the sultan's soldiers. I believe his mightiness suspects an uprising amongst the tribes. You had best keep your visit to Agmandeur's famed markets brief, my lord. Or else fare north for the wonders of Cappel Cormac, our second city. It's not too far from here and has much more too offer than rustic Agmandeur."

"Perhaps we'll loop back that way—after Agmandeur," replied Zallerak. He too had noted the soldiers behind them, though he heeded them not.

"There are fresh mercenaries in Agmandeur," growled a hard voice. It was one of Sulimo's armed fighters who had spoken. The merchant looked displeased that the man had opened his mouth.

"Ah... yes, I was going to warn you," he simpered. "Forgive me, it must be the heat!"

"Where are they from?" Corin glowered at the merchant whilst mouthing a silent 'thank you' to his hired man.

"The north," replied the fighter. "Like you and me. They are searching for something, or more likely someone."

"Enough, Marl! I pay you for your skill with a sword not with your tongue!" Marl's hard eyes flicked annoyance but he kept his lips together. "We had best be re-joining the train; I want to clear these dangerous hills before we set up camp." Sulimo awarded them an oily smile. "I bid you good day, Lord Bormion! Enjoy Agmandeur. But don't forget Cappel Cormac!"

Without further ado the merchant nodded at his two men, and struck his camel three times with a thin stick urging the beast clump towards the fading column of dust, his guards following on their own mounts close behind.

The soldiers on the ridge behind them waited until the merchant had passed, and then they too vanished from view. Corin watched the hillside suspiciously for some moments before urging Thunderhoof forward. He drew level with Zallerak who was already underway.

"What was all that about?" Corin demanded as Yashan led them on again with a sharp trot towards the distant ribbon of river. "That merchant..."

"He was no merchant," responded Zallerak with an irritated glance back. "Sulimo is a spy from Sedinadola Palace. One of the sultan's cleverest and most trusted advisors. The stuff about traveling to Shen was nonsense. His men were scouting these hills having got wind there are strangers about. And those wagons, master Tamersane, contained weaponry and reinforcements should they be needed. I suspect Sulimo's men had already spotted us while we were in the ravine. We had little choice but to reveal ourselves. He'll be sending a coded bird to inform the sultan soon."

"Thanks for the warning," muttered Corin.

"You're welcome."

Chapter 15

The Streets of Agmandeur

They made haste towards the city as the afternoon drew on; Corin wondered why Marl had warned them about the mercenaries when his master had not wanted him to. Still the mercenaries in Agmandeur need not have anything to do with the missing prince or their quest.

But why so many northerners in the desert? There were enough native freebooters in Permio without any need of fighting men from the Four Kingdoms and beyond. Merchants were different—they always employed outlanders as their travels took them far and wide. Even if that Sulimo had been a spy, his employing such fighters made sense and gave cover to his guise. But mercenaries stationed down here? That made no sense.

Yashan had told them that fighting was forbidden behind the walls of Agmandeur and that would satisfy Corin for the moment. He felt restless though. Trouble lay ahead. It was just a matter of where and when.

As afternoon waned and the sun slipped crimson behind distant dunes they finally arrived at the muddy banks of the Narion. This river was not as wide as the Liaho but was much livelier in its journey north to the ocean. Corin could see small eddies and whirl-pools amongst the strong currents, but worryingly he saw no sight of a bridge when they drew near to the eastern bank. Ahead the grey walls of the city soaked in the last of the sunlight. Close by, but still the issue of the river.

"So what do we do, fly across?" Corin asked sardonically as they rode on through the last dusty miles leading them down towards the steep banks of the river.

"There is a causeway," responded Yashan. "It isn't far."

Soon enough they arrived at the stony banks of the Narion. Tamersane laughed when he saw what Yashan had described as a causeway. Some forty or fifty worn flat stones showed barely above the river's weed-strewn, rushing water. Most of these looked treach-erous and promised to prove slippery underfoot. Beyond the ford, the walls and domed clusters of Agmandeur's houses bulked high against the darkening sky. These bastions appeared smaller than the walls of Port Sarfe but looked impressive enough from where they were standing.

They dismounted and led their thirsty mounts down to the river, letting them drink from its cool, muddy waters. Thunderhoof slurped and guzzled and snorted bubbles.

The crossing was even more treacherous than it had first ap-peared. Yashan explained that it was kept like it so inhabitants could get a clear view of who entered their city from the east.

Corin found that idea unsettling; he imagined what an easy time archers would have firing down on them from the narrow slots in the walls above, or higher on the lofty battlement. He could not afford to look up for long. The strong current tugged at his ankles and Thunderhoof's shod hoofs slipped on the fly and lice infested weed. Still, they made it over to the western bank without too much trouble. Bleyne's horse was nervous at first, refusing to enter the causeway, but the archer had whispered to it calmly for some moments and the mare had given him no further trouble. Even so, they were all breathless and panting by the time they had clambered up the steep bank and arrived at the city gates. These stood ajar as if they were expected. And perhaps they were.

Corin and Tamersane glanced around at the bastions which appeared strangely vacant. Yashan seemed relaxed as he led them forward, but Corin had the nasty suspicion that they were encroaching on a spider's web. But then his feelings toward Permio were anything but neutral.

That said, even Zallerak looked about sharply, as if he too were suspecting a trap. Bleyne was the last to lead his horse beneath the gateway. The archer was calm as usual, safe in his belief that the goddess watched his every move. Forlorn hope in Corin's opinion— Elanion held little clout down here. This was Telcanna's realm—the cruel petulant Sky God.

Corin tensed when he heard the gates creak shut behind them. Turning, he saw swarthy guards acknowledge Yashan with a casual wave. With a sigh he let himself relax.

"This way," announced their guide. Yashan led them into a tumbled maze of cluttered narrow streets, criss-crossing and twisting upwards in all directions.

These were not the ordered climb of Kranek Town, nor were they the narrow lanes and spirals of Port Sarfe. It was though the streets of Agmandeur had been deliberately constructed to confuse. It was not long before Corin gave up any attempt at trying to remember the way back down to the gates. Permio—nothing was straight forward down here.

People stared at them warily as they passed but said nothing; some nodded at Yashan, though no words were exchanged. Mostly the townsfolk merely glared at them in open disapproval. Corin was amazed by the variety of dress worn by these desert people; many of the faces that watched him pass seemed strange and foreign to his eyes. There were tall aloof tribesmen who whispered amongst themselves and stared at them suspiciously from dusty corners.

There were hard-faced warriors with wicked-looking curved scimitars at their hips, and dark-faced silent women who hurried by, their beauty hidden beneath alluring veils. Tamersane watched them pass with gormless gapes until Corin nudged him in the ribs.

"We had best not cause offence," he warned him.

"I was merely admiring," countered the Kelwynian.

"Your incorrigible charm might not work here," Corin told him. Tamersane scratched an ear and looked genuinely puzzled by that last comment.

Yashan led them up a steep hill that spiralled towards the right. They had climbed a fair bit by now, the walls were both behind and beneath them. They were almost level with the largest building: a broad dome almost reaching to the floor—the temple of Telcanna and city's central hub.

Corin noted that folk thereabouts looked quite well to do. There were silk-garbed merchants like Sulimo who chatted noisily, while their hard-eyed protectors watched warily from behind their dicing tables.

Not all the tribesmen were dark-skinned either, which Corin found surprising. Here and there he noticed a blue-eyed stranger amongst the throng, clearly not from the Four Kingdoms but not Permian either by their look. Afterwards Yashan explained to him that these men came from the far western desert beyond Golt and little was known about them. He didn't trust them, but then Yashan didn't trust anyone not belonging to his tribe, and not all who did either.

There was one man who caught even Yashan's eye. This was a giant, hugely muscled warrior with skin the colour of ebony. The black man wore a magnificent scarlet robe over his otherwise naked chest. He looked ferocious, broad sinewy arms festooned with golden rings and hoops. He wore gold earrings and sported close cropped silvering hair and beard. Surely this was some warrior prince from the distant south. Around his waist the warrior sported the hide of some spotted creature. The man grinned evilly at Corin, before ducking into a dirty alley where chickens clucked and capered about.

"That was one big bugger," Tamersane muttered in Corin's ear. "I wonder if he has a daughter, hereabouts. I like exotic women."

"If he has she'd probably unravel your tripes for gawping," Corin laughed.

Tamersane looked pained. "I can't help it, Corin. Foreign women fascinate me."

"Anything female fascinates you."

"There is that."

The smells were intense in the city as were the clamour of voices and the squawking of various beasts and fowl. Corin was relieved that evening was upon them, for surely things would quieten soon. Everywhere he looked in Agmandeur there seemed to be a mess. Skinny children scampered after scurrying mangy dogs, whilst thin pale-eyed lazy cats surveyed them coolly from the safety of faded whitewashed walls. The mainly mud-built houses leant towards each other like drunken comrades. From behind their doors middle-aged women berated small boys, these chasing leather balls through the dirt with their bare grubby feet.

And this was the expensive quarter.

It was almost dark when Yashan finally stopped. He dismounted outside a battered looking inn that bore no sign above its faded red door. Corin glimpsed some movement behind the blinds and curled his lip in distaste.

"This is where we will be spending the night," announced their guide handing his horse over to the care of a scrawny-looking dark-eyed youth with a squint.

"Must we?" Corin complained before reluctantly unbridling Thunderhoof and giving the boy a withering stare. "See that he is well fed and watered," he grumbled.

"Aye, sir—of course," the youth grinned after catching a friendly wink from Tamersane. He led their horses off to a stable hidden somewhere around the back.

"Relax, Corin, Yashan trusts this fellow" said Tamersane. "Besides he might have daughters.'"

"I don't trust anyone and nor should you," muttered Corin, sulking as he followed his young friend inside the murky inn, narrowly avoiding striking his head on the low lintel above.

Once inside Corin looked around at the room. He was relieved to discover the inn was much cleaner than it had appeared from without. They were promptly greeted by a portly man with a bristling black moustache who smiled warmly at Yashan before placing a kiss on either of his cheeks. Tamersane exchanged a disgusted glance at Corin, who shrugged in reply.

"This is Hulm," announced their guide. "He is my friend and here we can talk freely."

"Masters are welcome in my modest abode," said Hulm, his voice deep and urbane.

"It is hard to scrape a decent living on the edge of the desert but one tries one's best. I trust you'll take some wine with your supper." Hulm smiled knowingly. The innkeeper had a lugubrious face and easy tongue. He appeared genuine but Corin would keep his eyes open. Before anyone could respond Hulm began complaining ardently about the cost of goods this far away from the coast.

"Of course we manage well enough," he explained, "but one misses the big city comforts from time to time," he continued without so much as a pause for breath. "Agmandeur is quite provincial when one is used to the subtleties of Syrannos, not to mention Sedinadola."

"Then you have not always lived here, master Hulm?" Tamersane was the only one listening.

"No indeed not," responded Hulm with an expansive grin. "I hail from the sparkling streets of Syrannos on the Silver Strand," he informed them. "I'm a coastal Permian. Unlike my old friend Yashan here who is a true son of the desert."

Corin rubbed his eyes and wondered when the wine would arrive; Hulm's incessant chatter was giving him a headache. However he said nothing; Permians had their own way of doing things. And their words could be sharper than their scimitars. Corin knew that their host was shrewdly weighing them up as he spoke.

"I hear there are other strangers in Agmandeur this evening," cut in Zallerak who until now had not shown much interest and still stood gazing at the door.

Hulm shot a questioning glance at Yashan who nodded in return. Meanwhile Zallerak folded his cloak and took his place at a table. He launched an arm at a nearby bowl of olives.

"Hmm, these are good," he added, consuming another then another.

"Visitors, yes," replied Hulm, slightly taken aback by the tall bard and making room for Yashan at the table. Their guide had removed his faded burnoose and was tugging his long black hair free of knots.

"Mercenaries," continued Zallerak, his pale eyes appraising their corpulent host.

"We encountered a certain merchant in the hills who claimed to come from Golt. Sulimo, I believe he called himself."

"Then you are lucky to be alive." Hulm's face was suddenly serious. "Sulimo is a treacherous dog. He is a spy and one high placed in the sultan's service. The merchant's a wily rogue, I would guess word is already on its way to Sedinadola announcing your visit, Lord Bormion."

Corin gasped at this." How did you know that name?" he demanded.

"Silon's friend informed me of your imminent arrival, Corin an Fol," responded Hulm with a smile. "He told me to keep a wary eye out for one Lord Bormion who would be travelling south with young Yashan. When I enquired further he divulged the identities and traits of those accompanying him, though this Bormion's true name he wouldn't disclose. Don't worry, Corin—Silon and I go way back. And I know how you dislike this land. But not all Permians are your enemy. Take Yashan here."

Corin sunk into his chair. Silon was up to his old tricks again. He exchanged glances with Tamersane, who for his part looked baffled. "Silon's friend..." Corin nodded slowly. "Who would that be?" "Barakani the desert chief." Bleyne showed some interest. The archer had joined them at the table after washing his face free of dust and dirt in a ceramic bowl close by.

"The very one," replied Hulm. He turned to thank a thin, tired-looking man who had arrived with a large carafe of red wine, to both Corin and Tamersane's relief.

"My brother Olami," their host informed them, "has not been of the soundest health lately. You will forgive him if he eats alone." Hulm looked about the room in sudden frustration. "Where has that infernal Ragu got to? Ah, there you are, boy."

The squinty youth that had taken their mounts thrust his grinning head through the doorway.

"Have you seen to the horses properly?" Hulm demanded. Ragu nodded a breathless 'yes' before hurrying out of view to assist Olami in the kitchens. "Be quick, boy!" Hulm chided. "I've a task for you later."

The wine was excellent and Corin found himself relaxing at last, though he questioned whether their affable host would ever desist from his incessant banter. At present he was extoling the virtues of Permian women to a captivated Tamersane. Corin rolled his eyes and swallowed some wine. Zallerak was off lurking in the next room and Bleyne dozed across the table. Corin missed Barin and his dice. Much more, he missed Shallan and Ariane and wondered how they fared.

Outside the street was turning dark as dusk gathered pace and happily, thought Corin, there was now little noise in the city. Someone had lit lanterns at the corners of the houses. A quiet peace had descended on the streets of Agmandeur.

They talked their way through a delicious meal of spiced goat, lentils and humus. Zallerak, smelling food, had returned and now consulted their host with Corin and Tamersane adding the occasional helpful grunt. Yashan had retired to a dark corner of the room to smoke his weed, much to Hulm's disgust.

"A revolting habit," proclaimed their host, waving his fleshy arms at the swirling, sweet smelling smoke. Yashan shrugged, nonplussed.

"It keeps me content," he said, sucking at the device. Corin saw that Bleyne was watching something outside though he could hear no movement in the street.

"What is it?" Corin asked him.

The archer shrugged in reply. "I cannot be certain but I think that we are being stalked."

"Mercenaries?"

"No. something worse... something familiar." The archer's keen eyes gleamed like jet beads in the faintly tallow lit room. "You remember the valley near Kashorn?"

Hulm stood up warily. He closed the curtains, leaving a slight gap so they could see if anyone entered the street.

"Ragu!" he hissed and the sweating boy came into view. "I need you to get the supplies ready we talked about, and keep the saddles close to the horses. Also bring in those robes and stop jabbering nonsense with Olami!" The boy nodded and disappeared.

Hulm poured himself out a small glass of wine and sighed while they waited for Ragu's return. "Twenty mercenaries arrived two nights hence," he said, his tone suddenly quiet and conspiratory. "They came on swift Rorshai steeds and have been asking strange questions. Their leader is a tall man with nasty eyes, a badly broken nose, and long scar across his face."

"Hagan Delmorier," said Bleyne. Corin was cursing softly behind him. "Corin here broke his nose," announced the archer cheerfully. "He's in the pay of Caswallon of Kelthaine."

"I thought as much," replied their host. "This Hagan seemed quite agitated, as if it was imperative he found what—or more likely who—he was looking for."

"Aye, he has failed Caswallon before; I'd doubt the usurper

would forgive a second time," Corin muttered.

He was watching the silent darkness outside. He thought of the ugly winged creature that had listened to their conversation aboard Barin's ship—the Sodfin or Singefin or something. Bleyne had dealt with that goblin, but doubtless Caswallon had other weird spies, what with all his ghoulish antics. And what of Morak? Old Dog-Face was probably lurking around somewhere. Least that's what Bleyne suspected. And now Hagan was here too. The bastard certainly hadn't wasted any time. But was it Prince Tarin or them that he sought?

Corin looked up when Ragu reappeared staggering beneath a selection of faded desert robes. The boy handed them out to Zallerak, Tamersane, Bleyne and Corin, and the latter frowned when he saw them.

Not more cursed gowns! He'd only just got rid of the priest's cloak. However these robes were of a more practical hue. They were sandy white in colour and made of a durable fabric that would deflect the desert heat whilst keeping the companions hidden from hostile eyes. The garments were of loose appearance too, and could be worn comfortably over their other attire.

"You had best don these," warned Hulm. "Although violence is forbidden in our city, I doubt this Hagan will wait for long once he knows of your presence here. We might have to move swiftly, ere morning."

"Before that, I think," said Bleyne. Corin frowned seeing that the archer had strung his bow and had three long shafts ready on his lap. Just then Ragu emerged from the darkness behind them. His voice was anxious and his young face alarmed.

"There are men outside carrying torches! Big men, foreign by their look, armed with long straight swords!" Ragu's eyes were wide, the boy was clearly terrified.

Corin leapt up and warily approached the window. Outside the sound of hoarse shouts filled the nearby alleys. Dogs barked hearing the commotion. The sound of marching feet could be heard. A squad coming their way and closing fast.

Chapter 16

Ambush

"They sound close." *Tamersane looked peeved having* just settled into his wine. "Have you a back passage, master Hulm? Please pardon the expression," he added with a wink."

"Every house in Agmandeur has a hidden back door," muttered their host, incensed that men were openly bearing weapons in the city. "Left from the old smuggling days. Quickly now, follow me, good people, I fear my hospitality must end rather abruptly."

Hulm led them through his inn to the back room. At the far wall was a tall heavy cupboard filled with scrolls, pots and various clutter. This he slid sideways with a puffing grunt to reveal a wide crack opening on the emptiness of a dark alley beyond.

"Squeeze through," rasped Hulm. "Go!" He ushered them out with an anxious wave. "Make for the western gates as quietly as you can. The guards won't stop you. Ragu and I will meet you outside the city with your horses and supplies."

"Be careful," replied Corin but Hulm had vanished behind the cupboard, which was already back in its former position. Behind it

Hulm sank to his knees and counted to ten. This called for quick thinking and a cool head.

As Hulm returned to the main room there came a loud shout from outside the front of the inn, followed by an urgent rapping on the door. Corin, listening in the backstreet, heard a familiar harsh voice call out.

"Open this bloody door, innkeep, or I'll burn your hovel down. Quickly now!" It was Hagan. Corin fingered Biter's hilt. Then the boy Ragu appeared around a corner puffing, his eyes on stalks. "The master will deal with your friends outside," Ragu told him. "Best you look to yourselves."

"What about our bloody horses?" Tamersane hissed at the boy, wandering how Ragu had reached them so fast. They were not to know that the stables had a secret entrance too. You cannot have enough hidden doors in this world.

"Don't worry, sirs." Ragu waved a hectic hand, "we'll see to it you're reunited with them once we've straightened things out. We'll bring the desert robes too!" Tamersane nodded but Corin shook his head. Young Ragu's assessment of the situation was a touch optimistic in his opinion. He waved thanks but Ragu had vanished behind the corner whence he'd only just appeared.

"Coming, masters!" They heard Hulm shout from somewhere within the inn.

Corin reached behind to unleash Clouter. Now they were out in the street he'd have ample room to swing. Warily he scanned the darkness ahead.

"This way," announced Zallerak as though he knew what he was talking about. They followed, Corin tailing beside Bleyne who had an arrow ready on the nock.

Here we go again...

***

Hagan waited impatiently as the portly Permian emerged from the dingy looking inn. Hagan hated these people, like Corin he had fought against them for many years. The only thing a Permian was good for was a swift throat-slitting.

But Hagan sensed his quarry was close. This time there would be no buggering about. Caswallon had sent word to Hagan's new contact in Permio. The man in Cappel Cormac had told Hagan that Caswallon suspected Tarin would pass through Agmandeur, on his foolhardy quest, and that a certain Corin an Fol would be hard on the prince's heels. Caswallon had developed a curious interest in Hagan's former associate, the contact informed him.

"He wants this Corin alive," the Permian insisted. "No fuck ups—his words not mine."

"There won't be," Hagan had growled at the greasy merchant until the man backed away. "And tell Lord Caswallon I'll be back in Kella for my gold inside a month."

The contact had glared back at him before taking leave of the tavern where they had been conducting their business

They had reached the streets of Cappel Cormac while the rumour of the prince still echoed in the crowded hostile taverns. After meeting with Caswallon's man, Hagan's crew purchased fresh horses and supplies ready for the ride south to Agmandeur.

There had been a slight fracas with some nosy soldiers of the sultan. Hagan's men had been challenged by a squad twice their size. That had delayed them a while, but after a few slit throats and mangled limbs they'd broken loose and fled the city. Hagan's mercenaries had arrived in Agmandeur two days ago. They hadn't rushed as they took time checking the roads for evidence of their quarry. Once inside the city they'd kept a low profile.

Watch and wait, thought Hagan. *Patience wins. Let the quarry come to us.* And of course he was proved right. Caswallon's contact, the merchant Sulimo, had sent a fast rider to warn Hagan of Corin and company's imminent arrival. The man had followed them to the city and then steered clear and entered by the other gates. Thus by the time he got to Hagan, Corin and friends were already arriving at the inn.

Hagan had waited for the cover of darkness and then led his men out into the dimly lit streets. It was past time he called his debt.

***

Hulm opened the door with a polite smile. He bowed deeply at the hard-looking mercenary captain. Hagan ignored him, barging past and scanning the room.

"Who has been here?"

"Just myself and my ailing brother, lord," answered Hulm, relieved that Ragu had had the sense to hide the empty plates and wine mugs. "And a witless boy who serves us," he added rubbing his hands together. "Can I fetch you food and wine?" he simpered.

Hagan spat then turned on Hulm. In his left hand was a stiletto. Hulm hadn't noticed that before. In a blur of movement Hagan had the sharp point pricking just beneath the innkeeper's left eye.

"Who else has been here?" demanded Hagan in a quieter voice. "Talk to me, Permian, or I'll cut your lying eyes out!"

"It's as I said, master!" pleaded Hulm. "Just the three of us, my brother has the flux and is resting next door. You are welcome to go see but it is very contagious!"

Hagan frowned and told two of his men to go look. When they came back holding their noses, he turned and scowled at the innkeeper.

"I don't trust you, Permian. You're all fucking liars. But if I find that you have lied to me I'll be back to remove your tongue as well as your eyes." Hulm blinked like a startled bull frog. "Nobody fucks with Hagan Delmorier."

"Come on!" Hagan led his torch-bearing men from the inn to continue their search further up the street. Hulm sat down and wiped his soaking brow. He was getting much too old for this business.

***

Bleyne pulled back his bowstring; the archer's keen senses were alert. Something was stalking them through the night and it had nothing to do with Hagan's mercenaries. Then he smiled, recognising the smell that had guided him to the edge of the forest months earlier, and then again much later in Silon's garden. Groil. The dog creatures had returned.

Corin heard a noise behind him. He spun round on his heels, Clouter gripped in both hands.

Oh, it's you.

A hooded figure, the dog snout just protruding, stood some yards away, watching him with those evil yellow eyes from beneath the eaves of a storehouse.

And I thought Zallerak sent you somewhere nasty.

Corin felt the familiar fear and anger rising. He squeezed hard on Clouter's hilt as the sword had become suddenly heavy.

"Come on, slime breath—I'm ready for you now." Corin took a step forward then stopped. Morak's figure was fading and shimmering, within heartbeats the Dog-Lord had vanished completely. "Not quite your old bad self, eh howler?" Corin was rewarded by a sound like metallic laughter. Morak might have gone but he'd sent his creatures out to deal with them. Suddenly dog snouts and swirling cloaks were everywhere.

"Groil!" Tamersane yelled in Corin's ear, nearly deafening him. Tamersane hadn't seen the Dog-Lord and stood waving his sword about demonstratively. "Corin, watch out for that big one with the humped back."

Corin hurled his knife at the closest fiend. The dog creature slumped, but others hastened towards them materialising like liquid ghouls out of the dark.

"I think we better make a move," Tamersane added whilst stepping backwards and deftly skewering a Groil. "I hate these fucking things."

"Me too."

"Wait...what's that?" Tamersane tugged Corin's arm. "What's he up to?" There was a weird humming sound coming from Zallerak, and his spear tip was glowing with a blueish sheen. Already the Groil were hesitating, their doggy snouts snuffling with caution and doubt. "Excellent," said Tamersane who hadn't witnessed Zallerak in action before. "Does he do this sort of thing often?" The pale glow deepened to sapphire ice, cold steam exuding from the metal. "This is good stuff," Tamersane said. The Groil slunk back. A few dropped to all fours and began circling Zallerak. Then the bard thrust his spear at the nearest dog creature. The lance's tip fizzed and hissed as it scorched its black robes with petrified steel. Within seconds the dog-creature exploded amid wailing shrieking howls.

And then Zallerak was on them. Each time the spear touched a Groil they fizzled and exploded before shrinking back into nothingness. Only their black garments remained and these were reduced to cinders.

"Fuck, but that's impressive," allowed Tamersane. Yashan and Bleyne had joined them from further up the lane. Bleyne's shaft took three more Groil, and Yashan's scimitar joined in. The tribesman's face was ashen grey.

But it was hopeless for at least two score more had emerged, and these now rushed upon them. Howling and spitting, some on all fours, others on hind legs with serrated swords, and barbed pokers and spikes gripped in their blackened paws.

Zallerak's spear was working a fury but the Groil were closing tight and he was hard pressed for room. At last the bard drew back and yelled in Corin's ear.

"Hold them off! I need more room to summon extra charge for my battery!"

"What?"

"Just kill the bloody things!" Zallerak turned and fled around the same corner Ragu had recently frequented.

"Where's he going now?" Tamersane gulped when he saw the wizard running off. "He hasn't finished yet."

"He does that," Corin said before three huge Groil crashed down on them. There was no room now, Corin couldn't get a decent swing with Clouter. He gripped the blade by the leather band below the hilt that he reserved for close quarter work. Biter would have been better but no time to get that out.

To Corin's right Yashan sliced and lunged like a madman, whilst on his left Tamersane rammed his sword's pommel into a dog snout, and the thing coughed and fell backwards. Bleyne had stowed his bow and was slicing Groil with his long knife.

But still they kept coming—a wall of dog faces snarling and barking, forcing the four fighters back against a building. Corin levelled Clouter and readied for a desperate lunge.

I'm so tired of this.

A wall of flame shot past Corin's head, the glare temporally blinding him as Zallerak's spear sent a fire jet that blasted a score of Groil to ashes. The spear struck again and again, meanwhile the four fighters crashed into each other in the chaos.

"What are you doing back there? Must I do everything myself?" Zallerak urged them follow him through the gap he had created with his last blast. Scattered Groil parts fizzed and sputtered as the blue fire dissolved their flesh.

Corin grabbed Tamersane and shoved him forward while the other two launched themselves into sudden motion. Corin stole a wild look down the lane and then turned, fled behind the others.

Zallerak leading, they sped down through the now noisily waking streets, the remaining unsinged Groil giving furious four-legged chase close behind.

Some cityfolk emerged bravely from their homes. They gawped wide-eyed at the Groil before hastening back behind walls. Some took to drink with shaking hands. Others puffed urgently on their weed pipes. In the streets, dogs howled and scampered out of the way, and then finally the city guard arrived armed with crossbows and long spiky spears.

"Thanks for showing some interest, lads," Corin muttered as he slowed to a walk.

The guard surrounded and attacked the dog creatures, who

were circling and snapping, aware the coin had turned against them. Soon the Groil were all destroyed. As if on a whim, Zallerak turned and torched the last corpses to oblivion with his lance. Something he seemed to enjoy doing, Corin noted.

Job done, Zallerak shouldered his spear. He muttered some words and the blazing tip faded to a dull sheen. Then he turned, his expression imperious, and strode without a second glance down toward the city walls. Ahead the southern gates emerged reluctantly from the darkness.

The four fighters followed Zallerak, leaving the city guard shouting and kicking at barking hounds, whilst placating the few citizens braving the streets, who stood staring and pointing in horror at the fried doggy things piled in a heap.

Corin and the others approached the southern gate where Zallerak stood waiting with arms folded.

Corin turned to mutter something to Tamersane, but a blow on the back of his head sent him sprawling face first into a shop door. Corin rolled instinctively but his vision was blurred and he was seeing stars. He still gripped Clouter's hilt with his right hand. He tried raising the longsword but a heavy boot stamped on his hand and someone laughed. Corin let go of the weapon as his hand throbbed with pain.

"Finish it, you bastard!"

Nothing—just more quiet laughter. Familiar laughter. At last the street stopped spinning and his vision cleared. Corin saw Hagan leaning over him a smirk widening the scar on his face.

"Hello, Corin. I owe you a debt of steel, as I recall." Hagan's crossbow-bearing men had surrounded his friends. Even Bleyne had been caught out by Hagan's crafty ambush. Tamersane and Yashan looked miserable. There was no sign of Zallerak.

Corin gathered his knees together and glared up at Hagan.

"Go and shaft your mother, oh I forgot you haven't got one, you Morwellan shite."

Corin's head snapped back as Hagan kicked him hard in the face.

"I'm going to cut you open, Corin. Hook your guts out from balls to belly. But first I need a few answers. Borgil here can be quite persuasive. First up. Where are you off to in such a hurry?" He kicked Corin again this time in his stomach. Corin groaned, doubled over and spewed on the street.

"Up yours."

Hagan signalled Borgil over.

"There's much interest in you, Corin," Hagan told him. "I cannot think why. But who am I to question my employers?"

Corin stole a painful glance towards the gates. Zallerak had reappeared and stood there grinning at him.

And up yours too!

Borgil loomed over Corin, a mess of beard and pockmarks and fetid breath. He produced an evil-looking knife and smiled. The smile was shortlived. Borgil went sprawling after something slammed into his back. Before Hagan could react a huge black hand covered the mercenary's mouth, whilst a leaf-shaped dagger pricked his throat. The crossbowmen raised their weapons.

"I wouldn't do that," Tamersane advised them. The city guard had crossbowmen too. These already had the mercenaries in their sights.

"You took your time, Ulani," said Zallerak, having joined them again. Corin heard a deep resinous laugh, and turning painfully, recognised the huge black warrior they had seen when first they arrived in Agmandeur.

"You're Silon's acquaintance." Corin coughed blood and checked his teeth were still in his head. Reassured they were, he struggled to his feet. Once steady Corin squared on Hagan, still held by the stranger.

"Let him go, big fella, if you'd be so kind."

The huge warrior raised an eyebrow but obliged. Corin grinned a 'thank you' and lashed out at Hagan's groin with his left boot. The impact jarred Corin's leg and Hagan doubled over in pain.

Behind, the rest of the city guard had arrived led by a puffing, grumbling Hulm. The soldiers swiftly relieved the mercenaries of their crossbows and other weaponry.

"Tie these bastards up," ordered Hulm in a voice very different from his earlier tone.

"Yes, lord," responded a guard.

Tamersane and Corin exchanged quizzical glances.

"Will someone please explain what is going on?" Corin said.

"Wake up, Corin an Fol and wipe that face clean," replied Zallerak. "You are looking at the Castellan of Agmandeur!"

"Why didn't you tell me?" Corin snapped at Yashan, who was presently urinating over Borgil.

Yashan shrugged. "You never asked," he replied. Yashan gazed down at Borgil and grinned. "It's part of the ritual—I have to cure your fat northern hide before I skin it." Borgil paled visibly.

Corin turned to thank the black-skinned warrior who still stood guard over Hagan. "I am in your debt," Corin told him. The stranger grinned at him in friendly fashion. He folded his massive arms across his chest while his shrewd brown eyes watched Hagan for sudden moves.

"I enjoyed participating," he said in a deep voice, and held out a calloused paw. "I am Ulani of the Baha race. I hale from distant Yamondo."

Corin gripped Ulani's hand and smiled up at the warrior. He had never heard of Yamondo. Not that that mattered. Ulani of the Baha was huge, nearly as tall as Barin but much broader; his chest, arms and legs were all corded and contoured with ridges of muscle. Ulani looked like he could take on twelve men in a fight. The barrel chest was naked but the robe across his shoulders looked very expensive.

Ulani wore a kilt comprised of some spotted animal's fur, around this was girded a broad golden belt, and from this hung all manner of weaponry. He wore criss-cross sandals strapped around his ankles and calves, with a bone-handled knife thrust into a tiny sheaf stitched to the left one. Corin was impressed. This giant was a walking armoury.

"And what is to become of our friend here and his men?" Ulani enquired of Hulm.

"We'll strip them and leave them hanging outside the city gates for hyena, vulture and fly to feast on." Hulm's face showed no ruth. "Had I more time I'd punish them properly for baring their blades inside my city walls!"

"No." Against his better judgement Corin found himself pleading with a frowning Hulm to spare Hagan's life. "He was once an honourable man," Corin told the ruler, "before he sold his soul to Caswallon and Hakkenon for gold. Let his new master deal with him. Let Hagan and his scumbags contend with the sorcerer's wrath."

"Very well, if you wish it," shrugged Hulm. "My heart tells me you are unwise in this, Corin an Fol. I don't doubt you'll meet this rogue again."

"Neither do I."

The Castellan turned to his men. "Strip them of their weapons but let them keep their garments. Give them enough water to reach Cappel Cormac—just enough mind, not a drop more." After that had been done Hagan and his men gathered like restless hounds in a circle pinned by the guards. Hulm rounded on Hagan who was glowering at him with defiant loathing.

"If you or any of your filth venture near my city again, Hagan Delmorier, I will personally flay the flesh from your bones with a blunt knife and feed it to my hounds!"

Hagan nodded, stony-faced. He stole an acid glance at Corin, before allowing the guards to escort his men out into the towering dunes, rearing dark and huge beyond the western gates. Before he left Hagan turned to Corin a final time.

"We'll meet again soon."

"Can't wait."

Morning dawned clear and bright. Once again the streets of Agmandeur were teeming with folk as the blazing sun rose up beyond the River Narion. Ragu had arrived as promised with their mounts, robes and copious provisions including large gourds filled with fresh clean water.

Ulani informed Corin that he was returning to his homeland. Apparently the Baha ruled eastern Yamondo—a country far to the south of their destination.

Ulani announced he would be happy to accompany them on their journey to the Crystal Mountains. This was a cause of felicitation among the companions, particularly Tamersane who warmed to the big man almost at once.

They wasted little time getting ready; their mounts at least had received a decent rest. Thunder clomped toward Corin with a resigned look.

Zallerak thanked the Castellan and his men. Corin patted the boy Ragu on his shoulder and smiled before joining the others.

Once outside the gates they took stock of the desert ahead. Corin glanced up, squinting at the deepening blue above.

It was already hot and soon the sun would be unbearable. To think that it was nearly winter! He shook his head and waved farewell to the walls of Agmandeur.

They had sprung the trap again. Corin thanked Elanion for that much at least. But deep inside a small voice warned far worse dangers waited for him and his friends beyond the towering dunes of the vast Permian Desert.

Chapter 17

Syrannos

Shallan stood watching the clear blue waves break upon the painted bow of *The Starlight Wanderer.* Above her head the hot sun blazed down relentless, scorching deck timbers and melting the tar coating the stays.

She gazed up dreamily at the great sails, seeing crewmembers leap lithely across the yards to tend to knots and cleats. Behind her, on the aft deck Shallan could see the bulky frame of captain Barin, the ship's master, as he held their course steady southwest.

It was afternoon of the second day since they had departed from Port Sarfe harbour and they were making good progress. A warm breeze ruffled the sails. Shallan smiled, feeling her long chestnut hair lift and float about her face. She felt more alive than she had done for weeks.

Ahead stretched a low coastline of glittering sand dunes and gently swaying palms. Beyond these the tall domes of a white city could be seen rising up over the wall of sand, shimmering in the afternoon heat.

Syrannos—the captain had informed her whilst he sipped his liquid breakfast. Shallan decided she liked Barin. The huge Northman was a good-natured soul who helped raise her spirits. His jocular wit had cheered her father too, and she was grateful for that.

The crew were a rough-looking lot, especially the mate Fassof who had a fiery nature and a foul mouth. He sported a wild crop of red hair and often yelled at the men with the most colourful language Shallan had ever heard—and she'd heard quite a bit lately.

Barin was short of crew. He'd informed Shallan that he'd got four new recruits in Port Sarfe, but said he didn't hold out much hope for them, and needed another three at least. But good reliable sailors were hard to come by, and they'd been short-staffed since leaving Crenna. Though Barin's regulars had had a recent break they missed their northern home and were getting restless. They were all polite to her, not in a stiff dutiful Morwellan way; they were gruff, friendly. It was all she could ask for.

Shallan felt at ease on Barin's ship—almost content. Here was a freedom she'd never known before. All her life (and particularly the dark years since her mother's death) Shallan had been at the whim of her father or else her eldest brother's wishes.

Both stern proud men who would not be gainsaid. Father and first son were well meaning but bullish and unyielding in their attentiveness; it was something the free-spirited girl resented to this day. Her other two brothers were wild restless lads who went their own way in life. Shallan had always them envied their freedom, she knew she was as strong as any of them—stronger.

But now at last Shallan was free to do as she pleased. Duke Tomais had mellowed too; the loss of his city had hit him hard. He'd aged rapidly since the invasion, such was the weight of guilt he carried. First he'd lost his wife then his country. Tomais considered himself culpable on both counts. The duke relied more and more on Shallan these days, asking her opinion often, and even listening when she gave it. He suffered from depression though and mostly stayed below deck.

Shallan remained cheerful despite their predicament, she had found something amongst the cool leaves of Silon's vineyard that she never expected. A new thing—a love born from hope.

Shallan smiled dreamily as she watched from the dancing prow of the ship. She cast her mind back to that starry, jasmine-scented evening. Again she walked amongst the gardens of Vioyamis with the awkward, shaggy-haired Longswordsman from Fol.

Shallan had never encountered anyone like Corin before. He was uniquely unsubtle and had so struggled finding the right words. She had liked that. So different to the glib, garrulous courtiers Shallan had known back home. At first she'd felt a playful attraction, had wondered what it was about this uncouth stranger her cousin, Queen Ariane, so admired.

Shallan had felt so different that night. Adventurous and curious, and a small part of her had wanted to spite her cousin, if truth be known. Ariane was so frosty. But it was more than that. Shallan was known for being aloof but she had another side. A tricky conniving side that she didn't like. Almost sometimes she felt like another person lived inside her. Alien, cunning and mysterious—Ariane brought out that side of her nature though most oft Shallan kept it well hidden.

So Shallan had played a game with this Corin, but unwittingly the spider became the fly. She was caught by the steely eyes—the same grey/blue of her own. Shallan felt his inner strength and saw the passion beneath his anger; fusing, boiling like a cauldron about to overflow.

This was a dangerous man. Corin had excited her like no other. And now she was hooked and could think of little else save when she would see him again.

In the north—in springtime.

Shallan felt her inner voice calming her fears once again. Corin would survive the desert whatever the perils. He had to. Then as promised he would join her upon the high walls of Car Carranis far to the north. Together they would help repel the barbarians, whilst in the west Ariane's reinforced army would cast down the foul usurper of Kelthaine. Simple.

Shallan smiled to herself: it was a fanciful dream but she would not give in to despair. She would see Corin again and damn everything else.

Shallan had been discreet since their tryst; she'd kept her feelings for Corin quiet; still the perceptive Silon had noticed a change in her. She turned hearing soft movement behind her, smiled as he joined her now on deck.

"A fine autumn day, my lady," Shallan noticed how the small diamond sparkled in his left ear having caught the glare of the sun.

"It's beautiful," she answered, smiling at the merchant. "Captain Barin says we should make Syrannos harbour by late early evening if this kind wind holds."

Silon cast a wary glance at the sky before returning her smile.

"I do hope so, my lady," he replied. "I've a busy few days ahead." The merchant had not spoken of his business in Syrannos, but her new ally Barin had hinted Silon was plotting a coup with the renegade desert warlord known as Barakani. Together they planned to bring down the sultan, overthrowing his tyrannical rule in Sedinadola and returning power to the tribal princes that ruled there long ago. A dangerous business, Barin had said, and she didn't doubt that either.

But though she wished him well Silon's plots did not concern Shallan. Once they had dropped the merchant off in the harbour; traded some goods, sought new sailors, and sampled some Permian fare; they would sail north to Kelwyn, restock, then continue up the coast until they rounded the cape of Fol and made for home territory.

There at a secluded place beyond Vangaris, she and her father could disembark safely. They'd make their way overland to Car Carranis by secret paths whilst Barin sailed north to Valkador, his island home.

It would doubtless prove a long voyage with pirates snapping at their heels and Caswallon's probing eyes watching the western water. Morwella's fleet was broken, and Kelthaine's warships commandeered by Caswallon. Rael the Cruel ruled the Western Ocean now.

Shallan wasn't fazed by the danger. She was still young—quick of mind and hale of body. And she had her horn and her intuition. That inner voice that always calmed her so. Shallan curled a half smile. She secretly studied the hard, sun-darkened face of the merchant and wondered what he was thinking.

"You risk much in your ventures, Silon," Shallan probed, watching as the silvery coastline neared. Above the pale sands, the white multitude of minarets and spires of the city appeared to float suspended in the blazing heat. Gulls and terns weaved and swept low hurrying out to meet them, their wan cries carrying far over sunbright water.

Silon turned to face her again. His shrewd jet beads softened.

"We all risk much in this game, Lady Shallan," he answered quietly. "But amongst the teeming streets of yonder city lies a chance. Just a chance... if things go to plan I can help turn the tide of this impending war in our favour. But it's tenuous—fragile. Our riskiest gambit lies with Zallerak and company in the desert."

Shallan nodded. She pictured the enigmatic bard in her mind and wondered why Corin disliked him so much.

"Who is this Zallerak—I've never heard of his like before? A bard and songsmith—but from where?" When Silon didn't respond she continued.

"He is evidently more than just a bard. But just who is he, Silon?"

"No one really knows," Silon replied with a dismissive wave of his right hand. His look was guarded. Shallan suspected that he was withholding information. That something about the bard troubled him too.

"Zallerak keeps his own counsel and follows his own reeds," Silon embellished. "But he is a powerful ally and we would be lost without him. After all, Lady Shallan, Zallerak is our only defence against Caswallon and Morak's sorcery, until we have remade the Tekara."

"Corin doesn't trust him." Her eyes followed the gulls as they swooped high above.

Beside her Silon laughed. "Corin an Fol does not trust anyone, least of all himself!"

"He is a good man." Shallan tried to keep her voice neutral but the merchant smiled nodding slowly.

"That he is. None better, and one day, my dear young lady, with your help he may come to realise it too."

"My help?" Shallan's face had reddened. "I do not understand your meaning, sir. What help can I give?"

"You already have. Now Corin has something to fight for. A reason to strive. And he needs purpose, his was a rough past without direction. Corin strays—always has. I've known that idiot a long time."

"What of my cousin, Queen Ariane? What happened between those two?"

"That I do not know, though I suspect little. They are fond of each other of course, and Ariane was vulnerable after losing Roman in Crenna. Lovers? I think not. Besides, the queen has a vow to withhold."

"What vow?" This was news to Shallan, her cousin playing so close a hand.

Silon shrugged away her question. "*Your* love will keep Corin focused. That's what matters. And he needs to be focused."

"You speak as though Corin is more important than anyone else—even Zallerak and the queen." Shallan was puzzled. "I thought he was only a hired hand," she struggled, "a trusted Longswordsman and nothing more."

Silon did not answer her at first. Instead his gaze drifted landward across to the distant palms lining the pale sandy coast. Nearer now. "The Silver Strand," he mused as if lost in thought. "Enchanting, is it not? Beguiling yet perilous." Silon turned towards her again and smiled.

"Corin an Fol is a paradox, my lady. Orphan, brawler and rebel rouser, haunted by a harrowing past. But there is nobility within—

I've seen it shine through several times. Corin doesn't know himself, you see—not really. And he's scared to delve deeper."

"I don't take your meaning. How is Corin noble? Surely he is a common hireling—strong, brave and loyal, but there are many thus."

"Not like him. Corin hides from his feelings, but his strength lies in those nagging doubts that always make him look so serious. I thought he was wasted as a common soldier in the Wolves when I first espied him during the Second Permian War. That hidden quality was why I offered him a contract. He proved an asset in the main. Corin is a thinker and he has a good heart despite his own misgivings. But there is more..."

"Go on."

Silon spread his tanned arms wide and sighed as if suddenly weary. "We are all pieces of a cosmic puzzle: Barin, Corin, you and I, even Zallerak—all of us are pieces on a board.

"From their lofty towers in the skies the gods watch our every move through the passage of time. Mostly they let us be. There are myriad other worlds and their unfathomable minds wander the universe at will.

"But every now and then a mortal appears that captures their interest and piques their curiosity. King Torro was one such in ancient times, Erun Cade (Kell) another. And Corin an Fol is also such a one."

"How is it that you know all this, Silon?" Shallan looked up suddenly as Fassof's yell announced they were closing on the harbour.

"I study the stars, Shallan—read the cards that translate their meaning. I have done so for years. Within that vast tapestry above lie the answers to every riddle."

Silon drew his cloak about his shoulders despite the heat.

"We are at the threshold of a titanic struggle between good and evil. Between the servants of Law and the machinations of Chaos—led by Old Night the enemy of all worlds. He who we do not name. The Urgolais are his servants, Caswallon too—though the fool knows it not."

"Whatever the outcome of this struggle the result shall be pivotal. It will resound across the heavens affecting the fragile balance on many dimensions. These are the highest stakes, Shallan.

"This will be the culmination. The third and final war of the gods. The severed head of the Evil One has awoken deep beneath the mountains of Yamondo—so King Ulani tells me and I believe him."

Shallan had no idea who King Ulani was but she was captivated by Silon's words.

"Ulani rules eastern Yamondo. It's very far from here, south beyond the desert wastes lying at the very heart of Ansu, this troubled world of ours.

"Yamondo has been tainted by a canker of late. A creeping evil, Ulani says. Its source that terrible mountain somewhere amongst the steaming jungle regions in the west of that land. They say Old Night's head was incarcerated there after the Second War of the Gods. But He wakens—wants revenge."

Silon folded his arms and chewed his lower lip. "Even as we struggle against Caswallon and his warlock masters, the gods above us will be battling each other in heavenly conflict."

Shallan shook her head, confused. The answer had been so much more than she expected.

"But what has all this to do with Corin?" she pressed.

"Everything and nothing," came the elusive answer. "Corin has been chosen by the gods, Shallan. Don't ask me how I know this— I just do. Too many things have happened to that boy. Uncanny things. Like King Torro before him, Corin is the fulcrum. He is the central hub around which the wheel spins, and it is spinning quicker every moment. Corin comes from noble stock. At the moment he is hiding from that knowledge. One day he will have to face up to it and then he will change.

"You can rest assured immortals will interfere when they can, aiding him and assailing him both. Oroonin, Elanion and Her daughters the Fates; vain Telcanna the Sky God, down here in the desert where He holds sway. And Old Night through His minions and slaves.

"They will be watching Corin an Fol. They know he alone holds the balance in his fragile erratic fingers. They will meddle when they can. This I have known for some time. Corin's destiny holds the key."

"And I thought he was just a freebooter—a loyal hireling."

Shallan was lost for words. She wondered what manner of man it was that had strolled with her so awkwardly through the merchant's gardens. That had held her close and then so passionately taken her beneath that starry, blissful night.

"That he is. Though what Corin will become, who can say. I can guess. You see, I know who Corin's real father is, and I'm sure in time you will too.

"The wheel turns!" Silon's gaze softened, seeing the alarm on the girl's face. He smiled, placed a placating arm on her shoulder. "Do not fret. One thing I believe ardently; it is not Corin's destiny to die in the desert. You will see him again, Lady Shallan."

"I hope so."

Shallan looked up, hearing sudden noises. "Ah," Silon announced, "it seems we are entering the harbour of Syrannos."

Shallan watched Fassof skilfully steer clear of the harbour's rocky arm. Ahead lay a colourful jumble of sails and painted hulls. These were all sizes, bobbing to and fro as their mooring lines tautened and slackened in the late afternoon breeze.

The Starlight Wanderer's crew had furled the sails and tied off gaskets to hold them in place. They were now seated on benches sweating and heaving at their long oars, rowing steadily over to a wooden jetty jutting out from the main quay.

As she looked across at their dock, Shallan saw people everywhere dressed in all manner of garb; shouting, cursing, and laughing and doing wily deals with each other.

A cacophony of mayhem. Dogs barked and donkeys bellowed and kicked, whilst squawking fowl scattered and flourished feathers beneath their hoofs.

Strange spicy smells wafted across the water, making her hungry. Cart wheels clattered on cobbled stone. Women bickered and men swore as they struggled with heavy goods. There were grubby children running here and there. Everywhere was chaos, bright colours, hubbub and stench. Away in the distance came the scrape of saw on wood, carpenters erecting a platform that looked like a gallows. Shallan crinkled her nose. She hoped this stay wouldn't prove a long one.

"Welcome to Permio, milady." Captain Barin had joined her at the prow. Silon had just retired below deck to prepare for his jump ashore.

"I suggest you stay aboard my ship, lass. Else some greasy merchant tries buying you. We are no longer in the Four Kingdoms," he told her. "Anything is possible here!"

"That I do believe, Barin."

Duke Tomais had joined them on deck, scowling at the sights, smells and noises of the harbour. The duke shook his head in consternation at the shouting and clamour rebounding across the quayside. He looked visibly shocked, thinking of Vangaris's ordered harbour and neat mooring arrangements. Before the fires of invasion of course.

The moment Barin's men jumped ashore to tie off, eager hawkers crowded round them like flies, gabbling loudly in their ears. Fassof winced when a fat man arrived yelling oily expletives and peddling a battered trolley of sweetmeats and cheeses.

"Bugger off!" Fassof yelled but the man persisted stoically.

"How long are we staying here, captain?" the sweating mate asked, ushering the peddler away with an irritated shove. "I said bugger off!"

"As long as it takes to shift some of the goods we acquired in Raleen," answered Barin. "And I'm sending Cogga to the taverns to get some fresh crew."

"Is that wise?"

"Maybe not, but where else will we get the help you're always nagging me about? We've a long voyage ahead, Fass. Oh and keep an eye out for rubies in the markets. Marigold is fond of Permian rubies."

"I know—but they are expensive."

"I'll refund you."

"You didn't last time." Fassof growled at the hawker who was still lingering expectantly at the end of the dock. "You still here?"

"Just leaving, good sir—I'll be close if you change your mind."

"Just piss off."

"Thank you."

Barin watched Fassof fade into the crowd, then turned when someone coughed in his ear. Cogga stood there with the two recruits, Taic and Sveyn. The boys had been keeping a low profile since leaving Port Sarfe. But they'd pulled their weight, so Fassof had told Barin.

"You ready?" Barin asked Cogga.

"Aye. And I'm taking these tossers with me in case there's a scrap."

"Make sure they don't cause one."

"We're reformed characters, Uncle," Taic grinned at Barin.

Barin ignored him. "Return before dark, Cogga. I don't want to spend too long in this shithole. Soon as Silon's gone we're away."

"Will do. Come on, you pair." Cogga and the two younger sailors shoved and grumbled their way down the jetty and like Fassof, soon faded into the crowd.

Barin scratched his eyebrow and brushed a fly from his forearm. He watched in disgust as three ungainly beasts with humps on their backs deposited steamy lumps of filth on the cobbles and spat mucus at each other, whilst their owners (ignoring them) squabbled over coin. Barin hated Permio.

Silon's plan was to wait until dark before slipping ashore, lest prying eyes ask questions. Once the merchant had departed the brigantine would slip out of the harbour as quietly as was possible.

Syrannos, like most Permian cities, was best avoided after dark. Even the big men of Valkador would be in danger here were they to linger dockside.

Barin urged Shallan to go beneath deck but she would have none of it, laughing instead as she saw Cogga and the other two surrounded by a swarm of angry peddlers as they made their way to the nearest tavern.

"You wouldn't really sell me, Captain Barin, would you?" Shallan teased.

Duke Tomais looked at her sharply, hearing that.

"Shallan, get below!" the duke scolded, and reluctantly she heeded his words. Barin had spoken light-heartedly enough but Shallan accepted the crew would be in more danger if she were spotted on deck. Permian slavers prized northern women higher than their own. Shallan's was a rare beauty too. Nevertheless it rankled her to so meekly obey her father's wishes.

At least it was cooler below deck for a change. A helpful breeze drifted down through the master's sumptuous cabin from the open hatch above. Shallan found herself surveying the ornate tapestries draping the timber walls of the cabin.

Strange beasts patrolled scarlet forests, while pointed snow-clad mountains reared above. *Valkador*, Shallan thought, *must be an amazing place.* All ice and snow—no wonder the Northmen were hardy. And small wonder they hated this Permian heat.

Had Shallan known the hunt scenes on some of the tapestries depicted the forest of Enromer in northern Leeth her opinion of them might have altered. Valkador and Leeth were separate sides to the same coin. The same people, were it not for the feud.

Ruagon the portly cook emerged, grinning whilst handing her out a plate of piping fish fresh from the harbour. This Shallan ate gratefully and waited rather restlessly for evening's gloom to approach.

Time dragged in the cabin but at last evening arrived and noise abated. Outside the air grew cooler and the manic bustle of the harbour dwindled into quieter chat. The calm ended abruptly when Cogga returned with the two younger men dragging a screaming yelling creature between them. Shallan couldn't help herself, she'd clambered back on deck to witness the kerfuffle. She stood wide eyed beside her father. Both watched in silence as the scene on deck unfolded.

"What the fuck is that?" Fassof demanded. He'd got back an hour ago. He'd fretted and cussed beside Barin and was about to send a search party for Cogga and crew when they returned. And not empty-handed.

"I said what is...*that?*"

"Crew," replied Cogga. "As are these two behind." He motioned to where two dark-skinned, evil-looking men skulked behind Taic and Sveyn. Despite their unsavoury looks no one noticed them. It was the spitting, hissing, kicking, swearing, bony, black-skinned girl with the wild smoky hair that drew all eyes. "We're back to full complement, captain," announced Cogga as though this was something to be pleased about. "There wasn't a lot of choice," he added, seeing the bleak expression on Barin's face.

"Tell me everything," Barin demanded as they dragged the deranged-looking girl below decks lest her racket draw attention to the ship.

At that point Silon appeared from his cabin wearing a dark hooded leather tunic, which shrouded his features and covered the long curved sword at his side. The merchant shared a few friendly words with Shallan and her father before wishing them well. He nodded to Barin, glanced quizzically at the black girl still struggling between Taic and Sveyn, and then peeped his head above deck.

Silon watched and waited in silence for a moment until satisfied all was clear. He waved back at those watching from the cabin and heaved his body through the hatch. Within moments Silon had negotiated the jetty and slipped ashore. A flitting shadow, Silon's silhouette vanished swiftly from the quayside.

Chapter 18

A Change of Course

To say that their search for new crew had been a challenge was
an understatement. Taic nursed a black eye, whilst Sveyn had a small
chunk missing in his left ear. Both gifts from the she-lynx they'd res-
cued from the gallows. You'd think she'd be grateful. Instead she'd
kicked Cogga, tried poking Taic's eye out with a broken-nailed finger,
and then bit that chunk out of Sveyn's ear. Taic liked rough women
but this girl was something else.

They'd started with the taverns and inns. No luck. Most had
been empty (the sultan disliked taverns apparently, so soldiers were
always raiding them and arresting those within) and those few occupied contained wastrels that looked incapable of lifting an oar, let
alone climbing out on a yard in a stiff force niner.

Cogga had been on the verge of quitting and returning to ship
when he saw the gallows. The carpenters had finished and three ab-
ject figures stood dreary behind a huge shaven-headed fellow with
an axe.

Cogga deeming it worth a try, and believing Permians would

sell their mothers for the right price, took to strolling across and addressing the small crowd gathered below the scaffold. "Who's in charge here?"

"I am," answered three men in the crowd, and, "me," the grim lad with the axe above. Finally a voice with some hint of authority cut in with. "What do you want, Northman?"

Cogga turned to see a skinny shaven-headed man in a yellow robe glaring up at him. "I want two of those prisoners for crew. I'll pay good coin."

"Forget it. They are condemned for prompt execution by the city magister himself." Cogga didn't reply and the smaller man scratched his ear. "How much coin?"

Sveyn hoisted the small sack he'd stowed inside his shirt. "That much," Cogga said as the shaven-headed official's eyes gleamed seeing the sparkle of gold as Sveyn loosened the sack.

"Maybe something can be arranged," the official said. "Sixty percent and forty percent," the man addressed the axeman above.

"I'd prefer it the other way round," grumbled the executioner but nodded his agreement. "But what about this one?" He kicked the scrawny tangle of dark sinew and bones kneeling between the other two captives. "Hardly seems worth bloodying my axe on that scrawny neck. This third prisoner Taic suddenly realised was a girl (it had been impossible to tell up to now).

"We'll take her too," said Taic.

"What?" Sveyn said.

"Are you mad?" Cogga added. The executioner shrugged, leaned his axe against gantry and folded his arms. "Your call, boss."

The official grinned, seeing some amusement in the situation. "You can have that one for free," he smiled. Cogga, glaring at Taic, had bid Sveyn hand over the sack of coin to the official. The small man stared at the contents within then took a coin out and bit it. "Deal done," he said, still smiling. "Cut them loose!" The official tossed a small amount of coins on the ground to appease the onlookers, who were grumbling about missing the show. Minutes later Cogga and his helpers led the freed prisoners back toward the markets and the waiting ship.

That was when their problems started.

Her name was Zukei, the executioner had informed them whilst polishing his axe and wrapping it in leather cloth. "Be careful with her."

Taic hadn't grasped his meaning until they approached the jetty and the silent, pliant girl lashed out with sudden fury, kicking, punching, biting and spitting. It took Cogga, Taic and Sveyn, plus the other two prisoners to get Zukei under control. Which was understandable considering who she was. But then it wasn't until much later that they found that out.

***

Shallan watched on while the crew struggled to stow the newly purchased goods and made ready to depart. Cogga was already instructing the rough-looking new recruits in sail craft. Of the wild-haired girl there was no sign. Barin had ordered they lock her in the hold fast, or else he'd hurl her overboard. He looked furious about the business and was muttering something to Shallan's father, when Fassof's thin freckly visage silhouetted the sky above.

"What now?" Barin's frown deepened seeing the worry on the mate's face as he jumped down from the hatch.

"Permian war galley, big ugly bugger full of soldiers, currently entering the harbour."

Barin mouthed an oath. "How many soldiers?"

"A lot... I don't know. Two hundred maybe. It's a slaver—largest one I've ever seen."

"We must warn Silon!" Duke Tomais cut in.

"Too late for that," muttered Barin. "Besides, Silon can look after himself. This delays our leaving a while. Do not fear, sir Duke, soon as the Permians have vacated their vessel we'll slip away unnoticed."

Shallan looked at her father's worried face as Barin and the mate crept on deck to watch the lumbering galley enter the harbour. "I would fain see this ship," said her father, and Shallan nodded. She wanted to see it too. Carefully the two of them raised their heads above the main hatch.

As they waited the sound of oars approached, dipping and rising quietly in perfect rhythm, and then as they watched the approaching ship rounded the harbour's arm.

If ship was the right word for such a monstrosity.

It was a huge wooden galley, almost twice as long as *The Starlight Wanderer*, and at least three times the width.

It was ungainly tall, built square like a castle, with half score of turrets and parapets. The galley looked top-heavy and unseaworthy. Shallan (who knew a little about maritime matters having grown up in Vangaris) questioned how such a leviathan could sit so easily upon the water.

The vessel possessed three rows of decks: the lower two enclosed. From these the sound of whips cracking and drums penetrated the night. Shallan shuddered, thinking of the poor souls imprisoned down there. She deplored the concept of slavery but had never encountered it before as it was banned in the Four Kingdoms.

Crimson-cloaked soldiers paced about on the top deck carrying long spears, their faces concealed beneath full-face helmets that glinted in the moonlight. Above the soldiers, near naked sailors sprang lithely from rope to rope. There were so many. Shallan's eyes widened at the sight, it reminded her of a circus that had visited Vangaris when she was a child.

"Filthy slavers!" cursed her father angrily, making her jump. "There are probably some of our people chained below those decks, daughter. It vexes me so!"

It vexed Shallan too.

Permian slavers were not a common sight this far east. Most tended to trade goods and wage their wars in the mysterious lands beyond Golt. They were despised by the sailors of the Four Kingdoms and generally stayed away from their waters, lest the patrol ships stationed at Port Wind or Calprissa attack them—not to mention the Assassin's sharks who would revel at the chance of bringing such a monster into tow, nor would they have qualms about slavery, but rather take over custodianship of the unfortunates and sell them on. These huge Permian galleys were shallow-keeled, making them unwieldy in rougher seas, and thus lacking the fleet manoeuvrability of the northern vessels.

The large crimson triangular sails were being hauled in as Shallan watched. Swarthy sailors worked as overseers, mates and bosuns pointed about and swore.

Suddenly Tomais gasped beside her. The duke's eyes recognised the flapping banner on the foremost sail. A golden serpent on crimson background. The emblem of the Sultan of Permio himself.

"The sultan must be on board!" Tomais exclaimed. "They wouldn't fly his colours else. We had best lie low, my dearest. Captain Barin will want to think things through." Shallan nodded and reluctantly jumped down to join her father below.

Several minutes later Barin returned to his cabin and hastily poured himself a flagon of ale. "Moon's rising," he frothed. "We'll be able to slip away soon; most of the soldiers have departed with their royal passenger. Our leavetaking shouldn't cause much of a stir," he told them.

"What brings the sultan this far from Sedinadola?" Tomais enquired, gratefully accepting a tankard of ale from the master.

"I don't know, sir Duke," responded Barin. "But it worries me. Well is it known how much that fat greasy whoreson hates leaving his harem in the royal palace at Sedinadola. Perhaps rumours of insurrection have stirred his slimy flesh. I wish Silon had waited a bit longer, but we cannot help that now."

Barin had watched the royal palanquin carried ashore by four muscular naked slaves, swaying in unison whilst supporting their royal burden—hidden behind crimson drapes.

The palanquin was followed by strange-looking priests in dreary yellow robes. After these marched two columns of crimson-cloaked guardsmen; polished round shields of dazzling steel slung across their backs, at their sides broad tulwars, and short spears angled over their shoulders. The sultan's elite. They always wore crimson, whilst his regulars were garbed in purple. These were feared men in Syrannos.

Barin waited until they had entered the city and were lost from sight, then motioned his men to ready the ship for departure. Oars were carefully untied from their racks. Quietly the crew took their seats at the benches. Away to the right, some hundred yards, the great bulk of the sultan's ship lurked like a dozing sea monster.

The full moon and the odd stray cat watched them cast off. Aside from these, the city's focus was on the |sultan's unexpected arrival. Shallan stole another peep through the deck hatch as her father had retired. She watched as the sultan's galley slipped to stern. Nothing stirred on its decks. But below them Shallan heard coughing followed by a curse. The whip answered, she almost felt its abrupt lick and was filled with sorrow for the prisoners chained down there.

Her father was right; doubtless some of them would be Morwellans—captured and sold on by traitors like Hagan Delmorier. Relief flooded through Shallan when at last they cleared the harbour. Tired and saddened, she retired below.

Ahead churned the rollers of the open sea, dark and broiling beneath that watchful moon. It wasn't long before the city lights and empty beaches of the Silver Strand had faded to stern.

Again they were alone on the ocean.

It was calm and very still. Barin rubbed his eyes whilst fingering the wheel. He felt weary and edgy, and looked up sensing wrongness in the quietening skies. Cogga approached him and Barin offered him a begrudging nod. He was still annoyed with Cogga.

"I don't like this quiet," Barin said. "It's ominous, foreboding."

"That it is." Cogga shuffled his feet. "I'm sorry we cocked up. That girl."

"Who the fuck is she? And why is she on my ship? Has this

anything to do with my nephew?"

"They were going to cut her head off. We had already purchased the other two when Taic offered to buy her too."

Barin groaned and rubbed his eyes. "How much coin did you part with?"

"All of it. Look, Captain, those two villains will shape up quickly with Fassof growling at them. They're Permian fishermen who fell foul of the magister in Syrannos. They're workers and they know the sea."

"What of the girl?"

"She is something else entirely. It took all five of us to stop her running off."

"Tell Taic to haul her scrawny arse up here. I'll speak to both of them while I'm in the mood." Cogga departed and minutes later a sheepish Taic arrived and behind him lurked the black girl, her expression hostile and wild.

"Relax, I'm not going to eat you," Barin told her and her glare darkened to a vitriolic sulk. He shrugged and turned to Taic.

"You, nephew, are a boil on my arse."

"Sorry, Uncle," Taic scratched his own arse and grinned. "Things got a bit out of hand."

"They always do with you. Now go away before I hit you with something sharp and heavy. And, Taic."

"What?"

"You're banned from the ale barrel for three whole days."

"Thank you, Uncle." Taic sloped off to join Sveyn at the prow.

Barin turned to the girl, who was watching him in silence.

"They tell me you are called Sukei."

"Zukei," the girl croaked. Her accent was strange. She looked to be about twenty, though it was hard to tell as her face was lined and scarred. Her hair was thick and curly, a smoky grey-black, and her eyes, dark angry saucers. There was no fear in that gaze. Only anger and hostility. She was tall, skinny but wiry and her stance showed that she knew how to fight. But then Barin already knew that. Zukei wore shabby brown trousers and a torn shirt of dirty linen.

"So?" Barin reached across and offered her his ale. Zukei glared at it for a moment then took it in her bony hands and downed the contents with a greedy gulp. Barin took that as an encouraging sign.

"Are we going to get along, you and me?"

Zukei shrugged. "I've nowhere to go. No future back on land." The girl's voice was husky, even attractive in a weird sort of way. "I'm no sailor but I can learn. I learn fast. And I have other skills I can pass on."

"Fighting skills? Yes, I heard you're a handful," Barin smiled. "Where are you from, Sukei?"

"It's Zukei," the girl answered. "Get it right. I'm from Yamondo and have been seeking my father up here in Permio."

"Is he a merchant?"

"No, he is a king."

Barin didn't know how to respond to that.

"You have a nice smile," said the girl and then without further word left him with his thoughts.

Barin yawned and rubbed his beard. Why was life so complicated? He shrugged and returned his thoughts to their present situation. The night was treacherously bright; Barin witnessed the tension building amongst the crew, both new lads and old. He shrugged. It was time to go home; this had proved a long trip and one that had taken its toll on captain and men. Barin thought about his daughters and smiled. Same age as Sukei, though worlds apart.

Not long now.

The men stowed their oars when they felt the first swell lift the hull, then at Fassof's command the sails were set. Their progress was slow. They had to beat against a nor-wester that stiffened keen as the night wore on.

***

Shallan woke with a start. The storm had come upon them suddenly. A loud crack of thunder split the night, making her shudder

in alarm. Outside men shouted and cursed whilst beneath her, the
bunk rolled to and fro in sickening motion.

Duke Tomais appeared green -aced at her door. "Are you alright, Shallan?" her father asked. "We appear to have encountered
a storm!"

"Yes, Father," she answered, gripping the inner cabin rail, her
nightgown wrapped around her shoulders.

"You had best wait here; I'll go see how we fare."

Her father's expression was strained as he staggered above deck.
Shallan's cabin was lurching, the rolling motion making her stomach
heave. She summoned calm and waited until the duke returned.

Moments later Tomais appeared with Captain Barin. Both men
soaking wet and her father looked quite ill. Barin seemed his usual
ebullient self.

"A bit of a blow, milady," he shouted over the din. "They're not
uncommon in these parts. I felt something brewing in the night.
Don't worry we've fared through much worse!"

But the storm raged on through the night, increasing in strength
and violence. The wind shrieked: it tore a large rent in the mainsail
and Barin was forced to change tack.

Now they were heading due west, running before the howling
breath of Borian the Wind God. Borian was not a kindly deity nor
was His brother, Sensuata Lord of the Oceans. Both these immortals
worked against them tonight.

Lightning cast spears through the blackness above as the Sky
God Telcanna joined in. Thunder cracked and boomed. Again and
again, Shallan emptied the contents of her stomach into a basin. She
prayed to Sensuata to abate His watery wrath, and Borian to ease
back His violent blow. But both the Sea God and His stormy brother
were unremitting.

The dark waves rose higher and higher forming watery towers,
they smote the timber deck, sweeping men from their feet and hurling them at the rails.

Barin's crew struggled valiantly, furling and reefing sail, running and slipping on the rain-washed timbers. Then before they could get to it the mainsail was shredded to rags by a great bellow of wind.

The Starlight Wanderer floundered helpless at the mercy of the storm.

Barin clung tenaciously to the wheel, turning, spinning and heaving on the spokes, his massive arms soaked and bulging under the strain—anything to avert the swells battering the brig. A man fell overboard, his cries lost in the night. One of the new lads, there was nothing that could be done for him.

And still the storm raged.

For three days Sensuata and Borian assaulted them. Barin, tenacious as a boar in a pit and grimly exhausted, battled throughout. Shallan had never seen such redoubt. But the trader was in a sorry state: three sails were in tatters, the great sea eagle flapped wildly above as if trying to escape. Though no one else was killed, six crew had sustained substantial injuries; still Barin counted them fortunate when the wind finally eased on the dawn of the fourth day.

Shallan felt wretched and filthy. She staggered above deck for the first time since the storm had come, gulped in some fresh air. She was weak from lack of food, water and sleep and still felt sick to the bone. Her father the duke had mercifully been able to sleep. Shallan had not been so fortunate, riding the torrent of the storm wedged in her cabin, cursing and swearing like a fishwife, then retching enthusiastically until her throat hurt and her stomach cramped.

High above, outriding stormdragons fled east occluding the rising sun. Slowly, as day waxed clear the waves levelled and wind dropped to a spiteful breeze.

Ahead lay a rocky coastline of tangled dark forest and tumbling, chiming streams. Barin told Shallan they had been driven the entire length of the Silver Strand, miles upon miles. Way past Sedinadola and were hard against the coast of Golt.

"I do not know these waters," Barin admitted to her. "But we've little choice, save to heave to and find a safe harbour for repairs. At least there's timber on that shore. I fear our journey is delayed, milady."

Shallan helped the men clear debris from the decks, despite her ailing father's insistence she remain below and regain her strength. They were all exhausted including Barin.

"I've never known such a storm," he told her. "It's as though Sensuata and Borian were fighting each other and Telcanna edging on both sides," he said, shaking his matted sea-drenched head. He was doubly grumpy, one of the ale kegs had burst in the galley, flooding most the cabin and ruining his expensive rugs. Ruagon was still struggling with the mess.

Shallan nodded weakly, thinking of her conversation with Silon four nights past. The gods were readying for war. It wasn't a comforting thought. Telcanna, Borian, Sensuata, all hostile—only Elanion favoured mankind. Then there was the Huntsman and the Dark One no one named. All in all, a rather unsavoury bunch.

Eventually they spied a deep bay and heaved to. Barin sent men ashore to forage and Shallan helped her father up onto the deck. They had survived the storm but it had cost them.

Chapter 19

The Note

Syrannos at night. Silon flitted from building to building, a dark shadow in a darker night. He stole between wooden storehouses that reeked of fish and cluttered the quayside. The taverns were shut at this hour, the sultan having placed a curfew on the city to stop the frequent killings that occurred after nightfall.

Hungry dogs roamed otherwise empty streets, one showed its teeth at Silon, but he threw it a scrap of meat he had brought from the ship and it skulked off into the night.

Silon hurried into a backstreet, stepping over piles of filth and excrement, pulling his hood down over his nose to block out the stench. This was the poor quarter of Syrannos. Life was cheap here; murders a common occurrence among the mud-built hovels. A dockside shanty, it sprawled haphazard and filthy below the white walls separating it from the upper city.

Silon wove through the stinking labyrinth in haste. He had no wish to linger here, but must find the place he had discovered two years ago when being pursued by cutthroats.

Fortunately his memory served him well. Silon recognised a building with a crumbling gable leaning precariously against the wide bastion of the city walls and itself accessible via a tall olive tree. Silon blessed his luck—repairs in the lower quarter were tardy and infrequent, but you never knew.

Silon approached the tree, reaching up and grabbing a low branch he hauled himself up until he stood panting on the flimsy roof of the dwelling.

Beneath him, dark and silent, lower Syrannos bunched around the harbour. Silon could just make out the masts of *The Starlight Wanderer* in the moonlight. They should leaving soon—not like Barin to linger.

Tenuously Silon crossed the leaning gable and accessed the wall face. He glanced up at the sheer climb confronting him. It was hard to see anything in this light but Silon knew they were here somewhere.

At last he located the footholds he had hurriedly carved out with his knife on his last visit here. Faint scrapes allowing just enough purchase for three tough fingers followed by a nimble well-worn boot.

With infinite care Silon heaved himself up the twenty or so feet. At last gaining the top, he rolled over the parapet, pitched quietly onto the vacant stone platform that formed a narrow walkway below the ramparts. That was the easy part.

Silon waited there in silence for a moment. Nothing stirred.

Satisfied that he hadn't been spotted, Silon hurried along towards the distant gates. During the daylight hours these opened on the upper city, though now as was to be expected, they were locked in place with a lone sentinel at watch.

Beyond the gates a broad palisade led up the steep hill to the great domed temple ahead. Voices drifted out of the guardhouse as Silon approached. He saw three men sitting at table playing dice. Silently Silon slipped by. Once clear he jumped down onto the road, rolling his body into a ball as he landed. He was now in the upper city. If caught here he could expect to be flayed or worse.

Beyond the gates the lone sentry lolled lazily on his spear. Silon blew a sigh of relief. He hadn't been seen.

He took no time distancing himself from the guardhouse. Now for the next task—the difficult bit. Silon had to access the temple of the Sky God where Barakani would be waiting. He entered a wide street leading up, as all roads did, toward the temple. He ran.

Inside the walls, Syrannos was a complete contrast to the mishmash of the poor quarter. Here the streets were wide, tree-lined and ordered. They columned ever upwards in parallel lines towards the domed temple crowning the hill, dominating the other buildings with its pale gleaming minarets thrusting up into the dark—so many twisted spikes piercing the night sky.

Silon didn't know this city as well as Cappel Cormac but he had been here several times, when his cohort was unable to make the longer journey to the great city at the Narion's delta.

Barakani kept a secret camp close by on the Silver Strand. This gave him easy access to the city, enabling him to slip inside the walls from time to time, acquire information, and court new allies in the ensuing struggle against the Sultanate.

It was a risky business. Though the sultan himself seldom left Sedinadola, it was not uncommon for his elite crimson guard to wander the streets at will, searching for enemies of their ruler, (anyone caught out of place fitted that category). Silon hastened up toward the distant temple keeping close to the palms fanning the edge of the road.

It was getting late. A full moon had arisen to shine directly above his head. Its eerie glow cast silvery light on the tiled roofs of the houses. These were well spaced either side of the palm-shaded street. They were big villas with wide verandas and ornate gardens, about which the air clicked with the sound of cicadas and night thrush. The chime and tinkle of running water came from somewhere close by.

These were the sumptuous homes of the rulers of Syrannos,

mostly administrators and wealthy merchants, the magister's mansion amongst them. Shadows of trees hung low over clear pools reflecting the moonlight, while fountains trickled and chimed through the jasmine-perfumed gardens.

Directly ahead of Silon and terminating the road, were the ornate doors of the great temple of Telcanna the Sky God. He it was who was most worshipped by the Permians. It was a magnificent building of polished white marble walls and red mosaic floors. Silon paced swiftly toward the entrance—no time to waste. Seeing no one, he warily approached the great doors, inched one open and then silently entered within.

The smell of incense greeted him immediately, that and the crackle of candle flame. Silon saw yellow-robed priests kneeling in prayer by the stone altar ahead. This place was sacrosanct. It was death to enter here without permit. But it was the only place where men such as he could conduct their affairs safe from whispering walls. Only the priests of Telcanna, administrative elite, or high ranking soldiers of the sultan were allowed access at all times. Silon was aware he was breaking every covenant in this city—the thought wasn't comforting so he didn't dwell on it.

On sacred days the temple was open to all. During such times the meanest peddler could rub shoulders with lords of the city. But this wasn't a sacred day—worse, it was night time.

After dark the temple was frequented by the devout chosen. Wealthy and ambitious, they came to share secrets, plotting murder amid prayers in the secluded cloisters, and courting favour amongst their, even wealthier paeans. Such were the way of things in High Syrannos.

Barakani (guised as one such highborn) often came here to pay homage to the God. While he chanted prayer the old fox would listen to the whispers coming from the candlelit recesses lining the sides of the temple. Silon was new to the temple but his ally had left precise directions.

Silon passed beneath the huge chamber; above him a thousand

candles flickered and winked beneath the arching, lofty, ivory and mahogany vaulted ceiling. This was gilded both inside and out, braced by elaborately carved pillars parading the chamber. The pillars—six in all—were covered in intricate paintings depicting Telcanna of the Skies.

A tall priest glanced up to challenge Silon as he walked by, his head bowed in prayer.

"All praise to the bright one," Silon whispered, "I am here from Cappel on divine business." Silon handed the parchment over from the fold in his cloak where he'd kept it stowed. Barakani's forgery was good.

The priest's eyes remained hostile, but he returned the docket and resumed his mantra, cupping skinny hands to his bald head, walking forward and ignoring the merchant. Silon let out a long slow breath. He didn't like being here.

It was approaching midnight. Ahead by the concaves the priests of Telcanna were gathering for their hourly rituals. They knelt in front of the altar, gripping coloured beads and uttering words of humble prayer. All were clad in simple ochre robes held together by a scarlet tassel.

Silon walked on ignoring their monotonous chants until he reached the far wall. To his right the wide altar glistened with trickling water and carved statues of the gods watched him in silence. All were honoured here, though Telcanna ruled supreme, being lord of the desert skies.

Silon saw Elanion's green cowled features amongst them and uttered a small prayer to his own goddess, though Her eyes seldom looked this far south.

Silon glanced into the gloom, discerned the small entrance to the cloister he had been seeking. Third on the right before last column—the nook he sought came into view. Hood pulled over his head, Silon stepped within, quietly pulling the scarlet velvet curtain across to hide him from prying eyes.

The room was musty, damp smelling and cramped but it had served Barakani well in the past, being a place where he and cohorts could communicate at will.

It was also empty.

Silon frowned; he had expected the desert lord to be waiting for him and was taken aback by his absence. This wasn't good. Barakani was nothing if not reliable. Silon took a slow breath—*must remain calm, evaluate situation.*

Moments passed in silence. Ten minutes, perhaps twenty? Nothing.

Despite his iron control Silon became restless. Barakani was never late. It had been the warlord who had proposed this clandestine meeting stating it urgent.

Something untoward must have happened. Silon seated himself quietly on a stone stool, one of three residing in the room. He waited, feeling increasingly agitated.

Much depended on their meeting this night—he had news for Barakani too.

Still no one came. Silon got up to stretch and then noticed the folded parchment half hidden beneath a copper urn.

A note—but left by whom? It had to be Barakani.

Silon reached over and freed it, opening the folded parchment in haste to pore over the contents. The merchant held a candle close to study the manuscript. At once he recognised the clear hand of Barakani. The words were in archaic Permian, unreadable by most but Silon could decipher them easily. The merchant was a master of many tongues, in this business you needed to be. The note was short—succinct.

Silon, greeting,

Be warned the sultan has got word. I suspect from Caswallon. His slave galley has left Sedinadola bound hither, with a squad of his elite crimson guard on board.

It is no longer safe in the city; seek out my camp on the Strand.

The time is almost here. Telcanna guard you.

Barakani.

Silon shoved the parchment up his sleeve and turned to go. Too late. Footsteps coming his way! Voices, soldiers by their tone. Silon closed his eyes, he was trapped in a noose and the rope was tightening fast. The thud of feet was closer now.

Boots scraped the corridor outside. Someone swore, the soldiers were coming this way. Refusing to panic Silon glanced above, noticed the low beams framed a hidden attic, its small door unbarred.

A chance—I've still got a chance.

With the aid of a stool Silon's fingers could just brush the ceiling. He stretched out precariously on tiptoe, the stool rocking beneath him, at last grabbing the hatch handle and pulling it toward him. The hatch swung open and Silon heaved his body up through the tight aperture, rolling out of view and silently closing the hatch just as three crimson guard entered below. His ear to the attic floor, Silon lay deathly still and listened to their words.

"The rebel leader is somewhere in the city, we may be sure of it," growled a deep voice laden with authority. "We'll scour the streets until we have him and his followers in our grasp."

"I think we're too late," whispered another voice, cruel sounding with a lisp. "That Barakani's a slippery fucker; he's probably got word by now and sneaked out into the desert."

"How will he have got word, Gamesh?" asked a third voice, younger.

"Same way we did," muttered the lisping Gamesh. "Spies. Whole sodding deserts full of 'em."

"Hold that tongue lest I cut it out!" (The leader again—the first voice).

"Soon they'll all be crow bait," he growled. "Skin flayed off their backs and their limbs removed. It's the only way to deal with spies and traitors."

"You got to catch 'em first," hissed Gamesh, undeterred by the other's threat. "If our royal bloater hadn't insisted in joining us with his cursed eunuchs we'd have been here earlier and sprung the trap."

"You really should watch your tongue, Gamesh!" warned the first voice. "One day soon the sultan will have it on a plate."

"Only if you tell him, Migen," responded Gamesh with a sneer.

"And who's to say I won't—weasel that you are."

"We had best search this place all the same," whispered the younger voice, which seemed more nervous than the other two.

"No point, he's slipped the net," growled Migen. "Gamesh is right about that much. Still, Barakani's running out of hiding places in the city and that foul spy creature informed our master of his camp's whereabouts close to the sea."

"Aye, we're to send a hundred men there at first light," laughed Gamesh. "By noon the rebel's camp will be reduced to cinders. Barakani's pathetic insurrection will prove shortlived indeed."

"Then what?" enquired the young voice.

"We go south," growled Migen.

"Why south?"

"Because the sultan wants us to, you twat." Gamesh's unpleasant voice sounded alarmingly close. Silon tried not to breathe as painful cramp seized his leg. He willed it away.

"His Nibs got word of intruders in the desert," said Migen. "Fools were spotted by Sulimo who said they were bound for Agmandeur. But I know where their real destination is. The Crystal Mountains."

"Are they mad? How do you know this?" Gamesh and the youngster asked in unison.

"I listen when my betters talk," responded Migen with a superior snort. "That goblin creature—the spy—entered the royal palace last week when I was on watch.

"Gave me the creeps it did. But it held audience with his Ugliness. Told him about these villains—a nasty bunch apparently, especially the one with a bow. Seems they are wanted by its master, some warlock in the north."

"Warlock...?" The young one sounded worried.

"Yes, warlock—they're all fucking witches up there. What else is there to do in the freezing dark? It's always winter up there, so they say."

"But the Crystal Mountains lie close to the realm of the Ty-Tander! Hundreds of leagues across the desert!" snorted Gamesh. "Only lunacy would send them there!"

"Well, you had best prepare yourselves. For once we have tidied up this business with the rebels; it's into the desert we go, my brave lads!" Migen's gruff voice sounded smug as he spoke.

"Anyway, enough of this idle speculation. We had best be moving on, the big boss wants the whole city searched by dawn. If we don't apprehend the impostor we'll be on fatigues for a month. Pots and pans with naught but sand to clean them. And latrine duty to boot. Come on!"

The sound of heels scraping stone and boot treads walking away. They'd gone—at least for the moment.

Silon mouthed a curse. Barakani's camp lay several miles outside Syrannos, hidden by rocks above the beach. He'd never make it before dawn. By then the area would be crawling with the sultan's crimson guard.

Has to be a way to warn him—else we lose everything today.

He sat thinking for a moment, slowly stretching and easing the cramp from his thigh.

Silon lowered the hatch and squeezed his body out. Dropping silent to the floor, he let out a long slow breath, straightened his aching leg and rubbed his tired eyes. What to do?

He was caught like a bug in a jar, trapped in Syrannos while Barakani waited for him, unsuspecting down on the Silver Strand. Unaware his camp was about to be raided by the sultan's elite.

And what of the crown? How could Migen (clearly an officer) know about that? It seemed Caswallon's reach had grown longer than they'd suspected. If the sultan knew of the lost prince and broken crown, what chance would Corin and the others have? One thing certain, Silon could not stay here a minute longer. He pulled back the drapes. No sign of the soldiers but several priests were still roaming about. Silon smiled. There was only one guise that would enable him to pass through Syrannos unchallenged. And that was readily available.

"Telcanna forgive me!" Silon whispered as he struck the nearest priest from behind, and then dragged the prone body into the cloister out of sight.

Silon hurriedly threw the yellow robe other his head. The priest had been bigger than him and the garment easily covered his other clothes. He tied the scarlet sash tight and straightened the robe. The bottom of his scimitar's hilt was just noticeable beneath it, but there was little he could do about that.

Grasping the coloured beads the priest had been shaking, Silon distanced himself from the high altar and cloisters. A priest turned his way but paid him no heed. Silon walked on, beads turning in his fingers and mouth wording chants.

Reaching the far doors he eased one open, glanced about. All quiet outside. Silon summoned calm and stepped warily out into the night. He took to the main street again but this time walking boldly. Telcanna's priests were above suspicion normally.

Two purple-robed city guard watched him with cold distrusting eyes as he approached the gates to the lower quarter. They seemed on edge—no doubt having the superior sultan's elite in town had put their noses out of joint.

Silon ignored their hostile glances. He strode by chanting and hugging his beads, his heart thumping like a door knocker against his chest.

He reached the gates and motioned he wanted out. The lone sentry looked tired. He let Silon through without a word and closed the gates behind him.

Clear of the gatehouse and back in the slums, Silon stole a horse from a nearby stable. He saddled the beast quickly and rode past the harbour and out from the city under the cover of darkness. He noted *The Starlight Wanderer* had gone and thanked Elanion for that when he saw the huge vessel moored close by. The sultan's slaver, no doubt.

Tight-faced, Silon spurred his stolen steed west along the Silver Strand. As the horse galloped the sparkling breakers of the western ocean lapped around its sploshing hooves.

The sky lightened behind him. Morning dawned ominous and red. Beyond the city a storm mustered out to sea, its outriders swept shoreward like hungry smoky fingers. They pursued Silon as he urged his mount ever faster.

Elanion, please let me get there in time...

Chapter 20

The Faen

Barin's blue gaze moodily studied the wooded shoreline scarce a hundred yards to starboard. He didn't like this place and grumbled incessantly as his men hurried to repair the great rents in the sails of *The Starlight Wanderer*. They had already lost four days because of the storm. With winter's fast approach the seas would only get rougher, making their trip north more difficult.

Barin dared not hug the coasts of Raleen and Kelwyn. The Assassin's sharks would be prowling those waters intent on revenge. It was a confounded nuisance, but there was nothing for it. They would have to take their chances with the open sea in winter. The new crewmembers would have to learn fast. But they should shape up quickly. Taic and Sveyn, though lazy, knew sail craft and had served as experienced crew from time to time, when they weren't wenching and larking about.

The two outlanders, Wogun and Norman (Barin still had trouble with their names and where they came from), were hardworking and steady. And even better, experienced sailors. Haikon (the surviving fisherman from Syrannos), was tough and keen to learn, particularly after losing his friend in the storm. That left the girl. Barin didn't know what to think about her.

Time would tell. At least they were safe for the time being and it would not be long now before they could set sail again. That moment could not come soon enough in Barin's opinion.

This coastline had an odd feel about it. It was witchy and queer. Some of the crew (mainly Wogun and Norman who were more familiar with Golt than anyone else on board), whispered that they'd spotted tall horned shapes watching them at night from within the darkness of the knotted tangle of woods encroaching the shore. Trolls, witches and wood ogres, Wogun muttered under his breath until Fassof told him to shut up.

But even Barin had heard rumours about Golt. None were good. This misty land was veiled in dark mystery; tales of weird fiends haunting brackish pools and stalking these far-flung beguiling forests still terrified children in his homeland. But the truth was no one knew much about Golt. The lands west and south of Permio were wild and uncharted—at least by sailors from the Four Kingdoms, though the Permians were rumoured to fare that way. What those mariners saw they kept to themselves, thus Golt's mystery grew.

Barin lounged at the prow. He watched Shallan assist her father through the deck hatch as gloom settled in the forests ahead. Duke Tomais looked very pale and thin; his health having deteriorated in the humid air that clung to skin and clothes like spiders' webs—another thing Barin hated about this infernal coast.

The duke's daughter had a determined look as she aided her father onto the deck. Barin liked the girl. Shallan had shown remarkable courage during the storm despite being ill, and had since helped Fassof and Ruagon with dressing wounds and cheering those forlorn with pain.

Shallan was an unusual girl. Kept her own counsel most the time and when on deck watched the shore in thoughtful silence. A beauty, uncommonly graceful and slender. That said, it wasn't just her looks but her manner too. Proud, a bit stiff sometimes but when she laughed it was impossible not to like her. Barin noted how she often wore a dreamy look, seeming far away. Tall, willowy, yet strong and lithe. Thoughtful, intelligent and kindly of nature. Such was Barin's opinion of the girl.

Barin heaved up the gangplank as the last crewman clambered on board. They'd been hewing logs and were all exhausted. Barin's blue gaze surveyed the rocky coast flanking their anchorage. Those woods gave him the creeps too though he kept that quiet. Even as Barin watched, the familiar evening mist rolled in on silent wheels, clinging to and masking the mass of tangled growth. Weird howls and distant grunts sounded from deep inside the forest. Barin watched for several moments then shook his head in disgust and retired below deck.

"The sooner we're away from here the happier I'll be," Barin admitted to Shallan after the duke had returned to his cabin to rest. "How is your father?"

"I'm worried about him, Barin," she answered. "His eyes carry shadows and he is always so tired. I think he has lost faith in our world."

"This dammed heat doesn't help. Playing havoc with our ale supplies. I'm shedding pounds whilst slurping gallons. Still, we'll be under sail at first light. The repairs are completed bar those timbers Cogga's lads heaved up earlier. Cogga's ship's carpenter—he'll work through the night with my nephew and the other idiot." Shallan hadn't had a chance to talk to Barin's nephew though she'd heard a deal about him from Ruagon the cook (who didn't approve). Taic had winked at her once, he seemed cheerful and sunny despite his reputation.

Barin rubbed his chin and farted. He apologised and Shallan raised a brow. So different from the fawning nobles back home. "With a bit of luck we'll encounter a helpful wind that will carry us far away from this miserable coast."

"It is strange here," nodded Shallan, watching the mist gather apace. "I feel an odd temptation to go ashore and enter those woods. I cannot think why, Barin. It's almost like someone is calling me."

"Just your imagination," Barin rubbed his beard. "This place stinks of enchantment. Who knows what might become of you among those fly and mosquito-infested trees? This land gives me the willies; I'll not deny it." Barin poured himself an ale before continuing. Shallan sipped water and listened.

"The crew are muttering amongst themselves and giving me black looks. They haven't been happy since we left Port Sarfe. And now we have this new lot. I vowed never to employ foreigners. My old lads miss their homes and kin, Shallan, and their dead comrades. This run of bad luck has hit them hard."

"What about the girl?" Shallan had been desperate to ask about the wild-looking Zukei, but until now hadn't had the chance.

"Hmm. I don't know about her. A strange case. She'll probably prove trouble, just another reason to be grateful to my nephew. Stay clear of her, milady."

"I intend to." Shallan didn't. Rather, at first opportunity she wanted to speak with the black girl and learn all she could from her. They might be worlds apart but having another woman on board lifted Shallan's spirits. And what a fascinating woman too. Zukei kept to herself. But oddly she and Fassof the mate seemed to get on. The girl had worked close with Fassof of late and Shallan and noted how rarely he scolded her. Unusual, that.

Barin scratched his nose. It had become quite red and bulbous of late. Another legacy of the humid atmosphere of Golt, he insisted, and nothing at all to do with the copious draughts of ale he'd quaffed since their unhappy arrival at this place.

He wiped his chin and burped. "And now my lads are faced with a voyage across the ocean in winter."

"What chance our passage?

"We'll be fine as long as our provisions hold out and Cogga's repairs don't leak. And we'll have to be sparing with the food of course now it's a longer trip."

"And the beer," Shallan smiled.

"That too." Barin looked glum. "But not tonight—I need something to keep me sane in this bloody swelter."

Shallan watched Barin drain his tankard and immediately pour himself another. The captain was drinking way too much, she thought, even by his own capacious standards. Indeed they all seemed in poor shape, these tough islanders; as if the gloom shrouding the nearby coast had settled on board ship. The new recruits were more cheerful, except fisherman Haikon and the black-skinned Wogun who kept praying to Telcanna the Sky God.

Shallan, (often watching the crew of late), had noticed how Wogun shunned the girl, Zukei. Sailors were a superstitious bunch at best, and many didn't like having women aboard. But this was something else. Wogun—as tough a brute as could be imagined—appeared terrified of Zukei. Another story for another time.

Most the crew were dour and curt, Fassof spent every waking hour swearing at them whilst Barin looked glum, and her father frailer by the minute.

But Shallan would not be downhearted. She thought of Corin and wondered how he fared beneath that hostile desert sun. Silon's words haunted her from time to time but she didn't dwell on them. What would be would be. Corin had pledged to return to her and she would hold him to that. Until then she could wait.

Shallan politely excused herself from the brooding Barin. She checked in on her father who was sleeping soundly, and climbed on deck to get what little air there was.

Shallan wandered over to the prow, still her favourite place on the ship. She passed some of the crew who were playing dice, one or two nodded at her. She noticed how their faces looked uneasy—strained. There was none of the usual banter that accompanied dice.

Shallan leaned on the bow rail and let her gaze take her where it would. She watched the white moon rise like a ghostly face above the fog-shrouded trees. She shivered, feeling a slight breeze ruffle her shift. Shallan could hear the weird noises ashore but they did not sound evil to her, only strange. It was as though they had encountered another world here in Golt, and Shallan felt oddly drawn towards it. The crew retired and left her to it. Fassof sent a man aloft to keep an eye out, and then bid her goodnight as well.

Shallan watched the mate descend below deck. She was about to follow, for the hour was late. Instead she hesitated; something compelled her gaze to sweep towards the shore. Shallan's eyes widened at what she saw there. Pale figures waited at the water's edge. As the mist withdrew and moonlight settled on their forms she saw them clearly.

Shallan's heart raced. There on the shadowy shore stood three of the strangest figures she had ever seen. They were women; though their hair gleamed silver and their naked skin glistened with a pale blue light. Behind them were other figures harder to define, these watched from the mist-draped edge of the trees. She saw pale eyes in that mist and great horns that curled above its smoky veil.

And from somewhere close the lonely sound of a solitary harp drifted out reaching her across the water. It was melancholy and strange. The music filled her soul, reminding her of Zallerak playing in the gardens of Vioyamis. But this was different. More alien and remote and infinitely more melancholy. She felt sorrow accompanying every note.

The maidens were singing, their voices soft in the moonlight. Shallan could hear them calling her, beseeching her to come ashore.

"Shallan, Shallan! Come to us, sister," the women called. "Come home to your people, return to the Faen!"

"What do you mean?" Shallan heard her voice float across the bay. She hadn't realised that she had spoken.

"Search your soul, sister, on your father's side," the nearest of them answered. "Faerie blood runs deep in you!"

"I am from Morwella; I know nothing of the Faen!" Shallan called to them in an urgent whisper that seemed to carry far over the waves.

"Come to us sister, return to your kin!" The speaker had entered the water. The dark waves caressed her blue nakedness, and her hair trailed like silver thread down around her waist before vanishing in the brine below.

Shallan watched her wade through the waves, her pale, thin arms reaching out to Shallan as she called in that timeless lilting voice. The maiden was a vision of eldritch loveliness; her skin flawless, glistening like polished steel beneath the dreaming moon. She approached, oblivious of the lapping water.

Then the spell broke.

The lookout called out from somewhere aloft.

"Are you alright, my lady?" His shout sounded crow-raw after the beauty of the women's voices and the enchanting chords of the harpist. "I thought I heard voices!"

"Can you not see them waiting by the shore?" Shallan called up to him.

"I see nothing, lady."

"They are there!" She pointed to the maiden that had entered the water. She gasped. Both the wading maiden and her sisters had gone, as had the murky mysterious figures behind them. The beach was empty. The only sound the waves restlessly lapping the shore.

"There were beings, strangers calling out to me," she said, trying to convince herself as well as the lookout that she hadn't imagined their presence.

"It is a strange place, my lady, I suggest you go below," he answered, nonplussed.

Shallan nodded and waved thank you. She made to move but froze in dread when a grip like iron locked on her arm. Zukei the wild girl was glaring at her.

"You are faerie." It wasn't a question.

Shallan felt flustered and annoyed. "I don't know what you mean. You're hurting my arm!" Shallan glared back at the black girl and Zukei released her grip. "Did *you* see them?" Shallan asked the girl after an awkward moment's silence.

"That lookout saw them as well, though he's too shit scared to admit it." Zukei's accent was strange and her voice deeper than Shallan had expected. Shallan gazed up through the gloom at the dismal shape of the lookout. He sat huddled in silence. Either he hadn't heard them or he was choosing not to listen. "Your father must have told them you are here," Zukei said.

"My father is below and in poor health. You, girl, are talking nonsense."

Zukei smiled. Shallan was shocked to see that the girl had a front tooth missing. "I wasn't referring to that sick old man below. I was speaking of the Horned One."

"You know about The Horned Man?" Shallan was incredulous.

"I know many things." Zukei flashed Shallan another fierce grin before deftly slipping past her and vanishing in the gloom. Shallan leant on the rail and tried to quell her racing heart. What was going on here? She took one last questing troubled look at the shore and then hastened below deck. Shallan's sleep was troubled that night. Naked blue-skinned maidens called out to her while her father's coughs shook the cabin next door. And there were shadows in her cabin. Dancing, whirling and whispering shadows. Horned shadows.

Morning found Shallan as relieved as the rest of them when Barin hauled up the anchor and ordered the crew to set sail. By noon the coast of Golt lay far behind.

Chapter 21

The Silver Strand

Silon rode like the wind. Beneath his stolen horse's hooves the pale sand of the Silver Strand rushed by and behind him the sun broke free of stormclouds, blazing like a fiery ball. Wind whistled through the palms as he spurred the horse on, his head bent low behind the beast's neck.

To his right, Silon saw more black clouds bunching out to sea. Their ominous anvil heads lighting up in cobalt wrath as Telcanna hurled jagged lightning spears at the churning waters below. Silon hoped that *The Starlight Wanderer* was not paying the price for his blasphemy in the temple. Telcanna was a spiteful god, capricious in his moods and over-proud. Silon's yellow robes clung to him like an accusation as he willed his beast ever faster.

The Silver Strand spread out before him, serene and pure. It comprised of mile upon mile of white shells crushed by ocean over millennia and ground into a fine powder, giving the windswept shore its unique argent sparkle.

The beach was over a mile across from the heaving surf to the swaying palms ridging the southern horizon, hemming the desert beyond. The Strand ran for forty leagues from east to west and was compact underfoot, making it ideal for horses. In former times the princes of Permio had raced their stallions across its silver path, risking all in their breakneck speed. Even today the Strand served as the main trade route between the eastern cities and the sultan's palace in distant Sedinadola.

On Silon rode! Beneath him the horse's breath was ragged, the poor beast couldn't go on much further without rest.

High above dark cloud occluded the sun again and heavy drops of rain made chinking sounds as they pattered on the sand below. Then lightning lit the sky, and after the following thunder Silon heard the sound he'd been dreading. Hoofbeats.

Silon reined in. He looked back, saw the silhouettes of cloaked riders hurrying west in his direction. Doubtless the raiding party. They would spot him in moments. Silon cursed his ill fortune.

He spurred the beast into motion again, pressing his left knee into its flank so that the gelding veered sharply across towards the ragged palms. As he rode Silon's eyes were intent on the horsemen now closing on his left.

The crimson cloaks removed all doubt. There were at least forty of them, each armed with long spears and curved swords, and many had curved bows slung across their backs. A sharp shout announced they had seen him. Silon clung low in the saddle, his heels dug in as the tiring horse struggled on toward the wind-lacerated palms ahead.

"Come on, boy, we're nearly there!" Silon urged his mount faster. "You're doing well but don't falter now."

It was no good. Silon saw that other soldiers lined the ridge ahead and appeared to be waiting for him, their dark faces grinning beneath the trees and their hands locked around the hilts of broad tulwars.

Silon wheeled the horse about. An arrow thudded into the sand at his feet. Silon was trapped. He knew he had no chance of escaping now. He reined in and waited for the riders to approach. Within moments the sultan's elite had circled him with a thorn of spears.

Silon was trapped but he wasn't giving up. There was too much at stake. He waited coolly until the leader had pushed through his spearmen, emerging at last with face arrogant and accusing. Silon gave him look for look.

The officer's face darkened; he pricked Silon's stolen yellow robe knowingly with his gleaming scimitar.

"Strange is this," the officer said, "to find a dishevelled priest of Telcanna in such a hurry to vacate Syrannos. Most priests I know hate leaving the comforts of the city."

"Well, you must only know the lazy ones, officer."

The man's bearded face was hard and clearly he was no fool. He pushed Silon back with the tip of his blade, forcing the merchant from his saddle until he slid from the horse's back to lie prone on the sand.

"I think you're a spy!" The rider stamped his steed's left forehoof inches from Silon's face.

"Telcanna curse you for a fool, and a blasphemous one at that!" Silon's dark eyes blazed fury up at the officer. "How dare you assault me?" Close by, pale lightning smote the palms tearing one asunder in a piercing crack. The thunder answered booming like cosmic drums across the Strand. "See how you have angered the Lord of the Skies!"

Some of the troop looked alarmed but their leader merely smiled.

"If the Sky God is angry it's because one of his priests was struck down in the temple of Syrannos and his sacred robe stolen. I've just received word by carrier bird. You, spy, are no priest."

This officer's dark eyes were dangerously perceptive as he peered down disdainfully at the prone merchant. He leaned down, stretching in the saddle, and reaching low with his blade prodded Silon's diamond earring. "A most unusual trinket for a holy man," he said to his men and they laughed out loud.

"Let me be, fools!" Silon was playing for time, watching as the other men joined the riders from their stations at the trees. Silon counted their numbers as he pretended to cover his face.

There were twenty. He assumed that they had been searching for Barakani's camp when the riders had spotted him. Silon knew the camp lay close by.

If he could stall them for a time his ally might yet escape and they would at least save something from this disastrous day. Silon counted to three. Now for a few tricks.

"Telcanna blast you all!" he yelled in sudden furious rage that caught his would-be captors off guard. Silon lashed out with dazzling speed with his forearm, cuffing the scimitar away, and then rolled to his feet. Leaping up, Silon gripped the leader's saddle. He launched himself forward and up, snapping his open palm into the stunned officer's face, killing him instantly. The leader pitched from the saddle.

Silon caught the reins, straddled the saddle, and launched the beast into motion. His knife was out—he had no room for his scimitar. Still partially stunned, the spearmen closed in again.

Silon blocked a spear thrust with his left hand, and thrust his knife into the eye of another rider with his right. He reached down to grasp his sword hilt when something struck his head and pain exploded in his skull.

Silon slumped to the ground with a thud. A rider loomed over him, hatred consuming the dark face. The man stabbed down with his lance. Silon rolled to one side. The spearman raised his weapon again, and then lurched violently forward with a strangled cry.

And then Silon saw the long arrow sticking in his back.

Barakani—thank the gods!

Suddenly arrows were everywhere. Riders were screaming in agony as they tumbled from their mounts, some were crushed to death in the sudden panicked chaos.

Silon struggled to his feet, grateful that his ochre robes clearly marked him apart from the soldiers. The sultan's men were in complete disarray. The arrows seemed to be coming from all directions,

stinging like vengeful hornets as they struck horse and rider, shrieking like death hail from the storm-wracked sky above.

Silon, forgotten, yanked the robe above his knees and fled full
pelt for the shelter of the palm trees. He did not get far. A strong grip
seized him from behind and he felt himself hoisted up onto a vacant
saddle. A dark face grinned perfect teeth at him as he steadied the
spare horse's reins he was holding.

"Father sends his regards and apologises for missing you at the
temple, but the situation was becoming tricky in Syrannos."

Silon felt a flood of relief recognising Rassan, one of Barakani's
seven sons.

"I was coming to warn you," shouted Silon as they cantered toward a knot of stunted wind-wracked cedar trees. Rassan seemed in
no rush despite the danger. Above them the thunder rolled on, the
lowering clouds trawling their way across the angry sky.

Other riders joined them; all clad in the faded robes of desert
nomads. To a man they were armed with scimitar knife and bow.
Silon glanced behind, the sultan's finest were regrouping and more
were hurrying along the Strand from the east.

"We had best not stick around!" laughed Rassan, his tanned
handsome face alive with excitement. "We'll lead them through
these trees towards the rocks that conceal our camp. Once there we
can pick them off easily with our arrows!"

"What of your father? I feared I would be too late!" Silon ducked
his head as they wove through the pines; behind them the crimson
guard were closing, though Rassan seemed unconcerned.

"Father got word the sultan was on the move," he yelled, "so
he ordered the camp be struck and reassembled in the desert by the
turquoise oasis. That's some twenty leagues southeast of here."

Rassan reached over Silon's shoulder with his horn bow and
calmly put an arrow in the eye of a pursuer. He hooted as the rider
pitched from his horse and lay still.

"We'll join him once we have lost these dogs in the hills," he
grinned. "Make for yonder heights!" Rassan slapped Silon's horse on

the rump and reined his own back to cover their retreat.

The two riders fled with the enemy in hot pursuit. The storm was passing swiftly leaving smoky dragons in its tails. Moments later the sun returned to scorch the sand dry. Rassan motioned Silon follow him into a rocky maze of hillocks strewn above the palms and pines like broken marbles, as if discarded by some giant's petulant child. Beyond these rocks reared a steep rise. Mounts sweating beneath them, they crested that rocky crown, descending into a broad ledge awarding adequate cover.

Once out of bowshot they reined in, dismounted and took cover behind the sandstone. Other horsemen were emerging from everywhere. Silon borrowed a bow from a rider who kept a spare. He struggled to string it with his sweating hands, but at last got arrow on nock.

The shouts of the enemy loomed closer but were replaced by screams as another wave of arrows struck.

Then the sultan's bowmen answered.

Silon ducked as a crimson-shafted dart struck a rock to his left. Another whizzed past his ear before lodging itself in a tree behind him.

"That was close," Rassan grinned across at him. Silon grinned back more out of stress than joy. All seven of Barakani's boys were wild.

He peered over the ledge rim and saw that the elite had re-grouped and were waiting beyond bowshot whilst the newcomers joined them. Once bolstered by these reinforcements they'd attack again, but for the meanwhile they had reached an impasse. Rassan was undeterred. He jumped down to join Silon behind the rock.

"We've lost four men," he said, "and two others will be joining them at the silent shore of the Black River." Rassan showed those dazzling teeth again. Silon, looking at those flawless molars, recalled how all Barakani's sons courted danger like a wanton maiden.

"Our lads died well, those of us surviving will cheer them on their way across the Black River as we revel in my father's camp. The sultan has lost at least a score of his elite crimson," laughed Rassan. "The rest will not risk a full attack in daylight. It would prove too costly for them."

"So do we sit tight until then? We are still heavily outnumbered, Rassan. If we wait till tonight their numbers may have swelled again, enabling them to surround these hills and starve us out if they can't kill us earlier."

"I had already thought of that," replied Rassan. "That is precisely why you will slip away now, friend Silon. You are too valuable to lose. With you will go all but a dozen of us. We twelve happy stragglers will stay here to keep an eye on our crimson friends over there and stop any of them becoming overzealous." Rassan unfastened his quiver from his saddle pack and carefully placed a number of shafts close to hand.

"What of yourselves?" Silon's face showed concern. "I don't like leaving you here."

"Don't worry," replied Rassan. "We will give you a head start then lead them on a merry chase across these hills. Those fools are no match for my boys, merchant!"

"They are the sultan's elite, Rassan!" Silon rolled his eyes. "Dangerous bastards."

"And overrated. They don't know the desert like we do. Relax, Silon! Jarrof here knows the way to the Turquoise Oasis. He'll lead you to Father and we will join you tonight, after we have lost those crimson clowns in the dunes. Prepare to get drunk later!"

Silon was still worried about the risk young Rassan was taking but he agreed the plan made sense. The merchant had shed his priest's robe and re-mounted his borrowed horse. Calmly Silon waited for the word to flee. He was more than ready to leave the Silver Strand.

Rassan fired a casual arrow at the enemy still mustering beyond bowshot and then waved Jarrof depart. Hastily the others took to saddle joining Silon, keeping low and dodging the odd arrow—fired by encroaching scouts before Rassan's rear-guard brought them down. Within minutes Silon and company were out of range.

The silent bearded Jarrof led the way, threading his horse carefully through the maze of twisted rocks. Next rode Silon, glancing about warily while the other nomads followed close behind. Jarrof led them skilfully through the strewn rocks in a series of bewildering loops for what must have been well over a mile. Silon struggled to glean where they were headed. There seemed no end to this stony jumble.

At last they reached a high point awarding a wide view of the arid terrain south. The rocks fell away suddenly as though losing interest. Ahead was an ocean of sand. Nothing stirred amongst those dunes. Satisfied; they made their way down to the foot of the rocks and entered the desert beyond.

"We ride hard!" barked the lean-faced Jarrof. "I want to make the oasis by dusk! Are you fit, merchant?" Silon gave a breathless nod and Jarrof led them forward with a sharp click of his spurs.

"I'm just happy to be alive," he answered though no one heard him.

Elanion, Bright Goddess—I thank you!

***

Shallan watched the strange rocks loom closer. There were three of them, each rounded and caked with weed. They rose out of the waves like the humps of a slumbering sea snake.

"The Snags!" announced Barin from behind her.

"Many a ship's come to grief in the shadow of those treacherous skerries. There are hidden reefs joining them beneath the waves." Barin had regained his customary good humour when he saw the odd-looking rocks. They were back in familiar waters.

"If we held this course for a while, we would arrive somewhere between Port Sarfe and South Head," he told her. "That Assassin will be prowling the coast like a fire demon now that Corin's spoiled his good looks, so we'll fare north instead. You had best be prepared for a long spell at sea, lassie."

Shallan nodded, saying nothing as she watched the slimy black rocks slip astern. Two blue-sky days had passed since they left the coast of Golt. Still she was haunted by the memory of the creatures she had seen on the shore that night. She *had* seen them and Zukei had too. Their cool clear alien voices still echoed through her head.

Shallan cast her mind back, trying to remember what her tutors had told her of the mysterious folk said to dwell within the many uncharted forests of Ansu. The Faen. The faerie folk. They were an ancient people that had lived for thousands of years before her ancestors had sailed from Gol. Long before the time of the Aralais and their shadowy foe, the secretive Faen had walked the wide realms in freedom—or so the stories in her library had said.

Before Golt the Faen had just been another legend in a world of mysteries. Now, like the Horned Man, they were very real for Shallan. And like him they were her kin. Their faerie blood flowed in her veins also. Shallan was determined to seek out Zukei again, and this time press the strange girl into revealing all she knew. No need to rush, as Barin said this would prove a long voyage.

Those alien women had called Shallan their sister, and for some reason Shallan couldn't yet understand, she believed them. Though how such a thing could be possible she had no idea. The Horned Man had hinted at it, but she'd been so stressed at that time she'd all but forgotten his words. Perhaps he was Faen too.

The Horned Man is my real father.

Zukei was right about that. It was the only thing that made sense, though it made no sense at all. Another thing she had in common with Corin an Fol.

Shallan remembered when her eldest brother had ventured into the Forest of Dreams that lay close to the west of her country, after boasting his proposal to his friends. Although he had emerged safely the next afternoon later, he hadn't spoken for days and clearly had been badly spooked.

It was all so strange. She thought of Corin an Fol and the weighty fate that hung over him—hung over them both, she corrected. Her life was unfolding in ways she'd never foreseen. Shallan wondered how she would fare in the turbulent days ahead.

She shaded her eyes from the glare, and glanced up at the great sea eagle flapping proudly again above her head.

Duke Tomais was dying. Shallan knew that now. He wasn't eating and had lost so much weight since they had left Port Sarfe harbour. Shallan kept cheerful for his sake, but inwardly she wept. First her mother and now...

Shallan made her way to the dancing prow of Barin's ship. Once there she gazed down at the bowsprit as it plunged and lurched through the whitening waves. Shallan was lost on the ocean, caught between riddle and hint. The doldrums. Corin an Fol was so very far away. She was lost and alone. Only darkness and war lay ahead. The sea spray stung Shallan's face and mingled with her tears.

***

The riders arrived at the sparkling blue-green oasis just as the sun fell behind the sea of dunes ranging west into the shimmering horizon. Ahead of them a bold array of tents surrounded the fertile valley, the largest of which bore the emblem of a desert wolf—Barakani's flag.

Silon was bone-weary and travel sore, but once he had sated his thirst in the cool clear water of the oasis he felt revived enough to seek out the warlord.

Barakani, Wolf of the Desert, embraced him as he entered the huge tent. All about were rich cloths and drapes of many colours. Beneath his feet, the deep pile of lush carpets depicted desert scenes and ornate, jewel-adorned lamps, hung from golden ropes, giving light to the sumptuous surroundings.

Silon sat cross-legged in front of his friend and nodded in gratitude when the lean tribesman handed him a strong cup of coffee and a plate of figs.

"You live well, Barakani—even in exile," he said and the warlord smiled. Behind him were seated three of his sons, their sharp hand-

some faces reminded Silon of Rassan. He wondered how the young
nomad warrior fared.

"A diverting day, Silon," Barakani answered. "And alarming.
Now it seems we must act in haste, else all our plans shall be but
sand grains lost beneath the dunes."

"What brought the sultan out of his lair, Barakani?" asked Silon,
staring hard at the bearded nomad chief. "I overheard three of his
elite in the temple. Their leader mentioned a certain 'visitor' from
the north."

"Aye, it seems Caswallon has promised him aid in locating certain friends of yours," replied the warlord.

"The sultan has been informed of Prince Tarin's foolish quest
and his podgy mind has convinced itself a great treasure lies beneath
those far off mountains. Hence the bulk of his force will soon be entering the desert."

"But who told him?"

"That I do not know."

Silon thought of Corin and his friends having to watch out for
the sultan's army as well as their other enemies with only Zallerak's
spell craft to aid them. The merchant's face was lined with worry.

"What can we do?"

"Go see what the fuss is about," grinned Barakani. "It's long
years since last I saw the Crystal Mountains. Our situation here has
altered. The game's moved south. With that in mind I propose a trip
into the deep desert to see what we can find."

"What of the sultan's elite? They will be everywhere." Silon
sipped his coffee, letting the strong taste revive his flagging senses. It
was cold tonight but then the desert was always cold at night—unlike
the cities along the coast.

"We will take the longer road," Barakani replied. "By heading
southwest we should avoid both the Ty-Tander's lair and the sultan's
guard. We can gather allies along the way."

"That easy?"

"The tribes are stirring; we'll muster support, then meet with the sultan's army at the foot of the mountains. Yes, that easy." Barakani smiled. "Our presence should keep 'Old Greasy' (his name for the sultan) preoccupied while your friends engage in their subterranean venture."

Silon nodded approval, this made sound sense. He hoped Yashan's desert knowledge would keep his friends out of the sultan's reach before the nomads could intervene. Zallerak would know what to do in any case, he told himself. Despite everything things hadn't turned out that bad.

Silon sighed. He drained his coffee and smiled when Barakani produced a burning, bubbling water pipe. Gratefully Silon joined him in a smoke. He didn't usually partake but today had been a tad rough on his nerves. At last Silon could relax and he was so very weary.

They spoke deep into the night. There were many other matters to discuss and these two had known each other for long years. Silon was shattered when he finally staggered, slightly wobbly, into the tent that he'd been given. In moments the merchant was sound asleep.

At some point he was awoken by the sound of horses entering the camp. Silon drew back the rich folds of his tent to see that Rassan and the other fighters had arrived safely back in camp. He curled back to sleep for a time, the shouts of Rassan's boys faded. Silon smiled; they'd most likes be drinking till dawn.

***

At first the pain of the arrow had threatened to consume him. He'd been carried far below the waves towards a watery grave. Fish food he would become, a sad fate that for one of his ancient pedigree. He had called out the name of his master but Mr Caswallon hadn't answered—obviously big-ugly didn't care.

Gribble knew he was alone. No one liked him. No one ever had. He was misunderstood and now he was dying. It simply wasn't fare. And the pain was horrible. The wound throbbed beneath his left wing and puss bubbled. The Soilfin could see the pale shaft still sticking in his side, whilst the ooze trickled out, staining the dark cold waters around him. So cold.

Suddenly a great shark loomed above, its triple rows of teeth gleaming through the murk. "Hello fishy," gurgled Gribble. The shark was quick but Gribble was quicker. Ravenous, he sank his fangs into the shark's glistening flank.

The great fish leapt and snapped its terrible jaws. But to no avail. Its potential dinner evaded its jaws and instead clung limpet-like to its back. Steel-strong talons gripped the shark's gleaming skin with unnatural strength. The great fish wriggled but its unwelcome lodger hung on doggedly, his claws digging deeper.

"Take me to the coast and I'll let you be," Gribble said, as he rode the shark's back through the briny caverns of the deepest deep. "Try eating me and I'll eat you first—you're not in my league, big fishy."

Try as it might the shark could not shed its passenger. Eventually it succumbed and did the foul creature's bidding just to be rid of it. It raced to the surface and followed the faint scent of the shore. Soon tall cliffs reared above the waves. Once they were reached, the Soilfin hopped from the shark's back, carefully evading its vengeful jaws, and then limped ashore to rest.

He waited until darkness then found a village. After some hours eating the occupants, his strength returned and he bloated to cow size. Once Gribble had digested his supper and shrunk again, he winged awkwardly and flap wobbly, upwards into the thermals of the night sky. Half drowned and very sore, but at least able to fly again.

Through that clean air the Soilfin flew—a black spiteful lump of pain and malice and resentment. At last the Soilfin descried far beneath him, the lone tower where his master stood waiting beneath the single lantern.

"Ah, Gribble." Caswallon watched with mild interest as the Soilfin alighted on the recently repaired roof (Vaarg the dragon had paid a visit a while back). The sorcerer scratched his short beard with a dirty fingernail. "What has become of you?" Caswallon marked the creature's sorry state as it sulked and hopped ugly outside the window. "I was almost concerned."

He unfastened the latch and Gribble hobbled in. The Soilfin then recounted his dreadful tale. Caswallon listened patiently while he pulled the grey-flecked arrow out of his pet's rancid under-wing. He muttered a spell and the puss dried then vanished.

"No matter," said the sorcerer after the tale of woe concluded. "I have a new task for you, once you have your strength back."

So it was that a fully recovered, long flight ready Gribble, had journeyed south to the desert land the very next week. He'd made quite an impression down there, running amok in the fat sultan's palace, eating slaves and pawing at the nubile wenches that screamed their way through the ornate gardens—all good clean fun.

Gribble returned hours later with urgent news. From his high tower of pain Caswallon smiled. Again he rewarded his pet with warm, flaccid, greying flesh.

The sorcerer's coaly, far reaching gaze scanned the dark hills of Kelthaine, ranged south across the rolling wooded wilds of Kelwyn, and lightly touched on the rugged dry plains of Raleen.

They glimpsed the waters of the Gulf, came to rest at last on the high dunes and sweltering deserts of Permio.

Caswallon laughed then. He laughed loud and long at the folly of his enemies. Meanwhile Gribble crunched and dribbled at someone's severed foot in his cot beneath the table. Occasionally he would look up and squint at his master. On such occasions Caswallon ignored him.

Chapter 22

Wynais

The clear blue waters of Lake Wynais sparkled with early winter sunlight. Wind sighed through the reeds, ridging the glassy surface and distorting the reflections of the heather-clad hills flanking the lake's eastern hem.

Those purple crags rose up, ever steeper, until they embraced the timberline of the High Wall, the long mountain chain shielding the Four Kingdoms from the desolate lands beyond.

Even now the first snow was settling on the Wild Way, the ancient track threading the haunches of those towering peaks, making it nigh impassable till spring. The wind whipped ice chill out of those mountains and the call of skeining geese carried far over water, as they descended in their hundreds onto the marshlands rimming Lake Wynais to the west. Close by the lake, and wedged between two forest-draped hills, stood a gleaming silver city.

Wynais, home of the rulers of Kelwyn.

Walls of shining granite caught the sun's glare, as did the steel-polished helmets of the watchful guards, pacing back and forth across the battlements.

Beyond these ramparts the elegant lofty towers of the Silver Palace pierced the winter sky. Streaming banners ruffled in the sharp breeze echoing a pride of days gone by. A long peace now lost, when noble rulers had steered these fertile lands, second only in their majesty to the proud overlords of Kelthaine.

That time of peace, like the last king, had recently ceased to exist. Now this land's fate hung frail and fragile in the inexperienced, but confident grip of late King Nogel's only child, Queen Ariane.

But the queen had deserted her city in its hour of need. Few knew where she'd gone, and the glittering halls of the fairest palace in the Four Kingdoms seemed stale and empty these days.

Servants passed to and fro, whispering amongst the airy passageways and beneath the high-arched windows. Rumours were born of those idle whispers, portents of dread that wound their way down to the busy streets below.

That talk grew legs; soon the cityfolk knew fear. The freshly drilled soldiers muttered on the walls, rubbing their frozen hands and staring out at the wide lands beyond.

Nothing stirred. And still the portents were bad.

Then the black-clad messenger arrived from the north, and at his heels came the first heavy snows of winter.

"I bring greeting from the new lord of Kelthaine!" The man had shouted boldly up at the city walls. "Caswallon an Kella rules throughout the land. Only Kelthara and Car Carranis hold out in the east and that first city shall soon capitulate. Its inhabitants shall be punished for their folly, as were the citizens of Reln and Fardoris before. And Car Carranis has its own problems these days.

"But my lord Caswallon wishes only peace with Kelwyn, a land that has always been dear to his heart," continued the messenger with a haughty arrogance that rankled the guards above. He sat astride his sable steed scanning the walls with shrewd cold eyes concealed beneath the black horned helm.

"The lord of Kelthaine will protect this land despite its reckless queen fleeing the seat of power," he assured them. "Caswallon demands only this; that the renegade, faithless Ariane be brought to him on her return. Your foolish queen has plotted treachery against our lord and must be chastised. This is only reasonable.

"What have you to say to that?"

The messenger spurred his horse, trotting to and fro across the turf, awaiting their response with growing impatience. He raised his helmed head when a tall white-haired old man appeared on the battlements above.

Dazaleon had been informed of the messenger's arrival by the new captain of guard. The high priest of Elanion had left his silent vigil at the Crystal Temple at once. Aided by his sturdy staff, he'd struggled up the many steps, emerging red-faced on the west wall. Dazaleon was feeling all of his seventy-six years this morning, he was breathless and weary and worn down by worry.

But anger blazed within him too—gave Dazaleon just enough strength. He looked coldly down on the horn-helmed rider below.

"Who is this canard that dares mouth lies about our noble ruler? Speak, oh servant of night!" The high priest's voice rang out with clear authority but the armoured horseman below merely laughed at his words. He eased his mount forward and called up again.

"I am Lord Derino an Reln. High Captain of Caswallon's army, second only to Lord Perani in Kella City. I come in peace—this time. So be sensible, high priest, and do as I request."

Derino leaned forward on his saddle; Caswallon had told him to use diplomacy at first rather than force, to give their contact space to move inside the walls. If he, Derino, or their man inside could fool these weak Kelwynians into relenting and opening their gates to his force, then so much the better. Trouble was, diplomacy wasn't Derino's strong point.

"I assume it is you who holds council in this satellite kingdom."

"You are over-hasty, Derino an Reln," replied Dazaleon with a scoff. "Were our champion here you would not speak thus about our queen!"

"Your champion?" Cold metallic laughter could be heard issuing from beneath the helm. "Your champion is dead, Dazaleon! His headless body feeds the fishes of Crenna. Your little bitch-queen's feeble quest is in ruins. Soon she'll return here with her tail between her legs."

"Did you not know Parantios was dead?" Derino laughed when he heard the woeful cries beyond the battlements. "I so hate to be the bearer of woeful tidings!"

"Let me kill him!" Yail Tolranna, hawk-faced captain of guard, had seized a bow from a soldier. Eagerly he leant out across the battlements.

"Wait, captain." Dazaleon placed a placating hand on Yail's shoulder. "He is only a tool—this Derino. Besides I would know more. The rumour of Roman's death is no new thing. I had already suspected it were so."

Dazaleon stared coldly down at the rider below. "Have you come hither to gloat on old news, fool? Or do you carry real threats from your master?"

The black-armoured rider had withdrawn out of bowshot. He glanced up warily at the figures on the wall. "You are the fools," he answered, the voice muffled beneath the heavy helm. "Weak fools. I will return one month hence for the false queen Ariane. If I am refused, the full might of Kelthaine's new master will descend on Kelwyn and tear it asunder. You will perish in fire and ruin. You have been warned." With a mocking bow Derino whipped his sable cloak behind him and spurred his steed into motion.

Dazaleon watched in thoughtful silence as the horseman cantered off down the broad, tree-lined road, leading west towards the sparkling lake. Beyond that hallowed water the road met the Great South Way. That ancient highway ribboned up from distant Raleen to the city of Kelthara, five score miles to the north.

So Kelthara still held out against Caswallon. Good. Those few nobles that survived the earlier massacre must have fled there. But it was true they couldn't hold out for long. But would the Usurper crush Kelthara before invading Kelwyn? Dazaleon doubted that. Caswallon's deranged lust for Ariane would most likes take precedence. Kelthara could wait—Caswallon wanted the queen. And so their peril was grave indeed.

Dazaleon continued to watch the dust settle on the road ahead as the distant rider vanished from view.

"Derino will be back soon," he said quietly. Beside him the captain of guard slammed a mailed fist into the wall.

"I don't believe that villain!" Yail hawked and spat down angrily on the battlements below. "Roman Parrantios still lives. I am sure of it!"

"No. He is dead," answered Dazaleon in a soft voice. "Alas, that much is true, captain. The cold winds have carried his voice these last nights.

"Our champion's soul rides with the Hunt now. Roman is trying to warn us. I fear our queen is in direst need. Green Elanion, please protect her, your faithful child."

Dazaleon leant hard on the staff he always carried. At its tip the huge emerald glistened under the cold sun. He rubbed it thoughtfully, thinking of the visions he had had recently. His weariness abated and his thoughts cleared on touching the jewel. Dazaleon smiled bravely down at the worried faces of the young captain and his men.

"Fear not!" Dazaleon called out, his deep voice carrying easily down to the crowded streets below. "Queen Ariane shall never kneel before that sorcerer impostor. This much I have seen! We must have courage until our beloved ruler has returned. It will not be long."

After those words the high priest left them to their vigil and moody mutterings. Dazaleon made his way back down the spiral stone steps until he reached the crowded streets of the city below. People watched in respectful silence as their wise custodian strode across to the Crystal Temple close beside the palace. Nobody spoke as he disappeared within.

***

Captain Tolranna watched from the battlements. His thoughts were bleak and troubled. He felt like a traitor but what choice did he have? Dazaleon was wrong about everything. A noble old fool, blinded by naive devotion and unanswered prayers. Daring to hold out to a fruitless useless cause. Queen Ariane had already lost, and her rash actions only hurried the inevitable. Yail's careful manoeuvres would soften that coming blow. He owed that much to his people. Caswallon was rumoured cruel and twisted, but even he wouldn't wipe out an entire city without cause.

Caswallon's spy had sent word of General Derino's visit. Yail Tolranna had felt as much hatred as the others lining the walls when the arrogant bastard so openly scoffed their queen. Tolranna loved Ariane. He always had. That was his torture, his dread, the ice worm inside his belly. Yail loved the queen but was willing to sell her to the enemy for the greater good.

It was beyond hard. Fate had dealt him a cruel hand. Golden wonder-boy Tamersane would doubtless die valiantly, a hero in her cause, whilst he, the darker elder brother, would be cursed as a turncoat for evermore.

But that was of small account. Someone had to see a way through this mess. Kelwyn needed a steady ruler. A man for all seasons and situations. Tolranna was cousin to the queen so it was logical he fit that slot. Yail didn't relish it though. This wasn't personal, it was business. Hard brutal business that would enable Kelwyn's survival. Dazaleon was an old fool and Queen Ariane a deluded hothead. Between them they would prove the ruin of Kelwyn. He, Tolranna, couldn't let that happen.

That was why he had sent four coded birds to Derino after his departure, informing Caswallon's general that he would do as was required in return for the crown of Wynais—and his people's safety of course. Ariane was headstrong and reckless. She had dug her own grave.

And yet he loved her so.

***

When Dazaleon entered the temple he immediately cast himself at the feet of the serene statue of green robed Elanion. "Oh Queen of the Forests and Guardian of Ansu. Help us in this our hour of need! Protect brave Ariane and those who aid her. And protect our Silver City from the hounds of Caswallon."

As he prayed Dazaleon thought of the day he'd watched the brave young queen departing on her secret journey. Ariane was like a daughter to him, particularly after her father's untimely death. And Roman would be sorely missed in the coming strife. Without him to protect her Ariane was vulnerable indeed. It was two long months since her departure. Past time that she should have returned to them.

Elanion, Goddess—keep her safe...

Above Dazaleon's head the majestic serene face of the goddess watched him in silence. As he watched, Her fathomless gaze filled with sudden emerald light. Dazaleon felt the familiar fusion within. *She is answering!* All was not yet lost. As he stumbled to his knees, Dazaleon heard the words of his goddess fill the temple.

Ariane comes... even now she comes! And with her the first ravens of war...

***

Hooves drummed the well-worn road. Wind cried forlorn out of the east as the austere walls of Atarios faded into distance. Ahead rose the gentle slopes of the southern wolds. The Great South Way led up through those hills, its cobbled coating concealed by their wooded undulations.

For four days they had ridden hard since leaving Port Sarfe. Queen Ariane had set the pace. She was most anxious to return to her homeland.

She cut a proud figure in her borrowed Raleenian armour with rapier at her side, the steel-clad horsemen of Raleen and Belmarius's Bears clattering behind her, their spears and hauberks gleaming beneath the winter sun. A combined force comprising six hundred strong. When they'd reached Atarios they'd found two hundred riders waiting for them, the promised aid from Silon.

Ariane had spent a single night in that beautiful city, allowing Belmarius's rangers and their hard-faced captain, Valentin to arrive. Next morning they'd ridden out. A strong and confident force, Queen Ariane at their head. She might look magnificent but Ariane had no delusions. They rode north into the eye of the coming storm. A storm so dark and destructive it could bury them alive.

At Queen Ariane's side rode Galed her squire and the boy Cale. Both travel-worn and weary. Galed yearned for Wynais, his home. Cale was excited; he'd got over his disappointment of not being allowed to join the desert quest. Instead Cale was part of an army and that filled him with pride.

It was the first time he'd accompanied real soldiers. These Raleenians were smart and ordered, showing a discipline that made Hagan's band seem like drunken louts. And Belmarius's Bears were mean-looking and, (in Cale's military assessment), a doughty durable lot.

Cale grinned at Galed, who slumped in his saddle stoically beside him. His friend had a new blade hanging from his belt. Unlikely warrior he might be, but fierce determination had gripped Galed as he'd cantered behind his queen through the arid country of northern Raleen.

Then at last they came upon Greystone Bridge marking the gateway into Kelwyn. A brave sight, the riders clattered across whilst far below the icy, frothing waters of the Glebe tumbled through cloven hills on their quest west from the mountains.

Even Galed had managed a smile then. He'd winked at Cale and pointed down at the wild dancing water.

"We're in Kelwyn now, boy!" Cale had grinned back. They'd cantered beneath the creaking beech trees of Elglavis wood, and once free of that forest espied far off the deep blue lazy waters of Lake Wynais.

Cale's eyes were agog; the boy had never encountered so panoramic a vista. White-capped mountains, their shoulders cloaked by firs, held the east while due ahead the lake glimmered calm. Wedged between both was the Silver City he'd heard so much about.

Wynais.

Cale smiled with pride. The queen caught his stare. "Your new home, master Cale." Ariane turned in her saddle, raised her right hand to those following. "Behold the city by the lake! Silver Wynais! Ride content, my friends, we are almost home!" To the north storm clouds beckoned shrouding the mountain peaks. Queen Ariane spurred her mare to gallop; the last miles flew beneath them.

They reached the fertile fields between city and lake. Cale saw tiny figures watching and waving from the distant walls. They eased to a trot nearing gates. Those gates opened wide and the young queen's borrowed army rode through. There to greet them stood her people. In their midst Dazaleon, High Priest and Yail Tolranna, Captain of Guard. Dazaleon was smiling but Tolranna's dark gaze was haunted by doubt.

So it was Queen Ariane returned to the Silver City on the very eve of war.

Chapter 23

The High Dunes

Hundreds of leagues south that same winter sun scorched the shifting sand of the Permian Desert. Beneath its fiery mantle six men struggled over steep ridges of sand, their horses in tow. The High Dunes lived up to their reputation.

It was the third day since their departure from Agmandeur. Close by, the stone-strewn waters of the river Narion had shrunk to a babbling brook, whilst to their right the great mountains of sand that Yashan aptly named the High Dunes reared ever upwards blocking the way ahead.

Corin's throat was dry, he felt tired and irritated in the relentless heat. And Thunderhoof didn't care for the desert much either. "Come on, ya great lummox!" Corin urged the horse to struggle up to join the others. Thunder blinked at him but didn't budge.

Yashan had already left the ridge, and Corin's other companions soon caught up with their guide, stopping to survey the land ahead. Ulani laughed when he saw Corin struggling with his horse. Handing his own mount to the grinning (unsympathetic) Tamersane, the ebony-skinned warrior dropped down to assist Corin. Together they half dragged and pushed the reluctant Thunderhoof up the shifting face of the towering dune, until panting, they reached the crown.

Ulani laughed again, "He doesn't like the sand! He'll get used to it in time."

"He'll bloody well have to," growled Corin and then managed a wry smile. "He's got a strop on—misses his oats and good fresh water."

"Don't we all."

Ulani's good humour was infectious. Corin was glad the huge warrior had accompanied them. Such an impressive array of weaponry would doubtless come in handy. But it wasn't just that. Ulani of the Baha folk was witty, clever and resourceful—even Bleyne grinned at his banter. He had Tamersane in hoops.

Though bare-chested beneath his cloak, Ulani still sported his spotted fur kilt, girdled by a broad gold-studded leather belt. From this hung two curved swords, five knives, two heavy clubs and a crescent-shaped, evil-looking hatchet—all were of the finest steel, save the clubs that were capped with gold.

Fastened to his horse's saddle were three short ash spears and a horn bow with a bristling quiver of spotted shafts. Alongside those hung a great wooden mace similar to the clubs though double the size and again capped with gold.

Corin remembered Silon talking about the warrior king from Yamondo who had saved his life in Cappel Cormac. Ulani had been seeking the merchant for reasons of his own. Those now satisfied, the big man desired to return to his far flung land as soon as he was able.

Corin had asked Ulani if he really were a king. Ulani had nodded, and grinning added that he had three wives and nine daughters, though only two sons. "They are wild children," he'd informed Corin. "Particularly one of them. And my wives' tongues are sharper than my daggers."

"No wonder you need some time in the desert," Tamersane said.

Yamondo, so Ulani told them, was a huge country of steamy forests and green-cloaked mountains that belched flame hundreds of feet into the air. His people the Baha lived in the east of that country. To the west dwelt the Vendel, another proud folk who had no love for the Baha. Border skirmishes were common and even sometimes open war. Most times they traded to mutual advantage, kept their distance and remained content.

Yamondo, Ulani told them, was rich in savage beasts and weird coloured insects. There were worse perils too. Demons lurked the in the swamp-infested lowlands to the south of his country. And foul-tempered warlocks rode the humid night air on weird hairless birds.

Corin had enquired how far away Yamondo was. He couldn't imagine any land existing beyond these vast deserts. And a fertile one too. Ulani had responded that it lay many days south of the Crystal Mountains, their destination. Ulani spoke often about his country and the ways of his people. The tales amazed all his companions save the aloof superior Zallerak. However, he said little concerning his visit north. Corin remembered Silon's words at the council: 'dark days have come upon Yamondo'. He didn't press the matter.

Yashan kept his distance from Ulani. Whilst liking the king he was wary, having heard ghoulish stories about those southern countries.

Once he'd recovered from his exertions with Thunder, Corin took a look about. It wasn't encouraging really. He shaded his hand, surveyed the arid scene ahead and muttered something.

Mile upon mile of towering dunes ridged westward like some surreal golden ocean. To the south the distant terrain appeared flatter, though it was difficult to be certain as the shimmering heat distorted his vision in that direction.

Corin followed the Narion's journey with his eyes, the odd palm and show of reeds marking its path long after the sparkling water had faded from view.

"Well, now what do we do?" Corin said as he caught up with the others skirting the ridge of another dune. At least Thunder seemed resigned and was clumping behind him without issue. Corin's question was ignored, the others already deep in conversation. All except Bleyne who was scratching his ear, and Zallerak who was staring southwest with a mournful expression.

"What now, I said?"

Yashan glanced up in Corin's direction, his dark eyes troubled. Their guide shook his head, muttering something about foolishness. Corin had obviously missed out on a debate while he was struggling with Thunderhoof. His eyes narrowed when he caught Tamersane's rueful expression.

"What is it? What's the bloody matter?" Tamersane shrugged and turned away. But Zallerak answered readily enough. The bard looked edgy—coiled for a fight.

"Our time is short, Corin an Fol. The darkness musters against us already. Things have moved on in the game. I can feel it!"

"Feel what?" Corin could happily skewer this wizard sometimes.

"Tension. Eyes and spies. This entire desert is watched by our enemy. They know we are here." Zallerak shook his head and rubbed his eyes as though suddenly weary. "The river Narion is no longer safe," he added. "We cannot follow it to its source. That way will be guarded. Instead we must hasten due south flanking these sandy hills."

"But that is reckless folly, Sir Zallerak!" Yashan's dark eyes glittered like coals and the guide's voice was edged with anger. "That way lies only pitiless desert. No water, no shelter. And beyond that..." Yashan shook his head, unwilling to mention what followed. He changed tack.

"If we follow the river to its source, as was agreed, we can cross the stony hills around its basin, make for the oasis of Isalyos. That's only a few days' ride from the Crystal Mountains—ideal for replenishing before your journey in the dark. That was our plan, Sir Zallerak."

"Plans change," answered the bard, waving a dismissive arm. "That oasis like the Narion will be watched. Please keep up, Yashan.

My mind is set. Our only chance of success lies in speed—hence we take the direct route. Due south."

"Southwest isn't a good option either. I'd not think we'd make great speed traversing these dunes," said Ulani, rubbing his stubbly beard. "That would deplete our water supplies more than the open desert."

"Well, we had better make up our minds soon," grumbled Tamersane. "Or it will be too bloody hot to go anywhere!"

Corin listened to the words of his companions with growing impatience. He noticed how Yashan's voice appeared almost desperate that they follow his guidance. The tough desert warrior was clearly afraid of what Zallerak was suggesting. Corin didn't doubt he had good cause. Yashan was no craven.

Corin had had enough. He rounded on Zallerak.

"What plagues you? You keep hinting about this and that but tell us nothing! I say we take Yashan's advice and stop pissing around." Corin's mouth was dry and sore. Shouting wasn't helping. He spat a gobbet of grit down whilst pouring a few clear drops of water into Thunderhoof's gullet and then taking some himself. "Or if you know something we do not then may I suggest you come out with it!"

Zallerak gave Corin a sharp look. Those huge eyes were filled with sudden rage. He looked about to explode but then Bleyne, who had been watching the riverbank behind them, gave a shout of warning.

"Soldiers on the track behind! Over fifty I would guess. They are approaching with some speed!"

"Guess that's decided things for us then." Corin awarded Zallerak a withering glance. "South it is."

Cursing their luck, the six led their horses out of sight below the nearest ridge. Tamersane watched over the beasts as the others climbed back to see just who it was approaching in such haste from the north.

As Corin watched he saw the riders canter towards them, kicking up great columns of dust in their wake. They were still some distance away but the peculiar desert light aided his vision. He saw many horsemen in an ordered line, all carrying spears sloped across their shoulders, their steel shirts glinting beneath crimson cloaks. Beside him he heard Yashan curse.

"There gallops the cream of Sedinadola!" The tribesman spat in the direction of the riders. "The sultan's eyes are on the desert. Zallerak is right, our presence here has been reported. I imagine our encounter with Sulimo might have something to do with it. It could be the rogue knew more than he gave out.

"Or else it was that bastard Hagan," Corin growled. "I should have slit his throat."

"Certainly it's us they're after," said Yashan. "Why else would the Crimson journey so far from their sordid brothels on the coast?" Yashan's dark face was filled with contempt. The Crimson Guard was loathed by the tribes of Permio. "Even so our faring south is folly, trust me, I know this."

Corin turned to Yashan, who looked increasingly miserable. "What is it, Yashan? What do you fear down there?" Corin asked, dropping to his belly as the soldiers drew near. Instead of answering Yashan studied the horsemen counting their numbers and nodding slowly to Bleyne.

"You have keen eyes, sir archer," he said. "There ride fifty of the sultan's finest. See the gold trimmings on those crimson cloaks and trousers. Only the elite of Sedinadola may sport such garments. They are of the costliest cloth."

"But where is their destination?" enquired Bleyne fingering a grey-fletched arrow and watching the last horsemen pass below them. Corin noticed that the archer had an almost disappointed glint in his dark eyes, and, as often before, he wondered what went on behind that taciturn face.

They watched for several moments more, until at last the riders faded from view beneath the shimmering heat of the sun. Yashan was the first to rise. Grim-faced, the tribesman re-joined Tamersane, who recovered his steed and called out stiffly.

"You had better start out over the dunes," he told them. "Keep short of the ridges lest any more Crimson are close. I will see to our water supply." Yashan snatched a gourd from each of them and, after taking to saddle, rode down to the river whilst keeping a wary eye on the road ahead. Corin watched him go.

"What is it that scares so stalwart a man?" he muttered, shaking his head at their guide's edgy behaviour. Zallerak glanced knowingly at him but said nothing. Instead the bard turned and led his horse towards the next great ridge of sand.

You're a conniving bastard, wizard. Corin looped a hand around Thunder's rein.

"Come on, big lad—no antics now. I'm not enjoying this either." Corin was about to lead Thunder on when Ulani placed a huge knuckled hand on his shoulder.

"Think not harshly about the guide, he is a brave man," Ulani told him. "But some things test a man's courage to its brink. Yashan knows what lies beyond these dunes. His desert heart, though stout, misgives him. He is filled with trepidation. I know too, and the knowledge delivers small joy."

"The Ty-Tander?" Corin's blue/grey gaze pierced the other's warm brown sparkle.

"The very same," answered Ulani. "So his fame has reached the wild north country."

"No, I heard the name mentioned at Silon's council. Some kind of beast, I assume."

"That and more. Much more. The folk of this desert are a tough people, Corin. But they are also superstitious. I doubt Yashan will accompany us for much longer."

"Perhaps he is wise not to."

"There is that."

Corin gripped the reins and patted Thunderhoof's neck before urging him forward in Zallerak's direction. Thunder complied readily enough; Corin was grateful to the beast, Thunder obviously re-alised how tricky things had become. Ulani led his horse alongside. As they struggled through the soft sand the king told him what he knew of this fabled creature.

"The Ty-Tandii, or guardians of the crystal, were many once. But legend says that one by one they devoured each other until only the strongest, youngest of them remained.

"What were they—cannibal goblin-monsters?"

"Worse by far, and bigger."

"Giant cannibal goblins? Am I missing something important?" Tamersane had joined them with his own beast in tow, together they flanked the west ridge of the nearest dune.

"Even worse—this creature farts fire." Ulani made a roaring sound.

"Impressive," said Tamersane. After looking around Ulani continued in a quiet voice.

"That was so long ago nothing is known for certain. But rumours abound of this last ferocious beast of legend. Stories of his belching flame and horny hide have even reached us in distant Yamondo. It is said he cannot be slain, but neither can he escape from his prison amidst the Copper Desert."

"And guess where that is?" Ulani flashed them a grin.

"Due south beyond these dunes." Corin saw Yashan approaching. "You have it."

"Why was it imprisoned?" Corin pulled his grey hood down to protect his face from the blazing glare. He nodded thanks when Yashan tossed him a full gourd. When their guide heard the subject of their discussion his eyes narrowed. Yashan awarded the three an un-friendly glance and led his horse forward to join Bleyne and Zallerak, who were already cresting another rise ahead. Corin watched Yashan for a moment before tuning back in to Ulani's words

"As I said, the Ty-Tandii were guardians. Fashioned from fire made by Croagon the Smith: hewn from the very essence of earth crystal.

"But Croagon was tricked by his siblings. Those other deities were envious of His skill. It was Telcanna Himself who turned the creatures against Croagon. The Sky God was jealous, you see. Telcanna bid the Ty-Tandii form a ring of flame, trapping both the Smith and His great treasures under the mountains. Just because Croagon wouldn't share His craft.

"The Ty-Tandii ringed the entire Crystal Mountains at that time. Their fires kept Croagon holed up inside His forge. For though Croagon could craft things out of fire, He couldn't withstand it when raised against Him."

"These meddling gods have got a lot to answer for," Corin said. "This Telcanna sounds like a total twat."

"You are right, but such things are better unsaid. Telcanna has ears in the desert, Corin an Fol."

"I'm used to being plagued by immortals, one more won't make much difference." The other two stared at him quizzically. Corin shrugged. "Pray continue, we're captivated, Ulani. Aren't we, Tamersane?"

"Absolutely. But we had better speed up,, the other three are leaving us behind."

They closed the gap. Both riders and horses were getting used to the dunes, it was hard work but they were making progress. As for Thunderhoof—he seemed quite happy listening in to Ulani's tale.

"Then much later the Golden Folk arrived in their glass chariots," Ulani continued. "The Aralais were at the height of their power before the thousand year war against their dark kin. The Golden's cunning spellcraft fooled the guardians into letting them pass beneath the mountains.

"Hence they were able to plunder the mountains' crystal and cajole Croagon into crafting thirteen magical talismans. These they needed for their planned war with the Urgolais. The Crown of Kings was one such artefact, the sword Callanak, another. Rumour speaks of an enchanted bow hidden somewhere in my own country—a matter dear to my heart. Come on!"

Ulani led his horse over another sinking crest of sand, whilst Corin egged Thunderhoof on beside him. Corin wondered how it was this king from so far away owned such depth of knowledge. Corin berated his ignorance of the wonders of Ansu and listened intently as Ulani continued his tale.

"Croagon resented having been made to do the Aralais's bidding—to serve the needs of lesser beings. So He sought provocation against the Golden Ones.

"The Smith put his case to His higher kin. They were empathic. The High Gods run a select club. They might despise each other but They're not open to new members. How dare these newcomers tramp on Their territory? Even Telcanna—who loves bright things—resented the beauty of the Golden Folk's creations.

"With His kin's permission, Croagon was freed to work the crystal forge again. Telcanna even aided Him—together the two gods fashioned a new improved Ty-Tander. A creature wrought from purest crystal, far stronger than the others made earlier.

"All Croagon's malice and Telcanna's resentment went into their new creation. They say that it was the Sky God Himself that breathed life into the beast. His purpose, to drive the Aralais imposters from the Crystal Mountains where many now lived in affluence and comfort.

"But the Smith was not content with their evacuation; Croagon was vengeful and bid the creature rend the Aralais marauders limb from limb. And so a great slaughter commenced outside the mountains. It turned the region known now as the Copper Desert into a sea of blood—hence the name."

"Can't say I look forward to seeing it," said Tamersane.

"When he had consumed the impostors," continued Ulani, "this new Ty-Tander turned on his own kind, devouring them all. The monster grew even more terrible as his hunger waxed. Finally he assaulted the mountain, turned on his part creator and once again Croagon was trapped at His forge, and again His kin ignored

Their younger brother's plight.

"The knowledge that he was betrayed a second time and a prisoner again drove Croagon mad. He tore his eyes from their sockets in uttermost despair." Ulani scratched his beard thoughtfully before continuing.

"We in Yamondo heard that eventually even the other High Gods became afraid of Their brothers' latest creation. Telcanna was pressured into contriving an invisible cordon of power around the Copper Desert, trapping the Ty-Tander within. There the creature remains contained to this day."

"That must be one hungry beastie," said Tamersane.

"Aye," nodded Ulani, "that he is. Hungry and vicious. We in Yamondo know well to stay clear of the Crystal Mountains and their guardian!"

"Had we a lick of sense we would do the same," muttered Corin. "But why accompany us, Ulani? I doubt those soldiers would trouble you; the sultan has no quarrel with your country. Or does he?" Corin studied Ulani's face; the king was heavy set with blunt nose and square jaw. His close-cropped greying beard hinted he'd seen well over forty winters. Alone among the companions the king seemed entirely at ease with his surroundings.

Ulani grinned at Corin. "I have no quarrel with Samadin."

"Who's that?" Tamersane enquired.

"The sultan, you idiot," said Corin.

"Oh."

"But I would fain get a look at this Ty-Tander close up, maybe find a soft spot to put an arrow in his crystal hide. Hunting such a beast would prove an opportunity of a lifetime." Corin and Tamersane exchanged horrified glances.

"I thought you said it was unkillable." Tamersane was cursing his horse as the beast was slipping back in the sand. "I mean if it gobbled up half the Aralais we'd scarcely make a snack."

"So legend says," replied Ulani. "But then I never dwell too much on hearsay."

"And you said your people avoid that region." Tamersane scratched his ear.

"Yes, but I am myself and not my people."

"You're as bad as Barin," laughed Corin.

"Who is Barin?" asked Ulani.

"A great farting hairy lout from the north country. Your size, King Ulani, mayhap a touch taller and broader in the chest."

"Pah! I would like to meet this Barin," scoffed Ulani. "I'll challenge him to an arm wrestle. Where does he hail from exactly?"

"The far north," responded Corin, "an island full of ice and cold. You wouldn't like it there. Ride on!"

Chapter 24

Doubts and Delusions

On the second day after leaving the Narion the High Dunes levelled out. The ridges became less steep and there were broad level gaps between each, allowing the riders to mount. A welcome change after what seemed an age dragging and pulling their horses. At last they could make fair progress. They kept it slow at first, the sand was still soft and the horses needed to time to adjust. But it felt good to be mounted again.

They formed single file, Corin at the back with Yashan leading and Zallerak close behind. Next rode Bleyne, Tamersane and Ulani just a few paces in front of Corin.

Corin dozed in the saddle. The heat was oppressive and he hadn't slept well last night. His mind churned with nagging doubts and worries. He didn't want to be here. Added to that, Corin was convinced Zallerak was up to something. And after hearing Ulani's account of what lay south, it seemed to Corin they were courting disaster. He closed his eyes, allowing Thunder make his own way.

Easy, boy—you look after me and I'll look after you.

Time dragged. Days passed hot and relentless. The mood of the travellers blackened, even Tamersane was dour. The annoyingly cheerful Kelwynian now wore a constant long face.

Zallerak muttered and chewed his lip, while Yashan grew grimmer by the hour. Bleyne stayed hawk-alert but his mouth was set in resolution.

Ulani held cheerful but kept his thoughts to himself. Corin brooded and muttered expletives to Thunder. They were getting through their water supplies, the horses drinking most.

Corin sipped his gourd as he willed Thunderhoof ahead. He prayed to Elanion the sun move swifter, let night's cool release arrive to grant them rest.

It was telling on the horses, and Corin was becoming concerned for their plight. He regretted that they hadn't asked Hulm for some camels whilst they had the chance. An oversight, that. Thunderhoof remained hale but mournful, but some of the other steeds looked worn out. Yashan steered close and muttered in his ear.

"We'd be better served by camels, these horses are failing. Had I known our course would change I'd have purchased some in Agmandeur. Too late now."

Corin shrugged, wondering if Yashan had read his mind. "They'll be all right so long as they get good rest tonight. It's the water concerns me most."

"Me too," growled Yashan before urging his beast ahead.

At dusk they made a hasty camp. Yashan lit a small cheerless fire out of some twiggy logs he had brought with him from those last bushes by the river's edge. As evening deepened the temperature dropped dramatically.

"Some place, this," Corin grumbled to Tamersane. "Melts you by day and freezes you at night!" Tamersane nodded, his mouth full of dried mutton. The Kelwynian wasn't himself this evening. He crouched staring moody at the fire. Corin left him to it. Ulani seemed unaffected by the cold. He informed them cheerfully that it was always like this in the deep desert at night. You get used to it, he said. Or if you don't then you die.

Following those cheerful words the king bade his companions goodnight. He tossed his robe on the floor and was snoring within minutes. Corin rolled his lean body in Thunder's blanket and shut his eyes. He dozed.

Bleyne took the first watch and was succeeded by Tamersane. It seemed to Corin that he had only just managed to nod off when his young friend's face appeared in front of him.

"What is it?" Corin grumbled. Wide awake, he shook himself free of the blanket and stood shivering beneath the stars. "I'm alright," he said after a moment's blinking. "Get some sleep, Tamersane."

It was so quiet sitting there alone. Corin rubbed his tired eyes and warmed his hands on Yashan's struggling fire. Now and then his companion's snores pierced the silence. All else was deathly still.

Fidgety, Corin wrapped the desert robe tight about his shoulders and wandered over to check on the horses. He froze.

What's that?

Something had caught his eye in the distant dark. A flash of light, a bright winking stabbing glare. It lasted about a second and then faded. Corin watched: seconds later it returned. Far to the south a golden aura, swelling, flickering bright, and then vanishing once more only to reappear further away before disappearing again.

Ghost lights. Corin bit his lip; the eerie lights were disturbing and further darkened his mood. And it was so bloody cold.

Someone is here. That familiar creepiness stole upon him. Someone giggled close by. Corin recognised that laugh.

Urdei—child of the past.

Turning, he saw the girl watching with that knowing smile. Her dress was still the same, as were her long blonde braids and scuffed knees. Before he could utter a word she had faded into the night, her laugher echoing around his head.

"Be careful, Corin," she called out to him from the dark. "There are traps ahead. Trust no one..." Her voice trailed off, mingled with the night breeze.

Corin mouthed an expletive. Unwilling or not, he was becoming accustomed to these weird visitations and refused to dwell on them like he had before. He would take Urdei's advice—that was easy and it would start with her.

Corin studied the night sky in silence for several moments but the strange lights did not return. He felt strangely calm. Resigned. There was no way out so why keep struggling? Move forward and confront what lay ahead. That way he'd see the girl again.

Corin thought of his other friends riding north to face Caswallon. He thought mostly of Shallan, wondered how she fared aboard Barin's ship. That night in Vioyamis seemed an age ago.

A soft movement to his right announced that again he wasn't alone. Wary, with hand on Biter's hilt, Corin turned. It was Zallerak. The bard had arisen from his rest to join him in the dark. For once Corin wasn't hostile. Any company was welcome right now.

"There were lights, away south," Corin said.

Zallerak only nodded, as if such phenomena were to be expected in the desert.

The bard's expression was lost. He looked tired, challenged, and Corin thought that he'd aged overnight.

"Something on your mind, wizard? It's not like you to mope—that's my province, remember."

Corin watched Zallerak reach beneath his cloak and retrieve his harp. Thoughtfully the bard strummed a clear note before awarding Corin an elusive smile.

"We ride into peril, Corin an Fol," said Zallerak as he strummed. Choice words those. Again Corin heard Scolde's cackle by the River Fol. It seemed so long ago.

"What ails you, Zallerak?" The bard ignored the question. He continued to finger his harp whilst staring dreamily into the middle distance.

Suit yourself.

Corin took to his feet and left the bard to his reminiscing. Returning to the fire, Corin unsheathed his hunting knife and viciously swiped at a glowing faggot, pitching it high in the air.

It landed yards away on Tamersane's cloak and began to smoulder. The Kelwynian awoke with a curse, rolled free and stamped on his robe. Tamersane glared at Corin, muttered something as he quenched the flames and then slunk back into a deep untroubled sleep.

"I wonder if she is right about you." Zallerak had followed him over.

"What...?"

"You have strength inside you, but are driven by your own selfish desires...I wonder."

"What the fuck are you talking about?" Corin slammed the knife in its sheath and glared at Zallerak.

"The days ahead will be challenging for all of us," continued Zallerak, oblivious to Corin's angry question. "Are you worthy of your destiny, Corin an Fol?"

"And what destiny is that? Pray tell me, great knowledgeable one."

Zallerak shook his head. "I don't comprehend near as much as you think," he responded, waving a hand. "And again I ask that you stop challenging me all the time, Corin. It doesn't help either of us. We are on the same side."

"Are we?"

Zallerak shrugged. He glanced eastwards. The sky was pinking, it would soon be time to break camp. "We must reach those Crystal Mountains before the enemy anticipates our plan. Time is short; I can feel *His* malice in the chill wind. He wakens beneath that mountain—King Ulani is right."

"Morak?" Corin's steely eyes bored into Zallerak but the bard seemed not to notice.

"Morak is just another player, Corin. I speak of Old Night Himself. The Great Enemy whose real name is never spoken. The

Shadowman, they used to call Him. I have felt His terrible presence of late."

Corin was going to ask more but Zallerak quickly changed the subject as if he'd already said too much. "Tarin is the key. Our false gambit and bluff. Had I seized the shards for myself it could have proved our undoing. Morak would have been aware at once and used all his power to thwart me, instead of concentrating on aiding Caswallon. They will be watching Tarin when he enters the Crystal Mountains, they will be curious, excitable. Hopefully his sudden appearance will keep them occupied. Allow us to come to his aid unseen."

"They?"

"The Urgolais, of course," responded Zallerak with a curt wave of his arm. "They are stronger underground. It's their natural habitat. The only way I can defeat them there is by first distracting them—hence the prince as bait.

"But be assured, Longswordsman, the dog-lords will be watching all roads south."

Light filtered pinkish grey into the hollow of their camp, within minutes all shadows had fled far away. Corin noticed the others stirring as the glow reddened in the east.

Zallerak's face looked bleak as he watched the companions shake themselves into movement. Hurriedly they all snatched a bite and a gulp of water, before breaking camp and saddling their mounts.

"I feel a challenge coming, Corin," Zallerak said, watching the others get ready. "A trial awaiting me beneath those mountains. It's going to be a close call."

But Corin had already joined the others as they followed the dour-faced Yashan south for yet another parched punishing day. Zallerak watched them in silence for a while and then spurred his horse to follow. Mortals were difficult for him, always had been. They lacked his ability to think on several levels and had no concept how fragile the balance betwixt good and evil. But he wasn't their enemy, not at the moment—though that could change should the game shift its pattern.

Zallerak hoped it wouldn't change. It was hard being ageless and alone, his kin lost and scattered and his memory fading alongside his strength. Every now and then a kind word wouldn't go amiss. He rode on, his thoughts hanging over him.

For three dreary days they struggled beneath the torturous sun. Again Corin fretted about their diminishing water supply, especially since the horses needed more all the time. He questioned Yashan why they did not travel at night. Yashan answered that there were hidden quagmires in the sand that could suck horse and rider down to a choking death in seconds.

On the third day the heat was like a burning knife probing at their flesh and still there seemed no end to the ridges of sand. The High Dunes seemed to go on for ever. The riders spoke little, conserving their strength. Corin felt light-headed; his mind began to wander. Then the vision fell upon him.

...Shallan smiled as he helped her down from the saddle. She blew him a kiss and then plunged her knife into his belly. *Trust no one...*

Her cruel smile twisted into Rael's. "My vengeance starts here, peasant," the Assassin said whilst heating the hot knife inches from Corin's face. Above, a mountainous island loomed black over ice laden seas. Shallan's face burned with hatred. Beside her the Dog-Lord hoisted Golganak high. "They are mine, mortal, these friends of yours—all mine," Morak told him.

Trust no one...

Corin came to with a jolt that nearly pitched him from his saddle. Beneath his thighs he felt the big horse battling with exhaustion. *Steady, boy...*Thunderhoof's breath rattled noisily. Corin dismounted, let the animal drink more than he could spare. He felt giddy, sick.

Ahead someone yelled. Corin, squinting into the glare, wit-nessed Tamersane shouting and waving madly, spurring his horse cruelly on as though he had seen something that they had not. Corin yelled but the young rider was out of earshot. Worried, he heaved his shanks over Thunder's back.

"Come on, brave lad—let's go see what that idiot's up to."

Tamersane urged his weary mount forward. The beast was tir-ing fast but it wasn't far. The Kelwynian could almost smell the clear water surrounding the golden palace. Just a mile or so ahead. *Ride, beast—ride!*

He could see the girl smiling at him, her dress translucent and her dark eyes flashing mischief beneath those cool swaying palms.

Gone was Tamersane's weariness. He was fuelled with desire. She wanted him and he was on his way. *Almost there!*

Then the sand shimmered like boiling glass blinding him mo-mentarily. Tamersane reined in, shielded his eyes, straining to see through the glare. Girl and palace had disappeared, as had that beautiful blue water. Instead Yashan's hard face glowered at him from beneath the scarlet burnoose.

"Ware the desert!" Yashan shook Tamersane's shoulder hard. "It will lure you to a lonely death!"

"I saw a palace," stammered the Kelwynian. "And clear cool water!"

"A trick of the desert. You had best forget it!" answered the guide gruffly before making his way back towards the others who watched anxiously from behind.

"Is he unwell?" Ulani's voice boomed the question.

"He saw a vision of beauty that lured him on," responded Yashan. "Not an uncommon occurrence this far into the desert—caused by light, heat and wandering minds. We must stay alert!"

Minutes later Corin watched the embarrassed Tamersane re-join their party. Another day like this and they'd all be howling at the moon.

"What did you see?" Corin asked, trying to placate his miserable friend.

"A golden palace. And lots of water. Blue water. Lots of it and..."

"And a girl?" enquired Bleyne who had joined them.

"Er... yes. And a girl," admitted Tamersane. "A pretty girl: she wasn't wearing much."

"There's a surprise," smiled Corin. Beside him Ulani laughed and even Yashan grinned. Tamersane was undeterred.

"I'll recognise her if I see her again," he told them. "Dark flashing eyes and long black hair. She had a wicked smile."

Corin exchanged a quizzical glance with Ulani and Bleyne. They shrugged.

"You're hopeless, Tamersane," Corin told him.

"I know," moped the Kelwynian.

As the sun set like crimson pain on the sixth day since their leaving the banks of the Narion, the desert finally altered its mood.

The High Dunes dwindled to smaller mounds and eventually flattened to a shiny nothingness filling the horizon. As the sun sank low that level terrain blazed like polished metal—a deep dark reddish gold. They had reached the Copper Desert.

Chapter 25

The Copper Desert

They reined in, taking in the sight. All were exhausted from heat and toil. "Yashan will leave us in the morning," announced Zallerak, throwing back his blue cloak and allowing the cool evening air to revitalise him. The others framed the question why.

Yashan shrugged. "I'll not enter that," he hinted at the shifting colours due south. "I urge you to shun it also."

"It is our only way, Yashan. Have I not told you this?" Zallerak's tone was peeved and impatient. The tribesman ignored Zallerak's sharp glance.

"Down to you then." He dismounted briskly and set about making a camp. The faggots were all gone and it would be cold tonight.

"Tell me of the Copper Desert," Corin stared at Yashan, probing the man's reaction. Yashan shrugged as if to answer was pointless.

"It is the home of the creature we do not speak of," he responded. "No tribesman has entered that region since the fateful day Onami, Prince of the Golden Cloud, greatest warrior Permio has ever known, led an army hence to slay the monster."

"Monster?"

Aye—that's what you will meet down there."

Corin didn't believe in monsters really. Perhaps this Ty-Tander was a myth after all. If Yashan's people never went there then how would they know?

"So what happened to this Prince of the Golden wotsit?" Corin enquired.

"Cloud. He never returned. Only fools or madmen venture beyond these dunes, Corin." Yashan would not be swayed from his opinion. "Sir Zallerak is not without knowledge and power, I grant him that. I only hope he can ward you from the horror that surely awaits you down there."

"I hope so too," muttered Corin. Perhaps it was some giant elephant or something. He'd heard about those from Ulani. Bloody great things with long bendy snouts apparently. Perhaps a big one had broken loose and got all grumpy and horny in the heat. He couldn't blame it. Still... Corin unsheathed Clouter and worked his whetstone along its five foot steel. Doubtless he'd need the blade soon. Ty-Tander or not.

"I shall keep a watchful eye," continued Yashan. "Lest beyond all hope you return in one piece."

"Where will you go after we've left?" Bleyne cut in. The archer had unslung his bow and was checking his arrows with a thoughtful eye.

"I will seek out Barakani," replied Yashan. "With the Desert Wolf lies our only hope of finishing the sultan's rule forever. My curved blade is his to command."

Later that night Corin approached Zallerak where he sat tuning his instrument. Corin wanted answers this time, not innuendoes. "Yashan is no coward and he knows the desert better than you do, Zallerak. We cannot afford to lose him."

"I realise that."

"Can we not skirt this peril?"

Zallerak sighed in resignation. He rendered Corin a withering look. "When will you trust my judgment?"

"Maybe, if you explained things a bit more."

The wizard wrapped his cloak tighter around his waist then tickled the strings of his harp. "We cannot go round about. West: that way is too far, our water would run out and we would perish from drought. If we fared in the opposite direction we'd be plagued by Crimson Guard, all spoiling for a fight.

"But more importantly time is pressing! We cannot leave Tarin in the trap alone."

"What trap?" Corin had a nasty feeling.

"My trap. The snare we'll spring on our foe—I told you Tarin was the bait. His price for the folly of his actions, Corin. While the Urgolais are waiting to trap me at Croagon's forge they'll pounce on Tarin instead, allowing me to sneak behind them and trap them in turn. Cat verses mouse—but who is who, haha?" Zallerak chuckled at his own wit. It was entirely lost on Corin."

"But this thing... this monster as Yashan calls it?" Corin waved his arms in dismissal of the bard's words. "Both Ulani and Yashan claim it cannot be slain." Corin still hoped those two were just fuelling fireside weed-pipe stories, but he wanted to press Zallerak on the subject. "I mean, does this thing really exist?"

"It did once. Now...? I'm not certain." responded Zallerak. "Hopefully we won't find out. The Copper Desert is leagues wide, but only a score or so miles deep when crossing from north to south. We've just enough water left. With rest the night before we can cross in a single day. A hard one, granted. Once across there'll be streams coming down from the Crystal Mountains. We're nearly there, Corin."

Corin wasn't convinced. "What does this Ty-Tander look like?"

Zallerak shrugged as though bored with the subject. "Pray to your goddess you never find out!"

Corin gave up. Later he got from Ulani that the Ty-Tander of legend was a beast at least a hundred foot long. Its crystal hide armoured with thick, iron hard scales.

It had acute hearing and could outrun any horse on its huge cloven hooves. Three twisted horns sprouted from the head, Ulani explained, while the four eyes searched constantly back and forth in furious hunger, lidless like a lizard's. It belched flame, Ulani added with a grin, and the ground rumbled at its approach.

Corin wished he hadn't asked.

He saw the eerie lights in the sky again that night, as did his friends. Yashan said nothing but his expression left Corin in little doubt of their source.

Belches flame...

Dawn rose clear and sharp. High above, a wisp of rose-pink cloud glided north fading behind the High Dunes. They struck camp in silence and once mounted, made for the end of the dunes. That final motionless wave of sand towered over the level ground below. They dismounted and let their steeds down from the High Dunes for the last time. At the bottom Yashan halted his mare and turned to face them.

"Here is where I leave you," announced their guide. "I've just enough water to reach the nearest hole back east. After that I'll go seek out Barakani."

Yashan reached forward with his right hand. He yelped in pain and alarm. Blue light shot up his arm, "Fuck! I forgot about the fence!" The air shimmered and buzzed for a moment then all was still. Corin and Tamersane exchanged alarmed glances with Ulani.

What the...?

"Telcanna's fence," said the king, as though that explained everything.

"Beyond this invisible ward I will not go," Yashan told them, shaking his arm which was numb from wrist to shoulder. He'd only brushed the invisible fence with a fingernail. "Make haste towards Orlot," Yashan told them. "That's a lone height some miles south of here.

"Once there you will be clear of the Copper Desert. The Crystal Mountains are no great distance. Easily visible from Orlot's flat top.

I would advise you climb that knoll, scan all ways before venturing on."

Yashan held up a palm in parting.

"Go with care, my friends. I'll pray to Star-Bright Telcanna we meet again soon!"

The five saluted Yashan farewell. Within moments their guide and his mount had vanished in the dunes.

Corin turned to Ulani. "Still want to accompany us, your Highness?"

"Certainly," grinned the king. "I've been looking forward to this. Now then, we need to crouch very low else Telcanna's fence grill us alive."

But Zallerak was not going to get on his belly for anyone. He voiced some incoherent words and strode forward. There followed a flicker, fizz-pop and throbbing buzz. Sparks exploded around the bard's head and his cloak caught fire. Unfazed, Zallerak yelled at them to follow whilst beating the flames from his cloak.

Needless to say the others took Ulani's advice and crawled forward on their bellies. Corin, last up, felt a peculiar tingling sensation as he crossed beneath the invisible barrier, it made his head throb and nuts itch. All else was fine. Once through he heard a loud snap, and looking back saw a jagged line of sparks running from left to right. Judging by that, going back wasn't an option.

Despite their worries that morning passed without event. The Copper Desert was flat and its surface hard, allowing better progress. The horses were happier too with solid ground beneath their hooves. But the riders had to monitor their speed, it was vital they didn't push the steeds too hard in their anxiety to be across.

Even with caution they made fair progress leaving the dunes far behind them. As they rode, the five riders passed the water gourds around, sipping as sparingly as they could.

The Copper Desert spread out in all directions, the hard ground scorched to a dull rusty colour. Unimpressive in daylight, uniform and featureless—save for the odd standing stone glistening tall in the heat as they rode on by.

Corin glanced suspiciously at those wind-sculpted twisted rocks, recalling the statues that had sprung to life so horribly in Kranek castle. Whenever one loomed close he urged Thunderhoof past it in haste.

The day wore on monotonous; relentless heat bore down on them as the ground drummed beneath their horses' hooves. All else silence, heat shimmer and dreary featureless terrain. Then at last far ahead beyond the heat's shimmer, Corin spied an oval hill appearing to float suspended above the flat seething surface of the Copper Desert. That must be Orlot. They were nearly there!

Come on, Thunder—we've almost cracked it!

Optimism grew as the fiery sun passed high above their hooded heads. It couldn't be much further. The ground was rockier here than it had been at first and wherever they looked they could see the weird stones, standing erect and stark like the forgotten army of some long dead warlord, all awaiting word of their master's return.

Tamersane tried not to look at the stones, he disliked this flat desert even more than the dunes, and after his earlier vision no longer trusted his senses.

Bleyne lobbed Corin a half-drained gourd as he rode alongside. Corin took a sip before tossing it over to Ulani. The black-skinned warrior was still annoyingly cheerful, Corin couldn't help noting. The king's greying, curly hair had won free of his hood, but he seemed unaware of the ferocious heat. Up front Zallerak's horse set the pace, gathering speed, sensing its rider knew they had nearly made it.

Now for the last push.

What's that?

Corin noticed movement and a whooshing sound brushed past his left ear. He caught the flutter of wings as the raven settled dark on one of the tall stones. Oroonin's bird watched him pass in silence, then shrieked skyward vanishing in the painful whiteness above. Corin felt the familiar dread take him.

His eyes drifted reluctantly to his right. There he saw two great rocks leaning into each as if whispering dark and dangerous secrets. Beneath the rocks stood a tall man, cloaked—his bony hands resting on a spear shaft. His face occluded by that wide brimmed hat and a raven preening its wings whilst perched easy on his left shoulder. Sunlight danced from the tip of his spear. Corin looked away. He knew that the Huntsman was warning him of peril ahead.

"Did you see him under those rocks?" There was fear in Tamersane's voice. The young rider's face was ashen pale despite his tan.

"Aye, I saw him," growled Corin. Without any prompting from him Thunderhoof quickened his pace.

"Keep focussed!" Zallerak barked from up ahead. They rode on. Moments passing slow, the horses snorting as their hooves thudded weary into the dusty brown ground.

Tension hung like fusion in the air. How much farther? Minutes slipped into hours until at last the light paled toward blue and the cool wind of evening whipped the dust up around their horses' flanks.

Corin gazed ahead at the distant hill. He couldn't understand it. Orlot seemed no nearer than it had when he had first spied it hours ago. He screwed his eyes into tight squinty balls, straining to discern a cluster of strange shapes lying ahead of them in scattered heaps. Rocks? Hard to tell. There was something sinister about them. They looked *wrong*. The wind whipped suddenly sharp, wrenching the hood free of his head. Corin steeled his nerves as he felt the small hairs rise on the base of his neck.

"What are those things? Is that gold?" Tamersane had slowed his mount to get a closer look. The Kelwynian's eyes had seen something glistening yellow in the fading light. He cursed in alarm when he recognised the vacant armour of some long dead warrior.

"Look, there are many!" cried Bleyne. The archer vaulted down from his saddle and approached a nearby shape. This corpse was in sorry shape with bones blackened and charred beneath the glinting armour. Bleyne reached down and grasped the helm but the metal crumbled at his touch and the charred corpse turned to fossilized crystal.

Zallerak reined in. He turned in his saddle, face furious.

"Bleyne, come away from there!" Zallerak snapped. "Ignore the phantom army, and don't touch that crystal! Come on, all of you! We must cross before dark falls!" For once Corin agreed with him.

They rode on apace; Bleyne joined them as they guided their horses carefully amongst the dully gleaming mass of long dead warriors. Corin shuddered as he passed them, many were only charred bones but others were encased in multi-coloured crystal.

They were eerie and quite beautiful in their way, and Corin could only guess at the fate of the unfortunate souls lying cocooned within that glowing stone. He leaned low above one dead warrior. Was that movement? There were things, tiny black scaly insects crawling all over his face. Corin shuddered and urged Thunder on.

Tamersane let out a muffled cry, Corin reined Thunder in lest the beast crash into his friend's horse.

"What is it now?"

"Over there—don't you see him?"

To their right leaned another a great rock stained purple in the fading light. Sitting at its base, as though resting and not long dead, was the body of someone who had once been a massive warrior, dwarfing even Ulani. This corpse was clothed from head to toe in burnished golden crystal; a great helmet hid the long dead features of who must surely have once been the Prince of the Golden Cloud. Horror entered Corin's veins like creeping lead when he stared into those fossilized eyes. He goaded Thunderhoof to greater speed, trying vainly to quench the growing alarm threatening to take hold of him.

They left the army of crystal corpses behind. To the south, a sheer ridge of stone rose up barring their way like a forbidding seamless wall. Beyond that the rose pink heights of Orlot loomed closer at last. Telcanna's fence could just be seen shimmering in the distance.

They allowed their horses free rein, both steed and rider eager to be far from here. The dust trails danced beneath them and soon the crystallised warriors were left far behind. Ahead the ground slanted up abruptly, a steep incline revealing craggy heights on either side.

"Come on, we have to cross that fence!" Zallerak yelled.

Up that slope they rode, leaning forwards in their saddles. *Nearly there! We're nearly there!*

Then from behind came a blinding flash of light and the earth thundered beneath them with the sound of heavy hooves.

Corin wheeled Thunderhoof around. His jaw dropped when he saw what had caused the dazzling light. A great belch of flame hid the creature's form as it thundered enraged towards them, but Corin could tell it was huge. Beyond huge. A terrible roaring filled his ears and searing heat scorched his face like burning tar.

Zallerak yelled out again:

"Fly! Come on, we can still escape! Don't lose heart this close to the fence!"

They heeded his words, spurring their steeds on like madmen. None dared look back, but the roars were looming closer, second by second, as the fiend gave chase. Beneath its bulk the ground quavered and the desert echoed with the hollow clamour of heavy cloven hooves. Ahead the wall of rock split suddenly in two as if cut by a giant knife. It swallowed the road. At once they were plunged into a dark ravine, with sheer crags leaning precariously down from lofty heights on either side. At the far end fizzled Telcanna's fence—near and yet so far.

Time froze in fear and sweat. The scorching heat of the monster's flame burnt their backs. Zallerak, grim-faced, kept yelling, urging them on with increasing desperation. Beneath them the horses needed no prompting—they galloped like the wind despite their fatigue, whinnying in terror at the ancient horror giving chase.

Silence.

The dreadful roaring had stopped and the sound of leaden hooves trailed off. Corin turned, glimpsed the monster's glowing

bulk turn aside and fade into the fast approaching dusk. He sighed—
that was close. A flood of relief rushed through him as Thunderhoof
threaded along the narrow ravine, beside him his companions
breathed again. Tamersane even managed a pathetic joke, though
no one else heard it. It seemed that miraculously they had escaped.
Telcanna's fence lay scarce a hundred yards ahead, shimmering like
silver thread in the twilight.

The monster had lost interest or else was forbidden to go further.
That was the only explanation. Corin glanced up at the steep sides
of the ravine, the twisted rocks crouched over them in disapproval
as they steered their tired horses through, their thudding hooves the
only sound in the swiftly approaching dark. Long dead trees showed
bare roots still clinging with brittle grey sticks to the vertical sides of
the slopes. Now and then these ashen roots reached down, trapping
their limbs and poking at their faces like dead men's fingers.

Keep going—just a few minutes more.

The ochre pink flanks of Orlot loomed high and close. Then the
ravine narrowed abruptly, funnelling into a sharp cleft, Telcanna's
fence shimmering and sparking horizontal between it—almost in
arm's reach. Scarce more than a slice through the rock, the narrowing
crack forced them into single file again. But they were nearly through
and could see that it opened into a wide space scarce yards away.

Last push!

A monstrous shadow blocked their path. Something impossibly huge bulked out of the darkness, blocking light and sparkle of
fence ahead. Corin felt his heart sink like lead slingshot in a well.
The guardian had played them for fools. They had been willing par-
ticipants and now they would pay his price, trapped in this corner of
his lair.

Straddled across the cleft bulked the monster like a steaming
boulder, the cloven hooves pounding, shaking the steep sides of the
ravine and causing rocks to cascade down in front of them.

The Ty-Tander. He had come at last. Just when they thought
they had made it. They were trapped. Held fast like corks in bottles.

The brute raised its hideous head and bellowed in fury. A terrible din, the horses whinnied, even Thunder bucked and kicked and snorted. Somehow Corin held on. Tamersane's hands covered his ears. Bleyne was struggling for an arrow—though what shaft could pierce that hide, he alone knew. Ulani remained calm, but Zallerak was yelling his head off. Corin at the rear struggled to calm Thunder whilst cursing every god in the Firmament.

Their tormentor was in no hurry. Those four flickering eyes glowed down on them like marsh gas, mocking them with alien sentience and age old cruelty. Daring them do something—anything to prolong their pathetic little lives.

The triple twisted horns thrust out from the monster's thorny head like the curling poisoned blades of a Ptarni chariot wheel.

Slowly, indolently, the beast eased its bulk along the top of the cleft, sliding nearer to where they sat on their terrified horses. There was no room to turn the steeds about—they might as well have been encased in amber for all the manoeuvrability they had.

Corin, gaping up, saw that the Ty-Tander's entire hide was covered in gleaming flanks of steel-like crystal scales, sweeping up, and rising to sharp spiky ridges on its back. A tail whipped behind with smaller spikes adorning it like a cluster of knives, the end ball like in shape and heavier than any mace. That tail was the width of a mature oak and over twenty feet long.

The shimmering scales flickered in the fading light. They shone golden yellow, before turning rose-pink then crimson, then back to gold. The creature thrust its triangular head down through the crack toward them and bellowed outrage at their intrusion.

The noise was deafening, the ground shook and the ravine shuddered, the horses kicked and whinnied. Each rider clung onto whatever he could, lest he be crushed to bloody pulp in the panicked melee of hoofs below.

Steamy tendrils vented from the monster's two flaring nostrils, each one large enough to swallow a man whole. The ravine shook and trembled, spilling more boulders, blocking any possible retreat.

Then Tamersane's horse reared and kicked in sudden violence, catching the rider off guard. The Kelwynian was pitched from his saddle. His head struck the ground with a thud. Wild-eyed, Ulani grabbed the horse's bit and brought the beast back under control lest it kick its rider to death. Corin glared down at his prone friend. Tamersane did not stir, a dark stain oozed down the right side of his face. Corin reached back in his saddle. Face red with fury, he slid Clouter free and cut a triple loop in the air.

"Come on, then you acre of shite! Come play with a Longswordsman!"

Slowly, warily eyeing the monster watching him above, Corin dismounted and the other three followed suit, Bleyne sliding bow and arrows from his saddle in one fluid motion.

Corin's defiance had all the monster's attention. The beast wasn't used to this kind of bravado and glared down with angry bafflement. Corin used the brief impasse to whack Thunder's flank.

"Ride forward, old boy—the others will follow you. Crash through that fence and keep fucking going! Let warriors and warlock put paid to this bugger!"

Thunder showed his teeth, he didn't like leaving his master but recognised the logic of his words. He stamped a forehoof, bolted through the narrow gap between monster and rock, the other horses following urgently behind. Telcanna's fence fizzed and popped as they crashed on through. In moments they had vanished deep into the night.

And now it's our turn.

Corin raised Clouter high, took a step forward.

Then came the flame.

Chapter 26

Shifting Patterns

Shallan watched the dazzling dance of lights. For hours they had lit the night sky to the south, casting weird shadows on the ocean's restless surface. She watched in awe at Barin's side as the heavens blazed forth in fiery streaks of red and gold. Behind her the crew of *The Starlight Wanderer* gaped white-faced as the vision lit up the sky.

"What is it?" Shallan enquired of the ship's master. "I have never heard of such a thing before!"

Barin shook his head. He cast a wary eye up at the sails above as if expecting another storm. "I don't know, milady," he answered, tugging at his shaggy head and grunting. "A warning of changes perhaps."

"Changes?"

Barin shrugged. "I don't know—just a notion. It reminds me of the Giant's Dance."

"And what is that?"

"They used to say it's caused by the ice giants from north of my country throwing lightning spears at each other. But I know it for natural phenomena—something to do with the climate up there. The Dance is often seen in the far north beyond my island. "Yet this feels different, I sense real anger in those colours. It's a warning. Maybe the southern gods fight amongst each other. They are rumoured a quarrelsome lot."

"Or maybe it's just weird weather," Shallan said. She thought of Corin and the others far away in the southlands. She wondered whether they were watching the dazzling display of light in the sky.

"Weird weather? I hope that's all. And not some nonsense that Zallerak cooked up." Barin smiled at her. "You had better check on your father, girl," he urged her. "If his condition worsens we will have to alter our course and seek shelter."

"He won't allow that."

"He won't have a choice." Shallan nodded and went below.

For many days they had fared north over rolling waves, glimpsing land only once when the far off cliffs of South Head raised their sandy rim briefly above the starboard horizon. Tension on board ship had grown hour by hour; most the crew were still troubled by what they had seen on the coast of Golt.

They were a suspicious lot, these sailors, Shallan had discovered. Clearly terrified of the strange phenomena currently filling southern skies. The grizzled Wogun said it was a portent of doom. Most seemed of like opinion. Even the jocular Taic was tight-lipped.

Fassof ruthlessly quelled any such mutterings, barking at his crew relentlessly from dawn to dusk. But they weren't happy. Neither old hands nor newbies. Even the angry-eyed Zukei looked grimmer than usual.

Despite the tense atmosphere these last watery days had passed without much account. Apart from the Duke of Morwella's condition.

Duke Tomais's fever had spread. His mind wandered between consciousness and troubled sleep. Shallan's face was lined with worry. She had tended her father with loving skill, but lacked the knowledge of a physician. Neither had she the fresh herbs and medicines needed to aid his recovery. As time passed the duke's strength waned further. Shallan began to fear for his life.

She knocked the door, entered her father's cabin to check on his state. He lay there motionless, white and wan. Shallan placed a pale hand on the duke's icy brow. Her father's face was corpse white, but at least his sleep was untroubled for the moment. Shallan heard heavy footsteps behind her. She looked up, seeing Barin's concerned blue gaze watching her from the doorway. Shallan was surprised to see Zukei standing beside him. The black girl's face looked gaunt and her expression resigned.

"This girl knows medicine, or so she tells me." Barin motioned Zukei forward to sit by the duke. The girl perched at the edge of his bed and felt his pulse. Then she placed a callused palm on Tomais's sweating forehead and closed her eyes. She sat in silence for several minutes as Shallan and Barin watched on with worried expressions.

"He will die." Zukei opened her eyes and glared at Shallan. "His fever has taken hold and he's lost all will to fight it. He needs certain herbs and unguents. There is nothing I can do for him here."

"Thank you." Shallan's eyes were moist. Barin, frowning, bid Zukei leave them, and the dark girl departed without further word. Barin loomed awkward, Shallan could tell he was unsure what to say to her.

On a sudden whim Shallan reached up to hug his bearded bulk. "Barin, I'm afraid," Shallan said as tears held back for days at last spilled free. "So afraid—like this world is closing in on us. I feel trapped and alone. And now my father is dying."

But is he my father?

Barin held the tearful girl close for a time. He thought of his pretty daughters far away. He was getting old. He'd nearly seen fifty winters and had been voyaging too long. Barin wanted nothing more than the peace of hearth and ale, with lazy hounds lolling and kin laughing close at hand.

But his life had never been thus. Few knew the struggles of his childhood when the witch-queen ruled his island. When his father was cursed and his mother banished far from their home.

Barin sighed.

Mine is not an easy course.

He smiled down at the brave daughter of Duke Tomais. So beautiful. So lonely and lost. Barin had guessed that the duke was dying. He had hoped Zukei could do something, having heard from Fassof that the girl had healing skills. It saddened him that Shallan would be left to face the horrors of Car Carranis under siege without even a friend by her side. With a sigh he thought of his flaxen-braided wife. Marigold would understand. More than that, she would insist he do the right thing.

You'll have to wait a while longer, my love—but keep the hearth warm. I'll be home before spring thaws the mountain snows.

"We'll change course and head inland," Barin told Shallan. "Make nor' east for the coast of Kelwyn." Shallan hardly heard him. She wriggled free from Barin's grasp to lean over the duke's sleeping form.

"Zukei will be able to obtain medicines from the markets in Calprissa. That should help him some. If not then we'll hire a qualified physician." Barin believed the duke beyond help, but also knew Shallan needed something to focus on lest she despair.

"What of Rael Hakkenon and his pirates?" Shallan asked, trying not to show the relief she felt after absorbing Barin's words.

"We will keep an eye out for them. Don't worry that lovely head, girl."

Shallan smiled at the word girl. She much preferred it to 'milady', and it seemed more fitting here. "Besides the lads will buck up now," continued Barin. "They like Calprissa, and the off chance of a fight with that pirate prince will put fresh fire in their bellies!"

Shallan hugged him again and then smiled as Barin left her and bulked his way back above deck. Barin was a good man. He'd the manners of a troll but then so did Corin for that matter. Shallan didn't care a jot. She'd never encountered anyone who came a mile close to either of them. One was her heart's desire, the other fast becoming her best friend.

"We are bound for Calprissa, Father!" Shallan stroked his forehead. She felt fresh hope surge through her veins, charging her tired soul with energy. They had turned a corner and that now things would improve. "They say that it's one of the fairest cities in the Four Kingdoms. We never went there did we? Do you remember, Father? It was always Wynais, where King Nogel held court. Just a little delay to get you well again—so don't worry. You are going to be all right. I love you...Father. Captain Barin will save us!"

Back on deck, Barin watched the men clamber aloft as *The Starlight Wanderer* heeled hard to starboard. Morning's light would raise the Cape of Calprissa. Barin drained a tankard noisily and wiped a tear from his eye. The girl had gotten to him. He was getting soft and fat. On the upside the barrels were all but dry so at least they could replenish. Everything happens for a reason.

"Fassof!" Barin yelled up.

"What?" The voice came from somewhere above.

"Tell Cogga he's to accompany the Lady Shallan to Car Carranis. And he can bring those tosspots Taic and Sveyn," laughed Barin. "I'll need scrappers with me. There's a spot of trouble waiting there or so they tell me!"

"I thought we were makin' for Calprissa," yelled the mate.

"We are. I'm just planning ahead."

Barin turned to study the horizon, watching for some time as the dancing lights faded behind them in the southern sky. Shallan had stayed below with her father and Barin was left to his thoughts. His eyes widened suddenly as a bright flash of light shone out before vanishing into the night, taking with it the last of the surreal light display. Darkness followed. Barin poured an ale and stared deep into the night. Those lights meant trouble for someone, that was certain. A warning—but for whom? Barin suspected he knew the answer to that.

Take care down there, Longswordsman.

***

From His seat in the clouds Oroonin watches events in the Permio Desert. He silently applauds the hectic display of gold and blue jets shooting up into the night sky. Fireworks—He always loved them. Magic and mayhem caused by someone fighting down below. Someone He had a vested interest in. A fine spectacle, it would be seen for hundreds of miles. Oroonin hefts His spear in silent approval, and then stiffens sensing His younger brother's imminence. Telcanna's electric blue radiance fills the atmosphere. The Sky-God approaches. The Huntsman can see that He is angry. Oroonin shrugs: Telcanna is always angry.

"WHAT IS GOING ON DOWN THERE?"

"You should know. It's your desert, brother. And no need to shout, it's just us two sharing this cloud."

Blue fire leaks from the Sky god's mouth as He thunders towards His seated brother. "Someone's throwing thunderbolts. It's not to be borne, LIGHTNING IS MY PROVINCE, BROTHER." The Huntsman is unimpressed by Telcanna's blazing countenance. He's seen it all before.

The clouds around Him charge and crackle with cobalt fire. Telcanna looms over Him; fury encases His younger sibling in blue fire. The blazing light hides the beautiful face of the Sky God but Oroonin isn't dazzled. Oroonin sees through that brightness, can tell Telcanna is fretting again. No lesser being may look on Telcanna's image without being destroyed utterly.

But Oroonin is unconcerned. To Him, Telcanna is just a petulant spiteful youth. Oroonin awards Telcanna His single penetrating eye. A cold humour edges the Huntsman's gravely tone.

"Stop your carping, Telcanna," laughs Oroonin in a voice that grates like steel on stone. "You are only upset because your pet's on the rampage again. I'm surprised you care, brother. That Ty-Tander has long outlived its usefulness!"

"That's fine for you to say, meddler." The Sky-God leans over

His artful brother and blows in His ear, a mile high tower of majesty and light. "You just sit watching and waiting. Twiddling your thumbs, as ever wrapped in your riddles and cleverness while some of us plan DIRECT ACTION!" Telcanna's voice booms across the heavens parting clouds and upsetting the cosmic harmonies. His angry blue countenance starts to melt the cloud around Oroonin's seat. The Huntsman remains insouciant.

"Why fear this Aralais? He is no threat to us anymore," says Oroonin. "His kin—what paltry few remain—driven into the darkest corners of Ansu, together with most of their artefacts. Callanak, the Golden Bow and the other trinkets they tricked us with. All lost or broken."

"They can be found."

"Relax, brother, this Aralais is weak. A shadow of what he once was!"

"That schemer and his kin threatened our hold over Ansu once, brother," countered Telcanna. "Or are you so enmeshed in your own designs that you FORGET THE PAST."

"I forget nothing," replies Oroonin, His face darkening. Telcanna is starting to vex him. This always happens. He stands, points His spear at His brother's cobalt aura. The blue fizzles and pops then fades to dreary grey like a cosmic sulk.

"Forget the Aralais wizard, it's the mortals that concern me. Or rather one of them."

"More fragile slaves to swell your army of corpses, you old gallows crow!" Telcanna scoffs. "I never could understand your interest in the ways of men, Oroonin. They are pathetic creatures, I wonder why the Weaver allowed their spawning, He must have been having an off day when He fashioned such weaklings.

"In that desert land down there," Telcanna points contemptuously down through the cloud. "The priests cry out my name as if they think I care a cosmic shit what happens to them. They crawl on their bellies and chant in those grubby temples believing I care, when I'd happily fry their livers for breakfast. If only I could be bothered, that is and didn't have other, more pressing diversions. MEN ARE FOOLS!"

"They have their uses—some more than others admittedly."

"Many will serve Our dark brother when the time comes for war."

"Why do you think I recruit all I can for us now?" Oroonin wished His brother would depart to another planet for a decade and give Him some space. Why were His family such a pain in the arse?

"Someone has to plan ahead. When our dark brother wakes I for one want my army of corpses ready."

"He will blow them apart. His province is death, brother—not yours."

"No—His province is evil."

"And when He wakes I shall send His black soul screaming back to Yffarn. I don't need mortals to do my dirty work, Oroonin."

"Well you have yourself." replies Oroonin, waving His spear and taking to His seat again. "But don't expect a show of arms. You are in the minority here, brother. Sensuata stews in His fishy bath—what keeps Him occupied down there is beyond me."

"We don't need Him."

"Those connivers Croagon, Undeyna and Crun are all contained," continues Oroonin. "They can do nothing until their sentences are served out. And Undeyna will most likely follow Him again—there's no saving that one. So don't expect help there."

"I wasn't."

"Where then? Our niece Simioyamis is away with the faeries as usual. Tatiana Widethighs is contracted out to another galaxy—who knows when She'll be back. And Borian is no help, busy blowing up storms beyond the nine worlds."

"What of Elanion?"

"My wife? How would I know? She doesn't speak to me."

"AND WHOSE FAULT IS THAT?"

Oroonin ignores that last jibe. He feels miserable now, He always did when his Sister's name was mentioned. "She fiddles in her forests and plots and weaves against me. After all this time She still harbours resentment. It was only a brief fling with that water nymph—She's such a cold bitch, your sister. A mere dalliance—and She with all Her lovers too. Hardly fair." Telcanna isn't listening but His brother doesn't notice.

"I've never understood Her and now She has set my daughters against me. Vervandi especially holds a grudge. It vexes me. But Elanion likes to keep an eye on Ansu as do I. After all *He* will awaken soon."

"Let Him waken, brother. I AT LEAST AM READY FOR BATTLE!" blazes Telcanna, lighting the skies with livid electric blue.

Oroonin smiles at that. He has seen no future for the Sky God in His plans. He ignores His sibling; eventually Telcanna takes the hint. The Sky-God strides off moodily to His waiting carriage. He then spurs the electric steeds onward across the heavens whilst hurling thunderbolts at anything He encounters. Telcanna's cobalt chariot creaks and grinds beneath Him as He steers it through the clouds. The din sets Oroonin's teeth on edge. The Huntsman shrugs. He returns to his study below. Damn and blast Telcanna, he'd missed the show. The contest below was almost over.

***

From his high tower in the palace Caswallon had also witnessed the strange lights in the sky. He deemed them no natural phenomena. He knew there was sorcery going on somewhere, knew the stakes were getting higher in this paramount game.

The gods stir.

Caswallon had sensed a quickening lately. A shift in the firmament. There were others playing this game of his and he must needs tread carefully. He knew the signs—had read the stars. Next spring a conjunction, greater even than the one that pre-empted the fall of Gol would come into place.

A time of change. All nine planets would slot into their allotted place. A time of great opportunity. Or a time of unprecedented disaster.

The stakes were high. Knowledge was power and he was more knowledgeable than most. Timing was the key and so far that hadn't worked out too well.

It was frustrating. Months on, queen and prince and shattered crown still eluded him. They had had aid, that much was certain. The alien wizard—the stranger worked against him and his allies. But it was all down to patience really. This affair would be wrapped up in the desert soon enough. His allies had informed him of the prince's destination. Poor fool, Tarin could scarce imagine the reception awaiting him there.

The Urgolais would blast the remnants of the crown to powder—something he should have done, Caswallon admitted his failure there. Tarin would be slain—eventually. This Corin an Fol character Morak fretted about—he'd die in the desert too. Simple.

Gribble had informed him how the sultan had issued a prime mandate to capture these spies. His elite crimson guard would scan every dune. The renegades would be apprehended soon and their madcap quest fail.

Once he had knowledge of the crown's obliteration, Caswallon could concentrate on trapping that vixen Ariane. Too long she had thwarted him. Derino's army would break Kelwyn with the help of the traitor inside Wynais, then return home and smash the rebels still holding out in Kelthara. Then he could relax. This winter would see all such matters tidied up.

Small issues, they just needed resolving fast. What irritated him was how his enemies had stayed ahead of the hunt so far. They'd had a rare run of luck but that was fast running out.

A noise at the door. Gribble emerged through the special goblin flap Caswallon had had made for him. A Soilfin-sized door, wing friendly, with soft velvet hinges so he wouldn't scrape his claws. It was the smaller details that made the difference in this life. Caswallon didn't have many redeeming qualities. But at least he was fond of his pet. And Gribble was looking better these days (if a foul smelling, hairless fanged, winged goblin could look any better).

Caswallon's pet sported a new short sword at his waist. The scabbard was fabricated from a hundred foreskins (the only human parts avoided by the Groil—nobody really knew why). Gribble liked his shiny sword and used it to poke anything in range. It was very light and didn't affect his flight plans. He was Caswallon's only trusted confidante and kept both Groil and Perani in check.

"What is it, Soilfin, are you hungry again?"

"Yes, Mr Caswallon. But I'm here about my next scheduled flight."

"Ah, yes—I would learn how Starkhold is faring under siege, so take some sustenance and go pay visit."

"And, Gribble."

"Yes, Mr Caswallon."

"If you leave at once you'll get a special treat when you return."

Caswallon smiled to himself. Car Carranis would fall this winter and yet another cog would drop into place.

Caswallon watched the Soilfin exit his window, a dark speck arrowing out into the night. A useful servant, Gribble. Shame he didn't have more Soilfins. Caswallon took to his chair, warmed his bony hands by the fire and wondered just what really was occurring down there in the desert. Perhaps he'd send Gribble down there tomorrow.

Chapter 27

Fire and Ice

Corin dived low as the funnel of flame seared over his head, scorching the dead branches of the ancient trees and alighting them into crackling fury. His companions had already leaped for cover behind nearby rocks. They reached for their weapons, desperately trying to quell the panic surging through their veins.

All save Tamersane, whose prone form looked tiny and helpless in the fading light. That first gout of fire had missed him—just. The monster's dreadful bulk scraped the top of the cleft as it crawled forward, still with no urgency, content with its game.

The creature's hide blocked what little light remained. It loomed over them, close enough to fry them all. Instead the Ty-Tander raised its horny head and bellowed rage again. The roar deafened them; again shaking the ravine, and again spilling more rocks from the scree above. As one they covered their heads and ears. Burnt or crushed seemed the only outcome. Not a happy scenario.

"Back!" yelled Zallerak. "We've no chance stuck here!" The bard beckoned frantically then turned, stumbled over fallen rocks back down the ravine in a windmill of swaying arms and billowing cloak. In seconds he was gone from sight.

Corin spat in the fleeing bard's direction. Again he turned to face the horror.

"Come on, beastie, we're not all craven here. I'm going to poke your scaly arse with steel!" The Ty-Tander's roaring had ceased. Instead it drooled silver slobber over the inert body of Tamersane. Its eyes hovered like baleful lamps above the prone Kelwynian. It lowered a hooked hoof, commenced dragging Tamersane across the broken ground. Still he didn't stir.

Then slowly it lowered its three horns.

Tamersane chose that moment to open his eyes. It wasn't his finest decision. His jaw dropped as he stared petrified at the brute looming and stinking like decaying gallows feed just above him. He reached along for his sword but his fingers were slippery with blood. He couldn't grip the hilt properly. He tried again.

Down came the horns...

***

Corin saw those horns spear down, witnessed Tamersane roll free by a whisker. Again they jabbed. Again he rolled. The monster was still playing, it seemed—too idle to summon its ruinous fire.

But Corin wasn't playing. He wasn't idle—not today. He had enough attitude to bite the beast's fucking head off but lacked the molars. He levelled Clouter, yelled and then launched himself like a human missile at the monstrosity gloating and dribbling over Tamersane.

Whack...thud and groan. Corin's shoulder rammed into its ridged flank as a fly might bounce off glass, after striking that iron-hard hide with Clouter's length.

The blade clanged and wobbled in his grasp. Pain ran up Corin's arm, but he swung again and once more Clouter bounced off the dazzling scales surrounding the beast's horny face. This time his whole body quivered with recoil and Clouter rang like a holy bell. Corin clung to the hilt with both hands in desperation, gripped the rocky ground with his feet and made to swing again.

This one will hurt.

The monster, faintly distracted, turned its ponderous head in his direction and rewarded Corin with the full malice of its fiery four-eyed glare. Tamersane found that an opportune moment to roll over again and slip behind a rock. Once there he lost consciousness again.

The Ty-Tander's alien gaze fell on Corin. Those amber orbs were alight with contempt for this miserable bug daring to confront it. Never had it known such reckless valiance. But Corin felt his courage ebb rapidly as the full weight of that baleful stare fell upon him. Despite that fear he swung the blade—this time at the nearest horn.

Corin's stroke went wide, the beast having jerked its head back suddenly. Looking across, he saw Ulani's short spear clatter free of the monster's flank. Corin watched Ulani reach for another shaft and step defiant into the creature's path.

Behind the king, Bleyne (who had been waiting for his chance) held bow ready, seeking a clear shot at one of the beast's eyes. Of Zallerak there was no sign or sound. Gone. Corin cursed the bard for deserting them in their moment of need.

He raised Clouter again...

The Ty-Tander bellowed and roared. Seldom had mere mortals given it such trouble. This game had proved distracting but it was time to set a fire in their flesh.

An arrow pinged off its hide. The monster turned its head, nostrils flaring wide and launched a streak of amber fire that sent Bleyne whirling out of reach.

The Ty-Tander ignored Ulani's second spear. Instead it struck out at Corin with a barbed forehoof. Scarcely quick enough, Corin vaulted aside. Wild-eyed, he hacked at the leathery underside of the beast's foreleg. There were fewer scales here, bridged by small gaps of hoary foul smelling skin.

If I can puncture one of those.

He gripped Clouter hand over hand and stabbed hard at one such gap. The monster yammered as Corin's sword found entry, albeit shallow. Dark liquid oozed. It scorched the ground below. In sudden rage the creature lashed out, incensed this fly had pierced its armour. Forcing its entire bulk through the cleft, the beast tore down upon Corin an Fol intent on tearing him apart.

Corin dived for cover, the enraged beast close behind. Just then Tamersane (thankfully conscious again) rolled out from behind his rock with a yell. He stabbed up at the monster's nearest hind leg with a great two-handed thrust.

Again the beast was gored but only slightly. Roaring indignation more than pain, the Ty-Tander turned towards the blond warrior, summoned its fire and then bellowed like thunder again. But then the beast's roar changed key, rising to a searing wail of agony and outrage. Bleyne's next arrow had pierced an amber eye.

A dreadful wrath filled the monster. A hideous hate. Its hide blazed crimson fury and dark gooey ooze trickled from the pierced orb, Bleyne's slender shaft still showing like a needle in the iris. The Ty-Tander turned its full attention on the archer with nostrils flaring wide. Bleyne ran. The spout of flame tunnelled after him. Nothing could survive that. Trees crackled and hissed. Smoke filled the ravine. Bleyne the archer had vanished from view...

***

Corin still gripped his longsword in sweating palms. The Ty-Tander in its pain had momentarily forgotten him. Corin rolled beneath the monster's bulk, stabbing up towards the creature's belly but to little avail. Corin tried again but a hoof the size of an anvil (and just as hard) struck him square in the shoulder. That crunching impact lifted Corin from his feet, and sent him cartwheeling skyward, before sprawling onto the rocky ground with a painful thud. Corin's head whirled like a chariot wheel and his badly bruised side screamed at him. Despite that his body remained more or less intact.

He felt sick and giddy but clung onto Clouter like a life raft.

Shaky, Corin stood up but his strength failed him, his legs trembled and he sank to his knees, still gripping Clouter. Stubbornly he raised his longsword a final time as the monster's bulk loomed over him again. Then somewhere behind him Corin heard Tamersane curse. Dazed and nauseous, Corin turned his head witnessing the Kelwynian hack at the beast's tree-thick tail with his blade. Some hope. Impossibly quick for so huge a creature, the monster spun round, striking the fair-haired warrior with the iron hard side of a horn, sending him spinning.

And Tamersane lost consciousness a third time...

King Ulani strode forth. Boldly he confronted the Ty-Tander alone, his left hand flicking out with wickedly curved tulwar, whilst his right made ready with a golden-headed cudgel.

"Come on, demon breath—meet the king who will wreak your ruin! I am Ulani of the Baha!" Ulani dived forward, struck the beast's nearest horn with his tulwar. That was a mighty blow, the tusk was severed an inch from the monster's scaly crown and sent through the air like a juggler's baton.

The Guardian bellowed in outrage. It kicked and stamped down at Ulani with an anvil hoof, seeking to crush him to pulp. The king jumped aside, the horn missing his right ear by an inch.

Ulani struck out fast with the blade, severing the sinew behind the beast's left hind leg. The Ty-Tander roared in pain as the leg buckled beneath it. Ulani raised the tulwar again and closed in for the kill.

But the Ty-Tander was quicker. It had only feinted the buckled leg. Down on the king it pounced with cat's speed, catching Ulani off guard, sweeping the king aside with a thunderous blow from one of its remaining horns.

Thud—crunch. Ulani was knocked from his feet and sent flying. His face sprayed scarlet drops across the ravine, and his body crumpled on the stony ground with a hollow thud. He lay there lifeless and bleeding. The monster loomed close, its gaping maw revealing triple rows of filed crystal teeth. Its tongue forked like a snake's. Cobra-swift, that tongue danced out to lick the dripping blood off Ulani's battered face...

Corin shook life into his rattling bones. Somehow, he'd regained his feet again and with a great yell launched Clouter spear-like at the monster's ravaged face. The sharp steel cut into Corin's palms as he hurled the longsword but Corin didn't notice.

Clouter flew true—pierced another eye. The Ty-Tander roared in frenzy. The beast tore down upon Corin—twenty tons of dripping ooze and gleaming, rending fang. Corin reached down to his boot, gripped a throwing knife as the monster reared above him. He fumbled Biter free from its scabbard. He thought of Shallan—of Finnehalle. Queen Ariane, Barin; Cale and Galed. What a way to die.

Vervandi, Huntsman, anyone—help me now!

The monster's head was lowering upon him, the breath choking Corin and making him retch. Corin coughed as a barbed hoof thudded into his neck. Almost tenderly the creature lifted him up towards its horrible gaping jaws. Straining to breathe before blackness consumed him, Corin stabbed Biter up in a final act of defiance.

Eat this, fucker!

***

"Stop!"

The command echoed as dusk darkened to blackest night. The monster turned its head toward the voice. What new intruder was this?

Out of the corner of his squinting eye Corin saw that a tall shining figure had entered the ravine and stood defiantly facing the monster. The beast, sensing a new challenge, turned its attention towards this new adversary and unceremoniously dropped its prey.

Corin pitched to the rubble a mass of aches, saved only by his mail shirt from any broken bones. Forgotten for the moment, Corin wriggled free of the monster's range and staggered giddily to his feet. Ahead a new scene was unfolding. Corin gazed in amazement at the sapphire-blue aura radiating out from the newcomer and filling the night. Then he recognised him.

Zallerak. Of course. But a different Zallerak. Gone was the pompous bard, the elusive, evasive enchanter that so irritated him. Here was no wily warlock.

Instead confronting the Ty-Tander was a being of power and majesty, radiating blue light with eyes terrible and cold.

Corin remembered when he had first seen the wizard change form in the Assassin's castle. This time was different. This time Zallerak was clothed in gold from head to foot. A dazzling radiance of blue and gold emanated out from his form.

Over nine feet tall, Zallerak's eyes blazed golden fury, challenging and entrancing his foe. The long hair framing his ageless face was no longer silver, but rather shone with the brightness of the sun. That glare stung Corin's eyes, lighting up the rocky ravine and chasing shadows back behind rocks.

The Ty-Tander watched in deadly calm, its canny mind calculating and probing, reaching back into days long past. At last it identified this new challenger as coming from that earlier time.

Inside the beast's cold mind a seed of fear germinated. This enchanter was the source of the doubt that had awakened it from long slumber. The Guardian had sensed an old adversary had returned to challenge it. But who—and why?

Soon after the Ty-Tander had scented the mortals approaching across the desert, daring its domain—the first in so many years— its curiosity and cold fury had awakened, together with a terrible hunger rising up from within. Hunger so great only an immortal creature could sustain it.

Telcanna's guardian had watched and waited with growing anticipation for the intruders to approach. For not only was the Ty-Tander hungry, it was bored. But with the intruders came the feeling of doubt. A challenge from the past. Small wonder these mortals had proved hard to kill when one such assisted them from behind.

Now that mystery was solved. The guardian knew who confronted it. Here stood a great lord of that austere race vanished millennia past. A proud stern people the Ty-Tander and its long dead kin had scattered, chased and torn, limb from limb, until the surrounding desert became copper-stained with their arrogant blood.

The Golden Ones.

Thieves and plunderers, they had all but destroyed themselves in their apocalyptic war against their brethren. But now one at least had returned. The guardian had grown lazy. Never before had any creature touched its flesh as had these feeble men. These mortals had shown remarkable resilience. The wounds were a nuisance but they'd heal in time—even the eyes would grow back.

The Ty-Tander was invincible. But the beast remembered doubt and pain, sensations it had all but forgotten since the days of the Golden Race. They too had purged its skin. They too had had their little victory, then its flames had sent them to darkest Yffarn beneath that spewing mountain.

These mortal warriors would be broken then glazed with crystal to grace the desert like those before. But this newcomer wasn't just a golden one, but a sorcerer of old. The creature recalled a name of power, but names meant little to the guardian, a creature who in its glory days had defied the High Gods and caused even them to fret. Time to solve this riddle.

The Ty-Tander glared across at this adversary with its two remaining amber-fuelled eyes. The impostor warlock stood with palm raised out. The beast could smell the old hatred radiating outwards from the tall figure standing imperious just yards away.

The Ty-Tander channelled its rage and hatred. The pain of its torn and punctured flesh, the outrage of how that could have happened. Had it grown weak? Was it becoming old?

No. Such words had no meaning. The Ty-Tander was forever. The Guardian felt its belly surge with freshly summoned fire. A colossus of hide and crystal, it bore down upon the warlock.

BURN!

The flame surged through the monster's loins and up through the cavern of its throat. The air crackled and a great spout of flame engulfed the golden-blue aura of the wizard.

***

"Ice!"

Even as he heard Zallerak's command, Corin felt sudden chill enter the ravine and freeze the fiery blast of the monster. His head rocked, the ground heaved, and above the sheer cut of the cleft spewed stone, broken roots and loose detritus. The air crackled with fusion—raw untapped power.

Corin covered his ears as lightning smote the narrow canyon; the dead trees were torn from their roots, their fire consumed by freezing rain. Clouds rushed overhead. Weird shapes of blacker black, blanketing the stars, spilling great lumps of hail onto the desert floor. Bitter cold seeped into the ravine, quenching the monster's fire, freezing his dreadful breath.

Corin shivered. He watched in jaw-gaping awe, witnessing Zallerak step out from beneath the monster's last fire blast unscathed and unaffected. Corin could see that the enchanter now wore a golden circlet around his head. He looked younger, the sapphire cloak shimmering, half revealing symbols that meant nothing to Corin. In one hand he gripped his golden harp, whilst the other was raised palm forward toward his monstrous foe.

A grunt and groan close by. Corin was relieved to see that Ulani still lived. Cold chiselled deep into the ravine, stopping the monster in his tracks. It deepened in intensity, its bitter damp penetrating then splitting the dry rocks strewn haphazard in the gully.

Zallerak strode forward. His aura shifting between ice blue/white and gold, and his countenance stern. Zallerak now gripped his spear in his right hand, whilst the long fingers of his left worked a cunning dance along the harp strings. Alien, weird music entered the valley, growing in resonance until it drowned out the furious sound of the hastening storm clouds above. The monster loomed over him, snarling, reeking, the size of a house. Once again Zallerak spoke his incantation.

"Ice!"

This time a frozen lightning spear scorched the monster's hide like a meteor bolt. The Ty-Tander reared up in shocked pain before retaliating in fury by vomiting another jet of flame directly at its foe. And so the battle commenced.

"Ice!" commanded Zallerak again, once more stepping out unhurt from beneath the beast's blazing funnel. Gone were harp and crystal spear. This time the wizard clutched a glowing, ice blue javelin in either hand. He cast them at the two remaining eyes of the monster.

But the beast leapt backwards and funnelled flame, filling the ravine with crackling fire. Zallerak quenched the blaze with his icy bolts. Each time he hurled a shaft another appeared fresh in his hand.

Again and again he hurled his frozen missiles at the raging Ty-Tander. The monster responded with surging fire, roaring its hatred, spraying the rocks about with searing flame. Corin cowered in front of Ulani's prone form, trying to protect both himself and his friend from the terrible blasts. To his right he noticed Tamersane had once again regained his senses just enough to hastily seek shelter beneath a large rock. Of Bleyne the archer there was still no sign.

Pain pummelled Corin's body. His skin tingled as if an entire army of soldier ants were patrolling the length of his spine. His head pounded like a demon's gong; the terrible flames scorching his skin and smouldering his leather tunic. Adding to all that Zallerak's paradoxical cold clung to his steel shirt, freezing his sweat and snot and chilling him to the marrow.

I'll not lie here like a scolded whippet.

Corin leaned forward, retched on the floor and then squinted up at the continuing violence with morbid fascination. Corin had had better days but this was proving an encounter not to be missed. He willed aside his various woes and focussed on the conflict taking place scarce yards away. He saw that Ulani was watching goggle-eyed too, his own pain just under control. A sorry state—both of them barely managing to hang on to consciousness, but captivated as the titanic battle raged through the ravine.

Fire verses Ice: searing heat and numbing cold. Old adversaries free to do battle.

Zallerak's face was changing again. Gone were golden hue, and cool blue aura. Instead the enchanter paled to deathly white. His long hair flowing like freshly settled snow all around his face. The hands were blue/white with cold, the long fingers replaced with talons of ice.

The alien symbols and designs flashed neon on Zallerak's cloak. Dazzling the surrounding dark. The cloak had shifted to purest white, flanking him from head to toe. Statue still, Zallerak cast spear after spear at the monster, who in return belched gulps of fire down on its ancient enemy.

The ravine blazed and crackled like the pits of Yffarn. Moments melded into hours. Still they fought on, wizard and monster. Fire and Ice. Neither prevailing as the night deepened in the rift. This called for mortal intervention.

Tamersane painfully crawled across joining Corin and the still bleeding Ulani. Together they summoned their strength for a fresh attack on the Ty-Tander while it was locked in its epic battle with Zallerak. Here at last was a chance.

***

Zallerak sang as he fought this ancient adversary. His many chambered mind whirled back to the distant day when he had confronted this creature before. Zallerak had been defeated that time, his kin scattered, all but destroyed. He had been stronger in those days with many others at his side.

But the Ty-Tander was no longer the horror it had been. Telcanna's pet was old and, though it was still deadly with cunning,

Zallerak sensed the creature's doom was nigh. All things must pass in time. The bard could feel his own strength waning as the terrible blasts of flame continued to batter his shield of ice. It was weakening, thawing. He didn't have much time.

Zallerak tugged at his inner reserve, summoning latent power. Cat-lithe, he leapt boldly towards the monster now rearing up on hind legs above him. With a sharp cry that carried with it the last of his strength, Zallerak stabbed a shaft of ice upwards pricking deep into the creature's belly, freezing the pit of fire within.

The Ty-Tander shuddered and quaked as that chill drowned the furnace in its belly. Its deafening bellow drowned out both Zallerak's chant and the noise of the congealing clouds that still spilled icy hail down from above.

Slowly, painfully as one defeated, the creature sank down onto its haunch, the two remaining amber lamps half closed. Sensing victory at last, Zallerak approached the monster. At that point the three warriors seized their chance, jumping up, their weapons clutched in bloodstained hands. As one they launched themselves at the Guardian.

But the Ty-Tander was ready for them. The beast raised its massive head and belched forth a last great funnel of flame (stored in its throat thus unaffected by Zallerak's ice spear.)

And Zallerak was caught unawares. Too late the enchanter raised his ice wall. His alien cold withstood the fire but the force of the blast lifted him high like a rag doll. Zallerak's body was carried through the air, feather light, until he crashed into the wall of the ravine.

Zallerak slunk to the earth. There he lay still as death. The fight was over and Zallerak had lost again. The monster appeared stronger than ever. It turned its wrath towards the others.

Just then Bleyne reappeared on the top of the ravine. With a great shout he discarded his long bow and leapt down upon the monster's broad-ridged back. Balancing with a skill only he possessed, and tenuously gripping the sharp ridges of crystal scales, Bleyne commenced crawling along the creature's hulking hide towards the hideous armoured head.

The Ty-Tander whipped its long razor-sharp tail round to swat this new pest. Meanwhile the other three men charged it with spear and sword.

The beast was confounded; never before had its prey given it so much trouble. Its iron hard body shook with the pain in its eyes and stomach. Its flame was quenched by the wizard's ice, but it was far from defeated. Moreover, it was vengeful. Cold and cunning. The Ty-Tander still possessed its hideous strength and deadly guile.

Snake-swift, the monster lashed and hoofed out at Corin and Ulani, while Bleyne clung to its back in grim desperation, a slender knife gripped between his teeth. Ulani leapt out of the way while Corin ducked beneath a lashing forehoof. He swiped wide, got a clean hack at one of the creature's hind legs.

Beside him, Tamersane plunged his own blade deep into the muscles of the other leg and then leapt clear. The monster slumped on its belly. Its breath steaming like a venting volcano.

Meanwhile Bleyne inched along the razor-sharp spine of the Ty-Tander, heaving himself forward; the scaly ridges cutting his hands to shreds. He ignored the pain, continued to climb. The others kept the monster busy.

Bleyne reached the back of the creatures head.

"Oh, Elanion bright Goddess of the trees, guide my blade!" Bleyne gripped the knife with both hands, reached forward and then slammed the blade's point hard into the nearest amber eye.

That stab went deep. The Ty-Tander howled in pain and fear, kicking out and then rocking its head back and forth in agonised convulsions. Bleyne lost his perch. He was sent spinning through the air to join the prone Zallerak in a pool of melting ice. The archer's head hit the ground with a sickening crack.

The Ty-Tander vented steam. Acid mucus seeped foul from its many wounds. The beast pinned the full malice of its one remaining eye on the three still standing.

It tore upon down them. But as it reared for a final crushing blow the Ty-Tander's strength failed it. It stumbled, hesitated and stumbled again. Corin seized the moment, commenced hacking tenaciously at a leg with Biter, while Ulani rammed his spear into the monster's dripping gullet.

Tamersane had salvaged Bleyne's bow. He stood yelling and shooting arrows into the creature's underside until it looked like an inverted pin cushion, and the ground beneath its belly glistened with the steaming glow of liquid glass—the creature's ebbing life-force. Unbelievably it looked like they had won.

Defeated, the Ty-Tander slumped to the earth, lashing out one last time at Corin's face with its forehoof and catching him unawares. The Guardian lifted its terrible maimed head, bellowing defiance one final time. Then that last amber lamp closed forever. The Ty-Tander was dead.

Corin didn't have time to reflect on their victory. He'd felt his head explode with pain as the hoof struck him, pitching him through the air. The world spun as he careered towards the rocks, his arms flopping. Vaguely, Corin saw the monster's last death throes then his head struck something hard and he knew no more.

———————

Part Three

———————

Beneath The Mountains

Chapter 28

The Crystal Mountains

Painfully, Corin opened his eyes. He was alive. Battered, bruised and beaten, but alive. The world still spun with sickening speed, and the pain of a thousand hammers thudded mercilessly inside his skull—but then it wasn't every day one skewered a legendary monster.

Corin clutched his throbbing head and then tenderly probed his aching body for broken bones, discovering that miraculously, he had escaped with only a severe bruising. He squinted over to the left where the dead monster's stinking bulk was already a cluster of flies and huge evil-looking ants.

Corin saw Tamersane groaning in the corner. The Kelwynian looked frail as a day-old foal. Corin forced himself to his knees, found his legs and then staggered over to check on his young friend. Tamersane, despite everything, had fared remarkably well. The blond nobleman's face was bloodied and his voice was slurred when he answered Corin's questions. Nonetheless he rose swiftly enough to help Corin search for the others.

Ulani too had survived the ordeal, although the warrior king's body was badly gored and he had lost a lot of blood. Ulani was as tough as a boar. He'd pull through.

But when Corin saw the motionless figures of Bleyne and Zallerak his heart sank. Fearing the worst, he approached the prone archer. Bleyne's body was battered and darkened with bruises. There was a large pool of blood still oozing from his chest. Corin swatted away flies and put his hand across the archer's mouth. He felt nothing.

Corin straightened his back painfully and swore, cursing their ill fortune losing Bleyne. Angry, he viciously kicked out at a large stone sending it rolling towards the steaming carcass of the Ty-Tander. At that point he remembered Clouter, and staggered over to tug the longsword out of the monster's lifeless eye.

"Zallerak is alive," called Ulani, his face bleak when he saw Corin's look. "He seems to be in some kind of trance sleep, like the ones our sacred shaman induces on the mortally ill. Still, I think he will survive. His body appears intact." Corin hardly heard.

"How is Bleyne?" Tamersane's question did not hold out much hope.

"He is dead," croaked Corin. He sank to the floor in exhaustion, feeling tears of anger and frustration well up inside his aching eyes.

Ulani approached and placed a huge hand on his shoulder.

"Come, Longswordsman! Don't be glum, Bleyne wouldn't want you moping for him." Corin nodded but didn't reply. Sometimes there are no words.

"We had best see to our friend." Ulani signalled Tamersane. The two carried Bleyne's bloodsoaked body over to rest by a shady rock. There was no chance of burying the archer in this rocky terrain, so they placed his great bow in his tattooed hands, and spread his grey fletched arrows out in ordered fashion beneath him.

Corin knelt beside his lifeless companion; he had never really known Bleyne. He felt sorry about that now. A good friend and loyal companion. Corin struggled to say a few words.

"I expect we will be joining you soon, archer," he managed. "You were a valiant companion. Were it not for Zallerak's magic and your skill and astounding bravery, we would be lost. Sleep now, Bleyne of the Forest. May you wake refreshed to serve your beloved goddess once again."

Corin placed his hand on the archer's lifeless brow.

"If ever I return north to tell the tale," he vowed. "The whole world will know that it was Bleyne, loyal servant of Elanion, that slew the Ty-Tander in the Copper Desert. No small legacy. Farewell!"

"Surely we can't just leave him here to be pulled apart by scavenging beasts and marauding insects?" Tamersane's face was wet with tears, he had liked Bleyne.

"His goddess will watch over him," replied Corin. "Come, Tamersane, we must look to ourselves; we've still a job to do, though how we can achieve that without water and horses, I know not!"

They left Bleyne's body guarding the ravine. Ulani hoisted Zallerak's prone frame over his brawny shoulder, the bard was surprisingly light for so tall a man. Gone was the great sorcerer. Zallerak looked old and frail, his blue cloak faded and torn. Even his harp looked tarnished and dulled. Corin gazed down upon him.

What has become of you, wizard? Are you lost to us as well?

The ground hissed as the last of Zallerak's ice evaporated, filling the rocky cleft with a dense steaming fog. Far above, stars punctured the last of Zallerak's storm clouds.

"What do we do now?" Tamersane's face was bleak. He wiped his sword clean on his sleeve and then rammed it back in its scabbard.

"We make for Orlot," answered Corin. "From those heights we might be able to spot the horses. Who knows?"

They gathered what was left of their belongings, most of which had vanished with the horses. With one last sad salute in Bleyne's direction they slowly, painfully, made their way up the steep narrow ravine. It soon widened, allowing them greater progress.

They ducked below the fence half-heartedly. This time there

was no fizz or charge or even shimmer of light. Perhaps Telcanna's fence had dissolved when the beast died. Not that any of that mattered now.

They stumbled wearily on through the dark hours. Nobody spoke. Above and ahead, Orlot's black dome blocked out the moon. Eventually as the predawn desert light chased the shadows away the ravine fell abruptly to either side.

They had crested a sharp ridge. Below them the desert sprawled for several miles before rising up to greet the pink shrub-dotted slopes of Orlot. There it stood watching them. A lone hill drifting like an island high above the desert floor. It seemed so close and yet still was some miles away.

"I hate this fucking place," Tamersane grumbled.

"We'll never gain that height in our present state," muttered Ulani, Zallerak tossed over his left shoulder like a grain sack. "It will take the best part of a day to find our way down from this ridge. Suddenly he straightened. "What's that movement down there?"

Corin stared in the direction he was pointing and, as the first rays of golden sunlight gilded the plateau of rock on which they stood, he too espied shapes moving far below.

Tamersane's hoarse shout was excited. "It's the horses," he rasped. "See, there are five of them. They must have found a way down from this ridge last night. Or else they went around this plateau. We had better hurry!"

The knowledge that Thunderhoof and the other beasts still lived cheered them all. As Corin watched them far below, he saw that the horses were grazing on what looked like rough spiky grass. The terrain ahead, though still very arid, showed signs of bleak habitation. Here and there were acacia bushes, their thorny heads bobbing about in the wind.

"There must be water down there," Corin said. "Come on!"

They searched along the plateau's edge for some time, fretting, as the drop below was sheer and unmanageable. Eventually Ulani spotted a deep fissure in the cliff where loose stones and shale formed a giant slide, cutting in and snaking its way down to the ground far below. They ought to be able to manage that. Ulani slung the lifeless Zallerak across his back again, freeing his arms so that he could steady himself with his spears as they descended. Down they hastened, half slipping and sliding, clutching at bare roots and shrubs that clung tenaciously to the shallow earth.

Corin's hands were shredded by thorns that left painful splinters deep beneath his skin. The sun was fully up by the time they had reached the foot of the cliff. There was no longer any sign of the horses.

"We had best take shelter here," said Ulani. "We could use some rest and with luck the beasts will catch our scent and come running."

"They will probably gallop in the other direction if they've sense," grumbled Tamersane.

"Thunderhoof won't let us down," Corin assured his friend. "The others will follow him. They know him for a wise beast. Ulani is right; we would do well to rest here for a while. I don't know about you but my head feels like a sack of marbles. Have we any water left?"

They took shelter from the sun's merciless glare behind a large shoulder of rock. Ulani slung the lifeless Zallerak onto the ground and then slumped down exhausted beside him. Within moments the warrior king was fast asleep. Tamersane soon joined him in snores and Corin kept a watch out for the horses.

Hours passed; he must have fallen asleep too. When Thunderhoof's wet nose nuzzled Corin's face he jumped up in alarm. Corin shook the weariness from him and berated himself for sleeping.

He glanced up at the sky. The sun had already past high over their heads and afternoon was wearing on. At least their steeds had returned, and looked in better fettle than they did. Corin took a grateful slurp from the almost empty gourd tied to Thunderhoof's saddle. He passed it over to a waking Tamersane. Then Ulani's booming voice stopped him in his tracks.

"Where is Zallerak?" Ulani demanded. They scanned the rocks

about but saw no sign of the bard. Then Corin noticed that one of the horses was missing.

"What's that bugger up to now?" Corin again chided himself angrily for falling asleep on watch. Still it was probably Zallerak who had found the horses anyway, though what had possessed the bard to abandon his friends again, he couldn't begin to guess. Corin muttered to himself as he tightened Thunderhoof's saddle and then hoisted his battered body onto the horse's back.

"You had the right idea, Thunder," he said. "Now show us where that water is!"

They rode steadily for the rest of that day. Orlot's slopes loomed ever closer. Following their mount's noses they had found a small stream emerging babbling from beneath a rock. They drank deeply from its cold clear water before bathing their faces and replenishing their gourds. Refreshed and invigorated, they finally arrived at Orlot's north flank. Here they dismounted to lead their horses up the steep ruddy slope. They reached the summit quicker than expected. Orlot was not as big as it had appeared from the Copper Desert.

The hill's crown was flat and even, and its bare rock shone with a pinkish glow. From this height they had a clear view of the desert for many miles. Behind them they could see the cliff they had descended that morning, and beyond that the Copper Desert sparkling in the sun before dwindling from view north-westwards in a shimmer of heat, the High Dunes just discernible in the distance.

Opposite, great jagged ridges of rock marked the southern edge of the Ty-Tander's realm. These trailed off to vague lumps before fading from view in the heat haze.

Then Corin turned his gaze south. He gasped at what he saw. Seeming almost in arm's reach stood a range of mountains rising up like coloured clouds above the desert floor. Flawless triangles of blazing rock, their sheer slopes shone like mirrors. They looked alien as though they had crashed landed here from some distant world. Corin's eyes stung with pain at the glare from those flawless dazzling slopes.

"The Crystal Mountains," said Ulani, shielding his own gaze. "What now?"

Corin stared in awe for some moments longer, quite unable to answer. The mountains appeared so close but it had been the same with Orlot. He guessed they still had a full day's ride ahead. The sharp peaks shimmered rose-pink in the setting sun, and their smooth flanks blazed like burnished bronze.

"Is that a road down there?" asked Tamersane. The Kelwynian had been looking for signs of movement below. He had spotted what looked like a thin line beading towards the dazzling mountain slopes.

"Aye," replied Ulani, nodding his bearded head, still coated in dried blood and muck from their battle the day before. "There is rumour of a road that leads out of the desert. They say it passes close beneath the shadow of Orlot before reaching those mountains. The ancients built it when yonder peaks were mined for their crystal. I guess that must be it below," he added.

"Then we had better make our way down there," said Corin. "Hopefully it will lead to a gateway within."

"I know of only one entrance to the fabled caves hidden beneath the mountains," answered Ulani. "I saw it long ago," he told them. "It lies to the south of the range, still many leagues away. But it would make sense that there is northern entrance," he agreed. "After all, lore states that the Golden Ones dwelt mainly in this region. They'd hardly want to skirt the mountains every time they mined below. I expect Zallerak has gone that way to find his little prince."

"Little prick," corrected Corin. "I suppose we had better go see for ourselves. Finish what that shithead Tarin started." He made to start down the hill, tugging Thunderhoof's reins behind him when Tamersane's urgent call stopped him in his tracks.

"There are riders far to the west of us! See over there." They turned to see where he was pointing. "There must be over a hundred!"

"The sultan's elite, I expect," cursed Corin.

"It's hard to tell," replied his friend. "They are still many miles away."

"But those are not," barked Ulani, pointing across to where a thin column of horsemen were winding their way towards Orlot from the valley they had left earlier. Corin could see their crimson cloaks rippling in the breeze as they cantered on, the evening sun glancing off their pointed lances.

"We had better make haste," he said, tugging on Thunder's reins and briskly commencing the descent towards the distant road below. His friends followed without further comment. After a while they mounted their steeds. This southern slope was even gentler. It rolled without break down to the desert floor and thus their mounted progress was swift. Orlot's southern flanks were a mass of shrubby acacia bushes, which sighed mournfully as they hastened through.

The light was fading fast by the time the three riders reached the old road. The setting sun's reflection almost blinded them as they turned to face the towering heights ahead.

The mountains reared before them; a wall of mirrors ten thousand feet high, glowing crimson red to golden brown, casting weird light among the scrubland hedging the road.

Towards these peaks they now urged their steeds, shielding their eyes from the blinding glare of the nearest mountain until at last the pitiless orb was swallowed by western sand. As he rode, Corin marvelled at the road beneath them. It showed no sign of disrepair. Its surface was smooth and even, showing no crack nor pothole. Whoever built it had meant it to last.

As dusk's grey light descended on the desert, the painful glare faded from the mountains. They now appeared a dull pinky-blue, blocking out the sky ahead. The travellers were able to see more clearly. They could see no gap in those towering walls of crystal.

The smooth road led arrow-straight towards the peaks with no sign of any deviations, hence their progress was good and they made the most of the fading light. It was not long before they had reached the glistening slopes of the nearest height.

Corin stared in wonder at the scene ahead. Here and there rocks were strewn about its base, glowing faintly in a myriad of colours like giant gemstones. Above and ahead, the mountains were now stained dark purple, rising up flawless and sheer from the desert floor, their slopes reflecting starlight. The lofty crowns swallowed in the immense canopy of the heavens above.

On meeting the closest mountain the road veered sharply to the left. After that its course cut parallel with the peak's hem. They could see the faint thread-line of its surface ribboning higher, skirting the lower slopes before vanishing from view.

They reined in at the turn of the road; allowing their horses to drink and crop the stubby sparse grass while they sat their saddles, gazing wide-eyed at the surreal landscape whilst sharing a gourd.

Refreshed, they pressed ahead, looking forward to the cover both night and mountain would award them. Within an hour it was fully dark. Looking along the track as far as the gloom would allow, Corin noticed that the route became narrower ahead cutting into the sheer surface of rock. On reaching this point they were forced to dismount and continue on foot with care.

Up and up curved the road hugging the mountain's knees, the shining flawless rock looming over them. Polished by night to gleaming obsidian, the height's flanks bulged outwards on their right. To their left, dangerously close, the road edge fell away sheer in a single giddying plunge to the desert floor, now far below.

It was getting cold. The mountain air was intoxicating. Corin felt light-headed, dizzied by the vastness of the desert night seen from this lofty elevation. He watched the stars' reflections dance in the polished black surface of the road beneath his feet.

He felt like a trespasser—a bug on a noble hound's back. Surely this was hallowed ground. Here nothing lived. No insects scurried among those shimmering rocks, and no proud eagle swooped imperious above. Here was only silence and a growing feeling of doom. An alien place. The path wound ever steeper, wrapping itself like cord, coiling around the flawless rock like a sleeping serpent. Above, the silent aura of the mountains bespoke a chilling watchfulness.

They were about to give up on any hope of a northern gate when they felt (it had become too dark to see ahead) rock rising sheer to their left, hemming them tight on both sides. They had entered a kind of tunnel.

Corin bemoaned the fact that they had no timber for torches. Their progress was very slow and for some time their vision impaired badly. Then the sky appeared above them again, shedding just enough light to allow a quicker pace.

They saw a new path leading off to their right where the mountain folded behind a jagged spur. This deviant vanished in the blackness of the mountain wall. When their eyes adjusted they took stock. They stood on a high-scooped ledge overlooking the desert far below. To their right the almost hidden path looked like the gateway to Yffarn.

"That must be our way in!" Corin was relieved; he had felt much too exposed on the side of the mountain, despite the dark. "Let's go see."

They led their horses along the side cut until they spied a rough hole, a blacker blackness yawning deep into the rock. This they entered without hesitation, finding themselves in the cold damp atmosphere of what appeared to be a huge cavern. At first they were totally blind, but after a worrying time their eyes began to make out dim shapes and eventually the cavern revealed its secrets.

The cave was enormous its source hidden deep beneath the mountain. Here and there the strange rock shimmered with glistening veins of crystal. Each of these layers gave off an odd pale light that aided their way forward until, after what seemed hours, the three reached the cave's rear wall.

Here they were confronted by a problem. Their path had led them to an arched entrance. Beyond this portal were worn steps leading up, almost sheer, into the heart of the mountain.

"We'll not drag our steeds up those stairs," growled Ulani. "We had best return to the road and continue round until we reach the southern door."

"That could be miles away," said Corin. "We'd waste precious time." Corin could not rid himself of the feeling that they needed to hurry. That time was swiftly running out. "Besides, we can be certain Zallerak went this way."

"In which case his horse should be near," said Tamersane. "Come on, let's go find the animal."

They ventured back through the cave and returned to the mountain edge. Above their heads the stars blazed brighter than before and the air hung bitter chill. They searched about in vain for precious minutes. There was no sign of the bard's horse. Corin found his patience fraying fast. He was about to grumble that they were wasting time when Tamersane gave a warning hiss. Corin could see that the Kelwynian was watching the road to the west of them.

"Riders bearing torches," he spat. "Dozens of them, they are coming our way fast!" He spat again. "I would guess that they are only half an hour behind us." Corin and Ulani looked out to where he was pointing. Soon they both saw the weaving worm of torchlight flickering along the road up towards them.

"It looks like the sultan's got wind of your intentions," growled Ulani. "He doesn't want to miss out. We had best get moving." Corin watched the fire worm approach as the others waited, their eyes anxious. They looked to him for a decision.

"Come, Corin, what choice do we have?" Tamersane sounded edgy. "We had best make haste along this road and pray to Elanion that the way is not too far."

Corin looked at his friends. They both looked bone weary, even Ulani seemed deflated. The wounds left by the monster and his heroic carrying of the prone Zallerak had taken heavy toll. As for Tamersane, Corin's young friend was obviously still in pain from their encounter with the Ty-Tander the day before. Finally a decision reached him.

"We will split up," he told them. "It's the only way."

They both shook their heads in disagreement but Corin continued before they could answer. "Time is running out for us," he insisted. "Something inside warns me that our greatest peril yet lurks under these mountains, and that that loon Zallerak will need our assistance shortly. He thinks he's got it all mapped out, but I reckon he's over-optimistic." He paused to look at them each in turn.

"Ulani and I shall journey into the roots of the mountain," Corin said. "That's if you're willing to accompany me, I know this wasn't part of your plan."

"Of course," grunted the king. "I'd hardly let you venture in alone."

Corin nodded thanks, "Tamersane," he said. "You will lead our friends away, await our arrival at the southern entrance of which Ulani has spoken." Tamersane shook his head angrily but Corin placed a tanned hand on his shoulder. "It makes sense; you have more skill with horses than we two. It will give you a chance to hide up, recover your strength, once you have lost our pursuers."

Tamersane was still unhappy about the decision but Ulani nodded his approval. The king added that he knew of a fertile valley a mile west of the southern gate awarding cover, fresh water and shelter. Once there Tamersane could snare desert coneys and await them safely for as long as he needed to.

Reluctantly the Kelwynian capitulated. Without further ado Tamersane unslung a rope from behind his saddle, tied the other mounts' reins to his own, and glancing warily down at the approaching firebrands below, nodded curtly in his friends' direction.

The road ahead widened, allowing Tamersane to mount his own horse. He waved briefly, and in moments was clattering away out of sight and earshot. Behind the rider trotted Ulani's horse and Bleyne's animal, which had followed the others of its own volition. Corin saw Thunderhoof clopping doggedly at the rear, the big horse glanced back briefly in his direction with a look of deep reproach before being consumed by the night.

"Look after him, Thunder," Corin called out, "and watch yourself, you great lump!" He heard a faint snort then silence.

Chapter 29

Mercenaries

Hagan's luck had run from bad to worse. Ever since his humili-
ation at Agmandeur nothing had gone right. The hard-bitten mercenary captain rued the day he had accepted coin from Caswallon.
Things were getting out of hand.

Since that distant morning in Kella little had gone as planned.
His men, particularly Borgil, were awarding him sideways glances.
He knew they were losing faith in his judgment.

He couldn't blame them. Hagan Delmorier, their fearless captain, was totally out of his depth. Hagan was a fighting man, plain
and simple, not some warlocks go-get.

They were so far from their homes in the hills of Morwella—if
those homes still stood and hadn't been razed to the ground by some
Leeth war party. They'd been cajoled to partake in a foolish quest
that Hagan had no doubt would end in further trouble for him and
his men. It was his fault. He should have quit after Kashorn. But
then Hagan wasn't a quitter. And then there was Corin an Fol.

The only thought currently cheering him was that Corin was

almost certainly bound for the same destination. This time Hagan would make the renegade swordsman pay dearly for shaming him in Agmandeur. Corin would die soon, Hagan decided. Aside that they'd get this shit job done and return to Kella for their gold. Then Caswallon and Rael Hakkenon and everyone else could go fuck themselves for all Hagan cared.

Hagan and his mercenaries had nearly perished in the desert, their water supply barely enough to keep them alive on the harsh trek north to the coast. That wily snake Hulm had made sure of that when he had issued them with only half-filled gourds.

Hagan swore one day he would return to that desert city and burn it to cinders. Hulm and his people would be crow food then. The thought went a tiny way to cheering him further.

By the time they'd reached the great stinking fleshpot on the estuary of the Narion they were in a sorry state. Most of his men's feet bore bloody blisters. The soaring heat had tortured their bare faces, driving one fellow beyond the edge of reason, so that he cast himself into the river in a fit of madness.

Hagan had watched in horror as the unfortunate man had been torn apart by crocodiles, before disappearing screaming out of sight. They'd kept a wary distance from the Narion after that.

Then there had been the quarrel; three of the mercenaries spoke out against him, blaming his allegiance to Caswallon for all their woes. Borgil had fuelled it, of course.

Hagan had let it pass saying little, biding his time. He'd slit their throats two nights later when the three lay sleeping. Hulm's guards hadn't found the small knife Hagan always kept hidden inside the sole of his boot.

Next he'd woken Borgil, smiled at the horror on kettle helmet's face as he stuck the knife in deep with a twist. Borgil took a while to die. Hagan would not be gainsaid. But that left him with only nine men. These remained surly but there was no more talk of his failures.

When at last they entered the filthy streets of Cappel Cormac things only got worse. Hagan's plan had been to raid a tavern that night; snatch weapons and supplies from the sleeping guests, then creep across to the harbour and commandeer a light vessel across the gulf of Permio. Let Old Night claim Caswallon and his plots, Hagan's crew would take their chances in the Four Kingdoms. War was coming, with it plenty of chances for fighting men to get rich.

The renegades had spied a likely inn, were about to enter when a furtive movement caught Hagan's eye. They were being watched. The mercenary leader cursed under his breath when he recognised the scrawny bat winged shape of Gribble, Caswallon's goblin spy.

"My master is not pleased with you, Mr Hagan," dribbled the Soilfin. "You and your men have become a liability of late."

"What do you want from us, shitling?" Hagan wished he still had his sword so he could slit the ugly creature's gizzard. "I've done with your master. He can keep his money; we'll take our chances with the coming war in the north."

"But my master has not done with you, fuckhead," snickered the Soilfin. "He was informed of your failings at Agmandeur by another. But in his grace Mr Caswallon has blessed you with one final chance."

The Soilfin picked his nose with a grubby claw and swallowed the content, his ugly features half shrouded in gloom above them. "Tasty, that. I was sent to inform you twits of your new task," continued Gribble, eyeing them with cold contempt.

"Up yours, goblin."

Gribble made a sucking sound. "I'm not a goblin. I hate fucking goblins," he complained. "You, Mr Hagan, are to accompany the sultan's soldiers on their journey through the desert to the mountains of crystal. Easy peasy. There you will seek out the boy prince Tarin, and your friend Corin the terrorist, whom we believe are both in that region.

"These two, as you are aware, are still wanted by Mr Caswallon and Bad Chief Morak for interrogation. You are lucky, Mr Hagan. I've been good to you. Acting on my valuable advice, Mr Caswallon wishes you to gut this Corin, whilst keeping an eye on the sultan's guards. He doesn't want them getting their grubby fingers on his prize."

"What prize, goblin?"

"Ssssh. That don't concern you."

"Well, I say a pox on what your master wants!" Hagan swiped at the creature with his fist. The Soilfin spat acid mucus and retreated out of reach. "Did you not hear me, GOBLIN? I have done with your master!"

"As you wish, Mr Tosspot," replied Gribble almost purring, kneading the wall with his filthy talons. "However," he unlaced his trousers and deposited a steaming nuisance on the street. It hissed and fizzled, melting some of the stone. "You may soon come to rue your decision. You have been warned."

Before Hagan could react the Soilfin had hopped over the wall and vanished from view. Wing beats drummed skyward. Hagan angrily hurled a rock in their direction but Gribble had gone. The night air was clean again. Clean as it could be in Cappel Cormac.

Some of Hagan's men were worried by the creature's threats but their captain's harsh bark had bullied them into motion. "Never mind that imp!" Hagan growled. "We've work to do."

And so they had stolen into a nearby inn under cover of darkness. Grey ghosts, they'd slipped across to the sleeping quarters at the rear, stealing what they could find among the various weapons and provisions while their drink and weed-befuddled owners snored.

Hagan grunted in satisfaction when he lifted a huge broadsword out from underneath a sleeping northern warrior's bed. It was a fine blade, even better than his lost weapon had been; now at last he felt better.

Grabbing what wine and vittals they could, the Morwellan fighters slipped out into the nearest alley keeping a wary eye out for movement. The night air was sultry and thick. It was very quiet. They wound their way silently through the tangled, filthy streets of the sleeping city. Cappel Cormac sprawled and honked; a maze of ill-built hovels and stinking drains that led down to the broad muddy swirl of the Narion's mouth. Feeling uneasy, they stole through the lanes in the general direction of the city's dockyard. Somewhere a dog snarled and yelped, but all else seemed quiet. Too quiet, thought Hagan. Then he cursed himself for a fool. Crimson cloaked soldiers had suddenly appeared in the alley ahead, blocking their way. Turning, Hagan saw that others had followed behind cutting off any chance of escape. They were trapped! Caught neatly like bugs in a jar. Hagan cursed colourfully when he heard leathery wings beat overhead and saw a dark shape winging up into the night. The Soilfin had betrayed them. Hagan vowed to pickle that goblin alive if ever he saw it again. He levelled his stolen sword at the approaching soldiers but it was hopeless. They were greatly outnumbered and hemmed tight in the narrow alley. The sultan's elite bore down on them with long pointed lances. Swift surrender was the only option.

Relieved promptly of their new weapons; the mercenaries had been stripped naked, hog-tied to horses and blindfolded. Hagan demanded to know where they were bound. The only answer he received was a blow on the skull from the nearest lancer's spear butt. Hagan's head exploded with pain and nausea. He spewed.

The dark hours passed with hoof clatter and groans; Hagan lost consciousness once or twice, but his waking complaints only gained him another blow. He decided to suffer in silence after that.

At last the torment ended. The mercenaries were pitched unceremoniously from their saddles, to lie naked, bound and trussed on the ant-infested ground. Exhausted, some of them managed to sleep. Hagan wasn't one of them. At sun up they were kicked awake and beaten again. Then someone ripped the blindfolds from their swollen faces.

Hagan's eyes stung under the morning glare. He spat at a guard, receiving a painful kick in return. His head throbbed and his body was a mass of sores and minor wounds, nevertheless Hagan was defiant, determined to survive this last unfortunate turn of events.

He looked about, squinting painfully as the desert sun speared his eyes from out beneath a stubby grove of palms. Flies settled on his swollen lips, they buzzed around his face. Hagan ignored them. Instead he studied their surroundings, scanning for weak points where he could slip out were the chance to occur. They appeared to be in a large camp. Soldiers abounded everywhere, swiftly dispelling any hope of his escape. Here and there were oval tents flapping idly in the wind, the largest of which bore a long banner showing a golden serpent, coiled rearing over a crimson background.

Hagan and his men were given some water and were unfettered, allowed to don their rough clothes again. They were told nothing of the fate awaiting them and just sat bleary-eyed and silent under the relentless sun.

A score of lancers stood watch close by, their dark eyes cruel and mocking. Occasionally a guard would come over and award one of the prisoners a hard kick or else a sharp prod from his spear butt. Apart from those joyful moments their only company were the flies and ants, some of which were biting enthusiastically.

Hours passed and Hagan fretted. Sometime during the morning there sounded a peel of trumpets. The flaps of the great tent were opened wide to let a corpulent, balding man waddle out. He wore a silk robe of shimmering crimson tied fast by a golden cord. This he promptly untied and commenced urinating noisily on the dirt beneath him. The soldiers dropped to their knees instantly. The guards kicked their prisoners hard until the mercenaries lay face down in the dirt.

Hagan, glancing sideways, saw the balding man whisper something to another man who had just appeared at his side. This was a tall hawk-faced officer, resplendently garbed in purple and gold armour with crimson cloak on top. The balding leader fiddled with his manhood for a nonce then retied his cord. He pointed in Hagan's direction before vanishing once again behind his tent.

Hagan watched the captain approach. He noticed that the guards were looking nervous. This officer was clearly not to be trifled with.

"You there!" snapped the captain, pointing at the nearest guard. "Gamesh, isn't it?"

"Migen, captain," answered the fellow, his eyes down at the ground.

"Well then, Migen," snapped the officer. "See that this northern scum is scrubbed clean and made presentable at once. His Eminence wishes to address them shortly!" He turned on his heels and made for the great tent in clipped measured steps.

The guards leapt to obey. Migen ordered some camp women to scour the prisoners clean. A wrinkled crone seized Hagan's, hair pulling it back sharply. She spat in his eye and then assaulted his body with an abrasive cloth until his flesh felt like grilled bacon. He was relieved when the guards took over.

Prodded by lances, Hagan and his nine freshly-scoured men were led like sacrificial lambs beneath the open flaps of the great tent. The mercenaries gaped in awe at the riches piled amongst golden threaded carpets. Everywhere was diffused lantern light and the soft jingle of watery music.

Young near-naked girls danced skilfully before the prone figure of the fat man Hagan had seen earlier. It was apparent the man was nursing a growing bulge between his thighs as he idly watched the nubile entertainment. He turned away distracted as the troop filed in, allowing his fleshy hand to drop from inside his gown. He studied the captives with greedy currant eyes.

The tall captain ordered them to their knees with a sharp bark. Behind him, the guard named Migen gave Hagan another hearty kick, sending him sprawling at the fat man's feet.

"Prostrate yourselves, dogs," ordered the fierce-looking officer. "Pray that your deaths shall be swift!" He turned towards the fat man and bowed deeply, tugging his long black beard in submission. "Your Eminence," the officer continued. "Here are the rogues the wizard's creature informed us of. You wished to speak with them."

The fat man nodded. "I did, didn't I? But I'm already losing interest."

***

Samadin the Marvellous (a title he had bestowed upon himself because all his predecessors had titles), twenty-third Sultan of Sedinadola, Ruler of Permio and self-proclaimed overlord of Golt, glanced down with idle disdain at the pale-faced northerners lying prone at his feet. Caswallon's familiar had returned to him some days hence, informing him a great treasure lay as yet undiscovered beneath the Crystal Mountains, and adding that the rebel Queen of Kelwyn had sent an elite spy squad deep into his land to raid it.

The goblin reported that its master, in empathy, had dispatched mercenaries to help Samadin recover the treasure. Caswallon's only request was that the spies were to be handed over to these freebooters after their capture. They would then be taken north to await interrogation and public execution. The mercenaries had proved unreliable. The sultan got word of the trouble in the bandit city, Agmandeur.

This was followed by a gracious apology from the sorcerer in Kelthaine, carried hence on the wings of the Soilfin creature. Caswallon, the Soilfin said, was not pleased with the mercenary leader, one Hagan Delmorier. He requested that his eminence the sultan seize the brigand and his surviving men as they enter Cappel Cormac.

"Punish them, humiliate them, but spare their lives and make sure they can still fight," these were Caswallon's words. "They will prove useful to you as they know our enemy very well." The goblin left then, the trap having been set.

Samadin the Marvellous examined the northerners, regarding them with deep distaste, for they appeared ugly wretches. "Which of you offal is the man called Hagan?" demanded the sultan. His voice was oddly high and bespoke a serpent in a robe. His tone resembled that of an overindulged boy rather than a large man in his thirtieth year.

"I am he," came the gruff answer. Samadin stared coldly down at the hard unflinching grey eyes of the nearest brigand. Delmorier's face was a sunburnt ruin of bruises splattered around a broken nose, a wicked scar, and peppered with greying stubble. The Sultan marvelled at the inherent ugliness of northerners.

"You have committed theft and larceny in one of our cities," Samadin said, "and have trespassed out into the desert without our royal permission.

"Normally your limbs would be removed, your eyes gouged out and manhood cut off, before your bodies are fed to the crocodiles patrolling the waters of the Narion.

"But it seems we have need of you, at least for the time being. Be sure of one thing. There will be no escape."

The sultan waved his jewel-adorned hand, dismissing the prisoners. At once Hagan and his men were ushered out into the midday heat. The sultan, bored again, turned to the dancers but he wasn't in the mood for them anymore. Instead he would have one of the servant girls attend him at his leisure, that or one of the young men—it didn't much matter. Samadin the Marvellous had a variety of needs. He pictured the fabled treasures of the Crystal Mountains and smiled. He would be the richest of Permio's twenty-three rulers. That thought entertained him as he waited for the servant to arrive.

***

So it was Hagan and his men were reunited with their stolen weapons, given hooded cloaks to protect them against the sun's glare and ordered to accompany the sultan's royal guard on their journey south across the desert.

For some days they had ridden hard, passing close to Agmandeur until they reached the source of the Narion. They then turned due south crossing the open desert until the fabled mountains of glass hovered ominously before them.

Some miles northeast of the mountains lay the large oasis of Isalyos. It was here that the sultan set up his camp. Hagan was sent out to accompany a hundred 'elite' as they scoured the nearby desert for any sign of the spies.

On cresting the lone hill called Orlot, Hagan spied movement on the road ahead and he informed the Crimson Elite's leader. Led by that grim-faced captain (whose name Hagan had learnt was Damazen Kand), they had given urgent chase along the road that furrowed lance-straight towards the glowing heights ahead.

Evening loomed and the peaks reared tall; Hagan could see no sign of his enemy. He guessed that it had been Corin and co. on the road ahead. They would soon know for certain. Bearing torches aloft, the soldiers galloped up the ancient road skirting the mountain's hem.

Swiftly the sultan's captain led his troop on. Kand was eager to succeed in his mission, and no longer gave thought to the mercenaries accompanying him. Hagan's men found themselves slipping behind as they studied for signs of movement on the road ahead.

After some time they entered a dark tunnel of rock leading out to a high shelf, allowing a broad view across the desert below. Already Kand's troop were hastening ahead in their eagerness. Hagan let them go.

He reined in, glanced about in the dark—his instincts telling him Corin had stopped here not long ago. Then Hagan spied the hidden fork leading off to the right and tugged the sleeve of his nearest man.

"This way," Hagan motioned, grinning. At last things were looking up. Whatever else lay beneath these mountains, there was bound to be gold. Pox take the sultan and Caswallon. Hagan would get to the treasure first and if Corin stood in his way then Corin would die. Hagan smiled; at last it was time for revenge and reward. The coin had turned. They dismounted and entered the cavern with swords drawn. On reaching the gateway and steps, Hagan bid they abandon the steeds and pursue the quarry on foot. Once again the chase was on.

Chapter 30

The Warrior Queen

Queen Ariane woke suddenly from a troubled dream. It was the third morning since her return to Wynais. Each night the same dream had visited her, filling her heart with foreboding. Storm clouds coming their way.

She rose and dressed swiftly in practical garb, ushering her eager servants out of the way. They had all been so pleased to see her again and her welcome home had been gratefully received. But Ariane could see the fear in their faces. She could sense it in the city too. Fear was everywhere throughout Wynais. Almost it felt tangible—a stalking canker sapping the will of her people. One word summed it up.

Caswallon.

The apprehension was contagious, a chilling thread of malcontent weaving its insidious path through the noble heart of the city. Dazaleon had informed her of Caswallon's messenger and his menacing news; it seemed they stood on the brink of war. Alone against the sorcerer.

Ariane knew Kelwyn lacked the strength to withstand the might of Caswallon's ghoulish army, even with the aid of Belmarius's Bears and the riders from Raleen.

The rest of Belmarius's loaned rangers had arrived late last night and were barracked below. The city was full of soldiers but no one felt reassured. But Ariane's mind was resolved after her last dream. She would act as her father would have done, were he still alive. Queen Ariane would take the war to the enemy. Strike the first blow and strike it hard.

She remembered her dead father's warning just after she'd left the city. His hint that there was a traitor within Wynais. A worrying thought that had just returned to her on entering the city. There was much to discuss. Ariane bid Dazaleon join her later that morning, together with her new Captain of Guard, the dependable if stiff, Yail Tolranna. The queen was seated on her throne deep with her thoughts when Dazaleon's rod rapped on the doors of the throne room.

"Enter," she announced calmly. Ariane looked up briefly as the aging priest of Elanion strode into the room, the long staff clutched tightly in his rheumy hands as he paced towards her. At his side clipped hawk-faced Yail, looking very sharp in gleaming mail with polished helmet wedged under his right arm. Stiffly he saluted. Ariane nodded and let her gaze drift to the window.

"Be seated, my lords," Queen Ariane bade them take their places at the table below. This they did quietly. Dazaleon appeared thoughtful, reflective. Tolranna looked anxious and eager, looking up to await her further word.

"The Dreaming visited me again last night, Dazaleon," she told her mentor. She couldn't help but notice the worry lines on the high priest's face.

"Tell me of it, Highness," Dazaleon replied. He leaned forward, still gripping his long emerald-tipped staff with both hands. Elanion's sacred green cloak enveloped his tall form. Ariane noted how Dazaleon appeared thinner than he had when she had left months earlier. It irked her that so strong a man was wasting with worry.

"I dreamt of a great sea eagle struggling in the ocean, its wings broken and torn," she told them. "The eagle is harangued by sharks, drowning while they tear at its flesh.

"The dream shifted then after. I saw Calprissa our second city in ruins. Saw a rider in black leading Groil through the burning streets. Witnessed our people in that second city butchered like market beasts."

Ariane paused to draw breath. "My beloved citizens dying in horrible ways, Dazaleon. It was truly awful.

"Then the dream shifts back again. The wounded eagle is torn cruelly apart by the sharks so hungry for its blood. And during all this, darkness spreads down from the north, blocking out the sky and threatening to consume us." The queen paused to look down the sweeping columns of her hall before speaking again.

"What make you of that, Dazaleon? Obvious, is it not?"

The old man turned his attention to the high-arched windows filtering golden light into the throne room. "It is easy enough to interpret, yes. The sea eagle's no doubt the ship of your friend Barin, the sharks those of your enemy the Assassin, whose craft we know lie skulking in coves along our coast.

"You are worried about Barin and that is only to be expected. But my instinct tells me you will be reunited with your giant friend sooner than you think. I too have dreamed of the Northman.

"The blackness is Caswallon's wrath descending on our land. Your dream hints that Calprissa is where the usurper is planning his first assault. That makes sense. He's doubtless liaised with the Assassin. Take that coastal city, restock then push inland to Wynais. That murderer's sharks will be heading there, be sure of that. And Captain Barin also, I believe, caught up in the chaos."

"Why would Barin make for Calprissa?" Ariane asked. "Surely he would suspect Rael Hakkenon to trap him thereabouts?" She shook her head, trying to imagine what was going through the mind of that redoubtable mariner.

"Maybe he has no choice," replied Dazaleon. "One factor seems certain from not only your dream, but my foresight also. Both Barin and Calprissa will soon be in need of our aid. The black-garbed rider can only be that same Derino who paid us a call last month."

"Derino?"

"Perani's man. A brute," continued Dazaleon. "He leads Caswallon's horde. It will be this Derino that will head the assault on that city. With Calprissa and then Port Wind in his grasp Derino would cut off our access from the coast. From there he can harrow and burn at his leisure until all Kelwyn is laid waste and the Silver City surrounded and alone. Even with Belmarius's troops and the Raleenians we have on loan, we could not hold out here all winter. Wynais has not the fortified strength of Car Carranis, or even Point Keep for that matter."

"Aye, and we can expect no help from that quarter," cut in Yail, leaning forward at table. "Our friends in Kelthara are hemmed tight by the usurper's Groil. Our spies inform us Point Keep has fallen to Leeth. That leaves Car Carranis holding out alone in the far country, surrounded by a sea of foes. Car Carranis is strong—but to hold out indefinite against the might of Leeth? Added to that Starkhold cannot be trusted. We are alone, Your Highness. We had best look to ourselves."

"We have the two hundred horse from Atarios, and Belmarius's rangers under Valentin, all hardy veterans," she responded, accepting a cool glass of water from a servant and drinking deep, before returning her gaze to her sharp-eyed new champion. "They will both prove invaluable. And the rangers have small love for Caswallon having been stung by his treachery before. So tell me, how many fighting ships have we moored in Calprissa, Captain Yail?"

"A score, my princess, no more," replied Tolranna. "The fleet has dwindled in recent decades as you know," he answered. "But I cannot see the sense in rushing to aid that city. Rather we should wait here, as I see it, let Caswallon come to us."

"I disagree." Ariane cursed the folly of her father's fathers. They had lost interest in Kelwyn's navy, believing entirely in the Tekara's power. Even her father had scoffed at the notion that any threat could arrive from the ocean. Back then the Morwellan navy patrolled all coasts keeping the Crenise or any would-be invader at bay.

That said, it had been years since a Morwellan warship had last sailed into Calprissa or Port Wind. It was due to this that the pirates of Crenna had been so successful over latter years. Only Morwella had spent sufficient funds on her war ships. But Morwella was broken. Her fleet destroyed, torched and sunk by Redhand off Vangaris. Ariane had ordered more vessels built after ascending to the throne, but her time as ruler had yet been short and hence their fleet was still tiny. It was depressing.

The young queen felt suddenly weary. She ran a pale hand through her sable locks and sunk back into the throne chair.

Calprissa is the key—I cannot let that city fall.

"My lords, we must act swiftly," Ariane told them.

"I will leave for Calprissa this very day. Neither Caswallon nor the Assassin will catch us off guard." Dazaleon nodded slowly but Yail looked worried and seemed on the point of challenging her.

"Captain Yail," she turned her gaze to the fiery soldier. "I know how much you love Wynais. I need you here. I've no proof, but have reason to believe there is a traitor somewhere in the Silver City. Call it a hunch." Tolranna's face blanched, hearing that. Even Dazaleon looked shocked.

"Did you dream this too, my Queen?" the high priest asked her.

"No. I haven't spoken of this till now, but I was visited by my father's shade that first night after leaving this city. It was one of the things he warned me about."

"King Nogel?" Tolranna looked askance.

"Came to me that night to warn of the perils ahead."

Dazaleon said nothing but Yail abandoned his chair and stepped forward. "My Queen, I beg you let me accompany your army west. If you leave you'll need your best fighters with you. The city guard can flush out any traitors in Wynais once I've put the word out."

"Thank you, Yail," she waved him back. "But it's because of your vigilance that I need you here. Watching and listening and aiding Dazaleon. Who is your second officer?"

"Lieutenant Tarello. My Queen, I must insist -"

"Good," she waved him to silence. "Inform Lieutenant Tarello he will accompany me there with some handpicked men, together with the two hundred horse spearmen on loan from Raleen, plus fifty of our finest archers. You, Tolranna, will remain here with the rangers and city guard in Wynais, keeping watch over the city. Calprissa will hold out as long as it can. Caswallon will want fast results. He believes we are weaker than we are. And his main desire is this city and my throne." All three knew that Caswallon's designs went beyond that and focussed on the queen's person. Neither she nor her advisors felt the need to mention that at this moment. Ariane turned to Yail Tolranna, standing stiff and uncomfortable before her.

"Tolranna, I'm sure we've taken too much of your time already. Please convey my orders to your second and have the Raleenians make ready at once."

Tolranna saluted and without word departed from the room. Ariane's shrewd eyes watched him leave. "Something troubles that one," she said. "He appears ill at ease in our company."

Dazaleon shrugged. "He's restless and frustrated, a good man but he lacks his brother's sensibilities."

"I know, but keep an eye on him, Dazaleon. Yail worries me. He's impetuous and impulsive. That said,   he's loyal and dependable, and will ensure the city guard stay sharp. They are all wary of Yail Tolranna."

"I shall."

"We'll range wide throughout the lands between here and Calprissa," Ariane waved her arms, "burn crops and starve the enemy as winter takes hold. Belmarius's fighters can patrol the lands west of here, whilst my Raleenians goad Derino's force with petty raids, luring him away from Calprissa into the heartlands, until he is caught between Belmarius's rangers and my Raleenians. We'll decide on a suitable spot for that to happen. Meanwhile Tolranna can keep our Kelwynian soldiers ready, primed and waiting inside the city, should the enemy change tack."

"All good, and Tolranna is up to the task of minding this city. But your place too is in Wynais, my Queen," countered Dazaleon. "The citizens will take it poorly if you leave us again. Morale is bad enough already."

"That cannot be helped, Dazaleon. I must be decisive. Caswallon needs to know I'm at Calprissa—or in that region. I am Queen of Kelwyn, not just Wynais, and I will not let Calprissa fall! My word is final."

Ariane rose from her seat of power at the silver throne. She walked, calm-faced, down to join her high priest in gazing out the window. "We'll send word to Calprissa by carrier pigeon," she told him. "I will expect those few ships we have to be fully manned, refitted for war and awaiting my inspection on arrival."

Dazaleon's face was creased with worry. "A rash gamble," he told her. "Caswallon will fall hard on Calprissa. You risk much faring that way, my Queen!"

"These are perilous times, my old friend. Without risk there can be no gain. We must hold to courage. The die is already cast. I will speak no more on the matter." Their discussion shifted to the quest for the crown and Silon's council in far off Raleen.

Hours later the queen's party was ready to leave. All was resolved yet one minor issue remained. A stone in her royal shoe.

Cale. The boy had balked at being told he must stay in Wynais. "My place is with you, my Queen!" Cale had insisted. "To defend you or die at your side."

"Your place is at your studies under High Priest Dazaleon," she had snapped, being in no mood for discussion. Cale had sulked then. He'd told her he wanted to be a warrior like Corin or Tolranna, not a damned priest's scribe, or worse a kitchen scullion. Both he knew were normal routes to becoming a squire.

Ariane had told him tartly that the matter was closed and so their parting had been frosty. Cale had taken to the kitchens amid scowls. Ariane was annoyed with herself, believing she could have handled the situation better.

She was so fond of the boy and just wanted what was best for him. Enough. Graver matters commanded her attention. She sat her mare beneath the wintry sun and watched filled with pride, as her chosen Kelwynians under Lieutenant Tarello filed out of the city.

Tolranna had done well, each horseman rode with neat precision. The competent Tarello rode forth with a company comprising five hundred spearmen, and following behind rode the immaculate Raleenian lancers fresh out of Atarios. Two hundred strong, their heads held high and their garb spotless. At her side, watching astride his pale horse, sat the diminutive Galed. Ariane's scribe and loyal squire had insisted on coming along despite her disapproval. This was another reason why Cale had gotten so cross.

But Galed was a grown man; he had the right to choose to be at her side as he had been from the start. It still irked her though.

"You are not a warrior, Galed," she had told him. "Cale will miss your teachings. Besides, there is much you can do here in Wynais. Dazaleon and Tolranna will need help in the days ahead."

"Dazaleon and the captain will be fine," grumbled Galed. "So too will master Cale. I've come this far through thick and thin. I have grown accustomed to danger and will not desert you now."

"So be it, but you'd best ask Lieutenant Tarello fit you out in a suit of mail. This isn't a fucking parade. We ride to war, Galed!"

Afternoon came, the shadows lengthened on that bright winter's day. The cold clear waters of Lake Wynais ridged slightly in the easterly breeze. The tall swaying reeds sighed mournfully; they parted to reveal the shining host passing swiftly on the road ahead.

Into the west they thundered as sunlight glinted the tips of their spears. A brave sight. At the head of the host rode a slender figure encased in a coat of gleaming silver mail. Her determined features covered by a shining helm, crested by a flowing wave of silver horse-hair. So it was on the eve of winter, Ariane of Kelwyn rode valiantly out to war. Meanwhile all around her the storm clouds gathered.

***

A lone rider followed that bright host keeping a discreet dis-tance. Cale had purloined both armour and horse and sweated pro-fusely as he galloped toward the dust column raised by the distant army.

The sword at his side was heavy; it almost dragged him from the saddle. Cale knew he was in big trouble but didn't care. He was happy. Cale was a warrior now. No more dishes and prayers for him. No more errands and run-arounds and naggings from Galed.

He'd feed on the scraps left by her army after they broke camp. Once near Calprissa he'd filter in at some point and steer close to the queen. It would work out, Cale assured himself. Corin would have done it when he was fourteen. Cale wished that Corin was with him now. Together they were a match for anyone—and then if you had Barin alongside too. Invincible!

Why should Galed get all the fun? Cale grinned as he steered his steed into the west. He was becoming a hero. There would be stories about him one day—he just knew it. Cale the magnificent. Cale the Thrice Bold. Lord of Dreaming Towers. It was heady stuff!

***

A second lone rider crested the hill close behind Cale and watched the company ride out from the Silver City. He waited until the rear guard had vanished beyond Lake Wynais, before turning his steed about and bidding her wend north toward the Kelthaine border. Once there he would make direct for Kella City. His master Yail Tolranna wasn't trusting to pigeons this time.

Chapter 31

The Voice

Corin and Ulani returned to the cave mouth and hurried within. They were not far from its entrance when they heard the distant clatter of hooves passing on the road outside. It seemed their ploy had worked, the sultan's soldiers obviously knew nothing of this alternative route into the mountains. Corin hoped Tamersane would lose them in the miles ahead. He was a fine horseman and had plenty wit enough to lead them on a merry dance, as long as he didn't get distracted by phantom women.

Once again Corin and Ulani felt their eyes adjust to the weird light, but this time they made better speed. They reached the portal in minutes, passing beneath it without pausing for breath.

Corin led the way up the slippery crystal carved stair, taking two steps at a time. Behind him the great bulk of Ulani hefted his spears so that they wouldn't scrape on the low, sloping ceiling of rock.

They were now only two. Two fools against the gods only knew what. The steps climbed higher and steeper and the air grew stale. Corin clutched Biter in his right palm. Like Ulani, he'd had to alter

Clouter's harness so the long blade didn't scrape the walls and ceiling. No room for swinging Clouter here. His eyes scanned the dark above.

They had reached the final stage of the quest. Ominous quiet filtered down from the gloom ahead. Corin felt his heartbeat quicken with every step.

The stairs rose steep and were badly worn in places. The shining layers of stone around them wedged ever inward until there was scarce room for movement, and Ulani's multiple array of weapons kept scraping against the walls.

At least it was lighter than they had expected. Everywhere the rock face was lined with glowing veins of crystal, giving out a pale radiance that dimly lit their way ahead.

Time passed in silence beneath the mountain. They could hear queer echoes drifting up and down, that and the dull thud of their own footsteps. Strange creaks and groans resounded about them as if the mountain they were under disapproved of them being there, and was planning their ruin in its dark deep heart. Their own thoughts were grim as they strove up and up, panting with exertion at the steepness of their ascent.

It was hot. Corin melted in his steel shirt and leathers. He guessed that morning had arrived outside. Hours passed dreary and slow, hot and stuffy. The weird sounds came and went. Still they climbed. Their progress as ever hampered by the lack of room.

"The ancients must have been midgets," grumbled Corin. He felt entombed and wasn't enjoying the sensation.

"Thinner than me, that's for sure," grunted Ulani, dragging his spears behind him.

On and up they went until at last, greatly relieved, they reached an end to the stairs. Here they stopped for a grateful drink from a shared gourd. Resting a moment, they studied the way ahead. The stairs opened on a dimly streaked passage.

This yawned out at them, hinting at a wide smooth walkway that must surely lead towards the very centre of the mountain. Deep veins of coloured crystal lit the way ahead, casting light on strange shapes peering at them out of the gloom. Huge columns of rock stood there, vast stalactites descending from the ceiling like dripping glowing daggers. Beneath them the floor glistened as if wet. This too was a crisscross maze of glowing crystal. At least it was less stuffy up here. On the contrary the air was quite cool.

"Some place," whispered Corin, gaping through the gloom. He froze when Ulani tugged at his sleeve.

"We are being followed," said the king, looking back down towards the distant stairs.

"Are you sure?" Corin could hear nothing. Then he cursed when he recognised, from somewhere far below, the soft sound of footfalls approaching.

"Seems like some of the elite had sharp eyes after all," muttered Ulani. "We had best keep moving." They hurried on, leaving the narrow stairs behind. The passageway led smooth and straight as their road had been yesterday, deep into the mountain.

The crystal veins of light flanked their way, awarding enough light for good progress. They had copious space here; the roof of the tunnel was yards above Ulani's head. Occasionally a cold blast of air would reveal a dark passage leading off to right or left. These they rushed past with weapons held ready. Time passed, how much time they couldn't guess.

They had rapidly distanced themselves from the narrow stairway, whoever followed would be far behind. Ulani stopped often to listen but no longer detected any sound of pursuit. Perhaps they had imagined the footsteps. Had the mountain itself been trying to fool them?

They strode on apace. Eager to get the task (whatever it was) done, their feet almost gliding on the polished floor of the passage. The way was becoming much wider; a dozen men could walk abreast here.

The discomfort of the stairs was soon forgotten. Above them

were more weird stalactites hanging down like a forest of spears. These too gave off a translucent glow, casting baroque shadows on the passageway ahead. Corin had no idea how much time had passed in the tunnel. He'd stowed Biter and walked at ease with Clouter unsheathed and sloped across his left shoulder. Ulani clutched a spear in either hand. It seemed like a whole day had gone by when Corin noticed it was growing lighter up ahead.

"Looks like we could be drawing to the end of this passage," he said. "See how bright it is up there."

"Aye, but what lies beyond it?" said Ulani. As they drew closer to its source the light pulsated with rhythm, casting dust motes towards them. At either side the walls throbbed in reply, their radiance ebbing and flowing in answer to whatever resonated out from the centre of the mountain.

"I like this not," grumbled Ulani. "I sense spellcraft everywhere." The normally fearless king watched the throbbing light with deep suspicion.

"We've come this far, I'll not turn back now."

"Then lead on, Corin an Fol."

They steadied their nerves and continued towards the strange source of light. It seemed to be beckoning them forward, compelling them almost. After some time Corin thought he could hear voices chanting in some strange outlandish tongue. It was a disturbing sound. He slapped his head but the voices stayed.

It was becoming hot again, and the weird glow was filtering down the passage in long measured strobes. Glancing about, Corin could see faded paintings lining the walls of the passage. Here and there were broken lumps of iron that had surely been sconces and held burning brands in some distant time.

Wary, they ventured forward. Soon Corin could hear the voices clearly, they seemed to come from somewhere beyond the strange source of light.

Behind him Ulani said nothing, but gripped his spears tighter in either hand. Corin felt his skin shiver beneath the sweat. Something unnatural waited ahead. Of that he was certain. He felt a familiar dread enter his loins and suspected who it was that waited for them. Wet dog.

Urgolais.

Corin gripped Clouter in his sweating right palm and willed himself on towards the ever-brightening source of light. This time he wasn't fleeing the horror, he was confronting it. If the Dog-Lord was down there Corin would skewer him once and for all. Spells or no spells, old burnt face's days were numbered. So he tried convincing himself.

From somewhere the sound of water trickled and plopped into what must be an invisible lake. Corin felt suddenly thirsty and stopped to gulp at his gourd. Ulani joined him in a slurp, and together they listened in growing concern to the eerie voices beyond the light. There appeared to be several speakers chanting in unison, though one was much louder and deeper than the others. When this one spoke its echo sent a shiver through the passage.

There it was again, booming around their heads, followed at once by the other voices that sounded so much like hounds baying at the heels of a wounded bear. These lesser voices were higher pitched and snarly, a waspish drone accompanying the persistent boom groan of the deep voice.

"What do you make of it?" Ulani drained his gourd and wiped the sweat from his glistening brow.

"Sounds like a dirge," answered Corin. "Some kind of incantation, maybe. Guess we'll find out soon enough. Come on."

They approached the light with growing trepidation. The great voice was clearer now, its deep resonance echoing all about them in an endless chord of booms. Both disturbing and unnerving. The voice resonated pain like the tortured ravings of some madman. Accompanying it like a ghastly orchestra were the nasal cries and snarly barks of the other voices—the familiarly unsettling voices.

They walked on, two intruders trapped in someone else's nightmare.

Corin's head hurt. The great voice kept booming on. Like a toll it boomed—ominous and forlorn and relentless.

They were close. Hesitantly they approached the source of the light. Ulani thought he heard movement somewhere behind despite the din. He stole a glance that way but the passage was shrouded in shadow. He shrugged. There was no point in worrying about pursuit now.

Corin froze without warning and Ulani slammed into his back. They had reached an abrupt end to the passage. All around them pulsed a kaleidoscopic fusion of strobing light.

Corin and Ulani covered their eyes from the dancing, dazzling, bewildering glare. Squinting down, they saw that they had only narrowly avoided plunging to their ruin into what appeared to be a vast pit or cavern. Corin blessed whatever instinct had stopped him when it did. One more step and he would have been flying.

Beneath their feet the road fell away as if cut clean by an axe. The light throbbed out in rhythmic shafts and the great voice boomed up at them from somewhere hidden below and beyond.

Eventually their eyes were able to discern what lay before them.

"By Ugara's hairy nipples, that's a sight," Ulani said. Corin just gawped, witless.

They had reached the rim of what appeared to be a giant cavern. Like a vast scooped bowl of light it stretched around, a huge oval drawing their eyes downwards, towards its source.

And there it was at last. Far below their elevated position, huge and diamond bright, blazing like a fallen star. An enormous crystal.

The size of a palace or temple, the crystal's vibrant light resonated up from the very heart of the mountain. As it pulsed its heart's rhythm reached outwards in stabbing strobes of diamond light.

The walls of the cavern shook in time with that pulsation, and beyond it the tortured voice boomed its woeful cacophony. On and on and on. Through the throbbing, stabbing glare, Corin and Ulani studied the huge cavern encompassing the giant crystal. At its base were shining columns of stone leading up to the dome of light. Each of these tall stalagmites pulsated in time with the great crystal's throbbing heart.

An army of frozen warriors, they stood surrounding the crystal like so many sentinels of blazing light. Again Corin recalled the statues outside Kranek Castle. He didn't dwell on that thought.

Beyond the stalagmites glistened the silvery metallic waters of a lake. Dark and sombre resembling a sea of molten lead. The far shore was hidden from view. They would have to cross that gloomy water before reaching the giant crystal. It wasn't a comforting thought.

Looking down, it was difficult to gauge distance. It seemed like miles. Corin and Ulani felt like trespassers: paupers in the palace, or else two small children gaping down uncomprehending and incredulous from the parapet wall of a mile-high castle.

"This must be the great cavern Zallerak mentioned." Corin felt giddy looking down there. Worse, he didn't have any kind of plan concerning what to do next.

Neither did Ulani. "We must have reached the very centre of the mountain," the king said. "The answers must lie beneath that crystal. Come on, let's find a way down."

Corin couldn't think of any response to that so he just nodded. For several minutes the two men searched about in vain, seeing no access or break in the cavern's rim. But at last keen-eyed Ulani spied a narrow stair cutting clean into the side of the cavern, tight narrow chevrons disappearing into the throbbing light below.

"A way down—do you see it?"

"I do but it doesn't inspire me."

Ulani slapped Corin's back. "Chin up, this must be the very birthplace of the gods! Fortunate are we to witness this."

"If you say so."

Ulani had forgotten his former dread; instead he was eager to discover what wonders awaited them below. Even the dreadful voices no longer held him in check.

Corin remained nonplussed. "I hope Zallerak's down there somewhere."

They hurried across to the stairs, reaching carefully over the lip of the bowl and reeling with the vertigo assaulting them. The stairs were ladder steep and narrow, scarce more than scoops dug in the smooth surface of the cavern's shell.

The two gingerly made their way down, gripping the rock on both sides and mindful where they placed their feet. One slip would prove fatal here.

Corin was reminded of the worn steps cut into the cliffs above Kashorn. But this stair was steeper by far than they had been. The memory of that earlier trip tugged at him. Despite their predicament his mind wandered during the descent. So much had happened.

Corin thought of Bleyne and Roman, both gone now. He longed to smell the sea again; it seemed so long since he'd heard the crash of waves. He thought of Shallan and hoped she was safe. Would he see her again? Corin doubted it.

Enough. Focus on the task ahead.

Tenuously and painfully slow, they made their descent toward the great bowl of light. The throbbing heart of the crystal lit up their faces and dazzled their eyes. Shadows chased back and forth across the walls in a frantic, flickering dance. It was surreal.

At some point the light grew steadier as if the giant crystal was aware of their approach—two flies creeping down the cavern wall. It shimmered and glowed as though the moon itself were trapped within.

Down they worked, Ulani grunting and Corin mouthing silent expletives. Try as he might Corin could see no happy outcome to this venture.

The cavern seemed endless. It was as though they'd ventured uninvited into the lost halls of the gods. Enchantment hung like gossamer in the chilly air. Invisible cords hinting at dark power. And all the while the constant morbid drone of horrid voices rose and fell in resonance. Even Ulani's expression grew grim.

Down they journeyed, swifter now, both anxious to reach the base. The voices (still invisible) were all around them. Cruel alien words echoing about their heads and battering their senses. They dared not cover their ears lest they fall. Then Corin spied the base at last. Ulani grunted approval, they were nearly down. Then something made Ulani stop. Carefully, he turned, looked up at the high stair and swore vehemently. Corin arced his head back but couldn't see.

"What is it?"

"We have company," said Ulani. Corin turned, looked up. Far above, almost hidden by the throbbing glare, he saw a dozen or so tiny figures descending toward them. Corin shook his head in disbelief when he recognised the foremost figure. Hagan Delmorier.

Does that bastard never quit?

They hurried down that last stretch, no longer caring whether they slipped on the treacherous stone. A yell from above announced Hagan had spied them.

The chase was on. At last Corin and Ulani reached the final step. They plunged headlong into the cavern's basin making for the dazzle of the crystal heart, unable to see anything clearly in that glare.

They ran, weaving haphazard between the stalagmite sentinels. Corin eyed them with suspicion as he ran past but they remained cold impassive stone.

They reached the silent waters of the lake. It spread out before them, like an ominous pool of quicksilver. Metallic and motionless—its surface sheened by light, but the depths below dark and portentous. The lake's shoreline lapped silent against the base of the cavern. No evidence showed of any way around. The giant crystal floated like temptation just beyond that mercury expanse, seeming close but indefinable. The metallic sheen of the lake caressed the dark distant shore, fading into gloomy nothingness at either side.

Corin glanced back. Hagan was halfway down.

"Any ideas?" Ulani scanned the lakeshore before looking back toward the distant bead of the stairs. They could both hear Hagan yelling. The mercenaries would be upon them soon.

"No." Corin felt a familiar sense of panic welling up inside. The source of that panic came from the distant voices, (dog-voices, he now realised) baying somewhere out beyond the lake. "How many men do you see?"

"Nine...maybe ten. It's hard to tell."

Fuck you, Hagan. We haven't time for this. Again Corin slid Clouter free of its sheath. They were trapped by the lake shore. Corin squared his jaw, determined to take out as many as he could, then skewer his former dicing partner from throat to groin. They had five, perhaps ten minutes.

Ulani nudged his arm. "Surely that's a boat!"

"What?" Corin gaped at the lake and saw nothing.

"Coming towards us from far across the water." Ulani pointed out across the lake. Corin followed his arm's direction until eventually he spied tiny movement far out on the water. In moments they defined a small craft steering towards them at witchy speed from out of the light.

The craft was shadowy and hard to see beneath the glare of the crystal. A lone figure guided it. The boatman even more difficult to define beneath the brightness.

But Corin had a nasty feeling he knew this ferryman. There would be a price for their crossing—he felt certain of that. They said nothing, just waited for the boat to arrive.

It beached silent scarce yards away. Its lone occupant gestured with a bony hand, bidding them clamber aboard.

And what choice did they have?

Hagan's angry cries were close. The mercenary and his men had reached the cavern floor and were racing this way.

Corin took seat in the boat, Ulani beside him. Both looked pale. The boatman ignored them and commenced poling his pale-faced passengers toward the distant glowing dome. Once again the mercenaries' shouts were left behind.

Their guide's shadowy features were hidden from view by a long dripping cloak, his face concealed beneath a deep hood. The passengers said nothing. Both were awed by the power and menace radiating from their pilot.

Corin caught the cold gleam of a pitiless eye observing him shrewdly from under that hood. He recognised the Huntsman and shivered. Corin turned his gaze away.

Leave me be.

For a time the tiny figures of Hagan and his men could be seen at the shore waving spears and gesticulating. They soon faded from view as the silent craft slid effortlessly along the metallic surface of the water.

Far above their heads the crystal-veined roof of the cavern reflected back the dome's brilliant light. The cave was even vaster than they had imagined, its circumference supported by huge arches of rock. Miles apart and half a mile high. The roots of the mountain, their feet lost far beneath the water.

Like some vast cathedral of the gods, the cavern expanded beyond the confines of reality. Time appeared frozen in this place. Corin, bedazzled, felt as though he'd tumbled inside a cosmic dream.

Closer now, the giant voice boomed like judgement and the other dog voices rose and fell in their continuing snarly chant. Corin reached down. He trailed his hand through the leaden water of the lake. He shuddered, pulling it out quickly. The water's embrace was slimy and cold as death.

"Do not touch the water!" The boatman's voice sounded like gravel sliding down a scarp. The single eye mirrored the lake's bitter surface. It stabbed at Corin from beneath that wide-brimmed hat.

"Why do you help us, Huntsman?" Corin's voice was almost inaudible. Beside him Ulani's strong face looked gaunt. But the boatman didn't respond. Just turned away continuing his work with the pole.

The craft slowed to a stop. They had reached the far shore.

Their pilot steered close, poling onto the shingle. Without further word the two men leapt off the small boat, both keen to distance themselves from the ferryman's unsettling gaze.

Corin glanced back but ferryman had already turned his craft and was heading back swiftly across the lake at speed.

"We had better run," Corin said. "That spook is returning for Hagan and his boys. I wish I knew what his game was. I mean, why aid our enemy?"

"Who can guess the mind of a god?" muttered Ulani. "I'm certain he has his motives. We'll most likes never be any the wiser."

"He gives me the creeps."

More weird stalagmites loomed over them as they left the far shore of the lake. Soon its waters had vanished behind. Corin questioned whether lake and ferryman had actually existed at all. This whole place felt like an illusion. It was difficult to keep a sense of reality and time.

Focus—have to hold strong.

The crystal orb towered in front of them. An immense dome of light. It throbbed and pulsed with urgent speed, as though knowingly apprehensive of what would soon come to pass.

Corin shielded his eyes from the glare. He was well accustomed to the desert sun but this crystal colossus flared like a fallen star. Each throb of diamond light burned into his aching brain.

And still the great voice boomed continually from somewhere ahead, its heavy resonance resounding all around them as they hurried toward it. The other voices were clearer too, Corin could discern fell words uttered in some archaic canine tongue. The air of the endless cavern was deathly still. It was as though some weighty spell was about to be wrought.

"Shit!"

Ulani had stopped abruptly in front of him. The king grabbed Corin's arm just in time, yanking him back from oblivion. Blinded by light, they had failed to notice they'd reached the brink of another precipice.

This drop descended deep into what must surely be the roots of the mountain—immeasurably far below. More worn steps led down dangerously steep. But this time they didn't hold back. Both men sensed time was running out. Both knew whatever they had to do had to be done soon.

They hurried down, at last reaching the base of a ledge hovering close to the face of the giant crystal itself—its own base at least a mile below. An egg shape dome, it rested in the scoop of a massive pit—its bottom impossible to define in the brightness. An obelisk of pulsing light, the crystals' argent glow blazed down on them in fury.

But even as they stood gaping the light softened to a pale sheen of silver, and stabbing strobes withdrew back into the core. The crystal faded and shadows appeared, taking shape before their eyes. Corin and Ulani gasped in shared wonder.

At last they had reached the owner of the booming voice.

Chapter 32

At the Forge of Croagon

There He stood bathed in light, writing in pain and torment. A giant so broad He appeared squat: so huge He defied their senses. The tortured face almost reached the ledge where they stood spellbound. His bare feet and lower legs lost below in shadow.

Behind the giant, carved deep into the crystal's base, blazed a forge cavernous and vast. It was from here that the light emanated and pulsed.

Croagon's Forge. Blue and white fire roared up to meet them as they watched, too stunned to move. Both Corin and Ulani were lost for words. This was a scene beyond anything either had imagined.

And the giant was aware of them. Croagon the Smith God. He turned His terrible countenance upon them and they were afraid. That anguished face was a ruin of twisted scars, laced across a flat boneless nose. Dark gaping sockets were ridged by heavy shelved brows, these loosely fenced by thick oily coils of matted grey hair. The steely locks tangled down the naked scarred back of the titan, vanishing in His midst.

As Corin and Ulani looked closer they could see that the giant's wrists were bound cruelly to the sides of the fathomless pit by two heavy chains, and that Croagon's huge corded sinewy arms were stained with dark blood from where He tugged endlessly at the manacles.

Despite Croagon's blindness the giant was aware of their approach. He seemed to be weighing them up in His mind. But then the other snarling voices rose up in a seething surge from the base of the forge far below.

Corin, reaching out and looking down, could just make out three tiny cloaked figures standing there. They stood at the giant's tethered feet, a triangle of spellcraft, assaulting his body from their outstretched claws.

The voices were twisted with evil. Like hot knives they worked their thaumaturgy upon their captive. Again the giant cried out in dreadful pain. A terrible sound, deafening the two onlookers and shaking the foundations of the mountain, tearing great lumps of rock loose from the cavern's walls.

Corin was knocked to his knees by the violent shaking all around. Ulani lay sprawled.

"Who are those sorcerers?" The king looked more shaken than Corin.

"Urgolais—dog scum. Friends of Zallerak." Corin tried to grin through the familiar fear eating into him. He had to grit his teeth to force the next words out.

"I suspect that's Morak down there and two of his pals; see how they torture the giant. He must be the one we've come to see. The Smith God. We've made it, Ulani."

"Almost." The king gained his feet again and commenced forcing his numb legs into action. "Come on, waiting here achieves nothing, and that Hagan friend of yours can't be far behind."

"Don't remind me."

Shaken yet undeterred they descended the final leg of the stair.

Down and down they plummeted into the pit containing the huge crystal. The orb's light had faded to a dull sheen and its pulsations eased again, as if awaiting their approach.

Time dragged on the stair. They felt exposed and vulnerable and were halfway down when a shout from above announced Hagan's arrival at the edge.

Bastard hasn't wasted any time.

But Corin was no longer concerned with Hagan. There was worse awaiting them below—much worse.

Down they fared. All through that descent the Smith God writhed in his bonds as the hideous chanting of the dog-lords rose and fell like wind howling through an icy tunnel. Corin and Ulani were level with Croagon's hips; the giant's face lost in the shadows above.

Corin, looking down, could see the cowled sorcerers clearly. Was Morak one of them? He wondered if Dog-face would look up and fry him just for larks, or else send a spell up to swat Ulani and him like flies from their tenuous perch.

Fortunately the cloaked figures were preoccupied. The three spell-weavers seemed unaware of Corin and Ulani's approach, concerned only with the completion of their task. Then suddenly Corin noticed another figure emerge some yards beyond the plinth where the Urgolais sorcerers stood in triangulation.

It was Zallerak. He stood resplendent in his cloak with spear in right hand and harp in left. Briefly he glanced up in their direction. He waved his harp at them, beckoning them follow and then turned to run. Corin, squinting down, saw Zallerak was running straight toward the crystal's base and the yawning, white hot entrance of the forge.

"I see him," growled Ulani as Corin tugged his sleeve. "About time he showed up."

They hurried down the last few stairs, together leaping to the rocky chaotic base of Croagon's pit. Carefully they edged their way round its chipped and broken perimeter, avoiding the writhing and kicking, shackled, bleeding massive feet of the tortured god. All around was rubble and ruin caused by His lashing out.

Croagon wrenched and smashed His chains against the walls of His prison, breaking off more rocks which hurtled down around their heads.

They broke into a run, bolted towards the great gaping forge at the centre of the crystal's base. Running head on for that burning furnace.

A crossbow bolt bounced off a rock to Corin's right. He paid it no heed. Obviously Hagan was close behind. They fled past the low plinth of rock supporting the three Urgolais. Corin managed a grin of relief when they passed out of view of the sorcerers. Ahead the forge loomed close. The fire blazed huge, but there were passages through on either side. Just a bit further.

Then familiar canine laughter rose up like invisible smoke from the rock beneath them. *Too late.* Corin's stomach heaved. He gulped and once again the terror crept upon him. Ulani gaped like a trapped hare, the king wasn't used to this particular brand of terror and looked visibly ill.

"*Fools!*" The familiar dog snarl was colder than the wastes of Leeth. "*Did you think to pass unnoticed?*" The words were everywhere—icy spears jabbing into his nerves. "*My brethren are occupied as am I, but there are others here that will take your souls!*"

"Morak!" Corin shouted as the dog-voice faded like mist over water. "Show yourself, Dog-face. I'm ready for you now!"

Nothing.

Ulani gave a shout of warning. "Ware the walls!" The king had stowed his spears and now clutched his horn bow with arrow on the nock. Corin wiped sweat from his brow.

"What now?" Cloaked figures had emerged suddenly from the shadows, filing the sides of the pit. There were many. The faces hidden beneath dark hoods, though the occasional snout showed through. Some of the clawed hands wielded wickedly curved swords. "Groil!" spat Corin. And then the dog-things fell upon them.

Clouter clanged into a serrated blade in a blaze of sparks. The Groil barked, backed off, and then swung wide for Corin's neck.

Corin was quicker. He ducked beneath the black blade and, gripping Clouter in both fists, sliced the Groil in two. He leapt back just in time to sever the sword arm from the next.

Ulani's bow claimed two more but he was running out of room to shoot. He shouldered the weapon, seized his golden cudgel with his left hand whilst unsheathing his sword with his right.

The king waded in, stabbing and braining every dog-thing in reach. They were falling like leaves but there were so many. Corin panted as he leaped back and forth. As he slew he imagined each Groil was Morak. It gave him focus, he already had the attitude.

To his right Ulani fought with cool precision. A score of Groil lay dead at their feet. But more were coming and both fighters would tire soon. Somewhere close behind Corin could hear Hagan yelling as the odd crossbow bolt clattered around his feet.

Your time will come, Hagan.

Ulani sang as he slew, towering above the Groil in his death-dealing dance. But he was worn out and still the dog-things kept coming. It was Ulani's first encounter with the Groil. He wasn't impressed.

"They stink!" Ulani complained to Corin.

"One of their finer qualities."

A crossbow bolt grazed Corin's leg. He cursed, and turning saw Hagan grinning at him. Corin gutted a Groil with Biter (he had no idea when he'd unsheathed the sax but now fought with sword in either hand, which was beyond awkward, but then when you're pissed off enough you find a way). Corin leapt toward Hagan, but a curved blade tore through his tunic from behind and he narrowly avoided being skewered by a Groil.

Corin back swung Biter but his foot caught on a rock and he was pitched backwards, striking his head on the stony ground. Stunned and dizzy, Corin waited for the deathblow.

The Groil hesitated, dribbling mucus and growling. It stooped gaunt above him, its serrated-edged sword waiting for a clear thrust. Seconds passed in frozen silence. Corin wondered how many times he'd waited to get skewered during the last few months. Too many.

Do it!

The creature lunged down.

Corin rolled to his left. He sliced with Biter, cutting both paws from under the gaping Groil. Corin used Clouter's length to hoist his body up and, after regaining his feet, despatched the dog-thing.

But it was no good. Corin was still shaky and other Groil were rushing at him on all fours, amid howls from every direction, serrated swords raised high for the kill.

Corin was spent; his muscles refused to respond. All he could do was brace his body for the inevitable rush of pain. It was a shame—they'd done well. But then he always knew he'd meet with a bad end. His type usually did.

Time slowed. Corin heard Hagan shout something to his right. The Morwellan sounded alarmed. Perhaps the Groil had turned on him too in their hunger for flesh, and serve the bastard right.

It didn't matter much anymore. Corin was exhausted, could hardly lift Biter whilst Clouter hung limp and heavy at his side. A few seconds and they would have him.

Close by, Ulani grunted in pain as a sword scraped his thigh. Cursing, the king skewered his antagonist then his legs buckled and he fell, still gripping cudgel and sword.

"Farewell, Corin an Fol. I fear we are ended!"

And ended they were. Surrounded by Groil creatures, hemmed tight on all sides. There was no sign or sound of Hagan. Corin closed his eyes. A blow hit his back, sending him sprawling. He still clutched Biter but Clouter was missing. Again Corin waited for the deathblow but this time lacking the energy to strike back.

All things pass.

Corin should have expected this from the beginning. He pictured Shallan's face. Theirs had been a foolish brief dream. Corin cherished it now. He had never felt as happy as he had on that evening in Vioyamis. He thought of Ariane and how he loved her too. So strong so proud. And of brave young Cale and Barin, his friend. Corin waited. He heard snarls and scrapings. Why were they hesitating? Then Corin heard a whooshing sound swiftly followed by a dull thud. Something barked and hit the ground in front of him. Corin opened his eyes. He couldn't understand why he still lived. Then he saw the grey-fletched arrow protruding from the nearest Groil's throat. He laughed out loud.

Bleyne.

Other arrows whistled through the air from somewhere high above. With deadliest precision they rained down among the Groil now milling about in confused panic. Corin felt a joyous rush of deja-vu. Bleyne the Groil killer was alive!

Corin heard one of Hagan's men cry out in pain as a shaft pierced his throat. The man dropped his crossbow and pitched to the floor with a dull thump, his leg quivering once before growing still.

Ulani too had survived. He'd struggled his feet and was again fighting furiously, despite a savage rent seeping blood from his right thigh. Corin felt deliriously happy; once again he had cheated death. Or rather Bleyne had cheated it for him. He bayed louder than the Groil, wielding Biter like a madman—killing and killing. Then Corin found Clouter and really got stuck in.

Corin was charged with energy, both blades deadly blurs of steel, driving the foe back towards the far wall, crashing into Hagan's panicking men. The Groil had turned on the mercenaries in their confusion. Hagan was forced to defend himself with bold strokes. Beside him another of his men fell screaming beneath the jagged blade of a dog-thing.

Corin glanced up, noticing a slender leather-clad figure had joined them. Grinning, he rushed to embrace Bleyne.

"We thought you were dead!" Corin felt ashamed that they had left the archer to his fate.

"I very nearly was. But the goddess hasn't finished with me yet. For almost a day I lay prone in that ravine, nibbled by ants and flies.

But I endured, and at last found the strength to continue after you others. Some hornets' nest you've stirred up!"

"Indeed. And welcome back, you're always handy when there are Groil about!" He lashed out at another dog-thing who'd steered into range. The Groil's head sailed, trailing gore. Corin yelled at Ulani.

"Can you run with that leg?"

"I'll cope."

"To the forge then. Before they regroup and we are surrounded again!"

They fled. Corin and Bleyne supported Ulani best they could, though the king was nearly twice Bleyne's height and a full head taller than Corin. While he ran Corin laughed, hearing Hagan's desperate curses. It was the Morwellan's turn to be surrounded by Morak's creatures.

See you in the next life, Hagan!

Nearing the forge Corin spied huge shapes carved out of the rock base. These, it soon became apparent, were the tools of the Smith. Corin saw a huge crystal hammer and close to that a set of sparkling tongs. Both easily the length of three men. Ahead bulked what could only be a giant anvil—the size of a small cottage. Above that blazed the forge itself. The ground still trembled as the blind god continued His agonised dance at the mercy of His three tormentors. Both Croagon and the Urgolais had ignored the fighting in the pit.

The crystal reared close like a great wall of glass, its sheen reduced to pale silver and its pulsations a faint flicker. Despite its roaring flames the hearth gave out no heat. To its left was a path fading back into shadow.

Corin spied a postern gate leading to goodness knows where. Its narrow entrance had until now been hidden by the glare of the furnace. The three exchanged glances. Corin nodded. They hurried beneath the dome's entrance passing the hearth to their right, making for the tiny opening beyond.

The door was ajar. Corin saw someone beckoning them hurry with urgent gesticulations. "Quickly, fools! The Groil will regroup once they have dealt with those Morwellan idiots!"

Nice to see you too, Zallerak.

Corin stooped beneath the stone lintel of the postern and entered within. Behind him stepped Bleyne followed by Ulani limping at the rear. Zallerak stood flapping his arms at them impatiently. The bard seemed to have fully recovered from his battle with the Ty-Tander. He was back to his full on, cantankerous self.

"This way—quickly now!"

Zallerak fussed them into a long room. It was dimly lit by the glowing veins of rock, but seemed gloomy after the blazing brightness of crystal colossus and hearth.

The room narrowed into a tunnel leading deep within the dome's belly. Corin was about to demand where Zallerak was leading them when the bard stopped abruptly in front of a square rock. On closer inspection it was vaguely man-shaped and looked oddly out of place. Ulani gave Corin a quizzical glance.

Now what?

"Here we are and not before time." Zallerak looked pleased with himself. The three fighters stared at the statue nonplussed. Bleyne looked disinterested, Ulani tired and grumpy, and Corin resigned to being habitually pissed off.

What now?

Zallerak stood clucking like an old hen. He was clearly delighted with his discovery. He stroked his long fingers along the smooth contours of the stone figure. Corin still wasn't able to see the statue properly. It was too gloomy in there and his eyes hadn't adjusted properly.

"It's all down to me, you know—I planned this to perfection." Somewhere outside an enraged howling announced the Groil were once again after them.

"What is this crap?" Corin demanded "You've some explaining to do, wizard." Corin's eyes gleamed as they angrily pinned the bard's. Zallerak ignored him; instead he calmly turned to Bleyne.

"Master archer, would you care to mind that postern back there? Our doggy friends will be arriving soon. This final task is going to take a while." Bleyne nodded curtly. He unshouldered his bow and disappeared back the way they had come.

"Zallerak!" Corin's fist struck the stone statue in frustration. "What in Elanion's name are you up to? Tell me!"

Zallerak repaid Corin with a withering stare. "Wait and see, and in the meantime stop yelling in my bloody ear." He returned his attention to the statue with Corin's furious eyes welded into his back.

"Corin, look." Ulani grabbed his arm in alarm. The stone manikin was glowing with a dull greenish light.

"Ah," said Zallerak. "At last we're getting somewhere!" Outside the snarls of Groil grew closer.

Corin and Ulani watched in wonder as a column of light spread outwards from deep within the stone, revealing a figure captured within. Frozen. The green hue deepened until it revealed clearly the figure of a young nobleman sleeping soundly on a dais. Ulani rubbed his tired eyes in wonder.

"Extraordinary work. I doubt any mortal carved this. See how lifelike it appears."

The statue did appear strangely lifelike and, as the light grew around it, Corin was alarmed to see that the young man's eyes were fully open, and his face frozen in a mask of horror.

"What is this?" Corin asked in a hushed voice. He was hesitant to enquire further. Something very strange was happening here. Before Zallerak could answer, Bleyne's shout announced the arrival of the Groil.

"You must hold them off—you three," muttered Zallerak. "This will take some time to accomplish."

"Who is that?" demanded Corin, finding his voice again.

"Who do you think, idiot?" Zallerak snapped. "Why else would I be here at this perilous time risking everything?"

Corin ignored him. Instead he glanced closer at the man-shaped stone. He could see the prone figure clearly now. The green hue was filtrating within its prism.

The young man (if that's what he was) seemed frozen in some timeless state of pain. In his right hand he clutched a small bag. It was from within the bag that a pure prism of light pulsated. This dazzling essence grew stronger until it consumed the greenish glow encasing it, illuminating the long room and chasing shadows deep beneath the mountain. Ulani laughed. It was the same pure light as the crystal dome above them. And suddenly even Corin understood.

"Tarin," he said flatly. "That wretch is Prince Tarin."

"Yes," answered Zallerak. "And now shut the fuck up! I need time to free him from this witchy web of Morak's design. There are tricky spell-traps here—I can't hurry."

Corin stared at Zallerak until the bard rolled his eyes and blew steam.

"The Urgolais arrived here before I did, you see. Isn't it obvious—even to you? Now you can understand my urgency in the desert. Everything is down to timing, Corin. Our enemy pounced on Tarin, delaying their vital word spells on the Smith. My decoy sent to trick them, hah! I suspected they'd be waiting, the little shits.

"They like dark places, always have. When these Urgo found Tarin I knew they'd be diverted, they love little distractions. They'd soon suss his connection to me and assume I would be lurking somewhere—which of course I was.

"But the time they spent making that little trap allowed you idiots to arrive and me to assess our situation, which I have to allow could be better." Zallerak looked so pleased with himself Corin wanted to punch him.

"I knew they wouldn't kill him at first. They are like cats, they love to play. Their game this time was freezing Tarin and shards in limbo until they had consumed the mind of the crazed god Croagon, and coerce the Smith into obeying them. Among other things, they suspect Croagon knows the whereabouts of the spear, Golganak. Morak's principal objective is finding that spear. If he does we are finished, Tekara or no Tekara. Get it?"

Corin was still considering swatting the bard when Ulani's hoarse shout told him he was urgently needed at the door. Corin shook his head in disbelief, and after glancing suspiciously at the frozen form of the Prince of Kelthaine, Corin rushed back to aid his friends who were already exchanging fresh blows with vengeful Groil. Corin joined them at the postern. Ulani awarded him a questioning glance.

"Don't ask."

Beyond Corin's wildest expectations they had found both the lost prince and the shards of the Tekara. But this was no time for reflection. Again they were trapped. Again at some crazy ploy by Zallerak. This time in Croagon's antechamber, outnumbered and weary, and Ulani wounded to boot. Meanwhile on came the Groil, on four legs this time—sniffing and snuffling. Corin readied Clouter. He was getting so bloody tired of this.

Chapter 33

The Awakening

Zallerak crouched eagle-eyed in front of the solidified form of Prince Tarin. Outside the barks of the Groil grew in octave as the three men struggled to hold them at bay.

"This had better work," Zallerak grumbled. "Idiot Prince. You weren't supposed to get caught with the shards on your person. Lucky for us both they had other matters to attend to."

Leaning closer, Zallerak traced an invisible line down the edge of the glowing prism with his index finger. It had been long years since last he'd tried unlocking Urgolais ward spells. Tricky business—one false trace and he'd be blasted.

The dog people often left booby traps for those foolish enough to try countering their spellcraft. But if Tarin's mind was intact the boy still had a chance. That said, Prince Tarin's survival was a side issue. Zallerak's prime concern being regaining those shards. He worked on, breaking codes and unravelling mind-nets, fusing his thought deep inside the prism. So far he'd found seven traps but there would be more. Lots more.

A shout from the postern shattered his concentration.

Damn you—kill quietly, I'm concentrating here.

The fighters were hard pressed, he would have to work quickly else those Groil would get in and spoil everything. There was never enough bloody time. In all his long life Zallerak had had to rush about doing this and that for other people, and usually for scant appreciation. It vexed him so.

Willpower.

Zallerak closed his mind to the clash of steel and yells outside. He focused fully on the pulsating silver, forcing out the last of the cankerous green.

Better.

Click. Clonk.

Two more traps sprung. Good. Zallerak pressed his right palm flat against the throbbing stone; immediately it responded to his touch, the colour deepening from white to a faint rose pink.

That's good. The bard began to chant, softly at first, his right palm pressing hard against the stone and his left gripping the golden harp. Zallerak channelled his thought and his voice grew in resonance, the woven words eclipsing both the sound of fighting close by and the continual monotonous booming of tortured Croagon.

Zallerak let go his harp and placed his left hand hard on the surface of the prism. He leant into the statue, channelling, fusing with the boy trapped within.

It was touch and go. There were more snares as he'd expected. One by one he sprung the hidden traps.

Clunk. Clack! Fizz. Snap!

Excellent.

As Zallerak unravelled those inner snares, part of his mind reached back through the eons of his life, recalling a time when he had been foremost magician in the land. The good old days of golden splendour.

Zallerak dug down for some of that ancient strength, summoning a lost reserve from deep within his soul.

I've still got it somewhere. Yes, here it is!

Slowly the power flowed into him. He felt himself changing; becoming taller, younger. His words encircled the statue then passed within. The light flared in return. The crystal shards of the crown, clutched in the frozen hands of the prince, throbbed excitingly in answer.

Those sentient crystal slivers remembered the owner of this voice. Zallerak's tone deepened to a growl. The statue flared scarlet; the glittering shards blazing into dazzling life.

Almost cracked it.

Then a noise like steam escaping from a kettle filled the chamber. The spell was broken! Zallerak had done it. Slowly the stone containing the prince turned to liquid, melting and streaking before his eyes. Like spring's first kiss after a long pitiless winter, warmth filled the prism. Zallerak watched hawkish and tense. At last he relaxed. Tarin was alive. He could see the boy's chest rising and sinking.

It had worked.

"Zallerak, we need help!" came a desperate shout from outside. That was Corin's voice, a small part of Zallerak's mind acknowledged. "We are hard pressed out here!" The words seemed far away, trying to reach him from another time and place. Zallerak closed his mind to the desperate sounds. A nuisance but one easily ignored.

"Zallerak!" He resumed his incantation—he couldn't stop now. Moments passed, frozen in time. *Nearly there!*

Then at last the prone form of the prince stirred. The throbbing light of the Tekara's shards filled the room with vivid translucence. Their strident glares shifting from one dazzling shade to another; casting weird and wonderful beams of light across the passage and into the giant cavern beyond.

Zallerak chanted and channelled and focused. The prism had melted completely, leaving steaming puddles on the floor.

The fighting sounded closer (part of him acknowledged that the Groil must be in the tunnel). They'd just have to hold them there. It wasn't a lot to ask.

Then the prince groaned and shivered into consciousness. His blue eyes stared about in bewildered alarm. He saw Zallerak standing before him and screamed, stopping suddenly after feeling the hard slap of the wizard's palm.

"Wake up, you twit! Much trouble you have caused me!" Zallerak's eyes blazed cobalt fire down on the terrified prince. Tarin's own eyes squinted, accustoming themselves to the glare. Then he recognised the tall figure leaning over him.

"Zallerak!" he gasped. "I thought you one of them—the dog snarlers. They got inside my head. It was horrible!"

"Yes, they do that—nasty trick they have. Never mind."

"What has happened to me?" The young prince shivered and shook as welcome heat coursed through his veins. His face was flushed, but at least he was stronger now. He shook his stiff limbs into movement, took a step forward and wobbled a bit.

"Nothing that bad—you were fortunate, prince. The dog-lords have other matters concerning them. Matters I must needs spoil for them. Now hand me those shards, boy, there is little time."

This last statement became evident. A large Groil had won free from Ulani's spear and hurled itself through the postern. It clattered down the tunnel on all fours, teeth snarling and tongue lolling stinky.

Zallerak looked up in alarm. He grunted in satisfaction when Bleyne's hurled knife brought the fiend to the ground with a strangled cry.

"Well done," Zallerak said.

"The crown is my responsibility." Tarin still gripped the shards, unwilling to hand them over. "You told me that." Tarin hadn't seen the Groil. He gripped the throbbing translucent bag as if his young life depended on it.

"I must redress the harm I've caused," he insisted. "Who is that?" Corin had just appeared and was launching a tirade of profanities in their direction.

"No one important. Give me the fucking shards!"

"I cannot."

"Zallerak, for Elanion's sake hurry!" Corin yelled. Beyond the door the howls of the Groil filled the cavern. Zallerak eyed Tarin warily, saying nothing. A moment passed, their eyes locked in silent confrontation. Then snake-swift Zallerak snatched the bag containing the shards of the Tekara from the young prince's numb fingers. "Enough nonsense," he snapped. "I have work to do."

***

Corin's hands were drenched in blood; most of it fortunately belonged to the foul smelling Groil, but some was his own and he was tiring fast. Again.

Beside him fought Ulani, wielding sword and mace with fury, his bearded ebony face drenched in blood, a torn cloth binding the wound in his thigh.

Bleyne weaved between them, the long knife deadly in his sinewy palm. All the archer's arrows were spent. Groil lay scattered in bits all around.

Corin stepped back from the mound of stinking corpses. He let Ulani through.

Your shift.

The three had taken turns to face down the foe. Then that big one had got through, but Bleyne had followed and swiftly dealt with it.

But as always there seemed no end to the murdering things. Ulani waded out, allowing Corin a second's breather. His face and arms sizzled with Groil blood, the smell was beyond description. Corin yelled back at Zallerak. He had no notion what the wizard was up to back there.

Ulani fell back. The Groil were breaking through again. Corin heard footsteps behind. He turned sharply, saw Zallerak had joined them at last.

"About bloody time."

Behind him came the pale skinny prince, hobbling and shuffling. Corin glanced angrily at the bard. He noticed that Zallerak looked weary again.

"What kept you?" Disgusted, Corin turned his back on them. Leaning over Ulani, he despatched another Groil with a backhanded swipe of his longsword.

Zallerak didn't respond. Instead he reached down and retrieved his abandoned spear. His eyes were blazing jewels of rage. He pointed its tip at the milling Groil and resumed his chant.

The Groil hung back, uncertain of this new enemy. They could sense the raw power emanating from the spear shaft and were afraid. Their hesitation allowed the three fighters vital respite. Zallerak's flaming eyes beguiled the Groil; they milled in confusion. Slowly Zallerak reached down, brought forth the bag of shards. He touched the tip of his spear with the glowing crystal within the bag.

At that contact the spear's tip blazed golden fury. The Groil howled and snarled and jumped about, cowering from the burnished glow flooding cavern and forge. The spear tip fizzed. It was too much for the Groil. They broke ranks and fled howling from the pit.

Behind the fleeing Groil, the Urgolais warlocks ceased their chanting. Zallerak's witch-light had distracted them and drawn them away from their task. The three turned to confront Zallerak, angry their work had been interrupted.

Released from His torment and momentarily forgotten, Croagon the Smith let out a long exhausted groan. The chanting had stopped and with it the relentless assault on His body. Shattered and reeling with pain, the giant slumped forward, matted mane covering tortured face, His vast frame hanging limp and inert from the huge chains restricting Him.

"Wake up, you three," Zallerak shouted at Bleyne, Ulani and Corin who were taking a well-earned rest. "No time for shilly-shally. Follow me!" Zallerak led the way out into the cavern with an imperious stride, followed closely by the others.

All three fighters were filled with renewed energy. The Tekara's light had worked upon them too, but whereas it had terrified the Groil, the shards' sparkle filled Corin and his friends with new hope and strength. Corin noticed that Ulani no longer limped. Tarin the prince hesitated for a moment and then hurried after them. His young face stunned to silence by what he was witnessing.

But worse was still to come.

Outside the pit, the panicking Groil parted like an obedient wave to let three shadowy hooded figures approach. Corin felt the familiar dread return. His flesh crawled and his spine tingled but the Tekara's light kept most of the fear at bay.

The three dog-lords approached, a cold slither of menace emanating from beneath their sable robes. The largest one stopped. It sniffed the air, puzzled and confounded by the golden glow of Zallerak's spear.

"It's time," Zallerak strode forward to confront them. "Wait here—do nothing, I have business with these three." Zallerak's sapphire eyes shone cold and condemning. The three Urgolais sorcerers fanned out, forming another triangle surrounding Zallerak, their hidden eyes burning in yellow hatred from deep beneath the folds of their hoods. Then the foremost spoke. Its voice the dry rasp of frozen leaves tumbling down a wintry road.

"Aralais!"

The malice within those words caused the warriors to step back in alarm. Corin's palm sweated as he clutched Clouter's hilt. His mind was working overtime.

Aralais and Urgolais.

He really should have worked that out.

Prince Tarin's eyes were wide with terror. He kept swallowing but his mouth was dry. Ulani and Bleyne watched on from the shadows in numbed silence. Bleyne kept muttering to Elanion under his breath.

The air was dry, the atmosphere taut.

"You have failed." The closest Urgolais confronted Zallerak, its appearance whip-lean and stooping, with dog snout and flaring nostrils just showing beneath that hood. Though it was similar, Corin could tell this wasn't Morak. The snout wasn't burnt like old Dog-face's.

"The Smith is completely in our power, Aralais. With Croagon's skill we can forge new weapons for the coming war. Morak shall regain Golganak soon—the Smith alone knows where it lies. He will tell us before He dies—yes even the High Gods can die, Golden One. Their time is passing but we are stronger than ever.

"Callanak, your only chance of salvation is lost forever—that sword cannot aid you this time. Morak has grown weary of your meddling, Aralais. He knows who challenged him at Kranek. You were fortunate there.

"But your luck has run out. You have entered a trap!"

All three Urgolais issued a doggy growly laughing sound. Not pleasant on the ears. Behind their masters the surviving Groil were regrouping.

"Even now the sultan's little army hastens hither to block your retreat, like you, his greed gets the better of him," mocked the closest Urgolais. He pointed a cloak-draped claw at Zallerak and the four mortals standing behind him, then let it drop in a demonstrative chopping motion.

"Time to die, fools!"

Chapter 34

The Clash in the Pit

A great roar echoed beyond the cavern accompanied by the sound of many rushing feet. Corin leaned on Clouter's cross guard and shook his head. Would this ever end? Corin liked scrapping but it would be nice to have the odds in their favour now and then.

He swapped a wild glance with Ulani. "Permians?"

"I guess so—unless that horror is lying." They were both battle-weary despite the aid the shards' diamond light had given them. The thought of facing fresh enemies hung heavy on them.

Bleyne alone remained cool and ready, safe in his knowledge that the Goddess wouldn't let him die. He appeared unaffected by the Urgolais's malice, and had used the brief impasse to recover most of his arrows from the strewn bodies of the Groil.

The sound of steel-shod feet on stone was closing fast. The sultan's elite coming their way.

Corin glanced across to the far side of the forge where sudden movement had caught his eye. "Hey, Hagan, I haven't forgotten you."

The lean figure of the mercenary ignored him. Hagan, like

Corin, had had enough of this business. Limping badly, Hagan slipped from the pit vanishing into the darkness beyond. Of Hagan's men there was no sign. Corin assumed that they were all victims to the Groil. Too bad.

He turned his gaze back to the three sorcerers still checked by the power radiating from Zallerak's spear point. Corin stared hard at Zallerak's back.

Aralais...now I understand. Obvious really. You're a bloody alien.

Zallerak's eyes burnt into his foe, his silent challenge still checking them. The Urgolais waited, summoning spell-power.

Zallerak's words when they came were for Corin alone.

"Yes, I am of the Aralais. The Golden People who ruled these lands and will again in time. But we were allies before and you should trust me."

"Why?" Corin yelled at Zallerak's back.

"Because you have no choice. Come, Corin. Now is your big chance to rock this cave. Your grand moment. I'll mind these three— ignore their boasts, they are weaker than they once were and lack Morak's knowledge."

Zallerak's spear levelled at the sorcerers. Its crystal radiance again filling the cavern. Still the dog-lords hung back. Zallerak whispered a word and the light funnelled narrow, beaming outwards at the sorcerers.

Though unaffected by the glow they hesitated, unwilling to attack. Beyond their masters, the Groil slunk about growling and mewling on all fours.

"Take these shards," Zallerak hissed at Corin without turning his head. "Strike the chains that bind the Smith God."

"What? He's got to be bloody joking, surely?" Corin locked eyes with Ulani who shrugged. Meanwhile the cavern echoed with the sound of marching feet. The sultan's soldiers were somewhere behind the forge coming from the other direction.

"Bleyne will cover you. Do it!" Zallerak yelled at Corin.

Before Corin could respond Zallerak turned in his direction, tossed the bag of crystal shards his way.

"Go!" Zallerak hissed before returning to his silent battle with the three.

And Corin went. Of course he did. Just another job really. Why complain? He cut silent and fast toward the distant stair, leaving the pit behind. His left hand clung to the bag of glowing shards whilst the right gripped Clouter.

Groil sniffed the air. They saw him running and turned towards him. Corin ran for the stair. Two Groil barred his approach. He fended them off and won through hacking and slicing with Clouter.

Three more had fallen to Corin's sword by the time he reached the steep stairway leading up from the cavern.

But others milled behind. Sheathing Clouter behind his back, Corin clutched the throbbing bag of light as though his life's continuation depended on it.

Fuelled by Zallerak's words, he launched his battered body up the stairs. Up and up Corin climbed, hurrying towards the nearest chain link bracing the slumped colossus of the Smith. Below him Corin heard a great shout, and glancing down saw that a score of crimson-cloaked spearmen had spilled into the cavern from behind. More work for Bleyne and Ulani.

Corin's knees hurt, his hands were chafed and his entire body battered. But both the shards' light and his own bloody-mindedness kept him climbing up toward that nearest chain.

***

Meanwhile below the Permians fanned out, their spears and tulwars at the ready. Their captain took stock of the scene: four sorcerers—three shadow-dark and one radiating gold. Not what they expected. This could be bad. The crimson elite looked worried. Whatever was going on they didn't care for it. Both Zallerak and the Urgolais ignored them.

Then Ulani of the Baha strode out from the shadows. The warrior king's face was a mask of pride and fury.

"Let the spell-weavers confront each other. I will deal with you maggots!" Ulani hurled his spear at the elite's officer. The Permian collapsed gurgling, the shaft having passed clean through his neck almost severing his head in its passage. His men, shocked and enraged, circled the king of Yamondo. Ulani smiled. He would let them come to him.

***

High above, Corin hauled his body up the stair. Behind a small knot of Groil followed snarling and barking. Corin could hear their rasping breath below and knew they were closing on him.

The closest clawed at his exposed heel, trapping it briefly. Corin lashed out with a boot. The grip left his ankle.

The Groil pitched howling to the ground with Bleyne's arrow protruding from its snout. Other shafts followed, claiming more of the creatures. Bleyne never missed. But still they followed, closing all the time.

Corin was level with the giant's massive arms. He could see where the vast iron chains hung welded to the cavern wall, twenty yards from the stair. Corin gripped the bag of shards in his teeth. Time to be a human fly.

With both hands free Corin started reaching out tenuously along the sheer sides of the wall, his body flat against its smooth surface. There were narrow indents, ridges and bumps allowing just enough purchase for finger and toe. But one slip and he was curtains.

As Corin struggled the sweat trickled down his face, occluding his vision. Bleyne's shafts claimed more Groil but now the archer was preoccupied with the fighting below.

Someone yelled up at him. Straining his head, Corin saw Prince Tarin was climbing the stair. Somehow the boy must have slipped past the Groil unnoticed.

"Piss off!" Corin hissed between his teeth.

"Those shards are my responsibility," Tarin shouted across to him. "Only I can waken the Smith!"

A pox on your responsibility, shithead. If it wasn't for your stupid—

Corin's foot slipped on a glowing vein of rock. He hung suspended, legs flailing the in air for what seemed like an age. He kicked at the stone with his feet, seeking purchase however tenuous.

"I'm coming!" Tarin yelled.

"Fuck off!" Corin dribbled back. At last Corin regained a foothold. He braced himself, inched his way closer to the chain ignoring Tarin's shouts. Stubborn, the prince followed. Serve the boy right if he should fall.

Far below them the sound of clashing steel again rebounded through the cavern. Ulani's booming war cry accompanying it. Corin pulled his tired body across. One...two...three! He swung out reaching for the giant chain with his right hand.

***

Zallerak was drained by his challenge of freeing the prince. He was weary—uncertain he could win this battle of wills. But the Urgolais were weary also.

The week-long chanting spells to snare Croagon's mind had sapped their strength. Moreover they were only recently returned to flesh after millennia flitting about in shadow form.

Like many who followed Old Night they had awoken sensing He too was returning to wakefulness and stirring below His dreadful mountain. The dog-lords were vengeful, and now they had an Aralais intruder to deal with. Hungry for his destruction, they stepped up their game to break their enemy's will.

The three steadied their triangulation, tapped their full malice and spellcraft at Zallerak.

But Zallerak faced them down, his lips moving as he silently worded the blocking spell. So passed the silent battle with increasingly intensity. Power and light crackled all around the cavern.

Ignored, Ulani and Bleyne battled the crimson elite close by, whilst high above Corin approached the chains binding the Smith, with yelling Prince Tarin close behind.

Then the Urgolais took the offensive and resumed their doleful chant. As one they pointed to Zallerak's midriff. The chanting grew louder and more intense. Their searching fingers crackled with heat and potency. The air shimmered and popped, blue fire blazed forth from their fingers licking the ground at Zallerak's feet.

He leapt back, spear held high in defence. Desperation seized him. Zallerak yelled out the words to his blocking spell. Just in time he raised his astral shield, stopping the next blast of deadly fire bolts. The Urgolais chanting rose louder and louder. More fire bolts streamed forth.

Then Zallerak answered. Spear discarded, he stood before them. Tall and stern, a demigod from a distant time of fable. The golden harp rested in the fold of his left arm. His right fingers plucked chords of power, whilst with a clear resonant voice Zallerak sang his interdict.

His voice was intoxicating like strong wine. It filled the cavern, drowning out the Urgolais's dirge. Behind and above, the huge crystal dome pulsed strobes accompanying his words, filling the cavern with argent fire.

The tide had turned again.

The Urgolais's chanting took on a desperate edge. Above their heads a dark wave mustered threatening to consume the crystal light. It lowered over Zallerak like a great smoky bat, swallowing light and draining his power.

But Zallerak's spell shield held firm. Faster and faster he worked his chords. The song grew in definition. The blackness filtered and fell away. Zallerak's chords stung the Urgolais like winter hail. His song reached out, sapping the malice of their incantation.

Zallerak voiced a single word. The forge blazed in answer. A jet of silver fire shrieked out from the hearth, engulfing the three sorcerers and blinding their vision. The dog-lords screamed horribly as that crystal flame seared their flesh. They lost their balance and control. Their triangulation shattered and the three fell back in disarray, pain and confusion.

Zallerak didn't hesitate. He seized his spear from the ground, and leapt toward his foe striking each in turn with the glowing tip. As it pierced their faces the spear burnt deep into the Urgolais's flesh. They screamed and gurgled, then their cloaks melted away revealing emaciated starved bodies, mummified doglike skulls and thin twisted frames, all broken veins and blotches.

Zallerak, triumphant, raised his lance for the kill. He froze. An icy wind had entered the cavern. Zallerak stumbled—his concentration broken.

A huge shadow crawled along the wall of the cavern; where it passed the light petered and then went out. That darkness swelled like gangrene on ruined flesh, spreading outwards toward where Zallerak stood desperately gripping his spear and harp.

The shadow took on form and from it a cold voice whispered words of heavy power. Zallerak staggered as one struck by an invisible blow. His lips trembled and his body shook. The shadow was all around him, he couldn't withstand it. At last his knees buckled. Zallerak, defeated, collapsed in a crumpled heap. Then the shadow fell upon him.

***

Ulani was still holding his own. Just. He'd sent nine of the elite to Yffarn. But the rest were wary, they circled him awaiting a chance with their spears. One jabbed close, Ulani yanked the spear shaft forward and stove the Permian's head in with his mace. He spat bloody phlegm and dared them to come at him one at a time.

Instead all six lunged at him at once.

That attack never came. The elite's spears stopped inches from Ulani's face. He blinked. Glancing round in horror, the Permians and Ulani witnessed the shadow creature swelling like a bruise along the cavern's inner face. The sultan's elite muttered in fear. They had heard rumours of this place and hadn't wanted to come. They were terrified, eyes wild and panicky.

The crystal light sputtered and faded as icy darkness claimed the cavern. Ulani gasped, chasing breaths. He too watched in dread, shuddering as evil incarnate fell upon the Cavern of the Crystal.

The forge fire grew dim, the flames contemptuously quenched by he who had recently arrived. A shadow within the shadow. Bat-like, it settled silent on the hearth. The flames puckered then died.

Sudden chill filled the cavern. Bleak cold accompanied by stale gloom—the void of forgotten dead worlds spinning outside the Weaver's Dance.

Friend and foe watched terrified as the shadow took sinewy form in the hearth. Zallerak summoned his last reserve and struggled to his knees. The shadow was all around him. A face showed at last, grey black as burnt wood and canine in form. Yellow eyes and lolling tongue. Razor teeth and scarred tissue. Morak had returned.

"So there you are again, Arollas. Meddling where you shouldn't."

High above, Corin chose that precise moment to swing out for the chain. His wild swing went wide, Morak's grating snarl catching him off-guard. Desperately he clung onto a thin flake of stone, his fingers bleeding and the bag of shards dangling from his teeth.

So the scorched hound had come to join the party. Corin wasn't surprised. The more the merrier. A perfect finish to a wonderful fort-night's excursion. The crystal shards weighed heavy in his mouth. Close by Tarin yelled but Corin ignored him. He focused on the chain again.

***

Morak's ravaged visage grew to fill the cavern.

"You have failed, Aralais. I have unlocked the key to the ancient fortress. Golganak will soon be in my grasp."

"You're full of shit, Morak. You surprised me, is all. But now I'm ready for you." Zallerak had regained his feet. He clung to his spear again, weakened but not yet beaten. "You are still weak, Urgolais. All bluff and bluster and your spear's lost forever. Without Golganak you are nothing but a rumour. A shadow within a shadow. See how I snapped your kin like rotten twigs! Now it's your turn!"

In reply the shadow rose up from the hearth in icy rage.

"You are a fool, Arollas—you always were! You were lucky on that island. I was unprepared. This time you die!" Morak's shadow unfolded over Zallerak, choking the bard and again forcing him to his knees.

"DIE!"

***

Corin grabbed the nearest shackle. Swinging like a mad thing, he locked his left arm around the heavy chain. He opened his mouth and spat the bag of shards into his right palm. Corin's fingers closed around the crystal. He slammed the bag into the iron chain. There was a violent clang and a huge chunk of rock split along the cavern wall. A noise of growling thunder filled the cavern. Somehow Corin clung on as pain and giddiness tried to dislodge him.

BOOM!

There followed a blinding stab of light accompanied by a steely snap.

THUD—CLINK...TWANG!

Then the booming roar of a new voice eclipsed all other sounds.

Croagon the Smith was free of His bonds!

Chapter 35

The Smith

The giant crystal blazed anew. Dome, shards and veins of rock were all throbbing with urgent, hungry speed. The giant dislodged His remaining manacles as though they were made of paper. With a wrench Croagon pulled them from the wall.

Corin was sent swinging like a baboon on the severed chain. Barely hanging onto consciousness, he watched with bulging eyes as the next scene unravelled. He still clung to the bag of shards but his purchase was weakening. So was his strength, and it was a very long way down.

Terrible in anger, Croagon turned on His former tormenters. Behind the Smith's shoulders and forgotten, Corin swung and clung, and Prince Tarin gawped in stunned silence. Far below all eyes were on the giant.

Croagon reached down with a yard-thick finger. He scooped up the three Urgolais bodies and crushed them to powder in His hand. Bones crunched and dark ooze spilled out between His hoary knuckles. Croagon cast the mess into the hearth. It blazed afresh.

The blind god turned on Morak. The shadow containing the Dog-Lord had retreated beyond the hearth. Croagon moved a leg in that direction. The Smith's tread shook the cavern as He lumbered forward. His arms stretched with finger searching.

Morak remained defiant. He was the greatest of his people and not easily defeated, even by a god. The Urgolais lord worded a terrible spell and pointed a claw at the lumbering god.

Amber jagged spears of lightning lashed Croagon's knees. He bellowed, slammed His left foot down seeking to crush Morak were he in reach.

The Dog-Lord's shadow faded back along the wall. Again he struck out at the god and Croagon lurched like a ship striking shallows. His booming roar thundered through the cavern. Groil scattered like dust in a gale, while King Ulani, Bleyne and the crimson elite covered their ears and prayed this nightmare would end soon.

Corin and Tarin gaped down liked bugs stuck on the wall. Corin had found a foothold and got back some of his gunk. He wasn't feeling well, however. Even by his standards this was proving a shite day.

Morak sent another blast toward the god. But in his haste he misjudged. Croagon, more than any other being, save perhaps His twin brother Crun, was well accustomed to pain. And the Smith had a god's patience. He let that blast assault His bulk, absorbed it, and reached down fumbling for His great hammer, at last finding it and lifting it from its resting place at the forge.

Gripping the hammer with both hands Croagon brought it down on the crystal anvil with a deafening blow. He growled a command and the hearth fire leapt to obey.

Argent flame exploded outward from the forge. It fused with the crystal's light. Then like starburst exploded over Morak's shadow. The Urgolais screamed as silver fire tore deep into his half-formed flesh. It burnt and burnt and burnt, until Morak's tangible shadow had blistered to a hissing lump of charcoal. From somewhere very far away Morak wailed and mewed and then fell silent.

***

For a time there was silence, discounting the sobbing of Croagon who at last had come to terms with the fact that He was free. The Smith sat huge and horrible, moping on His anvil, staring sightlessly into the hearth pit, tears welling from sightless sockets. All around Him was carnage: broken stone and rubble, and corpses of both Groil and men. And a large gooey stain—the only evidence of Morak's social call.

Those crimson elite still living lay prostrate on the cavern floor, muttering and wailing. Ulani remained on his feet, his eyes wild and staring. Bleyne knelt grim-faced recovering arrows, whilst Zallerak managed a sly smile. High above, Corin and Tarin still clung to rock like stranded limpets at low tide.

One of the elite found his feet. He gaped about, kicked his closest companion who joined him blinking and mouthing unnecessariness. The other Permians followed suit and, ignoring the jeers from the king of Yamondo, fled back whence they'd come.

Ulani, face bloodied and scarred, slumped wearily toward Zallerak. The bard looked exhausted, more like a tired old wayfarer than the scion of an ancient powerful race. Despite that weariness he also looked smug.

He nodded weakly to Ulani who had offered him water from his gourd. The king watched on as Zallerak drank deeply before wiping his mouth and muttering thanks.

Ulani turned, hearing Bleyne's bow twang and saw the last of the Groil creatures collapse lifeless to the floor. Then a shout announced the return of Corin.

"Been having fun?" Ulani raised a brow.

"Lots."

"Been quite eventful down here too."

"Yes, I noticed." Behind Corin stood the prince. Tarin looked pale and wretched.

"Good job up there, both of you," muttered Zallerak.

"He didn't help," Corin couldn't resist saying and Tarin scowled at him.

"I wanted to," the prince said.

Croagon had been listening. The Smith wiped His ruined face free of tears and turned His massive head toward the sound of their voices.

"WHICH OF YOU TINY BEINGS FREED ME?"

"I did," Corin said

"And me," Tarin added. The god's blind face loomed over them.

"WHO?"

"Actually it was all him." Tarin pointed at Corin beside him, despite the god not being able to see him. The Smith, grunted, straightened His back painfully and then flexed those monstrous arms.

"YOU FREED ME, MORTAL? THEN I AM IN YOUR DEBT."

Corin yawned. "It's alright, I had nothing else planned for today."

"I MUST REPAY YOU." Croagon's ravaged face seemed to stare at the place where Corin stood with the others all gaping up at the god. Corin thought for a moment.

"I would like to—"

"Mighty Croagon," Zallerak interrupted. "We four questers and this young prince have sought you out deliberately, knowing your skills alone can help us."

"GO ON—I'M LISTENING."

"We seek to address the harm done by the traitor Caswallon and his advisers, (foremost of which you have just defeated. And jolly well done too!)"

"YOU DON'T SMELL HUMAN. WHAT ARE YOU?"

"Ansu is on the brink of a war so catastrophic it could unleash Old Night's malice again and warp the Maker's pattern. Your eldest brother wakes, Smith. We are confederates united against the return of Old Night. All friends here. We need your assistance in one small matter."

The giant's blind sockets rested on Zallerak. Something akin to dark humour accompanied His gravel voice when next He spoke.

"AROLLAS—NOW I RECALL YOUR ODOUR. YOU SMELL LIKE TREACHERY, YOU ARALAIS ALWAYS DID. WHY SHOULD I ASSIST YOU, WHOSE PROUD KIND ONCE SOUGHT TO TOPPLE OUR RULE IN ANSU?"

The Smith's booming voice echoed around the cavern. Zallerak's face was white but he showed no sign of giving in. "That was an old misunderstanding—we've all moved on since those days."

"HMM. YOUR LOT WERE ALMOST AS BAD AS THE URGOLAIS WITH YOUR CONNIVING AND BACKSLIDING. PERHAPS I SHOULD STEP ON YOU NOW AND BE DONE."

"You are ill informed." Zallerak's eyes blazed angrily up at the towering bulk of the god. "I was never your enemy. Neither were my kin. It was your other brother and His deranged pet started that misunderstanding back then. And it was the Aralais people that paid the highest price, as you should recall."

"THE TY-TANDER IS MY GAOLER. TELCANNA SERVES HIS BROTHER ILL."

"No longer—you are free. We few have slain the beast. Yes I know, we're quite a team. The Ty-Tander is no more. His scaly arse carcass feeds a billion ants beneath the pitiless sun of the Copper Desert."

"THAT WAS A VALIANT DEED—IF IT BE TRUE." Croagon paused in contemplation. He rubbed His filthy beard thoughtfully. He was about to speak but Corin got in first.

Corin never knew why he interrupted when he did. It was as if someone else put him up to it. And perhaps they had.

"These need attention." He waved the bag of shards in front of his head as if the Smith could see them.

"This idiot," (he motioned Tarin who glared back at him), "broke them last autumn. Apparently you're the only one up to the job, sir. We've come a very long way and we're all bloody knackered. So I ask of you, glue these shards together in payment for my freeing of your bonds.

"We'll call it quits after that. Reforge the crown so we can deal with this Caswallon bastard—and those doggy-bastards too, should any still be lurking about. And any other buggering bastard for that matter. You can do what you like with Zallerak. I don't trust him either." Corin winked at the bard who for his part failed to see the joke.

"YOU SPEAK BOLDLY."

"I'm tired—crabby. It's been a long month."

The Smith rubbed His bearded chin. Those black sockets gaped at down Corin.

"YOU ARE A STRANGE ONE."

"It's been said before. But never mind that. Are you going to help us or not? It's a long way back through horrible country—I'd hate for all this to have been for nothing."

Corin stared into the god's sightless face. Beside him his companions stood in silence as though frozen in time. Apart from Zallerak who was gaping at Corin with an expression comprised of irritation, wonder and profound dislike. Aside from that the forge crackled flame and the crystal strobed the cavern. All else was as before.

"YOU ASK MUCH, MORTAL," boomed Croagon after what seemed a ponderous age. "SUCH A TRAVAIL WOULD LEAVE YOU IN MY DEBT. IT IS NO SMALL TASK YOU REQUIRE OF ME. ARE YOU CERTAIN YOU CAN PAY MY PRICE, SHOULD I EVEN STATE IT?"

"Send the bill to Zallerak—this was his idea."

Croagon growled deep in his throat. It could have been humour but most likes wasn't. A sound not dissimilar to that of a great storm-blasted tree splitting open in the depth of night.

"SO BE IT THEN—WATCH AND LEARN."

Corin emptied the bag of shards onto the table flat surface of the anvil. At once the crystal blazed with furious light. On reflection this had also proved an interesting day.

"THIS WILL TAKE SOME TIME," said Croagon, and showed them his back.

Part Four

War

Chapter 36

Calprissa

Shallan had felt the tension growing all day. The ship's crew were on edge, almost spoiling for a fight as they drew near the rocky islet strewn coast of Kelwyn.

She watched diving birds swoop and disappear beneath the sparkling water, remerging seconds later before vanishing again. Earlier she had seen seals lazily observing them from the rocky crags that littered this coastline. Kelpies and sirens—the fisherfolk near Vangaris believed they stole the souls of sailors lost at sea. Shallan knew they were just beasts.

The sight would normally have filled her with pleasure but Shallan's heart was heavy today. Below deck her father's condition worsened by the hour. Duke Tomais went from waking dream to feverish slumber, his hold on life weakening.

The duke no longer recognised his daughter. Shallan was hard pressed to hold back tears in his presence. She kept her chin up though, determined and resolute that somehow they'd all pull through. They had to. The alternative was too horrible to contemplate.

Shallan looked up suddenly as wind whipped the canvas above her head. All around her ropes creaked and timbers groaned as Barin's great brigantine cut water, racing towards the rising buff-brown headland.

"Cape Calprissa," Barin announced appearing suddenly beside her and thoughtfully stroking his greying beard. "We will make port ere nightfall. Not long now, girl."

Shallan nodded. She glanced back across the dancing decks of the ship to the stern where the wild-haired Taic worked the wheel.

"Thank you," Shallan responded almost inaudibly. She turned to look up at him. "Still no sign of the Assassin?" Every minute she dreaded a cry from above announcing dark sails on the horizon.

"Not yet," replied Barin, looking troubled. He forced a smile on his lips. "Mayhap he's become bored with the game and slipped back to his island haunt to brood. Rael Hakkenon's known for his mercurial moods. Let us hope he's lost interest and found someone else to pick on, lass."

"I doubt we'll be that lucky, Barin. But thanks for your support."

Barin rested his huge hand on Shallan's shoulder. "Whatever happens, we are there for you, me and the lads. We're in for a tough winter and I don't mean the weather. But don't fret, you are not alone."

Shallan reached up and kissed Barin's chin. "Thank you," she said, a tear creasing her cheek.

Throughout that entire day Shallan watched from her vantage point at the prow. Her small hands clenched the rail, eager for them to gain the shore. Calprissa—perhaps Barin was right and someone in that artisan city could save her father.

That day dragged for Shallan despite the glorious weather. They rounded the cape and then hugged the coast eastward until an hour before sundown they entered into a rocky bay.

High above stood a gaunt watchtower. From its single window pale light filtered down to greet them. At least the sentinels would see the pirates long before they arrived, thought Shallan. Slightly

comforted by that thought she returned her attention to forward.
The Starlight Wanderer had entered a narrow, twisting channel
about two hundred yards across, hemmed by sheer sandy coloured
cliffs on either side. The rock face was pitted with holes, and watching, Shallan could see myriad birds dwelling thereabouts. A colourful sight, they swooped and dived low, their shrill cries abundant.

Through this crooked cove the trader weaved, the crew hard at
their oars. After a mile of twists and turns the channel opened to
reveal a wide sheltered harbour. In its midst freshly painted ships
bobbed gently, as the setting winter sun cast a rusty glow over the
most beautiful city Shallan had ever seen.

Calprissa. Kelwyn's second city.

Shallan had heard of Calprissa's cascading gardens whilst staying with Queen Ariane in distant Wynais. But nothing prepared her
for the sight greeting them now.

Calprissa's walls and buildings seemed to be sculpted from a
single vast rock, perched precariously on the extreme edge of the
east cliff rearing tall above the harbour.

Shallan was reminded of Silon's house in Raleen. Calprissa's
walls were the white of pearls. As she looked they sparkled and glistened reflecting the setting sun.

Tinkling fountains cascaded from those walls, their waters glittering in the waning sunlight. They cast rainbow shadows, and became babbling clear streams that joyfully wound their steep courses
down to the old stone harbour far below. These plunging streams
were criss-crossed with slender, elegant bridges, all cast from the
same gleaming, untarnished white stone.

Frail arches revealed hidden gardens high up on the cliff edge.
Shallan, her hand shielding the glare, spied brightly-dressed people
looking down from the lofty walls in wonder at the brigantine mooring up alongside their own craft. A few waved down and Shallan
waved back. She felt much better. These people were friends.

Barin addressed Fassof and the crew before disembarking. His
sailors were to remain on deck, saving Zukei and two volunteers to

carry the prone duke up the steep way to the city. Cogga volunteered Taic and Sveyn for that chore. Those staying put grumbled that they were thirsty for ale. Fassof cuffed a couple and the rest shut up.

Barin (feeling guilty) added that he'd make sure they had copious ale barrels brought down and some fresh vitals and salt. That appeased them a little, though most had envisioned a wild night wenching and slurping up there in the city. They all had cabin fever and wanted to disembark. Especially Wogun, who was still convinced something bad was going to happen. Barin, though sympathetic, was unmoved. He didn't want fights breaking out among friends.

After that was sorted, Barin vacated his vessel with Shallan and, struggling behind, the 'volunteers', Taic and Sveyn carrying the duke's stretcher. Last came Zukei, wrapped in her habitual scowls. The black girl stole silently behind Sveyn like a hunting cat.

Cheerfully Barin led the way towards the narrow walkway threading up from the harbour to the gleaming city high above. The way was steep but the steps were broad and even. Taic and Sveyn grumbled quietly with the weight of their burden but no one listened—least of all the duke who lay wan and pale asleep.

Shallan, taking the steps alongside Barin, marvelled at the steep terraces, the chiming water and trailing vines, still cropping despite the time of year.

Marble statues peered out from behind shady garden arbours. Their blank gazes seemed to question her presence there so politely, and looked almost lifelike in the fading light.

Up they wound: Barin striding, Shallan keeping up, the two porters grunting behind, sweating profusely as they carried their noble charge up towards the great city. And last up Zukei, lean and dour, her dark eyes hostile and resentful.

They capped the stair as dusk settled over Calprissa's walls. After a brief respite, allowing Taic and Sveyn to take a break, they entered beneath two wide arched gates, left open in welcome, and hastened on towards a large ornate turreted building. This, Barin informed Shallan, was the citadel. It was wide and spacious with cut lawns leading across to the circular walls.

Servants greeted them politely once inside. Seeing the prone duke they sent for a physician immediately. Shallan watched as the thin-faced doctor arrived with a worried look on his face. He frowned and pawed thoughtfully over her sleeping father's body. Zukei watched the physician, unimpressed. At a nod from Barin she vanished from the room, her quest to source herbs and unguents should the physician fail. Shallan watched her leave.

"Come, Shallan." Barin gently gripped her sleeve. "Leave the physician and Zukei to their work; hopefully one of them can help your father. Let us seek out the master of this city." Shallan nodded and reluctantly turned away. Taic enquired whether he and Sveyn need stay with the duke but Barin said they might as well come too, lest their stomping and gawping upset the medic who seemed the tetchy type, particularly after hearing that Zukei was off hunting herbs. "We have all we need here," he'd said witnessing Zukei's departure. "And I don't need *her* help."

A servant appeared, clad in a neat tabard of blue and yellow stripes over red stockings, these tucked into doeskin boots. He was smiling.

"I am Cormalian," the servant announced, presenting himself with a bow. "I will escort you to the first lord of the city. It's this way, please." The retainer ushered them through a series of airy rooms all with arched windows overlooking the ocean. Shallan's eyes drank in the stunning view.

They followed Cormalian through wide roomy passages, draped with scented plants and furnished with sumptuous carpets of red and gold. Brightly clad folk passed them from time to time, their handsome faces smiling in polite curiosity.

Shallan thought how boorish by comparison were her own people in Vangaris. Then she remembered that Vangaris was broken, her people leaderless and scattered far from their ruined homes. Maybe even dead. She wondered if her three brothers lived yet, and whether

Car Carranis would still be standing when she finally reached its mighty bastions. Time would tell. At least Barin was coming with her.

They were led up stairs to a lofty airy hall opening out onto a broad balcony, commanding more panoramic views of the city and the harbour far below.

Tolruan, lord of Calprissa, greeted them stiffly from the balcony where he'd been watching their approach from the harbour. The tall, aging man was dressed in highly polished armour with full-face helmet resting on his leather desktop. All that metal looked out of place on such gentle features. Barin raised a brow at the sight.

"You are expecting trouble, my lord?"

"Trouble is already here," responded Tolruan looking quizzically at Shallan, as if half recognising her from some time in the past. "Who is this young lady?" he enquired, rather rudely Shallan thought.

"The Lady Shallan of Vangaris," Barin replied. "Her father the duke is being tended by your physician. He has an ague." Barin's response was gruff as if he too were offended.

"Forgive my manner." Tolruan waved a dismissive hand. "I have slept little this week. Shallan? Ah, yes, I remember a pretty young girl playing with the then princess some years ago over in Wynais. You have grown into a beautiful young lady, I must say."

Shallan said nothing. She no longer had time for niceties. Barin coughed awkwardly beside her. Behind them Taic and Sveyn grinned like idiots.

"My lord, we have great need of haste," Barin explained. "The Morwellan duke is in no shape to travel. Your physicians alone have the skill to save him from a worsening condition. Tomais must stay here with you by your kind leave. But the lady and I—we cannot linger."

They had discussed this earlier and Shallan had been heartily against leaving her father. Barin had convinced her the trip north in winter would kill him, no matter what the physicians achieved here. Zukei would stay with him too, Barin had already paid the girl generous coin, and Zukei seemed happy enough having no other plans. Shallan, though not happy, had capitulated with reluctance and vowed to return to Calprissa when the duke was fully recovered.

Barin fingered Wyrmfang's beak. It felt good to have the axe strapped to his side once more. Tolruan's eyes widened at the size of the weapon. "I'm bound for Car Carranis with the first lady of Morwella here," Barin explained to Lord Tolruan. "Her brothers and the survivors of Vangaris should be there."

"Vangaris was sacked by Redhand or his father. Most free Morwellans are camped within the iron gates of Car Carranis. Surrounded, so rumour says, by innumerable foes."

"Much like us then," responded the lord of Calprissa, his expression bleak. Shallan felt her heart sink like a stone to the bottom of her stomach.

What now?

Tolruan's face softened when he saw her expression.

"A scout arrived here two days hence from Wynais, informing us that an army was bound hither bent on our city's destruction and ruin. A warrior in black armour leads them. They come from the north and greatly outnumber our garrison. It would appear that the usurper seeks to enlarge his domain."

"I am sorry to hear that, my lord, but we cannot stay with you," responded Barin. "We have our own battle to wage in the northlands. And we must leave in the morning, no later," he urged.

Tolruan nodded and, showing them his back, paced through the arched window to stand on the balcony outside. For a while he gazed out at the ocean below. Barin and Shallan exchanged glances, whilst Taic and Sveyn shuffled and looked glum. They had hoped to stay for a while.

Suddenly Tolruan tensed, and Shallan watching realised something else was wrong.

"Regrettably that's no longer an option." Tolruan turned to face them, his face blanched with fear.

"What's wrong?" Barin strode onto the balcony and stood glaring down. Beside him Lord Tolruan stood frozen with whitened knuckles gripping the balcony rail. His eyes were on the harbour below.

Shallan and the two crewmen filed alongside. They followed Tolruan's gaze down to the jetties. Shallan cried out and Barin, seeing what had captured their host's attention, cursed and slammed a massive fist into his palm.

The scourge of the ocean were back.

Nine sleek ships had stolen into Calprissa's cliff-locked harbour, their dark sails half furled in the lessening breeze. Bulky figures could be seen working the oars of the nearest vessel. A sleek craft—both its timbers and sail raven black. Shallan felt an icy pang of dread. She had expected this all along.

Rael Hakkenon had not forgotten. Rather he had been awaiting the right moment.

***

From the open roof of the lofty watchtower Rael had watched laughing as his sharks snaked silently into the harbour after sunset. Below him the motionless bodies of the watchmen still leaked blood on the granite steps leading down. Their lifeless eyes glazed as they stared up at their killer in disbelief.

Rael stooped to wipe his rapier on the nearest corpse then resumed his inspection of the harbour below. All was as planned; as the Soilfin had said it would be when it returned the other night.

The Assassin could see the dark banners of Caswallon's army high on the ridge to the north of the city. Already their campfires blazed beneath a lowering sky.

The goblin had informed him of its master's plan and for once the lord of Crenna found himself almost liking the creature.

"Mr Caswallon wants you to attack from the harbour," Gribble had said. "Bad Boy Derino will butcher all the cityfolk and I'll get the scraps. Then it's off to Wynais we go to join the others. I'm part of the army now, Mr Assassin—an advisor and valued asset."

Of course you are, goblin."

"Don't call me goblin."

Rael had smiled as the Soilfin took wing that night. This time there would be no escape for Barin of Valkador and the crew of *The Starlight Wanderer*. This time he, Rael Hakkenon, would be the victor.

Chapter 37

The Tekara

Deep beneath the Crystal Mountains the magician/bard Zallerak, the three fighters, and young Prince Tarin witnessed the re-forging of the Crown of Kings.

The Smith began slowly summoning His strength. At first Croagon crouched low, His beard brushing the floor. He worked the bellows, chest swelling and huge arms bulging and cording.

Like a sudden gale the hearth surged into life. White fire blazed dazzling the onlookers, sparks flew and shadows fled the cavern. Satisfied at last, Croagon scooped up the shards and tossed them into the flame. Corin's eyes widened in alarm seeing the Tekara's remnants vanish into the fire.

Croagon squatted over the forge, arrayed to His right were tree-long tongs, the hammer, poker and bellows. They watched forgotten at the edge of the pit, awestruck witnesses to the Smith God at work.

Croagon thrust the poker hard into the fire, He twisted it and rammed and shuffled. Then He reached in with His left hand and extracted the shards and arrayed them on the anvil. There they glowed white hot and shapeless. Croagon arranged them in a certain order and lifted His hammer.

And so the re-making began.

The Cavern was an amphitheatre of light and noise. The corded veins of rock throbbed in tune with the rhythm of the forge, as blind Croagon smote His massive hammer relentlessly upon the anvil table below. Each thunderous blow sent a dazzling whirl of diamond light dancing through the cavern and filtering off into the passageways without.

Croagon took His time. Painstakingly slow, the Smith shaped each shard one after the other, then with fuse runes, tongs, and His great gnarly hands, bound them together.

The process took hours. Nobody spoke. Prince Tarin covered his ears from the deafening hammer blows. Corin and Ulani were entranced and even Bleyne showed rare interest. Zallerak fretted at the time this was taking. He alone seemed on edge.

The hammer struck and struck, its impact slotting each piece into another, and after every blow Croagon sealed the link with a rune of power. The shards looked tiny under the blows of that huge hammer, but such was the Smith's skill that He never missed, using just enough force to fuse and not break the crystal. The ringing and clanging hurt their ears and the forge's crackle and spit kept them well back.

The crown took shape. Croagon eased the last shard into place between His gnarly fingers and then hammered down hard. He spoke the final seal rune and ran His huge hands over the surface of the crystal. The Smith looked strained and tired, yet pleased with His achievement.

And there it was at last.

The Tekara. The Crystal Crown made whole again. Flawless and glistening with diamond light. Looking tiny like a priceless jewel on the bare slab of the giant's anvil.

The Smith's sightless sockets fell on Corin then.

"TAKE IT, MORTAL."

"Me?" Corin hesitated, not sure what to do. Then shrugging he took a step forward, but Tarin leapt in front of him and made a wild grab for the Tekara.

"The crown is mine!" Tarin shouted. "I will earn the right to wear it." The prince held out his hand to grasp the blazing crystal coronet. But again he was rejected. The Tekara's light darkened to angry crimson. The crown's sentient source recognised the one who had betrayed it in the golden palace that autumn afternoon. Tarin looked horrified and upset.

"Why does it reject me?"

"That should be obvious, fool," snapped Zallerak standing behind him. "You cannot expect to wear the crown a second time. The connotations would be worse than before. We must find another to rule Kelthaine—someone worthy. We can fret about that later. For the time being I will take it." Zallerak stepped forward to the anvil, grasped the re-forged crown with both hands and lifted it high above his head.

"Kell's Crown forged anew! Now let our enemies tremble. The tide has turned!" As though responding to his words the crown's light shifted to a burning lightning blue.

Zallerak smiled. He reached out to the bag that had contained the shards. He spoke a command, the bag expanded to double the size. Zallerak placed the Tekara in the bag and fastened the drawstrings tight, finally lashing those around his belt.

"I thank you, Mighty Croagon," he yelled up at the god's ravaged face, then turning to the others added, "We should depart."

Croagon loomed over Zallerak. "WHAT OF MY PRICE?"

"Consider it paid, you are free for the first time in millennia. Take that and be merry, it's all I've got at the moment. I'd offer more if I could but we are pressed for time."

"I WILL TAKE IT, BECAUSE I KNOW WELL HOW TREACHEROUS ARE YOUR KIND. BUT I SAY TO YOU THIS, ARALAIS. YOU ARE IN OUT OF YOUR DEPTH. YOU CANNOT WIN THIS WAR ALONE."

After hearing these last words, Zallerak began beating a hasty retreat into the postern behind the forge. Ulani and Bleyne were hard on his heels, both eager to be gone. Tarin followed, dragging his heels; the prince's face was pale and drawn. Corin watched them vanish from sight. He wasn't ready to leave yet.

Corin turned back; he stared up at the ruined face of the Smith who slumped massive in deep fatigue beside His forge.

"What will become of you, Master Smith? You are free—will you leave this place now?" Croagon didn't reply, seeming lost in long forgotten memories.

A scraping sound distracted Corin. Perched on the anvil was a large raven watching him with cold clever eyes. How the bird had found its way in here Corin couldn't begin to guess, though he wasn't that surprised to see it.

The raven croaked twice, showed its wings and then took flight. Up it flew circling Croagon's head three times before perching on His hunched shoulder and hopping up towards His neck.

"WHAT DO YOU WANT, OROONIN?

Croagon's ruined face looked angry, resentful.

"I SHOULD HAVE GUESSED YOU'D BE LURKING ABOUT SOMEWHERE."

The raven cocked its head, opened its beak and issued a silent caw.

"I KNOW YOU ARE HERE, OROONIN. COME TO MEDDLE AGAIN?" The raven croaked a last time and then winged silently up towards the roof of the cavern and vanished from sight. Croagon laughed grimly at its departure. Then His huge head turned to the little mortal still watching Him in silence.

"YOU STILL HERE—WHY?"

"I would have answers." Corin looked around but there was no sign of the raven.

"WHAT ANSWERS? HAVE A CARE, MORTAL. HAVE I NOT DONE ENOUGH? WHY SHOULDN'T I CRUSH YOU LIKE A BEETLE?"

"Who is my real father?" Corin demanded. "Why does the Huntsman hound me from dawn to dusk?"

"YOUR FATHER—OH YES, I SEE THAT NOW. HOW INTERESTING. SEEK HIM IN THE MOUNTAINS ABOVE DARKVALE."

"Darkvale? I've heard that mentioned before."

"STAY CLEAR OF THAT FOREST LEST YOU FALL PREY TO HER SNARES."

"Her? And what of the Huntsman?" Croagon didn't respond. He had sunk back into deep contemplation. Corin wondered if the Smith had forgotten he was there.

"Thanks for what you did," Corin said after a minute gazing up. "I hope that you find peace in the days to come."

Croagon said nothing and Corin realised it was time he went. Without a backwards glance he made for the postern leaving Smith and forge behind.

Corin felt exhausted, but willed his tired legs to keep moving as he trotted through the tunnel. As Corin loped the giant's words pursued him like steely knives in his back. *Her... Darkvale...* in the coming weeks those two words would return to haunt him.

Corin ran. Behind him, back in the forge, a deep distant rumble like falling buildings announced Croagon slept at last. Corin shut out the voices in his head and sped on through the tunnel. He soon passed the place where they had found Tarin and entered into new passageways.

As he ran Corin marvelled at the intricate beauty of the many carvings on the walls. They were everywhere and, although it was much darker in here than outside in the cavern, Corin had just enough light to see his way ahead. The carvings were weird and alien yet beautiful to behold. Somehow they saddened him.

He forced his legs to move faster. The way narrowed, inclined and then levelled out again. The light faded darkening to gloom.

Corin hoped that he hadn't lost his friends. Why didn't they wait? He hadn't been long talking to the Smith. Or had he? It was so hard to measure time in this subterranean world.

He recalled how Zallerak had fled the cavern once he had the Tekara in his grasp. That thought more than any other spurred Corin on. He was going to have to watch that wizard closer than ever now. *Aralais.*

Corin wished he'd questioned the Smith about Zallerak's motives, but then Croagon probably wouldn't have told him anything. Certainly the Smith had no love for Zallerak's people. But then He didn't like His own lot either. Corin didn't blame him. These immortals were a twitchy lot. Too much time to weave their webs. Corin had no problem with that. Just wished they'd leave him out of it.

At last the welcome sound of footsteps ahead. Relieved, Corin hurried to join the others. Ulani grinned, seeing Corin running to catch up.

"What kept you?" Ulani was limping but still managing to shift along at reasonable speed. The king was a mass of scars and dried blood, but his grin raffish as ever.

"You need a wash," replied Corin. "I stayed behind to speak with Croagon."

"Was it worth it?"

"Not really."

"It never is. The High Gods love themselves and no one else. I don't like any of them," Ulani added after a moment.

"You've a profane tongue, my friend," said Corin. "Be careful lest one of them be listening."

"I care not. Lead on, Longswordsman."

The tunnel seemed endless. As he passed, Corin saw that there were many entrances to either side. He wondered what hidden secrets those passages would reveal. Best not know.

They stuck to the main path and Zallerak's pace never slackened. The bard led them on in haste despite his evident weariness. He looked stressed and edgy and was clearly desperate to be free of these mountains now that he possessed the Tekara.

Although it was tied securely to his belt, Zallerak jealously cradled the crown under the crook of his left arm, guarding it like a broody hen. Zallerak's other hand gripped his spear, the harp secreted out of view.

Corin studied the bard's body language from behind, wondering why he appeared so agitated. After all, they had achieved what they set out to do. As though aware Corin watched him, Zallerak picked up his pace, the blue cloak trailing behind like a cloud.

Behind Zallerak loped Bleyne followed closely by the young prince Tarin, his eyes still haunted and wary. Ulani kept up as best he could despite his leg causing him grief.

"You alright?" Corin asked the king.

"Fine—just getting older."

Corin drew level with the prince. Now for some answers.

Tarin was handsome in a blond freckly, blunt-nosed kind of way. Large boned, he looked strong and might make a fine warrior one day. If he lived long enough. He had courage, his rashness following Corin up the stair was proof of that.

Corin guessed the youth had seen about seventeen winters. He prodded the boy's shoulder.

"You've caused us a deal of trouble, prince." Tarin's eyes hurled daggers back at him. "Because of you Roman died. And for what! All Four Kingdoms are in turmoil. People are dying because of you and that fucking usurper!"

Tarin did not answer the accusation. His expression was hostile and his face red with emotion. Corin sensed the boy was about to erupt. He pressed further.

"How's your conscience, Tarin? What's up—lost your tongue?"

"Corin an Fol, it is not your job to question the prince!" Zallerak yelled back at him. "Tarin has paid a high price for his actions. He must come to terms with his guilt. The will of Caswallon is not easy to thwart. Give the boy a break." Corin desisted but the prince still glared at him.

"I will make amends," Tarin vowed, stony-faced.

"We'll see," responded Corin. He winked at Ulani who'd been watching the exchange with interest and then turned his attention to the gloomy passage ahead.

The path led arrow-straight for what seemed miles. Still the passages branched off into blackness on either side. They were all weary now. Worn out by stress and travail. Zallerak looked shattered.

Corin wondered how Ulani kept the pace up. The king never complained though Corin could tell he was in pain. His own legs felt like lead weights and he wasn't wounded.

It was dark in the passage; there were fewer veins of crystal on this side of the mountain. Time dragged on. Corin started to question if they'd ever escape from this labyrinth or were going around in circles and at some point would arrive back at that dark lakeshore. Perish the thought.

The stuffy gloom of these catacombs was weighing on everyone. The only sounds the soft thud of their footsteps and dripping water coming from somewhere far above.

Corin had lost all sense of time; he had no idea whether it was day or night outside. It felt as though they had been underground for a very long time. Perhaps they had, and time passed differently under these mountains. Corin drove such cheerless thoughts from his head and kept walking.

When at last bright light revealed the southern entrance up ahead, Corin felt a delirious flood of relief. Tarin shouted and Ulani grinned—even Bleyne smiled. Corin kept a hand on Clouter's hilt as they hastened to the entrance.

A huge wrought iron door hung half open. Neglected, its hinges rusted and skewed by the years. They passed through the gap between door and frame, emerging happily into the light.

Corin squinted, allowing his eyes adjust to southern sunlight. At his side Ulani was sitting in the sun grumbling about flies. Bleyne was scanning the terrain and Tarin stood blinking in the heat. Zallerak appeared as impatient as ever.

Corin glanced about. They stood on the edge of a wide level plain. Reddish sand, stone and rocks faded into shimmering distance. A mile off to the right were stubby trees offering protection from prying eyes.

"Those are the trees I mentioned to Tamersane," Ulani said. "Best we go see if he's awake."

Chapter 38

The Crimson Elite

A jingle of harness announced Tamersane had seen them coming and jumped into action. "About bloody time," he muttered, leading the horses toward them. "I've had all manner of aggravation with these beasts. That and Permian soldiers creeping about." Tamersane had obviously been waiting a considerable time.

"How long has it been?" Corin enquired.

"Weeks," Tamersane replied. Ulani raised an eyebrow at that. "Well, almost two days—but it felt like fucking weeks. I've been bored shitless perched under those trees like some lovesick buzzard. How did it go under the mountain? Do you have the crown all fixed and new?"

"Very exciting," responded Corin. "And yes, the Tekara is whole again, and no, I don't have it. He does." Corin motioned toward Zallerak standing a few yards distant observing the desert.

"Good. That's good! I found his horse by the way, roaming on that mountain path a mile or so beyond the place where we parted. And did I mention this region's crawling with crimson elite? They could turn up at any moment." Tamersane cast a questioning glance in Tarin's direction. "Is that young Prince Tarin? He's grown since last I saw him. I suppose it's good that he's still alive, but he looks a bit sick. What's his problem?"

"Don't ask," Corin replied and Tamersane shrugged. Tarin ignored them both. The prince was sulking.

They mounted without further ado. Prince Tarin shared a saddle with Bleyne, the lightest of the riders. They passed the provisions around and drank deeply from the gourds, Tamersane having replenished them at the nearest creek. Corin had forgotten how thirsty he was, he and Ulani had long since drained their own vessels.

"Which way now?" Tamersane asked Corin.

"I guess east past these mountains then north, but ask Zallerak— he's the one in a hurry." And Zallerak was. Without a backwards glance he kicked his steed into motion, guiding the beast out from the trees. The others followed.

They rode in single file keeping close to the hem of the nearest mountain. The glare from those dazzling slopes half blinded them. The Crystal Mountains no longer inspired Corin. They'd achieved what they set out to do and he just wanted to be gone from here.

By late afternoon they reached the eastern flank of the last height. Ahead lay flatness, sand and stone—the occasional weird, twisted tree breaking the monotony. They crested a small rise and reined in, taking a break and gazing around.

"We have company," Bleyne said after a few minutes. He had been watching the way they'd just come. The others joined him and groaned.

A large troop of crimson-cloaked horsemen had rounded a crag to their west.

"Get down!" Corin hissed but it was too late. They'd already been seen.

Lances at the tilt, the elite whooped and hooted closing on their quarry. Clouds of dust filled the sky behind as they thundered closer. Corin and Ulani exchanged a weary glance.

"It would be nice," observed Corin as he launched his aching hide up onto Thunderhoof's sweating saddle, "if just once, we could have a break from all this hair pulling and rushing around."

"You'd only get bored," grinned Ulani. "Time to go!"

They spurred their steeds forward, beating a brisk course away from the mountains. The enemy was gaining fast, their spear tips blazing in the golden sunlight, and their hoarse shouts carrying far across the wind.

Crossbow bolts whirred above their heads as they dug in their heels and drove their steeds ever harder. One passed clean through Zallerak's cloak. The bard didn't notice it. Corin questioned why they were riding due south into open hostile country instead of north. Again he had to rely on Zallerak's lead.

Behind them the shadow of the mountains shrank with distance. Ahead were only sand and sky and hot arid wind. Zallerak led them, his silvery mane wild and dishevelled. The bard was yelling something but Corin couldn't hear what it was.

A noise buzzed Corin's ear. A quarrel pierced his desert robe and lodged in his saddle pommel, nearly skewering him from behind and missing his groin by an inch.

Shite.

"They're gaining on us!" Ulani yelled from behind. "We'd better seek cover in those rocks and hold them off!"

The king pointed to their left. Corin saw a broken tumble of pinkish stones a mile or so to the southeast. Without a word he guided Thunderhoof in that direction.

"Not that way, you idiots!" Zallerak's cry was shrill and he was shaking his spear vigorously. Corin was about to yell 'why?' when he saw a score of elite emerging from the rocks ahead. Once again they had entered a trap. And more horsemen had appeared ahead of them hastening to cut off their retreat, whilst behind the pursuing riders swiftly closed the gap. This wasn't looking good.

Zallerak reined in, his eyes manic and staring.

"Make a fence around me—and quickly!" Zallerak ordered. "I'll need a little time to prepare a surprise for these fools. I can do without this crap, I've had a hard enough day as it is." The bard grabbed a startled Tarin and yanked him one-handed from Bleyne's horse. "You can assist me, boy," he told the gaping prince. "Up to now you've done nothing but sleep."

The four fighters formed a mounted guard around Zallerak and the prince, their weapons facing outwards. Corin spat in the dust and glared at the approaching riders.

The elite eased their mounts to a walk. They approached in precise order, spears levelled, tanned faces haughty beneath their shiny helms.

"Arrogant bastards," Corin muttered.

"That they are," responded Ulani. "Good fighters though, when not spooked by sorcery."

"Let us hope Zallerak does something soon," Tamersane added without much confidence.

The sultan's elite formed a ring of steel just out of range of Bleyne's bow. They waited, shifting in saddle and muttering. Their horses frothed and snorted and hoofed the ground.

Arrogant they might be but they looked splendid in their crimson cloaks, sparkling ring mail and polished half-helms. Corin could see that they had tight discipline and anticipated a hard fight ahead.

Bleyne had an arrow ready on the nock. The archer waited impassive as ever. The Permians tightened the noose. There must have been over a hundred of them.

Long minutes passed, Bleyne's arm was taut with tension as he pulled the bowstring back level with his right ear. He waited.

Still they hesitated: the riders jiffleling and cursing, their horses blowing and drumming their hooves on the dusty ground.

Dark faces mocked them from beneath those conical half-helms. Corin slid Polin's bow from Thunder's saddle. Time to give it a go. He wasn't the best shot but you never know. Eyes squinting, he picked out his man.

Attack, you shitheads.

He wished Zallerak would get on with whatever he was doing. But the delay could only help them. Corin could hear weird grunts and moans coming from the wizard's direction. Now and then a sudden puff of smoke announced that something was happening; however, it didn't amount to much.

"I think he's lost his spark," Ulani said, which wasn't very helpful.

Someone snapped an order from behind the crimson ranks. The circle of spears parted just wide enough to allow two swarthy horsemen through. Corin spat in disgust, recognising the oily Sulimo who they had encountered north of Agmandeur. The sultan's spy and Caswallon's man in the south.

It was the other man that held his attention. He was young and rotund, garbed in crimson and gold robes, with a gold and black turban wrapped around his head. He sweated on his gold-trimmed saddle and glared at them with contemptuous loathing.

The sultan?

Corin pulled back on the bowstring.

Ready when you are, fat boy.

Samadin the Marvellous stared coldly at the tiny knot of fugitives daring to show defiance in his august presence. His mood was black. He missed his harem and boys. He detested this relentless desert heat and was melting beneath his gold-laced purple robes.

Damazen Kand had failed him and the fool had got himself killed to boot. Just as well for him. Were he still alive Kand would be stretched out by pegs, naked and screaming—food for scavengers.

The sultan glared at the northerners who dared stare back at him in mutual loathing. His jaw dropped in surprise when he recognised the king of Yamondo amongst them. Permio had no issue with that jungle country; they traded coldly to mutual gain. There was little love lost but that didn't mean they were enemies.

"So you conspire against me also, Ulani of the Baha, siding with craven spies and impostors."

The sultan's nasal voice was like a fly buzzing in Corin's ear. It cut through the other sounds. "I know these villains you side with, renegades from the north countries. I will remind you of your folly, king, while my executioner separates your ugly head slowly from your shoulders with a rusty saw. After that your body will be dismembered, broken and fed to my slaves."

Ulani laughed. He had met Samadin some years past when the young sultan had received the king and his retinue in the palace at Sedinadola. King and sultan hadn't cared for each other.

Samadin's face mirrored his crimson robe, hearing Ulani laugh. No one laughed at the sultan. His men looked worried and Sulimo's eyes were everywhere.

Then Ulani stopped laughing. "Speak not of cooking the fish until the fish is hooked!" Before any could react the king had spurred his horse forward, brandishing a short spear in his ebony fist. He let fly, the spear slicing air toward the sultan's neck.

A guard leapt from his saddle, receiving the spear in his chest. The man gurgled and slid to the ground; Samadin glanced briefly down in disdain at the mess.

Then the sultan kicked the merchant Sulimo's horse forward whilst urging his own beast back through the ranks. Sulimo, terrified, tried to turn his beast around but left it too late.

Corin and Bleyne had both urged their steeds join Ulani's. Corin's wild arrow sang past Sulimo's ear, but Bleyne's pierced the merchant's right eye. Corin was fumbling for another arrow. By the time he had it on the nock Bleyne had punctured three more elite. Fortunately the sultan's archers were sluggish in response, being too stunned by what had happened to return prompt fire. But now they were getting their act together.

Time for Clouter—stick with what you know.

Corin slammed the bow back in its saddle harness and unleashed the longsword. Bleyne's bow twanged and another rider fell from his saddle. Enemy arrows answered and the rest closed in with spears parallel.

"Kill them all!" Samadin shrieked, kicking his horse back through the swiftly closing ranks. "I want them dead! And dismembered! And their fucking heads stuck on poles! I want to crap on their rotting corpses! Kill them all!"

The elite pressed forward eager to obey, their horses' hooves crushing the bodies of Sulimo and the other fallen into bloody pulp beneath them.

Corin gripped Clouter hand over hand and braced his battered body for the oncoming assault. Arrows thudded into the ground on either side. As yet no one had been hit. But they couldn't stay lucky for long.

The crimson lancers were almost on him when Corin was nearly knocked from Thunderhoof's back by the vortex of a colossal blast from somewhere behind.

"By Telcanna's seventh nipple—what the fuck was that!" Tamersane had nearly voided his smalls in shock, the blast having just missed his ear.

"Fireworks!" Ulani was beaming from ear to ear. "I love fireworks."

"A warning would have been nice." Tamersane rubbed his left ear.

BOOM! HISS. THWANG! ZING! All around the ground quavered and shook. Jagged javelins of lighting flared skyward, arcing, and then shrieking down on the panicked riders and horses of Permio. Most blasts thudded into stone and sand, burning smouldering rings at impact.

Others struck the elite's armour frying the riders alive, grilling them to charcoal as their fellows struggled in vain to remain seated on their terrified mounts.

Everywhere was panic and disarray. Men and horses scattered like dust as the lightning lanced mercilessly down from the clear blue sky above.

"Impressive," grinned Tamersane.

"Spectacular," added Ulani.

"'Bout bloody time," was all Corin could say. Thunderhoof wasn't impressed either.

It's all right—these pyrotechnics are not meant for us, old fruit. Thunderhoof wasn't convinced.

On boomed the blasts, each one striking a hapless rider, burning him to cinders and tossing his blackened corpse from his terrified steed. There was no sign of the sultan. Samadin the Marvellous urgently needed to be elsewhere due to a sudden development inside his smallclothes. He'd fled from his horse and squatted straining behind a rock.

Beside him, Corin saw Ulani carve a way forward into the tangled melee of horsemen, the king's golden club trailing scarlet as it whirled through the air.

Zallerak had remounted and joined them; beside him the young Tarin's face was flushed with excitement, a stolen tulwar already bloodied in his hands. Corin raised a brow at that. The surviving Permians cowed in fear of Zallerak. His eyes like molten sapphires, Zallerak urged his mount forward and broke through their tangled line, winning free to the stony flats ahead.

"Come on!" he shouted as the others urged their steeds to follow in his wake. "We can lose them under the shadow of night. See, even now evening approaches!"

It took an hour for the Permians to regroup. At least seventy were dead. Their surviving captains cursed and kicked their men into a semblance of order.

One of them found Samadin weeping behind his rock. The sultan emerged after a time with hands overhead. He'd soiled his robes but chose to ignore that. Instead he stood berating his elite for being worse than cowards.

"I'll see you flayed alive!" Samadin's face was as crimson as his robe. He still shivered in terror of lightning spears returning. "They're escaping! I want them hacked to pieces! Trampled into dust! After them, you filthy craven worms!" Samadin could say no more; he'd erupted into a fit of coughing.

Despite the sultan's rage it took another chaotic hour before the Permians finally gave chase. They were much too late. Again the trap was sprung, and as night approached their enemy slipped from view.

***

Eight lean-faced riders watched from the southern flanks of the Crystal Mountains. They saw the fugitives break free from the chaos occurring several miles away.

Barakani had raised an eyebrow at the uncanny lightning but his nearest son had laughed in delight. Rassan as ever was eager for battle.

"Which way will they go?" he asked his father beside him.

The Wolf of the Desert watched on in silence for a moment. "Silon believes the wizard will make for Isalyos," he said eventually, his thin lips showing a slight smile.

"Where the rest of the sultan's finest await the return of their most beloved ruler," grinned Rassan. "It's as we planned, Father. We will meet them at the oasis."

"Aye," laughed Barakani. "That we will, and put an end to this business at last!"

They rode northeast for several hours, at last reaching the dusky valley where Barakani's men awaited his return.

A force ten thousand strong. Their spears gleaming in the weird glow. The tribes of Permio had mustered for war. In the morning they would ride.

***

His body ached where it didn't bleed. Pain soared behind his eyes; two fingers were broken on his left hand, and his hair was matted with congealed blood. He felt sick and weary to the bone.

None of that mattered, Hagan told himself. He was alive. His men were all dead, broken beneath that dreadful mountain, but he, their captain had survived.

That said Hagan was in desperate shape and much weakened by thirst. He had half crawled his way back to the waiting boatman on the shimmering lake. The ferryman's cold stare had mocked him as he set him ashore on the far side.

Hagan shuddered at the icy glance of the waterman's single eye. He didn't wait as the shadowy figure poled his mysterious craft silently away. Nor did he look back.

Instead, Hagan staggered and hobbled towards the second stairway that led back up to the northern door whence he had entered the mountain. His mind wandered, he stumbled and fell, got up again. The climb almost finished him but somehow he made it to the top.

Got to keep moving—not going to die in this place.

Was he delirious? He heard strange sounds, voices in the passages below. Dark voices.

Must keep...walking...not...dying...here.

Other noises betrayed movement behind him but Hagan dare not look back. Something was stirring beneath this awful mountain. Something evil. Hagan didn't dwell, just limped on, stopping only when he heard the urgent sound of whispers carried across from the weird light behind him.

I am not alone.

Ahead was darkness. Hagan was far from the giant crystal's radiance now. He slipped into a side passage and waited in silence, allowing his battered body rest as his tired mind kept watch.

The voices grew louder accompanied by the clear ring of shod feet. Soldiers were approaching in haste. The elite—some of them must have survived. Hagan waited and listened as the whisperers drew near...

***

"He went this way—I know he did," insisted Migen.

"How do you know this bastard's got the gold?" asked Gamesh. "Those other brigands could have taken it."

"No, the Morwellan's got it alright; he's a sly one." Migen's growl echoed through the passage ahead. "Waited till all his men were done for by those hooded horrors, he did. Then grabbed the treasure and fled with it! I tell you, Gamesh, our reward will be great when we return with the gold and this villain's head."

Gamesh was about to reply when he stopped in surprise. He gave a startled grunt and stared down in disbelief at the long blade protruding from his belly. Gamesh shuddered and slumped trembling to the ground, his guts spilling forth as the sword slid free.

Hagan stepped back and swung again. Migen's head spun through the air, coming to rest by a sliver of crystal. The vein glowed scarlet. Hagan sheathed his sword and stepped over the thrashing body of the still living Gamesh.

"Gold," he snarled. "No fucking gold here—just death." Hagan opened the dying man's throat with a mercy cut from his knife. Hagan had few good traits but he wasn't sadistic, only cruel by necessity—or so he told himself.

After what seemed an age of climbing, crawling, hobbling and groping in the murk, Hagan, thirsty and weak beyond words, reached the stairway leading down to the hidden door.

Nearly out.

Hagan descended awkwardly, picking up his pace despite the pain and fatigue.

Something evil back there. Gotta keep moving.

Down Hagan clambered, half slipping and sliding until at last he reached the cave of stalactites marking the entrance to the mountain.

Hagan stopped to drink deeply in the dark pool of the cavern. Once sated, he lurched out from under the mountain and stared in wonder at the sight greeting him. High above a diadem of stars furnished the sky, a billion blazing jewels winking down on the silvery sand of the desert below.

There were horsemen down there. Hagan saw hundreds— maybe even thousands. Tribesmen garbed in dark robes. On their shoulders were strapped broad tulwars, the curved blades gleaming beneath the starlight.

Hagan sunk to his belly in utter exhaustion. He had survived but only just. And now what would he do? Ahead lay a sea of enemies and at least another week of hunger.

And if he survived the journey north...? What then? Caswallon's spy would be looking for him. That goblin was a spiteful little shit. The usurper would show no mercy this time. Hagan was a marked man, but then what else was new? He grinned suddenly, watching the army below.

You win this round, Corin, but I'll be back.

And he would.

Hagan had his stolen sword and his wits. He'd survived worse, though he couldn't remember when or where. Hagan nursed his painful shoulder and started the long starlit trek down the mountain road.

The game was far from over. He and Corin would meet again soon enough; in the meantime there were always those who could use a skilled blademaster. War was coming. He'd slot in somewhere. Perhaps Rael Hakkenon would take him back.

Time will tell.

Hagan felt sleep wash over him. He took shelter hidden by the road. Snatch a few hours here and there. Move by night, sleep by day. Survive. Then once back in the Four Kingdoms, Hagan would sell his sword arm to the highest bidder.

He would do what he did best. Kill. Then once he was rich enough, Hagan would gather more men, better than the last lot, and seek out the renegade Corin an Fol and his friends. This time he would kill them all. Hagan focussed on that happy thought before sleep stole upon him like a thief in the night.

***

Far below the mountain they stirred. Creatures older than time. Far below Croagon's forge deep in the roots of the mountain's heart. As the Smith's snores resounded through the chamber of the crystal, they began to manifest and swarm. Their master would have need of them soon.

It had been so long and they were all so very hungry. But it was almost time. They would have food aplenty before long.

And so the long slow scrape up the mountain began. One by one the thousand famished Soilfins inched their way up from the bowels of the mountain. They were weak and frail, their wings broken and rotted. But they would mend, become strong again. Because *He* was back.

Chapter 39

Ariane of the Swords

Snow fell in silent shrouds upon the sleeping hills of Kelthaine. The fields lay pristine white, barren and empty beneath a leaden sky. A raw wind cried chill out of the east.

High on the battlements of Car Carranis a lone figure braved the winter cold. Joachim Starkhold had risen early, as was his habit. He stood in silent gloom, a woollen cloak draped about his broad shoulders as he surveyed the wintry scene outside.

Starkhold could see the multitude of tents scattered like sleeping beasts below the dark canopy of the forest and out across the Gap of Leeth. There would be no attack today. The enemy waited for winter to ease or for Car Carranis to break under the withering embrace of the three destroyers: hunger, fear and cold.

Three long hard weeks had passed since that first attack. King Haal had lost many men to Starkhold's archers to no gain. After that day the barbarian king realised no swift victory could be achieved here.

But King Haal knew it was only a matter of time before the city would break. They had only to wait. Let winter take its toll.

Starkhold knew this, the barbarians knew this, and far away in Kella City Caswallon knew it too. The deceiver. Starkhold now suspected Caswallon had allied himself with Leeth. But why and for what gain? These barbarians had no concept of loyalty. Starkhold would probably never know.

So against his wishes King Haal had changed tactics, retiring from the first snows of winter and waiting while his brutish warriors feasted and whored their days away with camp followers at the edge of the forest.

And so the waiting game began again.

Joachim Starkhold was as tough as the granite walls he stood upon, but this watchful waiting was wearing even him down. Car Carranis was the greatest of Kelthaine's strongholds, wrought of iron and stone and cunningly wedged deep into the folds of the mountains, its flanks hugged by sheer crags awarding no purchase for attackers. There was a rear gate but the only way to reach it was via the high mountain passes, now buried in snow—hence that way was secure till spring.

The city walls were seventy foot high and twelve foot thick. The fortress had been raised on the flat crown of the lowest foothill, commanding wide views over the Gap of Leeth to the northernmost slopes of the High Wall.

Starkhold knew they could take long weeks of siege—maybe even months. But day by day the gnawing seed of apprehension and dread sapped their resolve.

And no help would come. They were alone.

Morale was ebbing by the hour. After the collapse of Morwella and the destruction of Vangaris, Starkhold received no news from the west. It was as though they were on an island slowly sinking beneath a relentless inevitable tide of evil.

Cautious as he was, Starkhold even considered a sortie into the enemy camp at night. If successful it would raise sagging spirits. But the risk would be great, and after thinking again he dismissed it as reckless madness.

Starkhold was a pragmatic man. He would not waste any of his soldiers on foolhardy ventures. Each fighting man was vital. The city guard remained vigilant. Those not manning walls practised battle-craft by the hour. When they weren't using their swords in mock fights they were honing them until they shone like silver fire. They ate sparingly and slept in steel. You never knew when the enemy might attack. They were unpredictable, these savages from the north.

Time was their enemy too. Days passed cruelly slow as winter's jaws took hold. Hour by hour spirits sank. Occasionally the enemy would capture a scout or some poor peasant and parade his naked maimed body in front of the fortress. Crows would circle and settle to feast.

Starkhold cooled the anger of his subalterns, especially Ralian. He was unfazed by the cruelty but it still depressed him to witness it. In his fifty-six years Starkhold had seen much conflict and savagery, but never before had he felt so helpless, so fenced in by lack of choice.

There was but one option. They must wait for as long as it took. Endure. Hold out in hope beyond hope that allies would come—from Elanion only knew where—to their aid. It was a fool's hope but it was all they had.

Joachim thought of his many years serving Kelsalion III. Good years on the whole. He had fought beside Halfdan of Point Keep and Belmarius the Bear. Both had been giants of battle. Both were prob-ably dead, murdered by the allies of Caswallon.

It galled Starkhold that the rapacious former High Councillor had got his claws on Kelthaine. He had never trusted Caswallon, had always suspected him of subterfuge. That said, the usurper's outright treachery had caught even the wary Starkhold off guard.

Now Caswallon was the most powerful man in the Four Kingdoms and his might waxed daily. They say the usurper had sold his soul to the people of the night. Starkhold didn't doubt it. Kelthaine, once so powerful and proud, was rotting from within. Morwella was lost, Kelwyn would soon follow, and after that Raleen, Joachim Starkhold's own beloved country.

Starkhold wondered what had become of the plucky young queen of Kelwyn. Ariane of Wynais had possessed wit beyond her years and a courageous heart. Last he heard she had challenged Caswallon. A brave and foolish girl.

Starkhold turned away from the wind, allowing his cloak to rebuff its relentless assault on his bones. He gazed westward, jaw set in resolution. Poor Kelthaine: an enemy within and an enemy without. Whatever happened Car Carranis would hold out until spring, he vowed. Come spring, change would come.

Wings brushed past him. Starkhold looked up surprised, saw a large raven settle on the outermost battlement. It watched him in mocking silence. There was something disturbing about that bird's beady gaze. Joachim felt a cold shiver running up his spine.

"Damn it all," he muttered, shaking his head in disgust; even the birds were getting to him. With a swirl of his fur-lined tawny cloak, Lord Starkhold of Car Carranis turned abruptly on his heels and then hastened below to seek the small comfort of a cold breakfast.

Outside the kitchens the guards were already queuing for their meagre morning rations. The raven watched him depart then let out a piercing caw, before winging up into the lowering cloud above.

Soon there would be more snow.

***

Far from Starkhold's snow-clad tower the sound of thundering hooves drummed across the wooded vales of Kelwyn. Rural folk stared out from their lonely crofts, eyes gaping at what they witnessed.

The host gathered pace, their queen at its van. Each time the riders passed a village or town the roads were lined with onlookers. Children whooped in delight as their elders stood gaping behind them, their toil-marked faces lined with worry of what waited ahead. Out in the fields peasants and yeoman alike stared in wonder, their tools forgotten as they watched their young queen gallop westward at the head of a large force of fighting men.

Ariane rode like the wind, her steel-clad host clattering behind her. For three nights ominous dreams had left her fearful of what they would find when they reached Calprissa.

Would they be too late? The road crunched beneath their horses' galloping hooves as they sped seaward, pausing only on occasion to allow their beasts drink.

The fourth day wore into night. Ariane showed no sign of stopping as darkness draped the road ahead. At her bidding they pressed on deep into the night. Squire Galed groaned at the breakneck pace his queen was setting.

"Surely we must rest," he pleaded. "It's still many leagues to Calprissa."

"I will take no rest until we have turned this evil tide, Galed," Queen Ariane answered without looking back. Her voice was muffled by the steel helm almost entombing her head. "Every minute counts if we are to save our second city from the foul stench of Caswallon. Steel your heart, squire. We ride to war!"

Galed gulped a short reply but curdled it when he caught the newly promoted Captain Tarrello's fearsome glance. "It's alright for you," he muttered. "You're a warrior and daft enough to enjoy this madcap capering."

Tarello grinned. The young captain was relishing every moment of this furious ride. This was his great chance. With Tolranna off his back Tarello stood to gain much, not least the queen's affections. Like most of her army, Tarello loved his queen.

He grinned across at Galed and the little man shook his head in resignation. "Warriors—you're all mad. How I wish I could have been born in quieter times!"

Behind him someone sniggered. If Galed had bothered turning he might just have pierced the disguise of the small soldier riding close on his heel.

**

Cale was grinning like a lolling pup. He'd joined the host slipping in last night, narrowly evading the watch as he raided the
leftovers by the campfires. That following day Cale had urged his
beast up through the ranks getting many a sideways glance from the
troops, Raleenian and Kelwynian both.

Cale wasn't fazed by those looks. He had a plan. He'd stay covert
until they reached Calprissa. Once there the queen would have to
accept him. She'd be livid of course but he'd win her round with his
invincible charm. It would all work out just fine.

Cale kept his head down and said nothing. He knew that he was
being rash seeking out the van, but he'd not been able to resist the
chance to ride close to his queen. It wasn't a problem, he told himself.
Before they camped for the night he'd slip back out of sight again.

But Cale's plans didn't take shape. The army's pace hardly slackened throughout that entire night and even he became exhausted. By
morning the boy began to wonder if he had been wise in accompanying this venture. He was hungry and cold and his buttocks ached
mercilessly. A bitter wind shrieked out of the east snapping at their
heels, driving them on even harder. Cale grumbled to himself but
decided it was all part of being a warrior; he would just have to put
up with it for the time being.

At first light they glimpsed distant towers shining silvery gold as
the morning sun embraced them.

Calprissa.

The city was still leagues distant but at last they were nearing
their destination. Cale's stomach grumbled but he ignored it. He felt
better now their destination was in sight.

"What's that?" Captain Tarello yelled, he was riding some yards
in front of the boy. The captain's gloved hand was pointing north.
Cale squinted that way; saw trails of smoke rising like grey wispy
columns along the horizon.

"The bonfires of the enemy," responded Ariane from somewhere
up ahead. "They are burning my country!"

"Then let us destroy them, my Queen. Onward!"

Tarello spurred his horse on to even greater speed. Behind him rode his chosen guard and fifty of Wynais's finest archers. Behind these steered the lancers of Raleen, two hundred strong and proud, all glittering in their highly polished steel. Last up rode Ariane's personal guard, a hundred crack fighters handpicked by Yail Tolranna, armed with spears, swords and throwing axes. Some had crossbows slung over their backs. Round shields hung from their saddles bearing the emblem of the Silver City.

Ariane brought her steed to a halt and her host reined in behind her. She turned to survey her army. They were few in number but they had the element of surprise on their side. Cale watched beneath his hood as the Queen of Kelwyn unbuckled her silver helm.

He was filled with love when he saw her sable locks spill free. From that moment Cale knew that he had made the right decision. Whatever followed he would be at her side. Ariane raised the helm high above her head. In a clear voice she addressed her force.

"Warriors of Raleen and Kelwyn!" she called out to them. "Ready your bodies and steel your hearts. The ravens of war have departed their crags!"

The host answered with a roar. Spears struck shields and horses whinnied. Cale, lost in the midst, was yelling defiance. It was on this day that he would become a warrior. He couldn't wait. Grinning, Cale watched as one of the Raleenians tossed a sabre across to the princess.

"Our swords are yours to command, Your Highness!" the warrior said. "We of Atarios are proud to ride at your command!"

Ariane flashed him a grin: she snatched the sabre from the air with her left hand, whilst her right latched onto the rapier's hilt and tore it from the sheath. They watched and cheered as the young queen deftly brandished a sword in either hand.

Beside her Captain Tarello applauded. "See how she masters both sabre and rapier. I give you Ariane of the Swords!"

"Ariane of the Swords!" The cry went up, Cale's tiny voice

drowned in the midst. They would follow her to the very gates of Yffarn were she to require it.

Ariane was filled with pride. She refastened her helm over her head and turned to face the distant fires.

"Calprissa, don't despair—we are coming!" Without further ado the queen of Kelwyn spurred her mare into the west. And her army followed.

Chapter 40

The Challenge

Barin had watched in deepening frustration as the Assassin's ships stole into
Calprissa's landlocked harbour. He glowered and fretted, witnessing them heel to starboard, making their way toward where his vessel lay moored and waiting. Just like at Port Sarfe, they'd been caught again.

Bastards.

They hadn't attacked during the night. Clearly they were waiting for a signal from Caswallon's army. Barin had spent all night waiting for the Assassin to move. But Rael Hakkenon was biding his time.

The Assassin's ships blocked any escape from the harbour. He had ordered the sharks to fan out across its narrow entrance, making sure that not even a rowing boat could slip out unnoticed during the dark hours. Throughout that long night they had waited with sails furled and oars ready for dawn's arrival.

Barin's men had joined him at the citadel; there was little they could do on board against nine enemy ships. Their swords and axes would be put to better use defending the city. They'd stowed the sails and drenched deck and cloth in seawater should the Assassin choose to play with fire.

Barin's first reaction had been to rush down and board his ship, then seize an oar and make straight for the enemy. Reluctantly he'd reined himself in, realising such a course of action would have proved suicidal. Nonetheless it galled him so to see *The Starlight Wanderer* looking so vulnerable and alone as the milling sharks of Crenna hovered close like probing wolves surrounding a bleeding, cornered bear. That evening Lord Tolruan had convinced Barin that the harbour was not as defenceless as it appeared.

"We have the odd surprise up our sleeve for that villain." The lord of Calprissa had managed a grim smile, whilst pointing down to where a tiny black-cloaked figure stood arrogantly poised at the bow of the leading ship, easily recognisable as *The Black Serpent*.

"What's keeping him?" Barin had snarled as evening deepened. "Is he waiting for darkness again? Surely he cannot expect to gain these walls at night. That would be rash indeed, and that little shit is no fool."

"I expect he awaits news from Caswallon's general," answered Tolruan bleakly. "Rael Hakkenon will wait for morning before he attacks, thus allowing Derino to position his army outside our land-ward walls. I fear we are to be placed like a horseshoe between the hammer and the anvil, my friend."

"Humph! They will find the horseshoe more troublesome than they expect," scowled Barin, accepting a cool tankard from a passing page. In seconds he'd drained it and reached for another.

That slow night had dragged, the atmosphere in the city one of tense apprehension. Few had slept before the first beams of sunlight alighted on the battlements announcing day's arrival. Barin was one of the first to witness that.

***

An hour passed in silence and watchful tension. A soft movement to his left. Barin glanced round, saw that Shallan had joined him to look down at the enemy ships below. Barin smiled gruffly at the girl, giving her a sideways glance as though he were weighing up her courage. She didn't smile back.

"How is your father, sweetheart?" Barin's eyes were full of concern at how tired she looked. Shallan's face was pale and drawn in the morning light. Her blue/grey eyes showed signs of weeping and dark rings shadowed them, betraying a lack of sleep.

"He is sleeping peacefully," she answered stoically. "Cormalian the physician has given him some strong concoction derived from poppy seeds. It has lessened the fever and enabled him to rest. The girl Zukei is with him now."

"That is good," replied Barin. "I'm glad she and the physician are talking to each other at last. I like that Zukei. Tough lass. Your father's in good hands." They heard a noise from the harbour below and watched stony-faced when a loud yell announced the Assassin had received his signal to attack. Barin and Shallan exchanged glances.

"And so it starts," the Northman said. Shallan didn't answer.

As one, the sleek ships of Crenna steered towards the quayside. All save three, the foremost being *The Black Serpent*. With rhythmic strokes these three craft headed straight for the place where *The Starlight Wanderer* was moored. Barin growled like a trapped bear. His huge hands smote the balcony rail as, red-faced, he watched his enemies bear down on his beloved trader.

Bastards—bloody bastards!

"So they are they attacking at last," Shallan said placing a taut pale hand on the rail. It looked so tiny next to Barin's callused paw.

"Yes—damn their fucking eyes." Barin glanced back hearing the sound of a ratchet tightening. "Please pardon my language but whatever is that racket?"

They both jumped in alarm when a loud snap issued from behind and above. Something whooshed and whirled overhead.

"Shite!" Barin ducked instinctively. "What the fuck was that?" Glancing up in alarm, Shallan saw birds winging skyward amid harsh cries. She watched amazed as a huge wooden arrow the size of a mature tree shrieked down from the battlements above to strike the churning waters just short of Rael Hakkenon's flagship. Another whoosh and whirl announced another giant arrow. This one pierced the deck of the shark alongside *the Serpent*. Barin roared approval.

The Assassin stood at the prow watching the missiles' descent with casual disdain. He raised a fist up at his enemies. Another projectile hissed into the water yards away.

At Rael's word *The Black Serpent* changed course, steering away from *The Starlight Wanderer*, seeking the protection of the quay. The other ship followed whilst the damaged one floundered as water claimed her decks. Crew swam like mad things for the harbour. Once there archers hidden in the terraces picked them off.

"Nicely done," laughed Barin. "First round to us, Assassin." Barin was grinning and thumping the wall. Shallan took heart from his optimism.

From somewhere behind, Shallan could hear the machine's ratchet tighten and snap free, sending more arrows lancing down into the harbour.

"Kill them all!" Shallan yelled then, slamming her small fist into the air. "Murder the fucking bastards!"

Barin grinned at her in new admiration. "My sentiments exactly."

A great cheer went up from the city as a shaft pierced the port side of the second ship. Within minutes it was foundering, decks awash with seawater as the crew baled in futile desperation.

Two down, seven left.

But the other ships were safe now. A shoulder of the cliff was between them, blocking the arc of the ballista's range. Moments later the seven vessels were drawing alongside the far end of the quay, allowing yelling figures to disembark and weave their way through the deserted harbour's cobbled lanes, towards the steep stairs that led up to the city above.

The hidden archers took a score and then repaired back to the battlements. The pirates' number was hard to gauge, though Shallan guessed there was more than two hundred down there.

Rael Hakkenon took the lead racing up the stairs, his rapier in left hand and a black crossbow with bolt ready, clasped in his right. The Lord Assassin danced contemptuously aside as arrows hailed down on him and his pirates from the defenders on the walls above.

Barin leaned so far forward half his bulk hung over the balcony. He felt the battle fury rising inside him. Growling, he slid Wyrmfang free of its loop, kissed the double blades and waited for the enemy to arrive at the gates.

Ready when you are, Assassin.

Just then a loud cry went up from the city behind him.

"Ware the eastern walls," came the shout. "Caswallon's army approaches!"

Barin cursed and dribbled into his beard.

Bugger the bastards.

He turned to Shallan who still gaped big-eyed beside him.

"Wait here, girl," he told her. "Don't go anywhere. I will return in a moment." Barin told Fassof and Taic to stick close to Shallan, then he shouldered his axe and vanished down into the citadel.

Minutes later, Shallan saw him emerge below. She watched wide-eyed and dry-mouthed as her huge friend strode into the city, soon disappearing amidst the maze of buildings behind.

She could hear the yells of the Assassin's men as they approached from below. Shallan felt useless. She needed to do something, not just stand here like a wallflower waiting for them to come. No good blowing her horn, even if she hadn't left it in her cabin it wouldn't help here.

To her right, Cogga winked reassuringly at her before rubbing his earring with a grubby finger and spitting down from the wall.

"We'll look after you, my lady. Taic, Sveyn and myself." Shallan turned away. She didn't want looking after, she wanted to help. But how?

"My lord," Shallan called across to Tolruan who still held his place at the other end of the balcony. "Have you a bow I could borrow?" Shallan asked him.

"Can you shoot, my lady?" enquired Tolruan, evidently impressed.

"I intend to learn how," she answered, and then thanked a nearby grinning archer who leaned across and handed her a small horn bow with a hastily tied bundle of arrows.

"It's my boy's," he told her. "But he's sick with winter ague down in the town house. So I brought it as a spare. You're welcome to try it, my lady." He strung the bow with expert ease and passed it over.

Shallan was delighted; she thanked the archer and received the bow with a grin. At last she could act. Shallan held the bow in her left hand and placed an arrow on the nock. She remembered what her brothers had told her after their hunting trips.

Be one with the arrow. Don't rush.

Shallan pulled back the sinewy cord, tensing her supple arms. Her face reddened slightly with the effort involved. She pulled harder, bringing the arrow's flight back level with her right ear as she'd seen her brothers do. Shallan held it there, mouthing the words to an old hunting song.

I am the arrow. I am the flight. I am the silent winged death in the night.

Shallan calmed her nerves, stilled her twitching arm, and focussed on the approaching enemy below. Though most were hidden from view, a score or so pirates were visible and well within even her small bow's range.

I am the archer at one with my bow. Fly true, brave arrow, fly straight—now go!

Shallan mouthed the words then on 'go!' she let fly, marvelling at the freedom she felt as she watched the shaft speed forth. Her first arrow went wide of the mark as did the second but the third one pierced the naked chest of a pirate. He slumped to the ground with a surprised grunt.

Die, bastard!

Shallan smiled and calmly placed another arrow on her bowstring; feeling a wild euphoria welling inside her. It was an alien emotion but she welcomed it with happy heart.

I am the huntress leading the hunt.

Something feral and savage and yet magical was happening to Shallan. She was changing. Gone was the duke's dutiful daughter replaced by a wildcat. 'We are kin', the Horned Man had told her. 'Sister', the faerie women had called her.

I am Faen. I am the huntress. Let the hunt commence!

Shallan fired fast and hard, taking down three more pirates. The bow felt so naturel in her grasp. She no longer strained to pull. It was easy—so easy. Shallan of Morwella was fighting back.

***

Barin sped through the panic-filled streets of Calprissa. He left the curving lanes that surrounded the dominant citadel behind him and hurried into a wide level street. A main artery, the broad avenue led arrow-straight toward the distant walls guarding the landward side of the city.

Everywhere people gaped in awe at the blond giant and his horrible axe. Barin ignored them and they parted like waves to let him through. As he jogged down the thoroughfare, Barin glowered thunderously.

"What are you gawping at?" The entire city's populace was out on the streets. Panicking, jabbering and nattering, eyes nervous and mouths full of the horror encroaching their gates. Another day Barin would have felt sorry for them. But not this morning. The rage was in him, taking hold. The *berserkergang*—the wild fury of the north. Barin's eyes blazed fury and he was filled with but one desire.

To kill.

They watched him pass, too confused and scared to comment. Men muttered whilst their women wept beside them. Little children scampered beneath their feet, blissfully unaware of the horror lurking outside.

Few of the townsfolk had ever envisioned this dire happening. Even the city guard were white-faced and agitated. Barin scowled as he listened to their jittery words.

The soldiers mustering outside the barracks he passed were unshaven and scruffy. They looked an incompetent lot. Instead of reassuring the people they were mixing with them in mutual disarray.

Tossers.

To Barin, Calprissa appeared a city already fallen. That thought darkened his mood further. He trotted on, ignoring hounds that yapped and snarled around his feet. The east walls loomed closer.

Calprissa was bigger than Barin remembered. He'd ran a mile already. Barin passed stables and shops, the traders stopping and watching him thunder by with slack jaws.

He smelt the tanneries and alehouses and heard the beasts stomping in the markets. To his right loomed a temple of Elanion, high and stately with carved archways and wide sweeping doorways. It was full of zealous worshipers, furiously devout in the face of the coming attack.

Barin jogged on by. On the pavements he heard wealthy nobles addressing lesser folk in panicky tones. Barin saw priests praying with arms raised to the sky. He shook his head in disgust and thundered on.

Pray and weep, you fools.

At last the street opened into a broad square. Here more troops were filing out willy-nilly in disorganised clumps. Ahead Barin spotted stairs leading up to the lofty battlements of the east wall.

He stormed across and took them three at a time. Minutes later Barin emerged, huge and horrible amongst the shivering guards, milling pale-faced and unsure of what to do next.

Enough.

Barin hulked towards them, his brows bunched like storm clouds. He shoved a gaping spearman out the way as if he were a sack of straw. Barin reached the parapet. There he stood in silence glaring out at the army marching toward them a mile or so distant.

Barin tried in vain to estimate their strength as the dark mass of Caswallon's host approached in shadowy jagged lines. He rubbed his beard and farted.

There were thousands of them out there. They would be out-numbered at least twenty to one. And that not including the Assassin and his men. The odds were dodgy but then Barin never worried much about odds.

He scanned the walls with a professional eye. They were built strong and high enough. If the defenders kept their nerve they could hold out indefinitely. That was the tricky bit. Not an encouraging prospect, judging by the shambles in this city. Someone needs to make them focus.

"Lord Barin?"

Barin turned, hearing his name mentioned. It was a tall guard who addressed him. The man had spoken to Barin briefly during the night. Barin remembered how the fellow had seemed less flustered than most of his peers. He raised a questioning brow as the soldier approached.

"We appear greatly outnumbered, my lord." Barin assumed he was an officer, judging by his garments which were more ornate than the other men's. The officer was young though, and his knuckles showed white on the hilt of his sword.

"I care little for numbers," Barin growled, turning back to the wall and looking out over again. "Let the fuckers come. Sharp blades and stout hearts is what we need today, my lad. Don't let those bastards intimidate you."

The officer made to reply but Barin turned away. Instead he watched the enemy approach Calprissa's walls like noisome swarming insects. All were clad in black. Most armed with long spears and crooked serrated swords. Barin saw many Groil among the ranks.

There were other more shadowy things too, however, most of the force comprised of men.

Men twisted by evil and fear. Broken men and wicked men. Losers every one, thought Barin.

These had once been the elite Tigers, who together with the Bears and Wolves had made up Kelthaine's prized and envied soldiery. The Bears and Wolves had always been far-ranging. The Tigers' task had been to guard the High King's city. They had always considered themselves superior to the other regiments. But the Tigers were no more.

Those remaining, like their leader Perani, had succumbed to evil. They were Caswallon's puppets, their minds horribly warped by his thaumaturgy, and by what they had done in his name. Perani remained in Kella. But his second was a man scarcely less feared.

The Tigers had long since abandoned their famous tabards. They were garbed in black chain mail, and sported long sable cloaks trailing behind them like storm clouds. Every soldier's face was hidden beneath a hideous death mask. It made it hard to tell them apart from the Groil, except they were taller and broader and didn't stoop to all fours. A few rode horses though most of this host went on foot. That comforted Barin. Perhaps horses hadn't sold out to Caswallon. They at least had more sense.

Barin saw that some of the enemy toiled beneath the weight of heavy crude ladders. These strode forth until they stood at the van of the horde. The ladders were raised skyward ready for purchase on the walls. Slowly, accompanied by drumbeats they approached.

"Archers!" Barin yelled. "Where are our bloody archers? Who commands here?" Barin turned to the young officer but he had gone. Another man stood in his place.

"I do," the soldier replied. This was a ruddy-faced guardsman who, despite the chill of the morning, was sweating profusely beneath his burnished steel coat.

"I am Savrino, second captain of Calprissa. I command the east wall."

"You won't command rat shit unless we get some archers up here fast." Barin barely kept a lid on his fury.

"I don't want those ladders getting close to our walls, matey. So bugger off and come back soonest with archers!"

The captain mouthed a word, thought better of it, and turned briskly on his heels.

"And, captain!" Savrino stopped mid stride. "Stop bloody shaking!"

"Aye, sir," replied Savrino, squaring his jaw, not stopping to ask himself why he was taking orders from this giant hairy savage from the north. He cast a furtive glance at the great battle-axe gripped in the outlander's paw and wondered at the strength it would take to wield such a mighty weapon.

"Archers needed over here! Hurry now!" Barin rolled his eyes hearing that. Savrino wielded authority like a milkmaid.

Elanion help us.

Moments later the second captain reappeared with a dozen bowmen in tow.

"It's left us vulnerable above the gates," Savrino complained.

"Well send some more up there, you daft twat. Just space them out," Barin yelled across to him.

"What?"

"Don't let them breach our walls, Savrino. You alone are responsible for the defence of this sector. Hold out, man, until I return. I am needed elsewhere."

Barin was about to descend from the wall when a harsh shout from below stopped him in his tracks. Looking out from his high perch, Barin saw that a solitary rider had emerged from the ranks of the enemy horde.

And who might you be?

The horseman heeled his horse up to the city walls, stopping just out of bowshot. This rider was clad from head to foot in polished black steel-plate armour. An ebony-horned helm of baroque design hid his face from the brightness of the morning. A sweeping sable cloak trailed behind the rider as he steered his great black stallion to face the Calprissans. The helm slanted back as the rider scanned the defenders on the walls above.

"Citizens of Calprissa!" The voice hailing them was deep and commanding, though it sounded hollow and metallic beneath the heavy helm. Despite that the leader's voice carried easily up to the walls.

"We need not be enemies! I bid you swear allegiance to my master the lord of Kelthaine. Open your gates and you will be spared. That much I promise!"

Moments passed. Men coughed on the battlements and shuffled their feet. The enemy flanked out in silent ranks like a midnight sea awaiting their leader's command to surge forward. The ladder carriers had stopped behind him with their poles still raised and ready.

All was hush. A sudden wind whipped ice chill from the east, lifting the black rider's cloak up behind him like a sail. He wheeled his horse about before turning to face them once more. When he spoke again his voice was less tolerant.

"Well? What answer do you give? I have little—" The rider stopped short when a mocking laugh cut across his words.

"Do you have a name, shit for brains?"

Barin grinned down at the rider whose flinty eyes narrowed beneath his helm. He scanned the lofty walls and soon saw whom it was that had spoken. Barin's bulk always gave him away. The leader smiled beneath the helm, recognising Barin of Valkador from Caswallon's description.

"I hight Lord Derino, barbarian scum," the black rider answered, staring directly up at Barin. "I am Lord Perani's second. I lead this army that confronts you."

"And a sorry-looking lot they are." Barin spat a dollop of phlegm down from the walls. "I wouldn't wipe my arse with any of them. Or you."

"Do you speak for this city now, barbarian? Must they rely on northern strawheads to lead them? I'll have your fat arse on a plate, Barin of Valkador, before this day is out." Derino let his gaze sweep the men on the walls.

"So, citizens, what is your answer?"

"Here is our answer, Derino." Barin had finally lost it being addressed as 'barbarian'—a sore point with him. He turned, heaved his trousers and smallclothes down around his knees. Then Barin shoved his rump on a crenulation and let rip a colossal fart.

Beside him the soldiers cheered and clapped. Grinning happily, Barin stood and reclaimed his breeches. Below Derino paced back and forth on his stallion, clearly not impressed by the display.

"Go back to your sorcerer, hornhead." Barin felt the rage buffet him like a winter storm. "Hide, lest I come seek you out and spilt you open like the rotten fruit you are. The tide is turning, Derino! Your army of slaves will break on these walls before nightfall!"

"You are a fool, Barin of Valkador!" Metallic laughter echoed from Derino's helm. "I know who you are, Northman. I heard how that witch butchered your grandfather so she could shag your father. I served in Leeth once."

"You know nothing," replied Barin, icy calm now. "But I will educate you before I split you down the middle. I tire of this conversation, so BUGGER OFF!"

"I'll see you soon, barbarian!"

"Up yours!"

The sound of laughter was cut short. Derino had already wheeled his steed away from the walls. Within minutes he was swallowed by the baying masses of his army. A great roar now issued from the horde. As one they surged forward. Ashen spears clattered on shields as the snarling faces and death masks glowered up at the defenders on the walls.

"Hold steady," Barin said calmly to the soldiers within earshot. "Remember these bastards are overconfident due to their superior number. And don't worry about those hoodies crouching on all fours—they're called Groil and are crap at fighting. The worst thing about them is their stench. Be brave, boys, with stout hearts we can hold this city for as long as we need to." Barin saw more bowmen had arrived and were lining up along the walls. Savrino had been busy.

"Archers, get ready!" Barin thundered as the enemy rushed forward with a scream of hatred. First in line were the ladder bearers, their wooden makeshift burdens thrust forward to rest against the high walls. They thudded into place and were immediately set upon by scores of masked warriors. Scaling up fast and screaming in hatred, long knives thrust in their mask clasps, and larger weapons slung across their armoured backs.

Savrino appeared by Barin's side. He looked calmer, more in control. With him was the young officer armed with sword and spear.

"You did well," Barin grunted approval. "Hold fast till I return. Wait until those ladders are full of men then shoot the bastards."

Satisfied he had done all he could for the moment, Barin left them with a few more brave words. They didn't look happy he was leaving but Barin needed to be elsewhere.

He winked at the young officer, shouldered Wyrmfang and commenced making his way back across to the other side of the city. A time-consuming trek. It was hard being in two places at once, but he needed to know how his lads fared with the Assassin's yobbos.

Again Barin broke into a jog. He hated all this rushing about but needs must. Harsh shouts announced the pirates were already attacking the west wall. Tolruan was right; they were caught neatly between the hammer and the anvil. Barin knew it would take a miracle to win this fight. He wished Corin were here with Clouter to make things ugly. Barin smiled as he approached the west walls. Lucky Corin, down there in all that sun and sand.

Hurry back, Longswordsman, you're missing the fun.

Chapter 41

At the Oasis

Corin an Fol didn't feel particularly lucky at the moment. Not with half of Permio on his tail. He was ready to be rid of this desert. But without all this stress and frantic rush. Zallerak's fire display had been exhilarating to watch but it was over. Corin was weary, as were his comrades. Thirsty, tired and worn out.

Tamersane looked sulky in his saddle, Ulani held cheerful but still suffered. Bleyne remained Bleyne, although he did appear a touch more cheerful after his near death experience. Sometimes he even smiled. Prince Tarin looked exhausted and Zallerak waspish and petulant. Corin and Thunderhoof remained objective. They just wanted out of there.

They rode north through the night. High above, stars studded the desert sky. The only sounds were the dull thudding of their horses' hooves and the relentless sighing of the wind coming down from the mountains.

Every now and then they heard a distant shout and spied the gleam of a spear in the moonlight behind them. The sultan was driving his men hard tonight. They kept the pace.

Slowly the shadow of the Crystal Mountains slipped behind and the stony ground beneath them softened to sand again. Fresh dunes reached toward them out of the darkness ahead, resembling frozen waves in the night. Corin asked Ulani if they had reached the High Dunes but the king shook his head, informing Corin they were many leagues east of that region. Besides these dunes were tiny by comparison.

Throughout that long night the six riders rode due north under Zallerak's guidance. The bard had said little since his pyrotechnic display the day before. Corin had seen how sorcery had an exhausting effect on the user. Power had its price. Corin hadn't softened toward Zallerak an ounce, but even he had been grateful to the bard yesterday.

Behind Zallerak the others also rode in silence; Ulani's bulk thundered to Corin's right whilst Tamersane flanked his left. The Kelwynian's eyes were despondent as he gazed up at the clear sky above.

"I'm bored with all this sand," he told Corin. "I'm ready for a plump wench and a horn of ale."

"Me too," grinned Ulani.

Corin, thinking of Shallan, didn't respond. He wondered how his friends fared. It seemed they'd been gone for months and Corin was desperate to ride north and find Shallan again. First they had to win free of Permio and that could well prove tricky.

They reined in briefly when dawn filled the sky, but Zallerak was in no mood for stopping despite his weariness. Tersely he urged them on.

"We dare not idle here," he told them amid grumbles and groans—mainly from Tamersane and Tarin. These he ignored. "Some way ahead is the great oasis called Isalyos. We can quench our thirst there before departing this desert."

Weary and worn, beast and rider had struggled on through the morning over waves of sand, battered and bruised and scorched beneath the leaden sun. Hours passed.

With the exception of the bard and Bleyne, the riders took turns dozing in their saddles, those close by ensuring they didn't fall.

Corin allowed his body to relax. A whole chunk of it still felt sore from his many scrapes. Nevertheless he felt better than he had done for weeks. They had done well. Against all odds they had recovered the Tekara and made it whole again, and now at last they were heading back.

To war.

So what? Corin didn't care. Soon he would be free to act as he chose. Free to seek out the woman who filled his waking thoughts. He just hoped Car Carranis was still standing when he arrived at its gates. A long hard trip through winter's worst awaited Corin before he reached that distant stronghold. No matter. He didn't intend to tarry on the way. Again Corin pictured the chestnut-haired beauty that had walked beside him in Silon's vineyard.

Where are you now?

It seemed more than just a few weeks ago. Corin missed Shallan more than he thought possible. Their brief encounter had reached deep inside him. Something that he—wayward stray and world-weary cynic—hadn't expected to feel about anyone. But Corin had loved Shallan from that first moment. He realised that now and yearned to see her again. He loved Ariane too and still felt guilty how he'd behaved with the queen. Corin couldn't control his emotions about these things. They just were. Besides, he was a warrior not a bloody philosopher. Head bowed in thought, Corin let Thunderhoof take the lead. If the horse had any views on Corin's issues he didn't offer them.

They watered and rested the horses only briefly under the full heat of the sun. Zallerak said it was crucial they made the oasis as soon as possible.

"But isn't the sultan going to make for it as well?" Corin had enquired, receiving no response from the bard.

During their quick rest the riders kept a wary ear out for pursuit. Nothing stirred. The only sound the sigh of hot desert wind caressing the dunes. It seemed at last they were putting distance between themselves and the Permians. For three nights they had ridden, stopping only when they must and snatching sleep at the saddle.

On the dawn of the fourth day Corin was heartily relieved to see the swaying shape of palms in a distant valley surrounded by the deliciously sparkling blue glimmer of water.

"Ain't that a pretty sight," Corin said. Beside him Ulani grinned. They rode on eagerly. The horses picked up their pace, smelling water.

Tamersane eyed the tall palms with distrust as they approached. He was still haunted by his vision of beauty and no longer trusted his eyes in this desert. He scowled at the palms, challenging them to vanish. They stayed put and finally Tamersane allowed himself a joyous grin.

This was no mirage. They had reached the oasis of Isalyos in eastern Permio. A large oasis ridged by reeds and thickets of palm on its far side. Isalyos was the last known water stop before the Liaho, still several days ride north.

Reeds echoed the breeze as the riders approached. They were wary at first, but soon abandoned all care hurrying down to the water's edge. Reaching it, they dismounted. All save Zallerak who remained po-faced and thoughtful.

They let the beasts drink and drank deeply themselves. The water tasted like clearest wine. Laughing, they washed the dust and filth from their tired faces. Bleyne kept watch while the others shed their clothes and dived blissfully into the blue water.

Corin, once free of his steel shirt and leather, scrubbed and rubbed his battered body. He emerged moments later to stand grinning, pale and naked beneath the morning sun.

Corin dressed swiftly, feeling exposed without his ring mail. He felt stronger but sobered by the knowledge that the enemy would still be hard on their tails and closing. That sultan wasn't about to give up. But they'd needed the respite and were better for it.

Time to get going again. Judging by their expressions the others were ready too. When Prince Tarin asked when they were leaving, Zallerak's answer had surprised them all.

"We stay put," said the bard. "Let the horses rest and get some sleep if you can. I will take first watch."

"But the crimson elite?" challenged Corin. "They'll be on us in no time if we stay here. Samadin Pain in the Arse must have guessed this place to be our destination."

"This is no place to be trapped, Sir Zallerak," grumbled Ulani. The king too was restless. He looked up at the reeds. Suddenly something felt wrong. Ulani tensed.

"It is too late you already are!"

The voice was deep and sardonic. Corin groaned. Suddenly soldiers were emerging from the tall reeds beyond the oasis where they had lain hidden awaiting their chance. There were scores of them. Corin grasped Clouter's hilt but it was fruitless. He couldn't believe after all they had been through they'd come to this sorry pass.

The Permians surrounded them with a cordon of level spears. Looking beyond the reed beds Corin now saw the tell-tale signs of a rudimentary camp at the far end of the water. Here and there were marks in the sand that had been half obscured.

What fools they had been not to notice. So eager to douse themselves in those clear cool waters, they had completely forgotten basic reconnaissance skills. The Permians must have spotted them and slipped in under the reeds. At least they hadn't caught them swimming. The thought of being skewered naked was intolerable to Corin. At least he could die with his pants on. Small comfort though that was.

Beside Corin, Ulani let out a remorseful sigh. Tamersane looked dreary and Bleyne's face was grim. He curtly notched an arrow to his bow. It wasn't like the archer to miss a trick and he clearly wasn't happy with himself.

Prince Tarin looked terrified and was pleading with Zallerak to do something.

Corin turned in the bard's direction, his anger (rather unreasonably, considering they were all to blame) levelled solely at the Aralais enchanter.

"Wizard, in case you haven't noticed we have a situation here." The Permians were grinning at them. It was apparent they were in no hurry to attack. Corin assumed they were waiting for their big boss to arrive and announce their prisoners' fates. These boys would most likes be in for promotion. Certainly they looked smug.

"Zallerak?" Corin glared at the bard. But Zallerak looked oddly distant as if nothing untoward had occurred. He turned in Corin's direction and his expression was, if anything, triumphant. Yards away the crimson elite waited with spears held ready, watching them in haughty silence.

Corin had had enough. He tore into Zallerak.

"You have led us into a trap!" Zallerak raised an eyebrow hearing that. Once again, Corin was on the verge of punching him.

A shout behind announced the sultan had arrived at the oasis. The spearmen grinned and cheered, anticipating a high reward for capturing such dangerous renegades. In Corin's opinion they were over-optimistic.

Everywhere Corin looked he saw crimson-cloaked soldiers descending toward the oasis, with many more filing in from the dunes behind. To Corin it seemed that the entire Permian army had descended on them. He squared on Zallerak again, determined to channel his wrath on the bard for want of better direction. He stopped short when he saw that Zallerak was grinning.

"It is indeed a trap, Corin an Fol. But not for us this time."

Corin gaped about. "What?" Ulani scratched an ear, the soldiers looked uneasy, and away up the hill the sultan was already yelling commands.

"It is time," Zallerak said in a quiet voice. "Get ready."

"Time for what—dying?" Tamersane still looked mournful.

"Listening," said Zallerak. "One...two...three—dive!"

Something twanged and Corin hit the deck. His friends thudded alongside him, the sound of bowstrings filling their ears.

"A second ambush!" Tamersane yelled gleefully as a sound like the drone of a thousand bees erupted from nowhere. Corin, glancing up, saw the sky darken with arrows. He watched in stunned silence as shaft after shaft shrieked down from above, raining death on the elite. The spearmen surrounding them were peppered with arrows. Within minutes none were standing. At that point Corin deemed it safe to grin. They had back up at last!

Beyond the oasis the sultan and his new arrivals were in a state of utter panic. Corin and his friends watched spellbound as men screamed and horses bucked and neighed. The arrows were coming from everywhere. How many archers were out there? And where had they all come from? Corin had the distinct feeling he was still reading yesterday's news.

Inside half hour the sultan's army was broken. The whole valley of Isalyos filled with groans of the dying. Men crashed into each other in their panic to reach cover. Soon the clear blue of the oasis was stained muddy crimson. Thus fared the crimson elite.

***

Barakani had watched with some satisfaction at the culmination of many weeks' careful planning. His scouts had reported back that the sultan was leading his entire force towards Isalyos, having rejoined his main army after the trouncing he got by the wizard.

Rassan, watching half a mile away, had seen the wizard's party arrive. He'd witnessed the elite stealing into the reeds, waiting to pounce, and had hurried back to their camp in the valley beyond.

Rassan had offered to kill those soldiers but Barakani had declined, stating it would be better to wait for the sultan to arrive before showing their hand. Instead the Wolf of the Desert signalled his picked archers to take their places and wait.

And so they had gone to ground. Hiding as only the true desert people can, invisible in the folds of the dunes. Samadin the Marvellous had no idea he'd been tracked for weeks. That a force many times larger than his prized crimson elite was stalking him.

Barakani watched the last of the enemy assemble in ranks around the oasis rim. Doubtless guarding their sultan. Smiling, he rose to his feet. Barakani was standing less than twenty feet behind the nearest soldiers.

The Wolf of the Desert raised his hand palm upward. Behind their leader a host of silent archers emerged from their hides. They readied their bows.

Barakani counted to three then brought his hand down in one swift chopping motion.

Beside him Rassan hollered "Fire!" They watched grinning as a thousand arrows screamed towards the sultan's guard. Standing beside the warlord and his favourite son was a diminutive figure. Silon of Raleen. The merchant casually watched the carnage unfold.

Back in Vioyamis he and Zallerak had agreed to liaise at Isalyos after Zallerak's mission was accomplished. Zallerak's rash gamble that Barakani and Silon would be at the oasis had paid off. Silon managed a curt smile when the laughing Rassan slapped his back so hard he almost lost balance.

"Remember this day, merchant," Rassan grinned at him. "This day the sultanate dies!" Silon, half choking, nodded that he would remember.

***

Corin, after recovering from his initial shock, ignored Zallerak's advice and launched himself at the wavering enemy, Clouter flailing in fury. The original spearmen were all dead but other elite were milling in confusion around the oasis.

Corin loped across to join them. Clouter clanged and thudded into flesh. Men screamed and died, riders were pitched form their bolting steeds. He looked across, saw that Thunder and their other horses were unhurt, still tethered to palms where they'd left them, a small distance from the shore. Corin noted Tamersane cutting a path that way.

Corin leapt at a crimson-cloaked warrior, but the man died with an arrow in his throat before he could reach him. Arrows were coming from everywhere. Corin had no idea who was firing them but assumed they were friendly, as he hadn't been skewered yet. It would have been far more sensible to stay put with Zallerak but he just had to be part of the carnage. Ulani joined him at the water's edge. The king was grinning like a moon-crazed hyena.

"I feel better now!" Ulani struck out with his golden cudgel, splitting an officer's skull. The man crumpled and the king leaped over his body to batter another.

An elite dived for Corin's waist with dagger in hand. Corin rammed Clouter's hilt down hard on the back of the soldier's neck, whilst bringing his left knee up and snapping the knifeman's nose. Corin stepped back, kicked the corpse out the way and swung Clouter.

Five spearmen rushed him. The first lunged. Corin stepped aside and sliced Clouter into the shaft, snapping it in two. He reversed the longsword and rammed the wolf's head pommel hard into the spearman's jaw, sending him sprawling.

Two more had slipped behind Corin but he was aware of them. The closest jabbed his weapon forward. Corin turned, caught the shaft in his left hand and pulled the man forward whilst stabbing him with Clouter. The spearmen gurgled as the longsword punctured his belly.

The next fellow attempted something tricky: he swung low and wide with his spear seeking to trip the Longswordsman. Waste of time. Corin vaulted over the spear and kicked the sultan's man in the face, breaking his nose. The spearman fell back on his knees and Clouter bit deep into his neck. The elite's severed head sailed through air before plunking into the stained water of Isalyos.

Corin grinned. "Who's next? Don't be shy."

The remaining two elite backed away from him in alarm. They exchanged glances, turned on their heels and fled back to join the main force mustering beyond the palms. Corin, joined by Ulani and a puffing Tamersane, gave hectic chase.

It was at that point that Corin turned and saw hundreds of figures had emerged as if by magic from the dunes surrounding the oasis. The tribesmen of Permio, united at last by the cunning and patience of the Wolf of the Desert. They were armed with bows and tulwars and dressed in faded robes matching the subtle shades of the desert.

Freshly mounted on their desert ponies, the tribesmen surged toward the enemy with tulwars whooshing and circling over their heads. The archers had done their work. It was time for steel on steel.

Across the water the last of the Sultan's army took stock, waiting grim-faced for the oncoming onslaught. Their yelling officers bullied them into disciplined ranks.

In their midst was the screaming, corpulent ruler of Permio. Samadin was beside himself. He couldn't understand what had gone amiss. He wanted to flee but there was nowhere to go. At last he fell to his knees and started weeping. The crimson elite formed a cordon around him. They were loyal soldiers. They would defend their sultan to the last. It was more than he deserved.

Corin and Ulani had also taken to their saddles amidst the confusion and hurried to join the attack. Tamersane was there too, and Bleyne with long knife held ready for close quarter work.

Prince Tarin and Zallerak stayed put by the water, watching as the two armies clashed at the far edge of the oasis. The boy prince had wanted to join the fray but Zallerak had grabbed his collar and bid him watch and learn instead.

Within minutes the sultan's force was surrounded on all sides bar the water. Slowly and inevitably they gave ground, backing away to the oasis behind. Corin rained death from Thunderhoof's back, savagely slicing Clouter into any exposed flesh. Beside him Ulani fought like a lion, and Tamersane yelled as he sliced and skewered.

Men groaned in agony as limbs were severed and heads hewn from bodies. To his right Corin spied Yashan wielding that wicked scimitar and urging his steed forward. Their former guide caught his eye and grinned back at him rapaciously. Corin laughed out loud. Against all odds they had won.

The sultan's army was breaking apart. Bodies were strewn along the oasis's banks in a tangled mess of gore and guts. Blood was everywhere. Doggedly the crimson elite fought on with stubborn courage. All save the weeping wreck of gaudy robes they protected. Samadin was still on his knees shaking and puking with fear.

The battle became a massacre. Swords sliced and spears jabbed; Horses neighed and kicked out, breaking skulls and crushing fallen bodies. Those remaining formed a tangled knot around their leader, shields locked and spears held ready.

Barakani ordered the archers in. One by one the crimson elite fell beneath those shafts. In seconds no one was left standing. The sultan's finest were no more. Amidst the corpses the pathetic figure of Samadin the Marvellous squatted hunched and shaking, his fat face soaked with sweat and his robes soiled and stinking from his recently voided bowels.

Barakani dismounted from his horse. He strode forward and reaching down, yanked the sultan to his feet. Barakani rested his scimitar against Samadin's exposed throat. The sultan wept for mercy, his podgy hands beating feebly at Barakani's chest. He soiled his robes again and was close to fainting.

Barakani's face was cruel with contempt. There would be no mercy today. He rammed the scimitar's jewelled hilt into the sultan's jaw, knocking him from his feet. Barakani then signalled to his seven sons. He bade them strip the sultan's flaccid body and stake him out naked beneath the blazing sun.

"Here let him wither at the desert's whim," said Barakani to all that stood there watching. "Let the prowling creatures gnaw at his weak flesh and the scavenging birds peck out his craven eyes.

"Let the desert heat burn down, hour upon hour, until madness claims him and his mind crumbles, even as his body rots and his soul flees screaming to Yffarn. Then let his bones bleach white and fade to dust beneath the golden sun."

"It is over." Barakani stood over the sultan's prostrate body. He opened his drawstring and let his steaming piss spill onto the sobbing wreck below. And so perished Samadin the Marvellous. Sacrificed to the desert he so despised. A most unhappy conclusion to the long dynasty of the crimson sultans. The pride of Sedinadola who had ruled in totality for so many years. There were none present felt any sorrow at his pitiful demise.

Chapter 42

The West Wall

Many leagues to the north another battle had only just begun. The bitter wind gathered pace as the defenders of Calprissa's east walls held back the first wave of attack. Savrino's archers brought down the ladder carriers with skilled shooting, and their captain ordered controlled volleys to be fired into the vast horde below. But they kept coming and the ladders were raised again until the wall was finally breached in several places.

It was then that the real fighting began in earnest. Throughout the city, bells tolled and priests knelt in supplication before the gods. Townsmen raced to aid the soldiers manning the walls. Together they heroically rebuffed the continuing assault.

Young boys stood beside greybeards each doing their part. Those not fighting ran back and forth carrying messages and taking orders from Lord Tolruan or Barin of Valkador.

Most of the women and children huddled beneath the sanctuary of the old citadel while their loved ones fought and died to defend them. There were some women on the walls, these having chosen to fight beside their men. Half a mile away, the halls of the healers were already filled with the groans of the wounded and the dying.

Barin watched from the balcony above the west gate. He stood with Shallan as she fired arrow after arrow at the approaching pirates below. But they kept coming. Then, with a theatrical show of bravado, Rael Hakkenon ascended the wall using a ladder of knives. He dodged arrow and missile. Within moments he'd cut down three men who had rushed to stop him.

Rael grinned as he vaulted the parapet, rapier and dagger in hand. A score of pirates were close behind, dropping lithely onto the wall.

"They're here. Stay put, girl. I'll go have a word. Come on, lads!"

Barin left the balcony and made for the spot on the wall where fighting had broken out. With him came Fassof, Cogga and Taic, Sveyn stayed with Shallan at Barin's bidding.

"Look after her—she's like a daughter to me."

"I will," Sveyn replied.

Rael's killers were already cleaving a path through the defenders. Barin loped along the battlements in monstrous strides. Shallan refusing to be left behind, followed Barin with bow in hand. Sveyn made to stop her but she slid past his guard. Sveyn rolled his eyes and followed close behind. This girl was trouble, he decided.

The Assassin, seeing Barin looming close, grinned and trotted to meet the giant Northman. Wyrmfang met the Assassin's blade with a clash of steel. Rael's skill deflected the huge weight of the axe, but even he was caught off guard by Barin's ferocity. The axe was a windmill of blazing steel, the rapier a needle dancing in between.

Rael's rapier darted toward Barin's midriff but instead collided with Wyrmfang in another a blaze of sparks. The force of that contact nearly broke Rael's arm as he was slammed back against the wall. Wincing in pain, Rael tossed the dagger with his good arm. Barin knocked it aside with a nudge from his axe.

"Time's up, Assassin."

Barin closed for the kill. The axe swung down. Rael rolled clear from Wyrmfang's path. Shutting out the pain in his arm, Rael launched his body like a missile into Barin's stomach and rammed his elbow up under the Northman's chin. Barin was caught off guard but still managed to bring his fist down sledgehammer hard on the Assassin's head.

Rael saw stars. Again he twisted free before Barin could finish him and swat him with the axe.

"You overestimate your chances, lardy boy." Rael spat in Barin's eye and followed on with a blazing series of lunges and stabs with the rapier. Barin blocked with Wyrmfang, but had to give ground lest the Assassin get inside his swing.

Meanwhile Fassof and Cogga were exchanging blows with Rael's men. Taic was presently rolling and biting with one on the floor. Shallan, ignored except by Sveyn (stressing beside her), was trying to get a clear shot at the Assassin with her bow, but Rael was far too quick.

She waited, saw a chance: pulled back the string but was pushed forward by someone from behind and her blow went wide.

A hairy arm grabbed her sleeve. Shallan's bow was knocked from her grasp and a fist cuffed her right ear. She saw Sveyn kneel with a knife in his guts. He winked at her and crumpled.

Sorry.

Shallan spat like a lynx but was held fast by those iron strong arms. Fassof, seeing her plight, rushed to aid her but was struck to the ground by a sword blow from a bearded pirate. Lord Tolruan ran the pirate through with a clean thrust of his blade and Fassof woodenly regained his feet. Fortunately the weapon had been blunt and his shoulder, though cut, wasn't sliced bad.

The defenders were surrounded as more pirates were spilling over the wall and rushing to assist their comrades. Cutlasses and spikes ready, they leapt down onto the battlements amid curses and jeers. Soon the west wall was overrun.

Lord Tolruan was surrounded but his armour protected him and his skill with the sword kept them at bay for a time. Yards away Barin and Rael Hakkenon circled each other like alley cats in moonlight. Sveyn pulled the knife out of his ribs and stumbled to his feet. Shallan screamed in rage and frustration. She stamped down hard on her assailant's foot and then rammed her elbow back into his startled face, catching his nose square on. Bones crunched. The pirate let her go. Shallan dived between his legs. She'd spotted an abandoned knife and grabbed it. The pirate tore after her. He yanked her hair from behind, pulling her back savagely so that he could slit her exposed throat.

Shallan was too quick for him. She spun on her heels with knife held ready. With a yell she rammed the blade into his belly. He crumpled sobbing, but soon others surrounded her, their sweat-strewn faces masks of lusty leers and scorn. They mocked her as she lashed out at them with the knife.

Shallan circled with knife held high. She knew she stood no chance. A kick sent her sprawling and then another in her stomach caused her to double up in pain. An ugly face loomed above Shallan. She felt rough hands grab her arms whilst twisting the dagger painfully from her grasp.

Two Crenise held her down while the grinning ugly fiddled with his trouser buttons. His laughter was cut short when a thin line of steel sliced through his neck.

The head rolled. Shallan blinked. The slender steel struck again. Another head went sailing past. She heard the brief clash of steel on steel and glimpsed flitting movement to her right. Another Crenise screamed, witnessing his arm leaving his shoulder. A dark wild-eyed scarecrow figure leapt between the wounded man and the three Crenise still surrounding Shallan. Within seconds Zukei killed them all.

The blood-soaked girl glared down at Shallan, then reached out with a dark hand and yanked Shallan to her feet as though she were a rag doll.

"The duke sleeps," Zukei told her. "The physician is with him, so I thought I'd be needed here." Shallan gaped at Zukei. The dark girl wore a red band of cloth around her head, in her left hand she clutched a thin curved sword, a type of weapon Shallan had never seen before. Her right clutched a small throwing axe, and around her skimpy shift she'd thrown a rusty hauberk of big-ringed steel.

"I stole them from the armoury," Zukei grinned. "Good weapons. This is a Karyia, a sword from distant Shen, and the axe is the sort the Ptarnian raiders use to throw at each other. Beautifully balanced. I've been after one of these for years."

Whilst Zukei was aiding Shallan, Rael Hakkenon stalked Barin like a prowling panther. Twice now he'd got beneath the giant's guard, stung him in the shoulder and right upper arm with his blade and then leaped clear of the arcing axe.

Barin coughed up blood from his chest. He staggered forward in pain. Eyes triumphant, Rael danced in for the kill. But Barin had only feigned weakness as his wounds weren't grievous.

Wyrmfang descended with renewed fury. Too late the Assassin realised his mistake. He ducked clear of the double blade's scything sweep, but Barin spun the weapon so that the flat of a blade batted into his enemy's shoulder.

That force nearly broke Rael's back. As it was it lifted him skyward and sent him spinning like a tossed coin back over the battlements. The Assassin's fall was eventually broken by a prickly rose bush which shredded his body like a cheese grater as Rael crashed into it. The rambler held him trapped like a caged baboon with legs dangling frantically twenty feet above the ground.

Rael lost consciousness at that point.

Barin turned: saw Zukei stab a pirate in the eye with her strange-looking sword. Shallan was with her and both girls were surrounded by corpses. Zukei's face was covered in blood and Shallan's eyes were wild and triumphant. Barin scratched an ear. He counted the corpses sprawled and oozing around the girls. Twelve. And not a mark on Zukei or Shallan. Impressive stuff.

"You alright, girl?" Barin asked Shallan whilst gaping at the blood-soaked Zukei. "Who did for this lot?"

"I did," Zukei said. "Though the faerie girl was doing alright for a novice."

"She killed them all," Shallan told Barin, who shook his head.

"Where is Sveyn?" Barin asked them.

"Behind you." Sveyn stood leaning on the battlement and clutching his chest.

"Wake up, you're meant to be looking after this girl!" Barin growled at him and Sveyn decided he'd had enough for one day. "You should nominate her," he pointed at Zukei. "That wee lassie could kick all our arses. I've never seen such fucking speed and cunning with a blade." Zukei flashed Sveyn a fierce grin.

A shout to their left announced Lord Tolruan was hard pressed. Barin and Fassof rushed to his aid, followed by Shallan, Zukei and Cogga, and a hobbling Taic (having just gutted his wrestling companion.) Last up Sveyn joined them, panting and clutching his stomach.

They were too late. Lord Tolruan was surrounded. Shallan saw the long spike of the nearest pirate find a gap in Tolruan's armour just below his breastplate.

The point went in deep and with a strangled gasp Lord Tolruan collapsed to his knees, gripping the spike with his gore-spattered gauntlets. Barin and Cogga fell upon the pirates, killing four between them. Zukei took three more, whilst Taic and Fassof commenced engaging the rest.

But now other Crenise came forward, forcing a wedge between the embattled Northmen. Taic and Fassof were forced aside, whilst Barin and Cogga were soon surrounded by jabbing probing blades. Zukei's lean blade sliced through a pirate's collar bone down to his crutch. She skewered another and then hurled her axe, felling a third who was on the point of stabbing Taic in the rear. But then the girl was surrounded by a forest of Crenise steel.

A pirate stepped over the dying lord of Calprissa. He raised his cutlass for the kill. Shallan hissed and waded in like a wildcat. The pirate turned and leered at the girl. She lunged out at him with her knife but he just laughed at her.

He signalled to another. A man seized her from behind and laughing the two dragged her swearing and biting to the floor.

Shallan spat in the pirate's pocked face as he straddled her hips and tore at her clothing. Zukei couldn't help her this time.

Down to me.

The Crenise held her pinned whilst his friend started clawing at her thighs with sweaty hands. Others joined in, grinning at this new sport. Shallan was pinned helpless. Six strong they leered down at her, their breath rancid and stale.

Shallan knotted her legs, trapping the second man's hand while his fellow tugged at her garments. Looking up in despair Shallan saw a shadow loom above her attackers.

Sunlight glanced off steel. Suddenly she was showered in blood as Sveyn's axe sent the first pirate's grinning head flying across the wall. The other man gaped until a second blow split his skull open like an overripe fruit.

Sveyn had got over his moping and forgot the shallow wound across his guts. The thing about Sveyn was he took a long time to get roused. But when he did get roused, shit happened.

Another head went sailing past her. Barin had arrived with Cogga tailing him. Steel rang and bones crunched. Zukei stepped out from a fresh pile of corpses surrounding her. Shallan blinked in astonishment, all the leering faces were gone.

The remaining Crenise hung back, wary of the Northmen's ferocity. Sveyn was making a weird howling noise and frothing at the mouth, Barin was glaring at them like a spring hungry bear, and as for the wild-eyed spitting she-lynx in the shabby chain mail suit— enough said. The Crenise looked about for their lord and, not seeing him, decided it a good time to vacate the wall and head back down to their ships.

Barin and co. stormed after them, taking two more before the others leapt clear. He met up with defenders further along the wall. It seemed all the Crenise had fled, though at least a third of their number lay gored open on the parapet.

With the west wall secured, Barin lumbered painfully back over to where Shallan sat cross-legged and staring. He leaned down and gently helped her to her feet. His tired eyes full of concern.

"Are you alright, girl?"

Shallan nodded and readjusted her garments. He shift was torn in places but on the whole she'd got off lightly. Barin wiped sweat from his brow. He was getting too old for all this.

"Go get something to drink then check on your father, Shallan," Barin said. "I must go see how the east wall is holding up."

"I will come with you," Zukei told him.

"I'd sooner you stayed with Lady Shallan," Barin replied.

"She can look after herself." Zukei awarded Shallan a tight grin and Shallan felt a warm flush at the compliment paid her. "I need to be where the fighting is thickest," Zukei said. "I'm a professional killer—in case you hadn't noticed."

A shrill shout brought bad news quicker than Barin expected. Glancing down from the battlements, Barin and the two girls saw a young messenger boy racing towards them. "The city is breached, my lord!" the boy yelled up at them in panicky tones. "Savrino is slain and most the guard also. All is lost!"

Barin awarded Shallan a bleak look before jumping down to speak to the messenger. The lad was almost in tears. Barin cuffed his left ear, knocking him sideways.

"All is not lost until I bloody well say so, boyo. On your feet!" Barin hoisted the youth up by his bloodstained collar. "Off to the east wall we jolly well go." In a kinder voice he added, "Don't fret, lad, the city will hold because I'm damned if I'll let it fall. What's your name?"

"Pont."

"Well, master Pont, come along. And you lot—we've still work to do." Barin disappeared followed by his men and the prowling Zukei. Sveyn (who had just calmed down again) looked at Shallan who waved him away.

"You're needed elsewhere," she told him. Sveyn nodded forlornly and left her alone. And suddenly everything seemed very quiet on the west wall, though in the distance the sound of fighting could be heard.

Shallan stared in horror at the mess of bodies strewn along the parapet. Most were Crenise though there were many city guard too, near the place where Tolruan fell. She was alone again; except for the haphazard litter of corpses, the battlements were deserted. All those who could still fight had fled to the east wall where the real battle was gathering pace.

The Crenise, lacking motivation without their leader, had slunk back to their ships to lick their wounds. Shallan suspected they would regroup for another attack once Rael caught up with them.

But where was he? Shallan no longer cared. Dead, hopefully, though she doubted they'd be that lucky. Shallan gulped in deep breaths and gagged at the stench of the dead sprawled everywhere. Twice she'd nearly been raped. If it wasn't for Zukei and Sveyn? Shallan shuddered. The assaults on her body had left her shaken and upset.

What if Sveyn and Zukei hadn't arrived and those pigs had had their way? Shallan felt ill. The stink of the fly-clustered bodies close by, the realisation that she needed others to fight for her despite trying so hard. Shallan was no Zukei. And she was no Ariane either. She was just a former rich girl doing her best in a cruel and nasty world. She felt older—stained. No longer a girl. Her earlier confidence whilst shooting the bow was shattered.

Shallan wished so much that Corin were here. That this horrible death all around her would vanish, and in its place she'd see her one-night lover's eyes smiling back at her as they walked, arms linked through Silon's vineyard.

I cannot dwell on that night. Got to be strong. Keep moving.

But it was so hard.

Shallan glanced at Lord Tolruan's dead face. His eyes stared out at her in surprise from beneath his helmet. She turned away, watched as blowflies clustered noisily around the gaping wounds of the bodies all around her.

So much death.

Shallan felt her gorge rise. She lurched forward and vomited again and again until her stomach cried out in rebellion. Then as the cramps subsided Shallan stood up. Her jaw was set with resolution. *You cannot go back—have to keep moving forward. That or perish.* Shallan was a duke's daughter and she would do as Barin had advised and see to her father below. It was time to stop fretting and care about others instead.

Shallan gave one last withered stare out across the city. The streets were strangely quiet now and empty of citizens. Apart from the distant sounds of fighting reaching out to her from over a mile away, the only sounds were the groans of the wounded under the surgeon's scalpels somewhere below.

Briskly with mind made up, Shallan descended to the street below and wound her way purposely toward where her father lay dying. If the city were to fall then she would die at his side. That was only fitting.

Shallan had reclaimed her fallen bow and collected a handful of arrows. She had her new knife too, which she'd thrust into her waist belt. Shallan sprinted across and down to the healing houses where the surgeons worked assiduously on the wounded, maimed and dying. Somewhere in their blood-soaked midst she would find the room where rested the Duke of Morwella.

***

Scarce moments after Shallan left the battlements, two bloody hands gained purchase on the wall. With an agonised heave Rael Hakkenon launched his battered body back over the parapet. He looked a mess: two of the fingers on his right hand were broken, his face was covered in tiny scars from the thorns and his silver hair matted with dried blood. He was in a rare foul mood.

Rael scanned the grisly scene with indifference before dropping silently down onto the deserted walkway. Not a good result for Crenna. A second time his hardy boys had fled back to the ships without seeking him out. Back on the island he'd grill the lot of them over an open fire and recruit new blood. But for the time being he still needed them, craven bastards though they were.

Glancing below, Rael saw Shallan running in the distance. He recognised her as being with Barin. She was making for the healing houses.

Rael smiled at this new development. Here was someone he could vent his stresses on. The girl vanished inside the building and Rael gave careful chase, hugging the walls and making sure nobody saw him. He entered the building, ignoring the groans all around. Rael glimpsed Shallan talking to a healer before vanishing behind another doorway. He waited a moment then stole across and entered unnoticed behind.

Chapter 43

The East Wall

When Barin reached the east wall he was confronted by total chaos. There were Groil everywhere, and the hard-pressed defenders were retreating in panic. He had to act fast lest all be lost.

With a yell the Northman and his men fell on the Groil from behind, catching them unawares with such savagery, they backed away from the windmill path of Barin's axe. Barin roared at the city defenders to stand their ground. Awed by his presence, they obeyed. Pont the messenger boy looked stunned as he watched the giant axeman and his ferocious warriors fall upon the foe.

Like a vengeful war god out of a lost saga Barin strode forth, eyes blazing blue fire and blond braids trailing down his back. Behind him came Fassof, wiry and mean, Cogga with curved blade and nasty knife, Taic and Sveyn, both hauling axes, and seven other shipmates they'd found along the way, Barin's men having been scattered all along the west wall during the skirmish with Rael Hakkenon. Lastly stalked Zukei, wild-eyed and murderous. A lean spiky-haired killer, armed with slender sword and throwing axe, both weapons hewing a path through the Groil.

The Groil fell back in disarray, not used to this sudden ferocity. They had relied on fear till now and that had worked. But with brutal efficiency Barin and company swept the Groil clean from the east wall and above the gate, earning the defenders a brief respite.

Barin paused to take breath. Beside him Fassof leaned on the parapet and belched down at the milling horde below. He turned, hearing a soft thud, and saw that another ladder now rested on the battlements some twenty yards away.

"We've got company," Fassof grunted.

"I don't know what's keeping that lot down there," Cogga said.

"Perhaps they didn't make enough ladders," suggested Taic. "They seem a bit dishevelled."

"Don't knock it," responded Cogga.

"Shut up, you twits, and follow me!" Barin was already beating a path to where the enemy were spilling onto the wall.

There were few guards over there and already two score men had climbed over the parapet. They were led by a huge warrior garbed entirely in black. Barin recognised Derino and smiled.

"Zukei, lads, kill those buggers. I'll deal with their leader. I promised him an education."

Perani's second was a huge man, almost Barin's size and from head to toe decked in sable armour. In his right gauntlet he heaved a heavy mace whilst his left clutched a broad serrated sax. Behind the leader were his prized bodyguard. All were ex-Tigers—huge burly men renowned for their prowess at killing.

Derino saw Barin approaching at speed and smiled. It was time he dealt with this Northman. Derino had underestimated the defenders. He'd expected the Groil to have terrorized them into surrender. Instead they'd fought with stubborn tenacity. Derino had promised Caswallon's spy he'd have the gates open by mid-afternoon. Now he realised he'd miscalculated. No matter, he would put an end to this charade himself. And that would start with Barin.

"Take the city," ordered Derino, waving the ex-Tigers on. "I will deal with this barbarian!"

***

Hoofbeats drummed the morning. Golden sunlight danced off steel-bright mail as Ariane of the Swords led her small army towards the bright walls of Calprissa. Ariane could see the dark horde spoiling beneath the eastern walls and prayed that they were in time to save the city. She saw no breaches and wondered why the enemy hadn't brought any siege machines or mangonels. Were they that arrogant? It seemed so.

She urged her mare on and her host followed behind, their horses at the trot. The road plunged narrow between two green hills. They entered a wood, forded a fast flowing river and then the road veered up to a high windy ridge. At its crown Ariane reined in. The city lay before them, two or three miles away. The riders could hear the sound of fighting coming from the city walls.

Queen Ariane wheeled her mare about and addressed her riders.

"I've no brave speeches," she told them. "Just want to say how proud I am of each and every one of you. Raleenian and Kelwynian both, I'm honoured to have you following me. For freedom from tyranny and victory against the odds," she shouted, "let us ride!"

The riders roared approval as Ariane guided her mare to face the city again.

"To Calprissa and victory!" Ariane pulled back her reins and leaned forward in her saddle. The mare whinnied and kicked its forelegs high. Men hooted and cheered.

"Elanion is with us!" Ariane yelled at them. "Come, my heroes! Ride with your queen to war!"

"To battle!" Captain Tarello shouted beside her, then in a quieter voice added, "Goddess, ward Queen Ariane from harm, her survival is paramount to our cause." She smiled at him then, and together queen and captain spurred their horses forward, and with a thunder of spear on shield her host followed. Like a thread of silver fire the riders streaked down from the hillside entering the level plain below. The walls loomed higher as they galloped at speed toward Calprissa. Three miles, two miles—the gap closed. One mile. At Ariane's right thundered Captain Tarello, his face flushed with battle fever.

Not far behind him rode 'Squire' Galed, eyes wide with panic as he clung desperately to his frothing steed and willed himself to stay put. Someone yelled in his ear. Galed glanced across. He nearly fell from his horse when he saw the boy Cale riding alongside him.

"You?" Galed gasped. "Idiot boy! I—" Galed's words were swallowed by the deafening rumble of hooves on stone.

Cale grinned back at him. The boy had been unable to contain his excitement any longer. Galed clenched his teeth. The queen would boil both of them alive but it was too late now. The east wall was looming close.

Ahead a shout announced the enemy had seen them and were turning to confront them. Galed closed his eyes and prayed out loud to Elanion. Beside him, Cale gripped his reins tightly with his left hand, while with his other he unsheathed his pilfered sword. He twiddled it through the air but almost dropped it. (Something he'd seen Corin do with that longsword of his but Cale hadn't perfected the art yet). He decided on caution rather than flare, clinging to the hilt with greasy fingers and releasing a manic yell, as his queen and comrades bore down on the startled foe.

Ariane's cavalry tore through the enemy camp like a silver tornado. At Tarello's orders the riders had formed a tight wedge with spears thrust forward and shields locked together. Like a huge silver arrowhead they pierced the rear of Derino's horde, ploughing a deep furrow through its ranks.

Everywhere was mayhem as the enemy fled from the sudden unexpected onslaught coming from behind. Ariane's face was flushed with excitement—all fear banished by the immediate. She yelled as her rapier slashed the mask from a fleeing foe. Then she hacked out with the sabre at a hooded spearmen, gasping when she realised it was a Groil. So it wasn't only men they were fighting. That only hardened her resolve. Caswallon's ghouls were no match for her army.

"Die!" Ariane yelled as she sliced the throat of another hoodie. Beside her Tarello's spear gored through two Groil but stuck in the last one's midriff. Tarello dropped the weapon and unleashed his broadsword.

"Time for some wet work!" Tarello yelled at his queen.

Ariane's wedge cut deep and fast into Caswallon's horde. In its midst were two terrified riders. Galed, shielded at either side by warriors, sat his saddle in gap-jawed disbelief.

He had actually asked to join in this lunacy. Why? His knuckles were white and his brow was sweating profusely despite the cold. Galed's prime concern was to stay on his saddle and not get crushed. No mean accomplishment. One slip would lead to a very nasty end. He hadn't even unsheathed his sword because he dared not let go of the reins.

Behind Galed, Cale swiped his blade at a passing spearman, reaching out too far and nearly falling from his horse. Bad idea. Then a Groil emerged from nowhere and swung a serrated sword at Cale's exposed legs.

Shit!

Cale tried to block but missed. He yelled in panic as the wicked blade slid across toward his unprotected knee. Then the Groil fell back, gored by the Raleenian lancer on Cale's left flank. The rider grinned at him.

"You're a crap warrior," the Raleenian told him.

Cale muttered thanks and clung to his sword, feeling suddenly very shaky. The boy hoped this battle wouldn't last too long. He clearly needed to invest in a training program. Perhaps he should have stayed in Wynais after all. Too late for regrets. Best Cale hang on and keep his head on his shoulders.

Queen Ariane and Captain Tarello urged their frothing steeds to greater speed. As yet they'd not lost a man due to the swiftness and surprise of their attack. The steely wedge parted foes like windblown wheat. But they were running out of space.

They had reached the walls and the enemy were closing again. Tarello yelled out to Darosi, the Raleenian captain, ordering his elite lancers to form a circle around the queen and cut their way across to the east gates. The Kelwynians would follow behind.

Once beneath the gates the combined force would yell to the guard to let them through to aid the defenders within. It would be touch and go but there was little else they could do, greatly outnumbered as they were.

The Raleenians complied, locking shields and forming a broad circle with lances lowered ready. Behind them were the Kelwynian guard and finally the archers awaiting their chance. At Tarello's signal, and keeping the wall behind them, Ariane's army pressed towards the gates. A shiny beetle surrounded by dark milling ants. The enemy closing in on all sides.

Ariane fought alongside the Raleenians, her silver armour drenched in blood. She hacked to left and right, killing men and Groil, often not knowing which unless the hideous masks fell to reveal the faces. Worried, the lancers closed ranks around her.

"I need more bloody room!" Ariane shrieked. But then Tarello intervened and, despite her protestations, Ariane was surrounded by a protective ring of steel.

"I lead from the front!" Ariane yelled at Tarello. She was furious.

"You're no good to us dead, my Queen!" the captain yelled back.

"Bollocks!" Despite her anger Ariane was forced back to where the archers stood nearest the wall.

It was then that the queen saw Cale lurking close by the archers. The boy's expression was one of sheer terror mixed with deranged excitement. Despite this he looked pale and sick and sat his horse with the grace of a sack of potatoes.

Ariane's face blanched white. She mouthed a question but the milling of horses and jostling of their riders widened the gap between her and the boy. Soon Cale was lost from her sight.

"Hold ranks!" Darosi was shouting as his lancers stoically inched across to the gates. Not much further but the Raleenians were taking the brunt of the attack. Fifty had fallen already and almost twenty of Tolranna's picked guard. "Hold!" Tarello added his voice to the Raleenian captain. "The gates are close!"

Ariane was beyond livid. She saw Galed struggling with his horse as he urged the beast across to hers. He didn't look happy.

"What's that fucking boy doing here?" Ariane screamed at him.

"I don't know," Galed yelled back. "I thought he was in Wynais."

But then Ariane was forced to forget about Cale. The enemy had broken through the Raleenian cordon, and were cutting and hacking their way to where she sat on her horse. But before they could reach her Darosi's defensive ring closed again, killing all trapped inside. They'd been lucky but time was running out. The gates were still thirty foot away.

They reached an outthrust buttress and were hemmed tight in its corner, trapped by the very walls they had sought to save. Groil and men pressed down on them. Ariane saw her fighters falling beneath that storm. The enemy surrounded Ariane's fast shrinking army like a winter sea lashing a lighthouse. Groil reached out with steely claws, pulling soldiers from their steeds and tearing them to pieces. Men screamed and died. Horses whinnied and trampled their bodies. She saw Captain Darosi pulled from his horse by snarling Groil, his screams lost in the melee below.

Then the enemy archers arrived. Shafts buzzed at them from all angles except the wall behind. Most bounced off armour or stuck to shields but some found their mark. They were so close but they'd never reach the gates now.

Ariane watched in horror as her valiant army began to crumble beneath the towering might of the foe. They were trapped. Her brave plan had failed. Soon she would die and her kingdom fall to ruin.

***

Barin bid Fassof keep the others back. "This is personal."

Derino's men filed back along the wall, allowing their leader room. There were only twenty present as most had already jumped down into the city below. These rash raiders proved overconfident. They died to a man, surrounded and butchered by Calprissan militia, the city guard having rallied at last.

Those militia now leaped up the stairs to the east wall, arriving just in time to view the confrontation between the Northman and his enemy.

"I've come to call in my debt." Derino loomed close like a steel tower. "Time's up, barbarian."

Barin felt the battle rage soar through his veins. This time he would put it to full use. He felt calm: the eye of the storm. Removed from the carnage surrounding him, his mind wandered as it often did at these moments. Derino watched him in silence.

"Are you ready, strawhead?"

Barin could see more ladders appearing along the wall, all teeming with masked invaders. The odds were getter worse by the minute. His instinct told him Calprissa was at breaking point. Barin thought of Shallan and her father trapped in the healing house. Soon to be surrounded.

He pictured his friend Corin somewhere far away on that crazy quest. All for what—a wizard's wild gambit? Lastly he thought of his pretty daughters and Marigold, his wife. So long since last he'd seen them. Barin tried to picture their faces but it was hopeless in the chaos.

Rage. Let it rain on down.

The defenders of Calprissa's walls were surrounded. It was only a matter of time before they fell. Barin could hear his men and Zukei engaging with Derino's thugs. The world stopped turning. Barin's vision sharpened and his mind narrowed to one thing. Killing. And thus Barin focused on the armoured figure bearing down on him.

He smiled feeling the berserkergang take hold. Rage and Fury. The Northman's hidden weapon, they called it.

"Yes I'm ready." Barin grinned and swung the axe.

Derino's mace slammed toward Barin's head, but Wyrmfang trapped it mid swing. Barin tugged, yanking Derino toward him, but his enemy disengaged and leapt aside.

Barin rammed Wyrmfang's beak up under the chin guard of Derino's horned helm. Derino leapt back and lashed out with the sax, scoring a cut down Barin's left arm. Barin hardly noticed it.

Again he swung the axe.

Derino danced aside, whirling his mace round in blinding speed and narrowly missing Barin's right ear. The Northman leapt back in the nick of time. He stabbed out again with the beak of the axe, aiming to pierce the thin gorget around Derino's throat.

Derino blocked his thrust with the heavy mace. Its long spikes trapped a blade, causing Barin to lose his balance. With a vicious jerk, Derino yanked the mace toward him, wrenching Wyrmfang from Barin's slipping grasp. He stabbed low with the sax but Barin's forearm impacted the flat of the blade, knocking it aside.

Derino kicked out striking Barin's groin with his steel-shod boot. Barin let his anger swallow the pain. Despite that he doubled over, trying desperately to catch his breath. Barin lashed out with his left fist, he grabbed the sax below the blade, twisted and wrenched it from Derino's grasp. He swung hard but Derino's mace battered the weapon aside again, leaving Barin exposed.

Derino grinned beneath his helm. He brought the spiked mace back for a killing swing but stopped short. A dark shape crossed his vision. Derino glimpsed a raven settling on the battlements a yard to his right. The gallows bird. Derino felt suddenly cold under that beady gaze. He hesitated for the briefest instant then swung the mace again.

Barin was ready. He ducked beneath the mace swing, then launched his bulk up into Derino's midriff. Barin's right fist impacted the leather padding of the buckle clasped under Derino's helmet. Derino's head snapped back with a jolt. Derino tried bringing the mace down but Barin twisted aside and slammed another fist into Derino's armoured gut. Despite his iron protection the force of that blow buckled Derino.

He swung wild with the mace. Barin stepped close, caught Derino's outstretched right arm. Barin tugged. With a sickening wrench the Northman brought Derino's armoured arm down upon his thigh and snapped the bone above the elbow. Derino yammered. Barin's upper leg was oozing gore from Derino's torn armour. Again he ignored the pain.

Derino slid a dagger into his palm. He jabbed hard at Barin's face with his left hand, the right dangling uselessly at his side.

Barin's fist battered the dagger from his enemy's grasp. It clattered loudly on the stone behind. Barin grinned horribly then rammed both fists hard into the broad nose guard marking the centre of Derino's helmet.

The helm bucket inward and Derino gagged as it pummelled his nose to pulp. Derino staggered forward, his vision blurred and the buckled helmet choking him. Barin kicked him hard under the groin, again ignoring the pain as his boot crunched into that armour. The force of that kick actually lifted the big man off his feet. Derino fell to his knees groping for a weapon—any weapon.

Barin calmly retrieved Wyrmfang from the stone, stored the axe in its loop and flexed his fingers. Silence settled on the east wall. Friend and foe both watched in awe waiting for the outcome.

Derino tried to get to his feet but Barin booted him in the helmet again, tearing the sole from his right boot. Derino groped.

Tired of watching, Barin reached down, seizing Derino by his broad leather mace belt with one hand and grabbing his helmet buckle with another.

Barin wrenched the choking Derino from his feet. He hoisted his enemy's body high over his head so that all on the wall and below could see. Then with a bear-savage roar, Barin tossed Derino's body far out over the wall. Derino screamed as he plunged from the battle-ments. His cries ceased when his neck and back snapped like twigs on the stony, blood-strewn grass below.

Two of Derino's surviving thugs leapt at Barin but Zukei cut them down, while Fassof, Taic and Cogga and company set upon the others. Beyond them, Groil and masked warriors crashed into each other in their confusion. Lacking a leader, they'd lost direction. Barin grinned. They might still be outnumbered but for now at least they were winning.

Seize the moment! Barin didn't hesitate.

"Come on, the day is ours!" he yelled, seizing the advantage and sensing possible victory. At his side, the surviving soldiers of Calprissa found new strength. They'd witnessed his fight with Derino and now believed Barin capable of anything.

The giant from the north who'd come to save them. The boy Pont had seen the whole contest with horn helmet. Pont's brown eyes were shining with pride as he took his place with the men.

At Barin's shout they hurled themselves at the shaken foe and their sudden fury turned events on the east wall. The enemy were driven back to their ladders, most hacked down before they reached them. The Calprissans fought with renewed confidence and direc-tion, mopping up the enemy until none remained standing on the east wall. They kicked the ladders away and scowled down at the remaining enemy below.

Barin, his rage having subsided, felt exhausted. He threw a bucket of cold water over his head and grunted. That had been some scrap. Derino was one hard bastard.

"Zukei?" The dark girl loomed into view. "Glad you're alive, girl. Do me a favour, go check on Lady Shallan and her father." Zukei nodded and sprinted off.

"Bloody good lassie, that one," Fassof said, watching her leave.

Barin nodded and yawned. "That she is." He glanced down from the parapet. "Who the fuck are they?" The mate joined him and gawped down. Below, and to their left nearer the gates, were silver-clad riders surrounded by the enemy. Who they were and how they had got there, Barin had no notion. But one thing was certain. They needed help and fast.

"Come on!" Barin bid Fassof follow him. Together they trotted along the wall to see more clearly. "Archers—we need you here!" Fassof yelled as he ran past.

Barin stopped alongside the gate parapet. He stared down, at last recognising Raleenians and Kelwynians fighting in a tight circle below. The enemy's entire might was bearing down on them. Within minutes they would break under that strain. Others joined them to watch, including some archers who started raining shafts down on the enemy horde below.

Barin studied the fight for a moment, trying desperately to discern who led the Kelwynians. He saw a sandy-haired warrior yelling orders, the helmet having been knocked from his head. Then he saw a slender figure with sword in either hand, petit for a warrior. Beside the armoured figure stood a boy waving a sword like a stick and jumping about. Barin knew that youth. Cale. And now he realised who it was stood beside him.

Queen Ariane.

Fuck.

And he'd thought her safe in Wynais.

"Open the gates, you morons!" Barin leapt toward the stairway leading down to the east gates. Men gaped at him but parted like chaff to allow him through. "Open those fucking gates before I brain the lot of you!"

"What? Why?" Two guards gawped up at him speeding like thunder toward them.

"Just do it!" The guards were still dithering when Barin leapt down amongst them.

"Must I do everything myself in this city?"

The seven gate guards just stared back up at him as if he had lost his reason. Fassof grabbed the nearest by the ear and threw him into the gate.

"Lend a hand," he said. Meanwhile single-handedly Barin was lifting the huge bars locking the gates and hurling them aside.

"But why?" someone managed to say.

"Because your queen is outside, dickhead." Barin tugged the left gate toward him. At least there wasn't a portcullis. Fassof hurled his weight alongside and then everyone else joined in.

"Thanks, lads," said Barin as the door swung wide. "Couldn't have managed without you." Barin loped through the gates, Fassof behind him. Taic and Cogga arrived at that point after tossing the last of Derino's thugs off the walls.

"Come on," Barin said. "Let's go tidy up." He unslung Wyrmfang and roared out into wasteground beyond the gate.

Chapter 44

The Assassin

The hall was a cacophony of blood and noise. It was filled with the groans of the dying and stank of sweat and fear. The anguished faces of the wounded bedridden stared up at Shallan as she hastened toward a backroom.

It was in that quiet room, a blood-soaked healer informed her, that the duke would be found. Kind Cormalian had placed Tomais as far from the carnage as was possible. Shallan reached the door to his room. She turned the handle, pushed it open discovering her father's unconscious body sprawled half naked across the marble floor.

"Father!" Shallan crouched down beside him. She lifted his frail head and kissed the thin bloodless lips. His rheumy eyes opened slowly. A weak smile greeted her.

"I heard the sound of battle... I fear Vangaris is under attack... see to your mother, Shallan. I always loved her despite that business with the faun."

"Father." Shallan felt fresh tears stream down her face. "Morwella has fallen, Father. It is lost and Mother is dead. Your wife. Oh, Father!"

Then a cold voice laughed.

"What a tender sight to behold."

Shallan turned. There he stood, not looking his best. Clearly Rael Hakkenon had had a rough day. The Assassin's bloodstained arms were folded and he slouched languidly against the door. The rapier he'd thrust point first into the floorboards.

Shallan's mouth framed a warning scream but the Assassin placed a finger to his lips. "Silence, lover. Let us not be interrupted, else I get careless. We wouldn't want that, would we? My patience has been frayed of late. I might...slip and do something nasty."

He leaned forward, plucked the blade free and almost affectionately placed his rapier's point against the groaning duke's throat. "It would be an act of mercy—judging by the state of him."

"Get away from him, you little shit!" Shallan yanked the knife free from her belt. "If it's me you want then take me and be done. But let my father live!"

"A tempting offer, my dear. If only I had more time, or indeed the inclination." Rael's expression was thoughtful, regretful even. Shallan lunged at him with the knife but he kicked it from her hand with contemptuous ease. She grabbed her bow resting by the bedside, swung it at him.

Rael caught her arm at the wrist, cruelly twisting it and wrenching the bow free of her grasp. Rael examined the weapon with a raised eyebrow. He smiled lovingly at her, then with sudden violence brought the bow down hard on his knee, snapping it clean in two.

"However," Rael watched her like a lazy cat surveying its cornered prey. "I have need of you both as insurance to get me safely away from these walls."

"You have failed again, Assassin," Shallan spat at him. "Your men are all dead!"

"Lucky for them, I'd say."

Rael wiped the spittle from his left eye. He licked his fingers and grinned at her. "And if they're not they will be before long, the useless tossers. But the majority of my chieftains remained with my fleet. That lies primed and ready just a few miles offshore. I wanted to be involved in Calprissa's fall, but not that involved. I do have other matters to attend to."

"You won't pull this off." Shallan's words lacked conviction.

"Yes I will." Rael traced the rapier along the duke's exposed back, scoring a shallow wound. Shallan's face tightened but she dare not move.

"Once I have bundled you and your decrepit father on the Serpent, I'll return with in full force and raze this irksome city to the ground, if that hasn't happened already. Caswallon will owe me big time.

"I didn't want to commit all my ships in the first instance," Rael explained reasonably. "I needed to witness how Caswallon's army behaved before getting too ensconced and risking my whole force. Just as well I did as I've never seen such a useless bunch of tossers. That Derino hasn't got a clue. They should have taken the city by now. Calprissans, like most Kelwynians, are cowards."

"You're wrong, villain."

It was a new voice that had spoken. Shallan recognised the thin face of Cormalian the healer. He had silently entered the room from the main hall. His expression was bleak but he confronted the Assassin without any show of fear.

"Your fleet was caught off guard and destroyed utterly by the queen's re-formed navy," Cormalian announced and a slow smile lifted the right corner of his lips.

"That little bitch has no navy, just sharp teeth and a foul mouth." Rael Hakkenon's eyes narrowed dangerously at the healer. His fingers stroked the ornate guard of his rapier. "You, physician, are a liar and will soon be a dead liar."

"I speak truthfully," replied the old man, giving the Assassin look for look. "Queen Ariane ordered her vessels refitted for war under secret hangers up in Port Wind. This was done most promptly. Her fleet is not vast but sufficient enough to deal with your vermin."

Rael's eyes narrowed to slits of jade.

Cormalian watched the rapier's point. "When Caswallon's army was spotted they sailed south from Port Wind and caught your lot lurking about. The navy captain sent bird to Lord Tolruan. We guessed you pirates would be predictable and rush to aid your accomplice in Kelthaine. You are trapped, Assassin. It—"

Cormalian gasped as sudden pain lanced deep into his belly. He sighed, looking down at the slender steel pinning him to the door. The healer gave Shallan an apologetic look and then slumped forward. Rael twisted the blade free with a savage jerk and Cormalian sunk to the floor in a pool of blood. Within seconds he was dead. As an afterthought Rael had dipped his steel in a jar of belladonna he'd found among the seriously wounded, deeming it might prove useful.

"Well then. I'd better take no chances in case there was some truth in that old fool's words." Rael studied the girl, who still watched him with silent loathing. "Oh come on, you didn't expect me to let him live, did you? You know my reputation."

"I hate you."

"So does everyone else. It's lonely being me." Rael examined a fingernail, pulling a rose thorn out from where it had been lodging since his encounter with the rambler on the west wall.

"We'll leave your father here, I think," Rael told her, sucking his finger. "I'll settle for your company just now, my lovely." He lunged at Shallan with his left hand and grasping her wrist, pulled her towards him with a savage wrench. Shallan lashed out with her fists but was rewarded by a hard slap that made her head spin.

"Come now, sweetest." Rael twisted Shallan's arm cruelly behind her back, making her cry out in pain. "I see you are in need of some training," Rael slapped her again, harder this time making her nose bleed.

Shallan tried to pull away from him but Rael's grip was like corded iron.

"Maybe I should have you here, after all. In this very room. It's not true what they say about me you know. All fucking lies. Besides, there are many ways of obtaining pleasure—not just the obvious. Imagination is a marvellous thing."

Rael's jade eyes mocked her futile resistance. "A last spectacle for your dying father. Send him on his way, the poor old fool." Rael laughed, pulling her closer into his embrace.

But Shallan had anticipated this move. She waited until his probing right hand passed close to her mouth. She drew her lips back in a snarl and her teeth crunched down on his bejewelled index finger.

Shallan bit hard. Rael snarled in pain and pulled his hand free. He gaped in stunned horror at the nearly severed index finger hanging from his right hand by a thin gobbet of sinew. Rage filled him. With a violent snarl he threw the girl across the room. Shallan's body struck the wall with a thud, bruising her badly.

"You fucking whore, I'll slit your throat for that and feed your body to the crows!"

Rael reached for her again. This time his eyes were murderous with outrage. He froze gasping in sudden pain. Unnoticed by them both, Duke Tomais had reached beneath the bed and retrieved Shallan's slender dagger.

With the last of his dying strength the duke had thrust it upward deep into the Assassin's exposed flesh. The dagger pierced Rael Hakkenon's thigh just above the knee. It passed clean through, narrowly missing the artery.

Rael coughed in pain. He sliced out with the rapier. The duke sighed as the narrow blade punctured his lungs three times. His emaciated body collapsed and lay prone on the bloody rush-strewn floor.

Rael stabbed him four more times and then turned toward Shallan.

And Shallan screamed.

Rael lowered the rapier. "Your turn, bitch." He stopped and, hearing a noise outside, cocked an ear to the door. The sound of many steel-shod feet approaching fast.

Rael Hakkenon reached down slowly, his eyes never leaving Shallan. With a grunt he pulled the dagger free from his gushing leg. "Time I wasn't here."

Rael gave her a last contemptuous glance then leapt one-legged toward the lone window at the far side of the room. With a panther's grace and swiftness despite his injured leg, Rael heaved his battered torso up to the high ledge above. He tore the useless finger free from his hand with his teeth, then spat it on the floor in front of Shallan.

"A trophy, lest you fucking forget me." Rael grinned like a gargoyle. "Until next time then." He smashed the glass with an elbow, wormed his bleeding body through the gap and then jumped clear, landing badly on the turf a score of feet below and hobbling to his feet.

Shallan staggered across to the window. She heard the Assassin shout out as he fell. "Gods curse you, Assassin!" No answer. Rael Hakkenon was gone.

Zukei arrived just ahead of the guards. Together they crashed into the room and were greeted by the sight of the Lady of Morwella stooped weeping over the prone body of her father the duke.

"The Assassin—capture him!" shouted the leader, seeing the smashed window pane. "He cannot have got far!" Half a dozen soldiers sped off to apprehend the pirate chief. Their leader stayed put, as did Zukei.

Shallan wiped her face clear of tears as her father smiled up at her through his pain. His fever had broken at last. His eyes now glistened with knowing clarity. But Tomais hadn't long, for the poison on Rael Hakkenon's blade would soon take hold.

"I am spent, my daughter," Duke Tomais whispered. "Finished. It is now down to you, my beloved. Return to our land, Shallan. You are Duchess now. Find your brothers if they still live and free our people."

"I will," she sobbed, cradling his head in her arms and unable to speak further.

"I always knew you should have been born a man, Shallan. Your heart is valiant, dearest. I never told you but The Horned Man is your real..." The duke's words froze on his lips and his eyes glazed over. Duke Tomais of Vangaris was dead.

Shallan wept. Zukei stood over her in watchful silence. Outside it had grown strangely quiet but Shallan no longer cared. She felt numb, her head light and her limbs weak. She turned to the door and the room started to spin. She fell, and Zukei caught her and gently lowered her body to the bed.

"I have failed," Shallan told the girl.

Zukei smiled. It made her look younger. "No," the dark girl said. "You have done well, Lady Shallan. You have courage and a good soul. The rest can be learned in time. And," Zukei's smile broadened, "you will have a good teacher. I'm accompanying you to Car Carranis." Shallan lost consciousness at that point. Her mind wandered down dark paths. Shallan saw a horseman tall and stern of face. He was calling out to her. *Shallan...Shallan!*

Clasped in his right hand was a blazing sword wrought of purest crystal.

Corin! But then he vanished and from far away she heard voices calling out to her. *Sister, return to us while there is still time...*

Chapter 45

A Sting in the Tale

Ariane controlled the horse with her legs and screamed as she skewered a masked warrior, she'd rejoined the fight when the enemy broke through. She'd lost her rapier in the melee earlier and now gripped the sabre in both hands.

There was no order now. No discipline. They fought back to back in tiny knots, their circle having broken. Most the Raleenians had fallen and half of her brave Kelwynians would never fight again. Despite that the survivors still fought on stubbornly.

The corpses of their enemies lay strewn in steaming heaps all about them. Ariane's helmet and armour were splattered with blood and filth. At her side Captain Tarello still bellowed orders like a madman. A good choice, Tarello. She hadn't known much about him before they left Wynais. Brave and smart. Shame he was going to die.

Tarello showed no sign of dying soon. He fought like a demon, stabbing and lashing out at enemy men and Groil whenever they broke through the defence, or came close to the queen.

Close by, Cale shared a horse with Galed. Neither looked happy.

Ariane had yelled at Tarello to order some guards cover them. She'd stared daggers at the boy but lacked time to render him the verbal lashing he deserved. That would come later—if by some miracle they survived. And that prospect looked woefully slim. They were hemmed in on all sides, the sheer weight of enemy bodies alone would crush them soon.

A giant two-headed Groil leered in front of her. Ariane slashed across at its face but this Groil was more cunning than most. It stepped sideways and trapped her blade in the serrations of its black sword. It twisted the steel and the sabre was wrenched from Ariane's grip. The Groil stood over her, dog tongues lolling, and its breath beyond foul.

"Queen, beware! "Tarello yelled a warning and tried to reach her but he was trapped between three enemies. Tw- heads swung its blade hard and Ariane dived low. Blood sprayed her from head to toe. She looked up just in time to see Wyrmfang split the Groil in two, sending a head each way.

Barin!

"This way, queenie!" Barin's axe was working overtime. Groil and men were felled like saplings. They fell back in panic, buying Ariane's survivors a modicum of time.

"To the gate," Barin roared "Run! We cannot hold it open for long!" Barin's sortie, though tiny in number had caught the enemy by surprise. They'd lacked motivation since Derino's fall and were easily confused. While they hesitated Ariane and Tarello seized the opportunity.

The captain led the way forward in a final push for the gates. Horses' hooves lashed out at the foe as they sought in vain to halt their escape. Barin's crew minded the entrance slaying all that came near, while the Northman single-handedly kept the path clear along the wall for the young queen's riders.

Ariane urged her steed forward. They reached the gates, clattered through and entered the city. In their midst Cale and Galed looked at each other in shattered relief. Neither could believe that they were still alive, and unhurt to boot.

Then just as the gates swung tight a huge Groil leapt through the gap. The dog-thing leapt high and seized Ariane from behind, its claws trapping her cloak and yanking her from the saddle. Together they tumbled between the small gap in the gates.

Ariane yelled out and tried to stab the Groil with her dagger but was caught off balance. The Groil cuffed her. Ariane fell and the Groil slunk to all fours and started dragging her out through the gateway. Black claws wrenched at the gates as its comrades sought to get in.

Amid shouts Barin, Fassof and Tarello all leapt for the gates.

But Cale was quickest.

Before Cale had realised it he had leapt from his saddle. Gripping his purloined sword with both hands, the boy stabbed down hard into the hind quarters of the Groil.

The creature's blood spilled over Cale, making him gag at the stench. Barin, looming close, heaved the dog-thing aside and slammed the gate shut crushing the claws still prising from outside. The guards hurried behind and slung the heavy bars across it.

Job done.

Ariane, shaken but unhurt, had regained her feet. She watched as the ashen-faced Tarello helped the boy up.

"That was well done, lad," the captain said and Cale beamed in return. Ariane's riders dismounted, allowing the newly arrived stable retainers to see to their steeds. Ariane glanced across at her men. They'd done well, nearly half the force that left Wynais were still living. She approached the nearest Raleenian, Darosi's second whose name she had forgotten.

"Your men fought with honour and courage. They will never be forgotten. From this day forward, Wynais is in your debt."

The Raleenian smiled a grisly smile. "An honour to fight along-side Ariane of the Swords," he said. "We still living are yours to com-mand, Queen of Kelwyn."

"Thank you. I don't recall your name, Captain."

"Jaan, your highness, and I'm only a lieutenant."

"No, you are a captain." Exhausted, Ariane managed a grin as Barin loomed over her.

"I was hoping you'd show up," she said. Barin beamed in delight when he saw the two figures behind her.

"So, Master Cale," Barin said. He lumped the boy a playful tap on the head. Cale felt like a tree had hit him but grinned back heroically.

"You and 'Squire' Galed here are warriors now," he grinned across to Galed. "I knew you would be, eventually. It was only a matter of time. You both have courage."

"Courage or madness," grumbled Galed, choking as Barin hugged him enthusiastically. "What difference is there?"

"It's a reasonable point of view." Barin rubbed an ear and yawned. It had been a tiring day and it wasn't over yet.

The queen, her officers and a score of fighters made for the east wall's battlements with Barin and his men. "We had best make ready for their next move," Ariane said. Once upon the wall they saw the enemy—still numbering several thousand—had withdrawn well out of bowshot. They resembled a dark untidy mass, leaderless and confused. Even now fights were breaking out between Groil and men. It seemed Caswallon's beasts were starting to squabble.

"I can't see that shower attacking any time soon. Think we've gained a respite at least." Tarello looked down on the horde with contempt.

"My guess is that they'll await fresh commands from their master in Kelthaine," Barin said as he watched the spectacle. "They were obviously at a loss without Derino's guidance. Caswallon shouldn't have put all his faith in one man. He may be a sorcerer but he's no general."

"Luckily for us," added Ariane. "And I suspect he won't make the same mistake again. Still—we've done well, my friends. Calprissa struck the first blow. Caswallon's ego will be dented at least."

Just then the boy Pont appeared sweaty-faced and puffing. He'd evidently taken it upon himself to act a messenger.

"Barin—sir!" Pont didn't realise who Ariane was. Covered in blood she hardly looked like a queen.

"What's up, Punk?"

"Pont, sir. The Assassin, sir—he's killed the sick duke and scarpered. There's a bunch of guards after him but none have returned yet."

Barin slumped against the parapet. In the chaos he'd forgotten about Shallan. If that girl was hurt...

"What of the duke's daughter?" Ariane demanded.

"She's sick, so they tell me. The crazy woman's minding her."

"Crazy woman?" Ariane awarded Barin a quizzical look.

"That'll be Zukei," Barin told her. "A stray we picked up in Syrannos."

"Poor Shallan. I didn't even know she was here." Ariane bid Captain Tarello stay and keep an eye on the enemy below. "I must go see my cousin at once." Ariane left the wall without further ado. Barin followed with Cale and Galed too. Barin's crew stayed with Tarello to keep an eye on things. All except Sveyn, who was feeling guilty that he'd abandoned Shallan.

Ariane ordered fresh mounts and, as they rode through the city streets, Barin told her their reason for being here in Calprissa. He was angry with himself for leaving Shallan and her father to their fate. Not that there was much he could have done—couldn't be in two places at once.

They dismounted beneath the west wall and hurried toward the physician's quarters. Everywhere people waved and cheered at their young queen (word having got out) and the giant axe warrior that had saved their city. The Calprissans worshipped Barin now. Master Pont had lost no time recounting the great fight on the east wall.

Citizens clustered about him much to his annoyance, but he said nothing, just waved and grinned. These Calprissans had done well despite Barin's misgivings. All of them were bone-weary. Most of the guards blood-splattered from head to toe. These drained kegs of ale while their womenfolk tended their wounds.

As he walked Cale studied the citizens of Calprissa. Considering the earlier chaos at the walls the cityfolk seemed rather dignified. Cale couldn't help but admire them. They were his queen's people therefore his people too. Cale was a Kelwynian now. A noble. And a hero. Gone was the cutpurse from Kelthara. That had been back then.

They reached the healing house and entered within. Ariane stopped several times to smile warmly and spare a kind word or two for the more serious of the wounded.

"Your queen has come," she told them. "Your brave deeds here will not be forgotten. We have won the day thanks to your courage."

Pride filled their faces as the wounded of Calprissa watched their beloved queen pass by. They didn't care that she was covered in gore. She was one of them.

Ariane entered the back room the others behind her. The lone guard greeted them. "She's been sleeping," he said. "The wild one won't let anyone near her till she wakes."

***

Shallan had regained consciousness some time ago. Zukei, hovering close, had offered her some broth, and feeling better she'd sunk into a long dreamless sleep. Shallan woke hearing voices in the room.

She looked up in surprise, seeing her cousin smiling down on her. Behind the queen, Zukei scowled and gripped the handle of her foreign sword until Barin emerged and placated the black girl.

"Ariane...Am I dreaming?" Shallan blinked. "I thought you in Wynais."

The queen reached down took her cousin in her arms. Shallan's eyes were bleak as she stared into the nothingness of the wall. She'd long since shed her final tear.

"Beloved cousin, don't fret." Ariane felt awkward as she always did with Shallan. "I heard what happened—your father died bravely, they tell me. He rests in Elanion's grace, your mother at his side."

Shallan gave her a stony look. "He wasn't my father," she whispered then in a louder voice added, "I must return north at once. Morwella needs me, Ariane."

"I know," answered the queen, forcing a smile despite the continuing friction between them.

"You will sail with Barin in the morning. He too has itchy feet." Barin, bulking beneath the doorway, raised a quizzical brow at that last statement. He had hoped to stay a couple of days at least to ensure no more attacks (and catch up with some serious ale draining).

They left after persuading Zukei to leave Shallan alone with the duke's body for a time to deal with her grief. Her father's corpse had been cleaned and adorned with fresh clothes as befitted his rank. The room too had been scrubbed clean of blood and Cormalian's body carried to his kin, so that they could see to his last journey.

Shallan had watched their tidy up in silence. Ariane had urged her get some air outside but to scant avail. Thus she had left her cousin to her thoughts with a heavy heart. Shallan hardly noticed them leaving. Someone stayed behind though. Sveyn had pulled up a chair and sat moping in the corner.

They retired to the citadel where Lord Tolruan's body rested in state arrayed in dignity on a long stone table. Outside on the balcony evening settled at last. It had been a very long day. The latest reports from the east wall stated that the enemy still lingered out of bowshot.

Barin, wielding a wine bottle in either hand, challenged the queen's decision about Shallan and himself. "What that lass needs is rest and plenty of it. She's been through a lot lately. And what of Calprissa? The enemy have not given up."

"Of course not." Ariane accepted a bottle from Barin. She spat the cork on the floor and glugged down half of it. "They'll be back tomorrow or the next day, on that we can count. Caswallon will be furious."

"He won't make the same mistake again. That Soilfin creature has most likes informed him of how things stand."

"Gribble." Ariane nodded. "I heard that little shit survived its drowning."

Ariane drained the bottle, belched and then smiled fondly at the Northman.

"Calprissa is my city, Barin," she said, placing a gloved hand on his arm. "And therefore my responsibility. I shall not let it fall. Not while I have men like Captain Tarello of Wynais and Captain Jaan of Atarios, and 'Squire' Galed by my side. Not to mention that valiant little shithead over there."

Cale, who had been skulking in the hall, perked up hearing her words.

"In here, Cale. Now!"

Sheepishly Cale approached with eyes welded to the floor.

"Whatever am I to do with you?" Ariane asked the boy. She placed a hand under his chin and made him looked up into her dark eyes. "Tell me, boy, how might I serve thee? A good whipping?" Cale blushed crimson, and then mumbled something inaudible.

"You blatantly disobeyed, not only my orders, but those of our high priest and your long suffering mentor, Galed. Such culpability could be punishable by death." Cale assumed she was teasing him, but you never really knew, and she had drunk an entire bottle of wine rather quickly. He pouted his lips and squinted back at her like a cornered ferret.

"I just wanted to be at your side," he muttered eventually. "I love you, I always have."

"Cheeky little turd," Barin was chuckling. Even Galed's concerned face softened with pride. The girl Zukei frowned at Cale. He caught her eye and gulped.

Ariane glared at him a moment longer, but unable to keep up her charade broke into a wicked chuckle. "

"You're a charmer, Cale," the queen said. "When you are fully grown you'll be big trouble. Elanion help the ladies at Wynais court."

She leaned forward and kissed the scarlet-faced boy on his right cheek. Cale gulped back tears.

"You saved my life at the gates and thus have more than redeemed yourself. From this day on you will be known as 'Squire' Cale. You will study lore with your senior, Galed, and will also learn the skills of a fighting man under the strict guidance of my Captain of Guard in Wynais, Yail Tolranna. Don't think you'll have an easy time. You won't. Tolranna's a bastard. Your training starts at once—report to Captain Tarello on the east wall for watch duties. You are dismissed." The queen waved him away.

Cale beamed and departed from the balcony. Galed accompanied him and was already imparting his wisdom but Cale wasn't listening.

He was Squire Cale now. Cale had no idea what a squire was but certainly it was another rung on the ladder. Once back in Wynais he'd work his way up the ranks. It didn't matter that they were still surrounded by enemies, or that a nasty sorcerer and his winged imp plotted their ruin. The only thing that concerned Cale was that finally he really was going places. As he trotted through the streets, Cale reached for a beer tankard left half full on a nearby table. Galed caught his arm. "There'll be none of that," said the elder squire.

Cale just grinned and gulped and walked on past.

"I will look after Shallan and see her safe to Car Carranis," Barin was explaining to Ariane. "Once she's safe inside that fortress I'll go home."

Ariane hugged him. "You are the best of men, Barin. Thank you for saving my city and my cousin." Barin had told the queen of his earlier decision to accompany Shallan to Car Carranis. She had been relieved and was deeply grateful to her friend.

Barin rubbed his beard and farted. He felt rather sad. His eyes were misting over. His thoughts filled with the snowy mountains of home.

Bloody red wine again—what I need is good northern ale.

"I shall be glad to see my home, queenie. It's been a busy time. I'm no longer young, and all this hair pulling and cavorting about is wearing my bones thin."

She laughed at that and Barin looked wan. He sighed theatrically, straightened his back with a creak and ran a battered hand through his tangled blood-crusted mane.

"Look at the state of me, I need a hot bath and proper ale. This southern wine does peculiar things to my head. Besides, we should celebrate."

"Celebrate?" Ariane's eyes widened at that.

"Aye, celebrate the honourable passing of two noble dukes," responded Barin. "And commend ourselves on our victory—however shortlived. But most of all take joy in the knowledge that we old friends are still alive."

"I am hardly dressed for a party."

"You look gorgeous, Ariane."

"You, haystack, are as bad as Corin." Ariane was on her second bottle.

"Nobody is as bad as Corin," Barin replied.

"True," responded the queen. "I miss him..." With that last comment still hanging in the air Ariane left Barin to his peruse from the balcony. At dawn Tarello woke her with word that Wynais, the Silver City, had fallen to treachery within, and that even now Perani's army laid waste to the streets of her capital.

At last Caswallon had shown his hand. They'd been taken for fools. The attack on Calprissa had been a ruse to lure her troops away from the capital. The real war had only just begun. Morning revealed no sign of Derino's force. Doubtless they'd received word to join their masters in the east. Within three hours Ariane was riding east.

The battle for Kelwyn had begun.

Chapter 46

The Return of Old Night

That following afternoon found The Starlight Wanderer already far out to sea, graced by a helpful sou'wester, her decks painted by the pale glow of a wintry sun. The cliffs of Cape Calprissa slowly sunk behind. They'd left early, retiring to the vessel after the celebrations and casting off at dawn.

Away south a trail of smoke revealed all that was left of the Assassin's fleet. Ariane's ships would return to Calprissa that evening. The sailors would bolster the garrison as it prepared for Caswallon's next move.

Shallan's mood was reflective this afternoon. She watched from the dancing prow as the lukewarm sun sparkled over froth-capped waves and a school of dolphins leapt joyfully towards them.

Shallan didn't share their joy. Last night she had watched the flames leap high above her father's funeral pyre. The Duke of Morwella's last words hung heavy on her.

The Horned Man was her real father not the duke. She was half Faen—one of the faerie people. Her blood alien and strange. The thought made her sad, thinking how Duke Tomais had lived with that knowledge all those years. That his wife had had a lover and his daughter was not of his seed.

Mother, what happened back then?

Shallan thought about Ariane and her mixed feelings towards her. She and the queen would never be friends, and yet Ariane had been so kind to her of late. She thought of Corin and wondered what feelings Ariane still harboured for him.

I know you still love him, cousin.

Time would tell. Shallan shrugged, turned to watch the dolphins approach. They were calling to her—her watery kin.

The crew were busy at their tasks and hadn't noticed them. Moreover, they were of a mind to leave Shallan to her thoughts. Even Barin gave her space to mend. Her only companion of late had been Zukei. The two girls had warmed to each other since the duke's death. Worlds apart: the duke's dreamy daughter and the savage dark-eyed killer from the distant south. Zukei seldom spoke, which suited Shallan well enough. The girl was away talking to Fassof this afternoon. Shallan had noted how those two seemed to like each other.

As Shallan watched from her vantage point she saw that some of the creatures had the blue faces and upper bodies of young maidens. As she listened Shallan could hear them calling her name from far across the water.

Shallan, beloved sister return to us…

I will one day—that I promise.

Shallan waved goodbye to her kinfolk, turned and made her way below to the master's cabin. The dolphins departed amid melancholy cries.

Later, as she took to her bed that night, and just before closing her eyes, Shallan saw three shadows watching her from the wall of her cabin.

Shallan closed her eyes, but not before recognising the duke and her mother's sad faces. Behind them the Horned Man's shadow faded and flickered from view. Despite the ghostly visitation Shallan slept far better than she had done in weeks.

***

Corin fed Thunderhoof fresh oats supplied by one of Barakani's sons, as he waited for the party to say their farewells. They had ridden north for several hours. During that time Corin had learned from Silon and Yashan of Barakani's gathering of the tribes, and of their journey south to the Crystal Mountains.

Once there they had waited for the arrival of the sultan—their scouts having reported his presence amongst the crimson elite. It seemed all had gone as planned and everyone was now congratulating themselves. And good for them too, he was very happy for them.

Actually he wasn't.

Once again he, Corin an Fol, had been a clueless participant in someone else's business. Silon, Zallerak and now this Barakani and his desert boys. For once it would be nice to play with his organ instead of everyone else controlling it. No matter—once free of this desert Corin would part with the lot of them. He'd miss Ulani and Tamersane—even Bleyne. But needs must. Car Carranis was waiting and Shallan would be there by now.

After some hours they topped a high ridge of sand and Barakani reined in his steed. Beside him his seven sons smiled as they grasped the hands of Corin and his friends and bade them farewell.

"Here we part our ways," said Barakani with a wave of his hand. "Go with my blessing. From now on you are always welcome in Permio. If there is any way I can aid in your struggle against the sorcerer I shall.

"A short ride north from here will bring you to the banks of the Liaho, near Helbrone Island. Upstream of that isle is a shallow ford where you can cross without difficulty.

"I suggest you make for the Fallowheld at the southern end of the High Wall mountain range; it commands a wide view of the lands there about. Farewell!" Barakani wheeled his horse about and signalled his sons to follow. Those left behind waved and said their farewells to the Wolf of the Desert and his fiery sons.

Ulani eased his horse alongside Thunder and thrust out a brawny arm.

"I wish you well, Longswordsman," Ulani said with a broad grin. The wound on his face had nearly healed and his leg no longer troubled him that much. "I ride south with Yashan," the king said. Behind him the lean desert warrior raised his hand in farewell as he took a pull at his weed pipe.

"Must you leave us?" asked Corin, returning the wave to Yashan with a smile. "We will have need of warriors of your prowess in the north. Besides, Barin will be most disappointed if he misses the opportunity to beat you in an arm wrestle!"

"He'll have to wait!" laughed Ulani. "My heart tells me I will meet this Barin one day, and that you and I, Longswordsman, will fight together again before this business is fully over. Until that bright day comes I wish you well, Corin son of Fol. I must return to Yamondo. There is trouble in my country too. Big trouble. My people will need my guidance in the coming strife. I have already been gone far too long."

Corin watched with Tamersane and Bleyne the archer as their friends, King Ulani of the Baha and Yashan the tribesman, caught up with Barakani and his seven sons and began the long ride back towards the oasis.

"I shall miss Ulani," said Tamersane, scratching his head and yawning as he reached for the water gourd. Ahead of them the young Prince Tarin and Zallerak the bard (or Arollas the Aralais as Corin had started calling him, much to the wizard's annoyance), were already trotting north towards the pale distant ribbon of the Liaho.

"He is a fine warrior, "added Bleyne. "I too would like to witness him and Barin in a wrestling match. That would really be worth watching; only the goddess would know who was strongest. Well, it's nice to have something to look forward to. By the way, we had best get moving, hadn't we?" Bleyne grinned at them both before trotting off to catch up with the others.

"What's got into him? I've never heard him talk so much," mumbled Tamersane.

"He's been in this damn desert too long," answered Corin. "We all have. I'm sick of getting sand up my arse."

"Aye, it will be good to return to fertile green lands of flowing ale and nubile winking lasses," grinned Tamersane. Corin rolled his eyes in resignation. There was only one thing they could be sure off in the north and that was trouble.

"Come on, Thunder," he grumped at the horse. "Let's be off. Back to the northlands; the mist and rain and sleet and sludge. Winter is waiting." Thunderhoof didn't respond to that.

The remainder of their journey passed without event until once again they arrived at the muddy banks of the River Liaho and made rudimentary camp by its waters.

They had survived the desert despite everything it had thrown at them. In the north the distant mountains known as the High Wall were capped with heavy cloud. A chill wind bore down on them from that direction confirming winter held court in their homelands.

Next morning they forded the river and left the arid land of Permio behind. Corin glanced back on a whim. He wasn't entirely surprised to see a figure watching them from the far bank. The tall figure of an old man, his features obscured beneath the shadow of a wide-brimmed hat.

Corin turned away. Let the Huntsman play his games. Morak was defeated and the Tekara re-forged. Corin had done more than his share. Let them do as they would. He was bound for Car Carranis. Corin smiled, picturing Shallan's beautiful face.

"Come on, Thunder—let's get cracking." Corin grinned for the first time in weeks. Despite Thunderhoof's indifference his rider was glad to be leaving the desert behind.

***

Gribble watched the shambles leaving Calprissa. What a sorry bunch they'd proved to be. Bad Boy Derino had got shafted by the Northman, and Perani would have to send someone else across to bang their heads together. Gribble wondered whether the time was right to request promotion. He had been an exceptionally good spy. Probably not, on reflection—Mr Caswallon was unpredictable these days.

And Mr Caswallon had other things on his mind. Queen Ariane. The noose was tightening around her at last. She had proved such a troublesome little minx. But her game was up. Tricksy Ariane had nowhere to go.

The traitor had opened the gates to them in Wynais. There'd be nice warm flesh there. Far better than munching corpses and dead doggy Groil. Gribble decided he'd need a proper lunch before heading back north to Kella.

Silver City, here I come. .

***

By the time he'd staggered into the harbour his ships had departed. Rael had taken to diving in the water, cutting across to the far side. Once there he would commence the long hike up to Kelthaine. From Fardoris he'd sail over to his island. When home he would disembowel the deserters and pickle their heads. He'd retire for winter and in spring return to cause havoc. Rael owed many debts. This was no longer business. This was personal.

A dark shape blotted the sun. Squinting, Rael glimpsed Caswallon's goblin flying overhead. Caswallon could play his own game. Rael had one thing on his mind. Return home and plot revenge on the bastards that had foiled him yet again. That thought kept him alive through the following weeks.

***

The Tekara re-forged closes one game and opens another. Oroonin smiles, this new game is starting well. Above Him the nine worlds turn and spin ceaselessly on their axis. Oroonin listens; He feels the Maker's presence far away, senses the time so long awaited draws close. He chants the rune-words summoning Uppsalion the corpse-horse, His steed for countless millennia. Together they depart from the desert land where He has been watching events unfold to His satisfaction.

Uppsalion carries its rider high, far beyond the place where the clouds wrack the skies. Time and matter shifts; Oroonin crosses dimensions, seeking that high lonely castle in the sky.

Telcanna is expecting Him. The Sky-God awaits His brother's arrival whilst holding court from His cobalt throne. The courtesans in the Sky-God's palace are beautiful too, they gather in their hundreds to adulate at His feet. Telcanna's raiment is a shimmering dazzle of sapphire: it hides His face. The Sky-God calls out to Oroonin as His brother rides close.

"So you return, gallows bird. Can you not sense it? OUR BROTHER WAKES!" Telcanna's voice echoes across the heavens. As He speaks shafts of lightning spear out from His cobalt mouth.

"Already he challenges his bonds. The final war has started at last! WAKEN YOUR HOUNDS, OROONIN! UNLEASH YOUR CORPSE LEGIONS WHILE YOU STILL CAN!"

Oroonin says nothing, choosing to ignore His brother's rant until Telcanna, in irritation, dismisses His court. Castle and court vanish. Telcanna glares at His brother before turning and fading into nothingness.

The Huntsman watches Him go in silence and smiles that calculating smile. And so it begins: the final war. Deep in the roots of Ansu, He feels His other brother stirring. Ansu. The world where it started and the world where it will end.

Oroonin allows His mind to journey back down there again. There is something still to do. He mounts Uppsalion and swoops down through racing skies.

His journey this time takes the Huntsman far south of the desert realm to the steaming jungles of Yamondo. It is here that He seeks for the second time, that forgotten fissure beneath the fiery mountain in the jungles' midst.

Oroonin spies the lonely peak's trail of smoke rising up above the lush vegetation surrounding it. He bids Uppsalion wait, while in astral form He ventures toward the mountainside.

Oroonin is wary. There is much danger here even for one such as He. A pale ghost. The Huntsman passes beneath the dreary gates where the demon lies sleeping. He finds the sconce flickering stairway and follows its winding path, down and down, in darkening spirals. Passing stinking pools of filth where fear holds sway, and shadowy things gape at him from churning, oozing pits.

Down and down and down Oroonin's shade hastens, towards the final catacomb from whence comes the hidden icy fire. Fell unspeakable creatures snarl at His passing. The Huntsman is invisible to their eyes but they can sense His hidden presence.

Fangs snap and talons claw toward Him as the creatures of Chaos waken from their ancient sleep. Oroonin ignores them as He draws near to the fiery heart of the mountain. Light fades as the mountain sleeps, its fires content to wait.

At last the Huntsman reaches that final awful place; the cavern men call Yffarn, and even He knows fear at what He sees there.

Big Brother.

Eyes set deep in that huge severed head watch His approach from the high plinth at the edge of the fiery lake.

Cul-Saan.

In this place the sentient head of the Huntsman's eldest and most feared brother, branded Old Night, has been imprisoned for aeons.

Oroonin approaches slowly, warily. He is careful to avoid the fumes of Old Night's contaminated breath. The Huntsman's single eye narrows when it sees how the blood drips endlessly from its owner's severed neck to rest in smoking puddles on the lava lake below. So the contamination still spreads.

Silence chokes the air; glowing translucent mould clings to

slimy walls like a canker of despair. The head of Old Night rotates slowly on its plinth. His terrible eyes see who has come. His are the eyes of futility: darker than the jungle night, colder than the tundra wastes, and yet veined with living fire.

Then the head of Old Night speaks through the ruined crack of His mouth, filling the cavern with the stench of rotting flesh. Blood salivates around Cul-Saan's black, snake tongue. He yawns, spraying the cavern and walls with his detritus.

"SO YOU RETURN."

The words are like poison. They shake the roots of the mountain, His tomb/dungeon, and waken the last of His nightmare brood. The dark acolytes that chose to be incarcerated with Him. Here in Yffarn beneath the mountain. Despite His fear Oroonin is not to be swayed. His single eye blazes icy blue in return.

"The time comes."

"WE FEEL IT." The head stares down at Him from its fiery mantle. "OUR CHILDREN AWAKE, THE TIME FOR OUR VENGEANCE HAS ARRIVED. WHICH SIDE WILL YOU TAKE THIS TIME, DOUBLECROSSER?"

"I play my own game as you know well enough," responds the shade of Oroonin. Behind Him the dark sinewy shapes of Cul-Saan's acolytes manifest and gather, their insect eyes glaring like bloody swabs of hunger.

Old Night laughs. The sound splits stone sending tremors through the mountain and out into the jungle night beyond, where savage beasts pause in their hunt quailing suddenly at an unknown fear.

"CHOOSE WISELY, LITTLE BROTHER."

The ghastly head rocks on its plinth. Oroonin's god sight can see that most of the invisible bonds binding His brother's head have rotted into spidery ruin.

Now as the head moves a dark river of blood glistens beneath it. Sizzling, it gushes forth corrupting the fire and melting the stone beneath it.

"WE ARE ALMOST FREE."

Those ice-fire eyes are fully open now. Behind the plinth the stained children of Old Night stoop to drink deeply at the gushing river of blood seeping from His neck. They sigh like lovers as their long banished strength returns to them at last. Again the head speaks.

"I AM THE LORD OF CHAOS AND FUTILY. SOON I SHALL BE ONE WITH MY BODY. THEN SHALL THE FINAL RENDING BEGIN.

BEHOLD, BROTHER, YOU ARE WITNESSING THE RETURN OF OLD NIGHT!"

At those terrible words the mountain rocks in sudden violence shaking its foundations to the core. Stone crashes and splits asunder. Jets of fire surge forth into the heavens.

At the gate the demon wakes in fury and discovers itself bound helpless in writhing flames. Oroonin flees. He alone is no match for the might of His eldest brother, even in His present dismembered state.

The children of Old Night shriek and wail behind Him as He runs. They can see Oroonin clearly now. They chase His departing spirit up from the roots of the mountain.

The Huntsman passes between the ruined broken gates; He glances down at the writhing tortured demon trapped by its own bonds of fire. Oroonin summons Uppsalion and the corpse-horse bears Him aloft just as the mountain spews gobbets of black flame a thousand feet into the sky.

That flame takes form. A tyrant tall and beautiful garbed in glossiest black. The spirit of Cul-Saan the First Born, soon to be free again. Old Night. The earth shakes with the sound of His laughter. His form shimmers—splits into a billion fiery splinters and then settles like choking dust on jungle below.

***

Here concludes Book Four of *The Legends of Ansu*.

In the next Legend, *The Glass Throne*, we find Corin an Fol trapped in the meshes of Darkvale, Shallan enduring Car Carranis under siege, whilst Barin battles barehanded with a troll. Ariane of the Swords leads a guerrilla war against Caswallon, and Zallerak is faced by the fury of Vaarg the firedrake.

~ JWW

Get a sample preview.
J.W. Webb's...

The Glass Throne

Chapter 1

The Rider

The Ptarni Plains surrounded both rider and horse, a vast expanse of featureless grey. No solitary tree or hillock broke the monotony. Just mile upon mile of tall grasses, swaying and sighing, as the bitter wind carried with it the fresh promise of snow. A desolate landscape, its only occupants wild birds and prowling beasts, and the odd thin river struggling through. Men said the Ptarni Plains were endless or that nothing but void lay at the other side.

Olen Kaanson knew better. He alone of the Rorshai people had seen the other side. A journey of many days—during which he nearly starved—had revealed dark mountains, and beneath them an alien city high in the clouds. Olen had told no one of his journey, the arduous task he set upon himself, after taking advice from the Seeress of Silent Mountain. She who had warned so long of the coming war.

Four weeks ago he'd ridden to Silent Mountain, climbed the long winding, wind freezing stairs, and then entered the horse skull cave that led to her silent chamber. Once there he had lain with her, as was expected—paying her price for counsel and warning. No one knew her age, though they say she was around in his grandsire's day. The Seeress appeared a woman in her forties, wild-haired and dark of eye; her body sharp and lean. Her voice husky with the drugs she took to aid her inner vision.

"What brings you here, Kaanson?" she had asked Olen, knowing well the answer. Her eyes teasing him and long fingernails tracing a thin line of blood down his cheek. "Are the dreams taking shape inside your head?" She smiled as she loosened the drawstrings of his breeches.

"They are, wise one," Olen had replied after they were done, and then told her of his nightly visions. Dreams of war and dreams of blood. Nightmares where dark silent creatures stirred in empty tombs. And the stranger, the reflection in the water. The harbinger of war. A warrior, scarred of face, across his back a huge sword and in his eyes intense purpose.

"The fulcrum, yes I've seen him too." The Seeress crouched by the fire. She'd thrown a cloak over her nakedness to shield her from the chill. She held something in her left hand. Olen couldn't see what it was. He gasped as she tossed it into the fire and the flames roared and crackled with sudden urgent life.

"He is coming soon," the Seeress told Olen. "Him and another, arriving from the south. They bring with them the first snows of winter. They also bring death."

"What must I do?"

"You must fare south, Olen of the Yellow Clan. But before that you need to ride east."

"East? I don't understand. That way lies only grasses and wind and the edge of the world."

"Not so." The Seeress tossed another tiny object into the fire, and again the flames surged and fizzed. "Beyond the plains are mountains and past those wide fertile lands where men and women dwell, fight and screw and starve and hunt, much like any other land. The closest of these lands is called Ptarni, the furthermost Shen. There are others but they don't concern you. Ptarni does. Those ruling that land have long had their eyes on the Four Kingdoms."

"I have heard of Ptarni of course, but I thought it myth. A place of whimsical fancies, a city in the clouds lost to dream and mystery." The Seeress showed her secret smile. Her teeth were perfect though her eyes were shadowed with darker purpose. She turned toward him, her nakedness revealed again. Despite who she was, Olen felt his loins stir anew.

"You've seen the riders out on the plains? Where do you think they come from, fool?" The Seeress's laugh was cold and brittle, like cracking ice on a thawing lake. Her eyes were charcoal daggers of sardonic wisdom.

"There are many lands both north and south, perhaps those riders are from these." Olen struggled to make his point. "We Rorshai watch over the grasslands in constant vigilance. And yes, I have seen strange horseman watching from afar. I deemed them merchants, or else maybe scouts from Permio, or Raleen across the mountains."

"Raleen across the mountains?" The Seeress cackled and rounded on him, pulling Olen toward her and kissing his lips hungrily. The need was upon her again but Olen wanted answers. He pulled away and wiped her spittle from his mouth. She glared at him in frosty silence.

"I have been out on the steppes, as far as any of our people. I once road east for three long days, seeing nothing but wind, eagle and sky. An empty land, I deemed it."

"You need to travel for thirty days, Olen Kaanson. Then you'll see the mountains, and amongst them the city in the clouds." She reached forward, smiling again. "Come, fill me again with your urgent seed, then shall I tell all I know of the threat in the east." And so Olen had loved her again, hard and fast until she yelled out his name in sated rapture. As he stood above her, donning his garments in watchful silence, the Seeress had crouched close to the fire, whispering words and tossing rune charms into its hissing midst.

At last she had stopped, and as Olen stood waiting at her cave's entrance, the Seeress had stood before him naked and bleeding. It was then that she told him what he must do.

That had been a month ago.

And he'd done her bidding. Ridden mile upon wind tossed mile, over grasslands, low hills and craggy slopes. Passing beneath wind torn trees and fording icy rivers that hurried to the gods only knew where. On the thirtieth day Olen had reined in sharp, at last seeing the mountains revealed by winter dawn. Tall and stark they stood, and in their midst a golden city, just as she'd described it.

Ptarni—the fabled realm. Olen had ridden closer throughout that day. He'd stopped at the west bank of a huge brown river. Its mile wide waters sluggish, the banks rimed with ice. In the distance that golden city glimmered some twenty miles ahead, appearing to float in the mist surrounding the mountains.

Olen gazed north along the river. A mile or so that way, a great bend stole the river from his eyes as its midst was lost to willow and grasses. He turned south. Here the river flowed more or less straight. Olen shielded his eyes and stared harder along its banks. He saw shingle strands and iyots, where lone cranes stood as patient sentinels. Beyond the islands and birds, Olen could just make out the square shapes of what looked to be buildings on his side of the river.

Intrigued, Olen guided Loroshai—his black stallion—southward along the banks until the buildings revealed themselves alongside a road. A road leading west away from the river and vanishing into the vastness of the plains.

Olen urged Loroshai forward until he reached the road. To his right the building loomed high. A great storehouse, it appeared. There was no one around so Olen slid from Loroshai's saddle and tied the beast to a stunted tree. Silent—as only his people can be— Olen stole close to the building. A single door waited ajar.

He ventured within, only now realising just how huge this building was. Huge and empty. But Olen could see where wains and carts had been stowed as there were wheel tracks and runnels everywhere across the cobbled base of the building. He wandered through, seeing stables and rooms with hooks where tools or weapons must have been racked and stowed.

For what purpose? Olen guessed he already knew the answer to that. Grim-faced, he left the building behind, and remounting Loroshai, urged the horse follow the road into the maze of grasses ahead.

For five days Olen followed that track. It was pitted and churned by wheel and hoof, evidence that a large company had passed this way recently. As night fell the track faded into the gloom of a steep ravine. Olen chose that moment to take shelter beneath a quiet cluster of trees a half mile ahead of the ravine.

He woke to the distant grumble and grind of metal on stone. Olen rolled free of his blanket and reached up to Loroshai's saddle where he retrieved his horn bow and a half dozen arrows; his golden hilted scimitar was already strapped to his waist. Rorshai riders seldom parted with their swords.

He spoke a few cool words to Loroshai and then, silent and painstakingly slow, crept and crawled closer to the ravine. Behind him the sun rose glorious and bright. The creaking grew louder, announcing wagons on the move, and Olen could hear voices too. Guttural accents speaking a tongue he didn't understand. Ptarnians, no doubt.

Olen reached the point where the track channelled into the ridge. Here he left it and took to scaling the sharp rise on the left. Half hour later he crested that shale slope and gazed down in astonishment at the sight greeting him below.

An army was camped in the wedge between the hills. Down there a stream glittered in the morning sun, on either side were scattered bushes and clumps of stunted trees. Amongst these and as far as his eyes could see along the ravine, Olen saw men, horses and various carts and wagons of all sizes and construction.

He tried to count the wagons but there were too many. They filled the deep cut of the ravine, spanning its fifty feet basin for at least a mile until a shoulder of rock thrust across his vision and Olen could see it no longer. Instead he focussed on the men, antlike and scurrying to and fro below.

They were strange to behold. To his Rorshan eyes they appeared clumsy and awkward, weighed down by heavy plate armour of various colours and hue. The few faces he could see (most were hidden behind chained masks hanging from the pointed helms they wore), were hard, scarred and swarthy, their hair long oily and black. Occasionally a man would doff his helm to wash his face in the stream, or else wipe sweat from his forehead. There was no doubt in Olen's mind. These were professional warriors.

For almost two hours Olen crouched in discomfort, watching and listening, as the strange men shouted and yelled at each other as the army broke camp and made ready to move. In the distance he see could the wagons already rolling out of view. There must have been over a thousand. A thousand wains loaded with weapons, supplies, food and ale—all the things needed by an army on the march.

He watched as the nearest soldiers saddled their ponies whilst the wagon riders whooped and hollered their oxen and mules into noisy movement. Another hour passed as the winter sun climbed the ridge behind him. Though some rode the shaggy ponies most went on foot—a comfort to Olen on that cold morning, and those ponies he'd seen would prove no match for Loroshai. Olen waited until the last soldier had vacated the ravine's valley. Then he stood in one fluid motion, easing the cramp in his legs.

He needed to warn his people—and fast. Olen returned to the spot where Loroshai grazed in the sunshine. He saddled and mounted the horse and bid him trot northwards along the edge of the ridges away from the ravine. After several miles the terrain flattened out, returning to the familiar carpet of blue grey grasses and pale winter sky.

Olen turned west, deeming himself a safe distance from the foreigners. He steered closer and soon spotted the endless train of wagons wending across the steppe lands. Again he tried to count their number but it was impossible. At least they were moving slowly, Olen guessed it would take them many weeks to reach Rorshai. With that last thought in mind the lone rider spurred his war beast to quicken his trot. Olen was desperate to get back, but he must needs pace himself. Loroshai was one of the finest horses owned by the Yellow Clan, but even he needed rest and breaks from the arduous journey ahead. It had taken Olen thirty days to reach the foreign river. It took him twenty-three to return.

During that entire journey the words of the Seeress echoed through his head. "He is coming via a dark road. You must be ready! He is the harbinger and the war cannot be won without him."

"How will I know him?" Olen had asked her.

"By the length of his sword and the smell of destiny that surrounds him," she had answered. And so Olen Kaanson rode.

***

Rogan froze as he saw the distant trail of dust rising up to greet the afternoon. Could it be? Then he smiled, recognising the rider as their own beloved Olen, his war chief and eldest son of the leader of the Yellow Clan, or the Tcunkai (thinkers) as Olen's father the Kaan liked to call them.

"Teret! Your brother comes and he looks in bad need of ale!" Rogan yelled laughing at a dark-eyed girl who was crouched behind him in the stockade, milking a cow's teats into a wooden bucket. The girl stood, wiped her comely face with a sleeve and, after hurdling the fence, came and stood beside Rogan. Teret's face lit up when she saw her eldest brother guide his lathered steed into the corral.

"Brother! We feared you were lost! It's almost two months since anyone has seen you. Where have you been?" Teret ran forward to hug Olen as he slipped exhausted from his saddle. The smile fled from her face when she saw the worry worm eating at his brow.

"What is it? What have you seen?" Teret's dark blue eyes were haunted by worry as she threw her brown arms around her brother, noting how weak and thin he appeared. "You need rest," she told him.

"There is no time!" Olen shoved his sister back. "Take care of Loroshai, Teret. He needs sustenance and rest—and lots of water. We ride out on the morrow!" Teret made to question her brother but his bleak gaze left the question in her mouth. Obeying, she turned and led the big horse towards the stables behind the homestead.

Olen turned to Rogan.

"Summon the clan! We fare south in the morning."

"South?" Rogan scratched an ear. "That's Anchai country—they'll not like us trespassing." The Anchai were known as the Red Clan, due to their love of blood sports and troublesome nature. They kept themselves aloof from the other clans. The Anchai settled the land near the great arm of mountain that thrust east from the High Wall ranges marking the southern borders of Rorshai. "Why south?" Rogan pressed.

"Because that's the direction he'll be coming." Olen thanked a youth that had just appeared with a large flask of ale. He downed the flask and sent the boy for another. "From the mountains," Olen added—as though that explained everything.

"Who?" Rogan's eyes were saucers. No one came from the mountains these days. There was rumoured a pass but the Rorshai steered clear of that region—even the Anchai. Word was that secret way beneath the mountains was haunted by an unknown terror.

That evening Olen spoke before his father, the Kaan and the thirty war chiefs of his clan. Olen told them of his dreams, his journey to see the Seeress (many paled hearing this), and the long hard trek across the steppe lands. Nobody spoke whilst Olen recounted what he had witnessed, first from the river and later looking down into that ravine. Olen was respected here. Even the Kaan had learned to listen to his eldest boy. But it wasn't just that. Olen Kaanson had the Dreaming.

"War is coming," Olen told them. "A pivotal strife unlike any other. The clans must be summoned at the Delve!"

"Good luck with that," wry Rogan had muttered under his breath. Olen's word might be respected by his own clan, but the shamans and head clan of the Delve were unlikely to be affected by his passionate call to arms. Moreover they probably wouldn't even listen.

"This stranger? The harbinger of war?" The Kaan leaned forward in his heavy chair and stared deeply into the fiery blue of his eldest son's eyes. "What did the Seeress say about him?"

"That he comes from the southlands, but he's no southerner. And that he brings with him a destiny that even he cannot comprehend. She hinted he was a Longswordsman and man of few words. He journeys with another—a younger brighter soul."

"A name?"

"Corin an Fol."

Early next morning Olen of the Yellow Clan led his hundred horsemen south toward Anchai country. They passed the Red Clans' lands during the starry dark of night, thus avoiding certain conflict. Two days later the hundred reached the folds of mountain leading to a crack in the rock from which darkness yawned like a smoky mouth.

The hidden pass. Or as most there liked to call it, the haunted pass. There they fixed restless camp, waiting until the appointed moment when the stranger would appear. In his tent Olen was late to sleep. Sometime ere morning he must have dozed, only to wake minutes later to the sound of urgent thunder rolling out across the grasslands far to the east.

On instinct, Olen rolled free of his blanket and eased his way out of the tent. No sleep tonight. Away east the thunder growled and boomed like prophesy. Olen nodded in silence to the watchmen posted at the edge of their camp. Uneasy, they watched their leader stride off into the gloom. Olen walked toward the rolling doom of thunder. A mile away from their camp was only open sighing grasses, and brittle breeze lifting the long shadow of his untamed dusky hair.

It was then that Olen saw Him. The owner of the thunder. Far out across the plains He strode, a giant figure, eyes blazing and dark cloak billowing like thunder cloud behind Him. For an icy instant Olen felt that heavy gaze fall upon him. Then the giant was gone, storming off into the distance. Olen paled: it did not bode well to see Borian the Wind God whilst alone in the night. It was later that morning when the strangers arrived, and with them the first ravens of war.

Glossary

IMMORTALS

The Weaver/Maker

THE WEAVER'S CHILDREN, THE HIGH GODS

Cul-Saan: first born, leader of rebellion against the Maker; now known as Old Night.

Oroonin/The Huntsman: God of War and Trickery, he plays his own game.

Elanion: wife and sister of Oroonin; guardian of first planet Ansu.

Telcanna: Sky God, vain and capricious.

Borian: Wind God, currently working on projects in different solar system.

Croagon: the Smith, imprisoned beneath the Crystal Mountains.

Sensuata: ferocious Sea God, destroyer of the continent of Gol.

LESSER GODS AND DEMI-GODS

Crun Earth-Shatterer: a treacherous giant imprisoned on Laras Lassladan.

Undeyna: Old Night's twisted daughter, known as the Witch Queen. Haunts the forest of Darkvale.

Simiolanis: golden-haired demi-goddess known for her beauty and infidelity.

Argonwui: the Virgin, a cruel and vengeful deity, her beauty having been ravished by her uncle, Old Night. Eldest daughter of Elanion and Oroonin.

THE FATES

Urdei: blonde child, representing the past.

Vervandi: mysterious redhead, representing the present. Also serves Elanion, her mother.

Scolde: ancient crone who represents the future.

SUPERNATURALS

Zallerak: maverick wizard with an agenda.

Morak: the Dog Lord, warlock, Urgolais leader, seeking to return to power.

The Horned Man: a fawn-like creature of the Faen.

ALIEN PEOPLES

The Aralais: the Golden Folk, golden warrior wizards that once occupied parts of Ansu.

The Urgolais: Dark cousins of the Aralais, a subterranean people who coveted their cousins' wealth.

The Faen: the faerie people, Elanion's chosen and the first occupants of Ansu.

Dark Faen: those Faen who sided with Old Night and his daughter against the Light.

CREATURES

Flail Six-Hands: Caswallon's retainer, a Groil, who are soulless killers fashioned from sorcery by their masters, the Urgolais.

Drol Two-Heads: Flail's lieutenant, a Groil.

Gribble: a Soilfin, one of the surviving winged goblins used as spies and messengers by the Urgolais in the Aralais-Urgolais war.

Vaarg: Morak's former servant, a dragon, or Firewyrm, who survived the Aralais purge.

Ty-Tanders: legendary desert creatures, rumoured unkillable, feared guardians of the Crystal Mountains.

MORTALS

THE FOUR KINGDOMS

Kelthaine, The First Kingdom

Kell: legendary first ruler; exile from Gol.

Thanek: Kell's son, second ruler of Kelthaine.

Kelsalion the Third: late High King, descendant of Kell and Thanek, recently murdered.

Prince Tarin: Kelsalion's renegade son.

Caswallon: sorcerer and usurper of Kelthaine's Glass Throne, schooled by Morak, the Urgolais.

Halfdan: outlawed leader of the Wolf regiment, the High King's younger brother. Believed missing or dead.

Belmarius: exiled leader of the Bear regiment.

Valentin: an officer in the Bears, leader of Belmarius's Rangers

Perani: previous leader of the Tiger regiment, now Caswallon's henchman.

Derino: Perani's lieutenant.

Cale: young cutpurse who falls foul of Corin.

Ulf: Cale's companion, a brigand.

Starki: Ulf's twin.

Jen: crofter and wise woman.

Cullan: Jen's husband, formally a soldier.

Dail: Jen and Cullan's son.

Bleyne: mysterious archer.

Starkhold: leader of garrison in Car Carranis. Formerly a warlord from Raleen.

Ralian: his eagle-eyed second in command.

Kelwyn, The Second Kingdom

Wynna: Kell's other son and first ruler of Kelwyn.

King Nogel: Wynna's descendant, recently killed in a hunting accident.

Queen Ariane: Nogel's daughter, new to throne.

Dazaleon: Ariane's high priest and councillor.

Roman Parantios: Ariane's champion at arms.

Yail Tolranna: Ariane's newly promoted captain of guard.

Tamersane: Tolranna's brother, joker and wit.

Galed: Ariane's head scribe, called "squire" by Roman.

Tarello: Tolranna's first officer in Wynais.

Raleen, The Third Kingdom

Kael: warrior exiled from Gol, founder and first ruler of Raleen.

Raleen: Kael's beloved daughter, after whom he named his country.

Silon: merchant, Corin's former employer.

Nalissa: Silon's daughter and the reason for Corin's departure north.

Rado: proprietor of The Crooked Knife tavern in Port Sarfe.

Darosi: a captain of horse from Atarios.

Jaan: his lieutenant.

Morwella, The Fourth Kingdom

Jerrel: another survivor of Gol's destruction, became first Duke of Morwella.

Tomais: present and sickly Duke, Jerrel's descendant.

Shallan: Tomais's headstrong daughter, First Lady of Morwella. Haunted by visions of the Horned Man.

Hagan Delmorier: hired hand and killer. Outlawed from Morwella, he now serves Caswallon and Rael Hakkenon; Corin's former drinking partner, now bitter enemy.

Borgil: Hagan's brutal lieutenant.

THE OUTER REALMS

Fol

Corin an Fol: contracted mercenary and former soldier in the Wolf regiment.

Burmon: kindly innkeep in Finnehalle, Corin's birthplace.

Holly: Burmon's daughter.

Polin: former blacksmith, once Corin's friend.

Kyssa: Polin's daughter.

Tommo: her husband.

Crenna

Rael Hakkenon: Killer of Kelsalion. Called the Assassin. Rebel prince and pirate chief, in league with Caswallon.

Pollomoi: Rael's captain of guard.

Cruel Cavan: Rael's chief pirate and master shipwright.

Scarn: a pirate.

Leeth

King Haal: Barbarian ruler of Leeth.

Daan Redhand: heir and eldest son of King Haal, bloodthirsty warrior prince. Sworn foe of Barin of Valkador.

Vale The Snake: King Haal's second son.

Corvalian: King Haal's youngest son.

Valkador

Barin: giant axeman. Master of the brigantine, The Starlight Wanderer. Sworn foe to Daan Redhand.

Fassof: Barin's foul-mouthed first mate.

Cogga: one of Barin's crewmen.

Ruagon: The Starlight Wanderer's cook.

Taic: Barin's wayward nephew.

Sveyn: Taic's sidekick and nephew of Cogga.

Permio

Samadin the Marvellous: sultan of Permio.

Damazen Kand: leader of the sultan's crimson guard.

Barakani: Wolf of the Desert. A tribal leader.

Rassan: one of his seven sons.

Yashan: a tribesman.

Jarrof: a tribesman.

Migen: an officer in the sultan's crimson guard.

Gamesh: a sergeant in the sultan's crimson guard.

Sulimo: a merchant.

Marl: a mercenary in Sulimo's pay.

Hulm: an innkeep in Agmandeur.

Olami: his sickly brother.

Ragu: his stable boy.

Haikon: a fisherman

Prince of the Golden Cloud: legendary warrior lost in the desert.

The Far Countries

Ulani of the Baha: warrior king of Yamondo.

Normacaralox: known as Norman, a sailor from the distant east.

Wogun: another sailor from distant Vendel and Norman's friend.

Zukei: a crazy girl saved by Taic from execution.

Subscribe to our email list at <u>legendofansu.com</u>
Get the Twitter app and contact J. W. Webb, @LegendsofAnsu
Please, leave a good book review for J. W. Webb.

Printed in Great Britain
by Amazon

22188497R00310